Asher

Wolves of the Wiltshire Pack Book 1

Mia Fury

Copyright & Disclaimer

Names, characters, places and incidents within this book are either the product of the author's imagination or are used fictitiously, and any resemblance to actual persons, living or dead, business establishments, etc. is purely coincidental.

Copyright © Mia Fury 2022

All rights reserved. No part of this text may be reproduced, scanned, transmitted, or distributed in any printed or electronic form without permission.

Cover Copyright © Anya Kelleye Designs 2022

Website: anyakelleye.com

All rights reserved. No part of this image may be reproduced, scanned, transmitted, or distributed in any printed or electronic form without permission.

Trigger Warning

This book isn't your typical romance. This is a paranormal romance, set in a world of magic and wolf shifters, with some dark or violent themes. Please note my wolf shifter world may differ from those you've read before. *This is NOT omegaverse, and there is no knotting.*

That said, if you have triggers, then sadly, this book may not be for you. The book features mental health issues including flashbacks, nightmares, and anxiety attacks, references to past sexual trauma, graphic sex scenes, threats, violence, murder, oh... and bad language.

I do not condone *some* of the behaviour within these pages, nor do I believe it has a place in the real world, but for the purposes of good old fashioned paranormal romance, I really hope you enjoy this book!

Stalk Me

Join my mailing list to stay up to date and gain access to bonus materials:
https://mailchi.mp/1c8fb54b3542/newsletter-signup

If you want early access to everything, including bonus scenes, exclusive covers and more, come and join my Patreon group:
www.patreon.com/miafury

Want to be involved in discussions and have access to tons of giveaways? Join my reader group on Facebook:
www.facebook.com/groups/miasfuries

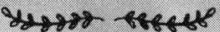

https://linktr.ee/MiaFury

Chapter One

Asher

I RAN A HAND through my dark blond hair and groaned. "I know." My Beta, Jase, was bitching at me again. *What else is new, right?*

"Alpha, it's only a matter of time, and you damn well know it," he repeated unnecessarily.

I glared at him. "Did I stutter?"

He lowered his eyes, trying to fight the internal submission he felt, when my Alpha wolf spoke.

"I'm only trying to advise you. That's why you chose me as your Beta, when most wouldn't have." He'd said this before too.

"Aye, but he had no choice now," Derek spoke up. He was my Delta, and these two were the backbone of my pack, with me at the top, and how did I end up there? My fucking father. Yeah... I should have been sad that he died in that last battle, but he'd left me leading the remains of this pack, and I'd been fighting tooth and claw to see off every other damn Alpha who saw fit to 'absorb' us into theirs.

I'd become the Alpha of the Wiltshire Pack, and there were only fifty of us left. That was thanks to the older bastards who died in that battle, or left soon after, declaring a vote of no confidence in their new Alpha. *Me*. Alpha at only forty years old, so young for a shifter to lead a pack.

What the hell did I fucking know about running a pack? I'd been Alpha for a year, and all that had happened so far was that we'd managed to negotiate our way out of two attempts to challenge me, and those attempts wouldn't stop any time soon though.

I'm not weak, but as an unmated Alpha, I'm apparently not as strong as I could be. That fact ate away at me every day, mostly because I didn't even believe in that shit. My father was as tough as nails, and he didn't marry his 'mated' wolf. He married a wolf he fell for; my mother, and she never failed him.

"You're not listening. He always does this when the subject matter gets tough." Jase was complaining to Derek.

"Let him have his peace, brother. It's lunchbreak, and we have beer. Just enjoy it." His Irish brogue always made his words sound more musical than they were.

I was glad that he'd joined our pack when he did. He'd been a lone wolf passing through town, and we'd instantly connected. He knew his role, and he was a savage, dirty fighter. We needed that, especially right now, but that still didn't make me weak.

"*I don't need a mate*," I spat, with both men turning to me in surprise.

"We didn't say a word, Alpha," Jase said quietly. "I know you don't believe in mates."

I stared at him, feeling an urge to prove my point, while I tried to keep my tone conversational.

"Neither of you have found yours. In fact, there are only three mated wolves in our entire pack. Maybe if you males all go out there, and find a fucking wolf to mate with, we could double the size of our pack. Ever think of that?"

Derek flashed that grin, the one that meant something dirty was coming up.

"Ah sure, boss, but then she'd have to enjoy fucking all the extra girls I bring home with me. I'm not really a one-woman wolf, you know that."

I snorted, tossing back the last of my beer.

"Okay, bring the committee together after work today, and let's discuss options. Jase is right, another Alpha is going to try his luck with us soon. Let's do our best to be ready for it. I doubt it'll be settled by giving up rights to assets, or finances, this time. We don't have much left to give up, and I won't split our territory."

They both nodded in agreement. They finished their beers, and stood up first.

"I'll just take a leak, and follow you guys," Derek said, but we both caught the sidelong glance he gave the barmaid, as he stood up and sauntered in that direction.

She finished wiping the glass she held, and put it on the shelf. We watched as she commented to her colleague, and headed after him, smoothing her skirt as she walked. I don't know why she even bothered. The damn thing would be up around her ears in no fucking time.

"That boy needs a fucking leash," I said to Jase as we left, and he snorted.

"I think he'd probably enjoy that."

We both laughed, and started walking the short route to where we'd parked, to drive home to the pack house. We ran a small IT Security business, which we housed at the pack house, to save money. We weren't poor, but it helped to stay close to home, particularly with regular challenges on my leadership.

"Do you believe in mates, Jase?" I asked, as we headed to the last corner, where the small garden centre was.

"I actually really hope they're real, Alpha. I like the idea of staring across a crowded room, and meeting the eyes of the one I'm meant to be with. It'd be better than being with the wrong person." He was shrugging as he spoke, but I knew he meant every damn word.

I made a gagging sound. "You should write those chick books, Jase. You'd make a killing." He laughed.

"As a side-line, you mean?"

I laughed, but something stopped that laugh in my throat, and I made a choking sound instead. *A scent filled my senses.* A delicious scent, that washed over me, and went straight to my cock. I groaned, rubbing a hand over my face. Suddenly all that mattered was that scent.

"Alpha?" I had stopped moving, my feet locked in place.

"What's that smell?" I asked, staring around me, blinking languidly, because everything seemed to have slowed down. Everything except my heartbeat, that is.

Jase sniffed. "I don't know, Alpha. We're by the nursery, so maybe the flowers? I can smell-"

"*No...* It's not flowers." I knew that much. No, this was something else entirely.

I cast my eyes across the front of the garden centre, and I saw *her*.

She was kneeling over a patch of soil, busily planting something. She was wearing the company uniform; dark dungarees, and a pale yellow shirt. Her blonde hair was cropped adorably short, and she must have felt my stare, because she suddenly lifted her eyes, meeting mine. A gasp and a shudder went through me.

"*Oh, fuck*," I whispered.

Jase chuckled, suddenly catching on.

"See something you like, Alpha?"

She had cast her eyes down immediately, almost seeming to be afraid of me, and I guess, for men around here, we were pretty tall and bulky. Wolf genes being what they were, of course. It could be intimidating for others though, humans, specifically.

"*Fuuuuck.... She's human.*"

Mina

I LOVED PLANTING THE front patch at the nursery. It had to look pretty, with seasonal flowering plants, and had to stay well maintained at all times.

When I started working here six months ago, Daisy had quickly realised that I had an eye for planting combinations, and nurturing the plants to thrive, so she put me in charge of this patch. Once the plants were past their best, they were lovingly potted up for sale as slightly more established plants. It was a win win, and a joy to work on, because it gave me purpose, and structure. Something to quiet my mind, even just for a little while.

Today's patch was for spring flowers, my absolute favourites. I'd planted the bulbs some time ago, and they were starting to flower, so it was time to add the other flourishes to go with them. I sighed happily, staring at the vivid daffodils already in bloom. *Nature was beautiful, and safe; it didn't deliberately try to hurt us.* It calmed my soul, and it always had.

I needed the calm, any calm I could find, because the nightmares were still extreme, and frequent. I barely slept at nights, so this was the only respite I could get. Three days a week at the nursery, and two days a week to myself, plus those damn weekends.

I could feel someone staring at me, and it was such an intense feeling, that my stomach clenched. People didn't look at me, because I'd worked really hard to make sure they didn't notice me at all. The staring continued so eventually, reluctantly; I risked a glance up.

A few metres away, a man stood, tall and muscular, *and staring right at me*. His mouth had dropped open, and he seemed frozen on the spot. I looked down quickly. Did he know me? I didn't want him to recognise me. Oh shit, what if he'd recognised me? What if he knew me, because of... no...

I moved here for a fresh start, and I loved it here. No, *please*. My heart was thudding in my chest, and I couldn't breathe. No, not now. I couldn't show my vulnerability to them. I patted the soil around the last plant, and gathered up my kit as quickly as I could.

He was still there, watching me, and there was another big guy with him, also staring, although he then turned to talk to the other one. My hands trembled. Two of them. No, it was too much.

I went inside, panic almost overwhelming me.

"Done already? I can't wait to see it," Daisy said, moving across the small nursery to join me.

"Jesus, are you okay? You're as pale as a ghost." She reached out to put a hand on my shoulder, and I flinched away.

"Sorry, *no touching*, I forgot. What happened?" I stared at her, my hands trembling enough to make me drop the stack of plastic pots I'd been holding.

"I, uh... I feel..."

Daisy dropped to the floor, picking up the pots.

"Do you need to go home, Mina?" I nodded fast, when she stood up again.

"I'm so sorry."

She shook her head. "Don't apologise, Mina, I understand. You explained all of this to me. Are you safe to drive though?" I shook my head.

"I walked in today. It'll do me good to uh…" I glanced at the front of the nursery, where he might still be waiting. *They.* I wished then that I'd driven in today after all.

"I'll head out the back. It's faster that way."

She nodded, waving me away.

"Feel better, babe, it's all good."

I left fast, seeing her glance at the front entrance, and then head there to peer outside. Was he still there? Panic made it hard to walk, but I forced myself to take one step at a time. To put one foot in front of the other.

Breathe, Mina, focus on the flowers in the gardens as we walk past them. I had to use the best of my techniques for reducing panic, just to get me home.

For once I wished that my home was further from the nursery than it was. I'd been lazily driving to work during the bad weather, but it was really just a ten-minute walk, and I'd started challenging myself to do it.

As soon as I wrenched the door open, and slammed it shut, locking the lock, deadbolt, and chain, I leaned back against it, trying to slow my breathing.

I'm safe now. I'm safe now. I'm safe now.

Chapter Two

ASHER

I saw Daisy peek outside, and glance at both of us. She looked behind her again, and stepped outside, checking the garden patch for a moment. Almost against my will, I moved closer.

"Daisy..."

"*Alpha*." She lowered her head submissively, and then nodded at Jase as he stepped up beside me.

"Daisy, good to see you."

"You too, Beta. What brings you both to my business?" She was one of my pack by marriage, so we didn't know her very well yet, but she was still a trusted member of the pack, nonetheless. She was married to a valued wolf on my committee, Ned.

"We were just at the pub for a pint over lunch. We're on our way back to the pack house now." Jase was speaking, but I struggled to focus on anything but that scent, the thought of that woman. *It consumed me*. It lingered in the air, even without her here.

"Uh... the garden looks good," I finally said, lamely, because I didn't know how to proceed. I was completely out of my depth, floundering and uncertain.

She smiled in response. "Mina does lovely work. She has quite a gift for planting, and nurturing growth. This patch is completely her domain now."

Mina. Mina... my mate is called Mina. No, she can't be my mate. She's human.

"She's human," I finally said, and she nodded.

"No rules against them, Alpha." She sounded like she knew what was really happening.

I stared at Jase for a moment, trying to get my faculties back. Even with the girl gone, *Mina*... the scent remained, taunting me, arousing me. I wanted her like I'd never wanted anything before.

"She... uh... she from around here?" I tried again, wondering why I didn't just shut up and leave. I couldn't seem to make my feet move, and Jase was just watching me, grinning like a smug bastard.

"And you can stop that right now." I jabbed a finger in his direction, and he tried to smother it.

"Yes, Alpha."

"Man... what the fuck's going on here. Ya didn't have to wait for me, it was just a quickie," Derek said, coming up behind us.

"Hey, Daisy, looking fine as always."

She laughed, but she was shaking her head at him.

"Thanks, Derek. My condolences to whichever barmaid you just slobbered all over."

He snorted. "Ah... I did a bit more than that, baby, don't you worry."

I turned to glare at him, and he quieted, lowering his eyes, although he seemed to be the only one who didn't have a clue what was going on.

"Where is she?" I asked Daisy, and she glanced behind her.

"Mina?"

"Yes," I gritted out, completely frustrated by the events of this fucking day, and the way my priorities seemed to have shifted in one single moment.

"She went home. She wasn't feeling well." She looked sad, and my heart thudded painfully in my chest.

"Is she okay?"

"Jesus, what's goin' on here? Are we going back to work or what?" Derek moaned, and I turned to glare at him.

"You both go. I'll follow. *Now.*" They turned and started walking, leaning together to talk. Great, the whole pack would know by the time I got back there.

"Alpha... should I take this unexpected interest in my employee to be rather important to you personally?" Daisy asked delicately. I groaned, running both hands through my hair, which anyone who knows me well will tell you, is the maximum frustration level for me.

"I don't understand it," I finally replied, a heavy sigh following straight after.

She nodded. "Might I offer you a cuppa, and a chat?" She gestured to the garden shop, and I found myself agreeing, and following her lead. She had put up a 'closed' sign, and locked the front door.

A cup of tea then found its way to my hand, in a ridiculously tiny cup, and she laughed.

"Oh my... that looks just as silly in your hand as it does in Ned's. Hang on." She took it away and returned with a proper mug of tea.

"Thanks." I laughed a little, even though quite honestly, my world had just been upended on me.

"So she's your mate?" She asked tentatively.

"I think so? How do I know for sure?" I shrugged as I spoke, like it wasn't a big deal. *Fuck, it's a huge deal.* I thought that this 'mated' shit was a damn myth.

"The scent should be your first clue." My head lifted, as I met her eyes.

"A heavenly scent that you can't ignore, that goes straight to your... *I mean*... that overwhelms you completely?" *Idiot.*

She laughed. "Exactly. She likely won't feel the mate pull, because she's human. That could be a problem for you, but sadly not the biggest one you'll face."

I stared at her warily.

"She's married? Gay?" My heart was dying a slow death in my chest, at the thought of anyone else with her. *She wasn't meant for them; she was* **mine**.

She shook her head slowly.

"Sworn off men forever. I can't tell you the details, but clearly just having you staring at her today sent her into a major anxiety attack. She was shaking, and couldn't breathe."

"Couldn't that be a mate pull response?" I'd been known to grasp at straws out of desperation.

Daisy shook her head again.

"No. She suffers from several anxiety disorders, but I can't tell you more. It's not my place to share that with you. Getting her to trust you will be damn near impossible, and at the risk of insulting my Alpha, I'll say this... you're going to have to tread lightly, and listen to her. If she backs off, or is afraid of you, you have to give her space. If you get all up in her face, she's going to run. *Again*."

I stared at my mug of tea, feeling an unexpected surge of anger. *Again*, she said... as in, she'd come here to escape something or someone already.

"I see."

"I apologise for my words, Alpha."

I snorted, looking her in the eye.

"Daisy, hardly anyone speaks to me like I'm just a person. It's nothing to apologise for. When we're the only ones in a room, you can speak to me however you like."

She smiled, her shoulders relaxing a little.

"Ned said you were a good Alpha. I hoped we'd meet properly and get to talk, although this is obviously not what I thought it would be about."

I drank some of my tea, and the sweetness seemed to help my faculties return to some semblance of normality.

"So she's unlikely to return any feelings I may develop for her... and *hell*... she's human... I should just let her be, right?" I stared at her, feeling like my heart was breaking, like I was being pulled in two directions, both polar opposites of each other.

On one side was the desperate, burning urge to claim her as mine, and on the other, the sobering realisation that I should back off and leave her in peace because she'd been so upset even by my presence.

When did I turn into such a sappy fool? An hour ago, everything had been normal, and I'd been a staunch non-believer in exactly what I was now desperate to experience.

Daisy smiled at me.

"Listen, I think that you'd be good for her. If we can get her to talk to you, and start to trust you, then maybe there's a chance. She needs to feel safe, and if she's the mate of an Alpha, then she never needs to fear for her safety ever again, but she needs to make that decision for herself. I can talk you up a bit to her, I mean, obviously I won't mention the wolf thing, but I guess we need to broach that in a way that won't scare her, and soon."

I suddenly wanted to be the one to open her eyes to wolf shifters, to introduce her to our world, but I also sensed that it could be even more terrifying for her that way. It was a sobering thought.

"Maybe you should slowly bring her in. Tell her, show her. She trusts you, so hopefully it won't scare her. That way, if she's ever willing to speak to me, she won't fear that part of me. Jesus... what am I saying? I can't have a human mate. She won't strengthen our pack, not like a wolf mate. Hell, I have no idea what I'm doing here..."

I stood up, setting aside my empty mug.

"I should head back now, but please look after her. Whether I can proceed with this whole mate thing or not, I can't let anything hurt her. But, Daisy, she should know the real you. That could make her feel safer around you, knowing that you could protect her in a way that no other would ever expect."

Daisy lowered her head.

"As you wish, Alpha, but please, don't disregard the mate bond purely because she's human. She could strengthen the pack in ways you can't even imagine. She will strengthen *you*, that's how it works. *A stronger Alpha is a stronger leader.*"

"You are wise beyond your years, Daisy. Thank you."

As I headed back to the pack house, my mind was whirling. How could the mate bond be a real damn thing? And how could my destined mate... an Alpha's mate... be a fucking human? Wolf shifters are not immortal, but we live for hundreds of years, and a human won't.

That meant this was doomed to fail right from the very start.

Chapter Three

Mina

I STARED THROUGH THE window at the back of the nursery. Daisy was sitting chatting with *that* man, the one who'd terrified me outside. Why did I try to be brave, and go back to work? Why did I risk walking back? Why was I now hiding behind the door, like a total loser?

It was a wonder that I could even leave the house alone at all. *But that's what I am; alone*, and until today I'd actually felt safe here. I really didn't want to leave this place, and have to start again elsewhere.

She'd made him tea, and she chatted easily with him, like she knew him. She was respectful of him, dipping her head to him now and then, and he seemed like he might even be okay. Not scary as such, not while he was sitting down, at least. He looked less terrifyingly tall, and overpowering.

His dark blond hair was long, and a little scruffed up, like he'd been pulling at it. He had a rugged beard, which covered the bottom part of his face, but wasn't very long. Not that it was neatly trimmed either, it was just a beard.

I never saw what colour his eyes were earlier, but they were intense, I already knew that. They burned into me like I don't know what. They seemed to reach into my soul, like they knew me, and I panicked. Who wouldn't, having this huge guy suddenly staring at you? It was normal to be afraid, or at least it was for me.

I suddenly realised that all they'd have to do is turn their heads, and they'd see me peering in the window like a peeping tom. I turned and ran, because without the anxiety, I could actually run.

Being steady on my feet felt like bliss, after the shaky walks home and back. Why wasn't I freaking out now? I had no idea, but it wasn't something to be understood. It just was.

Once more at home, I locked the door securely again, and headed for my chair in the corner. The doctors had suggested a safe place at home, somewhere to retreat to when the anxiety is at its worst. Somewhere I can relax and breathe, and feel calm again.

My recliner chair was situated in the one corner which had no windows anywhere near it. It was safe because nobody could sneak up on me, or be behind me, watching. I pulled the cushion into my lap, hugging it, as I curled up in the chair. Would I ever be normal again?

A knock at my door an hour or so later, set my heart thumping, and a new panic starting to rise. As if the person on the other side of the door knew that, they called out.

"It's me, babe. Just checking in on you." *It was Daisy*. I sighed with relief and stood up, then remembered that she'd been with *him*. I approached the door cautiously.

"Are you alone?"

She was quiet for a moment, maybe surprised at my question.

"Yes, Mina, of course I am. You can take a look with the chain on, if you prefer."

She was right in suggesting that I'd want to check first. I did, and I couldn't catch a glimpse of anyone near her. I didn't think she'd lie to me about that anyway. She was the only person I'd ever told about what happened to me, well, bits of it, anyway.

I let her in, carefully locking the door behind her.

"I brought something to cheer you up," she said, holding up a bag; it was a giant chocolate chip cookie from the bakery next door. She knew I loved them, and despite everything, I smiled.

"Thank you, that's so kind. Look, I'm sorry about today." I'd felt awful for letting her down.

Daisy sat down on my sofa, giving me a warm smile.

"Mina, you were clear with me about your past, and how it affected you. I'm hardly going to complain if you have a bad day, am I? Not with the great work you do every other day."

I set the cookie down, pushing the bag far enough back to break off a piece. I offered it to Daisy, and she took it. I broke off a second piece for me.

"Who was he?" I asked, knowing that she had no idea that I'd seen her talking to him.

She tilted her head, smiling slowly.

"You returned…" I widened my eyes.

"You can't possibly know that."

She laughed. "You did! Oh, good for you, although I'm sorry you didn't come in."

"You were having tea with *him*." She nodded.

"He's a good man, Mina."

"You knew him already?" She nodded again, then shrugged.

"I've known him a while. Not closely, but I've known of him, through my husband. You'd like him, I think."

I shook my head firmly. "*No.* No men, you know that. I can't be around them." She sighed sadly.

"You might change your mind."

I shivered as I pictured him again.

"Did you see the size of him compared to me? He could overpower me in a heartbeat, and I can't risk that." Daisy looked sad.

"And if I said he'd never do that? To anyone, let alone you?"

I watched my hands as they trembled, dropping the last piece of my cookie.

"It doesn't matter. *No men.*"

"Okay, I won't pressure you, but if you ever change your mind, I'd love to introduce you. I'll even stay, if you feel safest that way." She offered me a big smile.

I shook my head again.

"No. Men. Ever." She groaned.

"Okay, so... on an unrelated subject, I was thinking of taking a drive tomorrow, up to that hiking route you've been wanting to try. You up for that? You know I like to spend my day off getting muddy in the woods."

I laughed, despite myself, because Daisy was the most elegant woman I'd ever known. I mean, she was perfectly groomed at all times, so I couldn't imagine her getting muddy by choice.

She even wore gloves when planting at the nursery, and her luscious red hair was always pulled back in a perfect French plait, and her makeup always pristine. She was taller than me, probably tall enough to never be a victim like me. *I wished I knew how that felt.*

"You're planning to say yes, right? Please do, because I hate doing this alone. Ned can't come this week, he's got pack... uh, *packing up* to do." She grimaced at me.

"Packing up?" She looked flummoxed.

"I just mean he's got some work to do. Uh... with stuff..." I laughed.

"That's nice and vague, but yes... count me in." A sharp shock ran through me with a sudden thought that occurred, chilling the blood in my veins.

"Wait... this isn't some trick to get me out there to meet this guy, is it?"

She looked horrified.

"Mina, I don't ever want you to feel you can't trust me. I promise you that I would never do that. If you say you want to meet him, I'll happily help arrange it, but until you do, it's not my business. This will be just you and me, I promise, and it'll be fun!"

I nodded, feeling a wave of relief. A walk outdoors, among the wonders of nature, would do me so much good. My doctors had even noticed that it calms me, so they'd practically prescribed it as a therapy.

We made plans for the next day, and Daisy left. The house felt unnaturally empty after she left, and I realised then that in six months, she was my first and only visitor. *How pathetic was that?*

Chapter Four

ASHER

I COULDN'T CONCENTRATE ON anything. I just sat there with the committee, at the meeting I'd called, and all I could think about was her; *the human*. The human mate that the moon fates had sent to me. What the actual fuck?

Do you have any idea what it's like, sitting around a table with a bunch of fucking male wolves, when you've got a semi in your pants? I'd been semi hard since I'd smelled her earlier today. It was so fucking uncomfortable, and I couldn't do anything about it.

What did I want to do? Find her, fuck her, sink so deep into her that I couldn't tell where either of us began or ended, but it wasn't going to happen. Why? Because she was human, or because she was afraid of men. *Afraid of me...*

"Alpha?" Jase was speaking to me, but I hadn't even been listening. I cleared my throat.

"Uh... yeah?" He grinned.

"I was just suggesting that we call it a day. Any objections?" I glanced at him in surprise, and relief.

"Uh... no. Thanks, guys." I stayed in my seat while they made a swift exit, with only Jase remaining.

"Were we done?" I asked him quietly, and he chuckled.

"Alpha, your head isn't in the game, so I thought it best to reschedule."

I groaned. "I'm a fucking failure." I rested my head in my hands, trying to compose myself.

"If I might be a little personal here, Alpha. I hear this is perfectly normal for males, when they find their mates. You know, if they don't complete the bond immediately."

I stared at him in horror.

"You mean I'm going to be out of it, and have half a boner for days, or weeks, or... *fuck*... months?" He laughed.

"I'm going to focus on the timescales you mentioned, and steer clear of the... you know... why do you think it'll take that long?"

"She's afraid of me."

Jase frowned. "She doesn't know you, Alpha."

I glared at him. "I'm more than aware of that, thank you. I mean, she's apparently afraid of all men."

He'd lowered his eyes at my tone, but met them again now.

"Afraid of all men?" He frowned deeply.

"You know what that suggests."

I growled, long and low, because I knew exactly what it fucking suggested, and if someone had hurt her, they'd better be prepared to feel their dicks being ripped off and fed to them.

"Daisy is going to teach her about wolf shifters, and then... *we'll see*. She may refuse to ever come near me, and I'll have to find a way to deal with that. Is there any way to cure this damn mate bond thing?"

He stared at me, his eyes wide and shocked.

"Why would you want to-"

"If she doesn't want me, or is afraid of me, I can't function like this, Jase. I'm in a permanent state of arousal here. It's no wonder I can't fucking concentrate." I wanted to scream out my frustration.

He quirked an eyebrow. "If it's that bad, maybe go and get your end away in town tonight. Might help for a while. I have no idea, but it's worth a try, right?"

The thought of sex with anyone but Mina felt distasteful, all of a sudden. *Wrong, so wrong*. This woman had ruined me with one whiff of her damn scent.

"About the fact that she's human..." Jase began, nervously.

"I know, she can't help me restore the pack's strength. Fuck... this is a nightmare. Why have the fates done this to me? We need to strengthen, or we're all dead." I adjusted myself in the chair, fed up with all of this crap.

He cleared his throat, watching me fidget in my seat.

"We could ask the witches for guidance. Maybe they can help with the bond."

I considered his words. Witches were the only other supernatural beings that existed, despite what people wanted to believe. Some could be trusted, but most couldn't.

We had a few locally, a small coven, who were supportive of the pack, and in fact, one of them had married into the pack, and her gifts made her a powerful ally.

"Perhaps, but let's try a night on the town first. Maybe this is just a blip, and I'll get a good shag, and feel better." I grinned, despite the sinking feeling that it wouldn't work at all, despite the way my words had practically turned my stomach.

Two hours later, and we were in one of the two bars in our small town. It was full of wolves, so seemed like the best idea, but... fuck it... it was like all of a sudden, no women were getting me hot. They were wolves, for fuck's sake. They were exactly who I was made for, but suddenly my inner wolf was saying 'nope, just her, just our mate'.

Every now and then, I thought I could catch scent of Mina again, and I'd look around, eagerly hoping to see her petite form, cropped hair, and wide eyes. I hadn't even been close enough to know what colour they were, but they were tired, afraid. I'd noticed that much immediately.

What had happened to her, to make her so afraid? I was worried that there was only one answer to that question, and damn, it really pissed my wolf off right along with me.

If someone hurt her, we'll hurt them, he growled in my head, and I nodded. I already knew that part. Whether she accepted me or not, I'd avenge her. I couldn't not, and that meant I needed to know more about her, because all I knew was her first name.

I was pretty sure Daisy would tell me more about her, apart from what she'd already refused to tell me, but I could find out the rest. I could take away the thing that she was so afraid of, and give her back her life.

"Nobody getting you hard, boss?" Derek asked with a smirk.

"What's your point?" I snapped back.

He laughed, enough beers in him that he didn't care about my tone. I was beginning to think that my Alpha pull wasn't even working on him. Why did he stay, if he didn't feel submissive to my wolf? He'd always called me 'boss', rather than 'Alpha'. Was it an insult, or was it just his way?

"Ah come on... you normally get your end away, when we come to the bar. What's stopping ya tonight? How about her?" He jabbed his thumb in the direction of a young woman. She was gorgeous, with long luscious dark hair, curves in all the right places, and... *nothing*. Not a damn thing. Was my cock now completely fucking dormant, unless it was Mina in front of me? I groaned.

"Let's get some fucking hard liquor out here. I need a real drink." Jase returned with tumblers of bourbon, and we all put away a good few of those. The frustrating thing about my wolf was that he seemed to stop me getting drunk quickly, and right now that was pissing me off too. I needed peace. I needed to forget about her, even just for a while.

I growled, running a hand through my hair.

"Fuck it, I need a piss." I headed for the restroom, wondering if I'd seem like a pussy, if I crapped out early and went home. Maybe if I could jerk off, and get her out of my system, I'd be able to shake this cloud over me.

As I was leaving the restroom, a woman stepped up in front of me, her hand on my chest. She was one of the unmated wolves from a nearby pack. Although we pack Alphas were in charge of our wolves, we allowed the unmated ones to mingle as they wished.

If wolves paired up, they could choose which pack they moved to, meaning that these females could bring more wolves to another pack. If they mated with my wolves, they'd better damn well join ours, though.

"Wolf got your tongue?" She cooed, slipping her other hand down my body, to my pants.

I stopped her hands, and her eyes came back up to mine, confused.

"Is something wrong?" She asked, biting her lip. Fuck... just a day ago, I'd have dragged her into the restroom to fuck her brains out, just for that. What is wrong with me?

"I... uh..."

She gasped, and stepped back.

"Oh my god, you're mated. Fuck, I'm so sorry." I frowned at her assumption.

"Why do you say that?" Was there some kind of fucking visible mark on me now?

She winked at me then.

"I only ever get turned down by mated wolves." She tossed her luscious dark hair back. It was the same girl that Derek had pointed out to me, and I felt suspicion creeping in.

"Did someone send you to try and seduce me?" She blinked at me.

"Say what?"

I growled, low, dangerous, and she groaned, her eyes lowering instinctively.

"*Alpha!* I'm sorry, I didn't know. I've never been in this area before. The girls in my pack told me it's full of sexy wolves, and I'm looking for my own mate. Until then, I'm having some fun."

I sighed. "You don't need to submit to me, wolf. I'm not your Alpha, although if one of my boys turns out to be your mate, I hope you will be." She laughed.

"Well, if he is, he's not here tonight, Alpha. I'm told I'll know."

I groaned, banging my head back against the wall with frustration.

"Yeah, apparently so."

"So you're not?" She asked tentatively.

I shrugged, trying to act carefree when I felt anything but.

"I can't stop thinking about her, but it's not going to happen. Fuck... why am I even telling you this? I came out tonight to try and put her out of my mind."

She grinned suddenly.

"I'm told that's not easy to do, but if you want me to try, I'm more than willing." She winked at me, and slipped her hands back down to my pants. I groaned, fighting the urge to push her away, even though this was exactly why I'd come here tonight.

"Fuck..." Grabbing her by the hair, I dragged her back through the restroom door, and slammed her up against it, my mouth taking hers in a hard kiss. *I can do this.* Her hands worked their way into my pants, and slithered over my cock. I groaned as I kissed her harder, and the scent of her arousal wafted around us. *I can fucking do this.*

It took a hell of a lot more attention from her hands than it should have, than it would have before today, but as soon as I was hard, I pushed up her skirt, tore her pants away, and thrust inside her. She moaned, and wrapped her arms and legs around me, as I pounded away at her, up against that door.

There wouldn't be a single person in that bar, who wouldn't know that someone was getting their brains fucked out right now.

A dim voice in the back of my head was cursing me for even looking at another woman now I'd found my mate. My wolf was seriously pissed, and nothing felt right about this moment.

On top of the wrongness of the whole fucking experience, I'd also forgotten a condom in my rush to get inside her, that desperate need to get on with it before that fucking mate bond destroyed my ability to even try. I growled with frustration.

I never even checked if she was on the pill, and I should have, because shifters were just like humans, and unprotected sex led to wolfy fucking babies.

Before I got too close, I pulled out and pushed her to her knees, praying my dick would stay hard, even though no part of me wanted anyone but Mina now.

"Finish me," I snarled, and she was only too willing to comply, wrapping her hands and lips around my cock, and working me up until I finally came in her mouth, my hand pressed against the door for balance. She swallowed it down, and stared up at me, her eyes wide.

"Um..."

I nodded, feeling like an absolute bastard.

"Sorry, I forgot a condom, and didn't want to take the risk. Stand up." She stood up, awkwardly pulling her skirt down.

"What are you doing?" I asked gruffly, and she stared at me, a frown creasing her forehead.

"You're done, right?" I grinned half-heartedly.

"You're not."

I slipped my fingers up under that skirt, and started to tease at her clit, slipping two inside her, while my thumb pressed and circled her clit, her breaths coming in heavy gasps. I circled her throat with my other hand, pressing lightly and holding her gaze, wishing the wide eyes staring back at me were Mina's.

"I never leave a woman unsatisfied, wolf. So I'm going to finger-fuck you, until you scream my name."

She shuddered, trying to stay upright on her legs, as her orgasm started to creep up on her.

"I don't even know your name."

I forced a grin as I stared at her.

"Then you'll scream 'Alpha'."

She did, and then I sent her on her way, staying behind to frantically wash my hands, as I tried to rid myself of the essence of a woman who wasn't Mina from my skin. Already I hated myself for everything I'd just allowed to happen, and knew it wouldn't happen again.

Pasting a grin on my face, I strutted out of that bathroom like the Alpha I was, even though every step felt like a fucking lie. At the table, I ignored the smug grins of my two subordinates, and grabbed my jacket.

"I'll see you guys back at the house." I left before they could respond. I was pretty sure that one, or both of them, had sent her to me, but who cares because even though it was so wrong, it had rid me of that fucking arousal at last.

Maybe my brain would start to work again now that I'd cleared myself of that fog of fucking desire for a woman I couldn't have. Hell, maybe the attraction to Mina was just that; attraction. The smell could have even just been some flower I'd never smelled before.

My temporarily blissed-out brain was pretty ready to declare the mate bond thing bullshit again, despite how wrong it had felt to be anywhere near another woman. I sighed with determination, turning the corner at the bottom of the street, just past the garden shop.

A scent wafted at me, and my legs trembled to a stop. *Fuck*. She wasn't even here, and I could still fucking smell it, or did that mean it really was something growing there that was doing this to me?

I wandered up to the small garden I'd watched her plant, crouching low to sniff the flowers. Nope... it wasn't coming from any of them, although it was in the air all around me.

I stood up, looking around me when I suddenly realised what a pussy I'd have looked like. Crouching to smell fucking flowers? I'm a fucking *Alpha*. I growled at myself, angry with my behaviour, and glanced at the windows of the garden shop.

Wide eyes stared back at me, and the face disappeared as soon as she knew I had seen her. *Mina*.

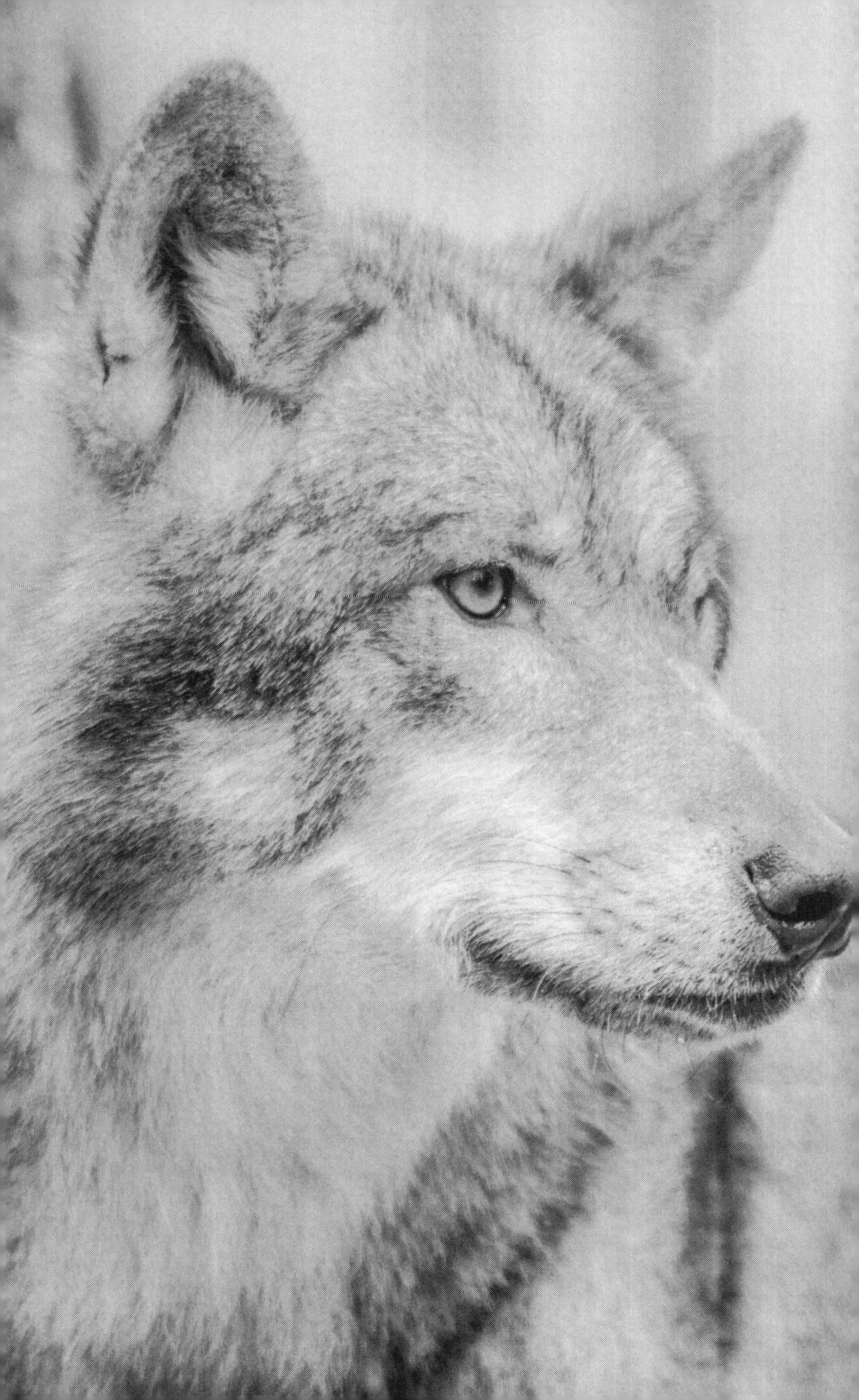

Chapter Five

MINA

Crap! He saw me! He really saw me. I stood away from the window, my entire body trembling. How could I get out of this? I needed to escape.

Daisy had always let me spend time after hours in here, if I wanted to, and tonight I'd just needed to be somewhere other than my empty house.

Being able to drive practically to the back door was all that made it possible, only now...now I was too afraid to try leaving. What if he came after me? I wouldn't be able to fight him off, because he was huge.

He was clearly stronger than me, and that was the danger of letting him near me. I wouldn't stand a chance. Light tapping at the window stopped me breathing for a few seconds. *No.*

"Mina?" A voice called. He knew my name? Daisy must have told him. Oh god, what do I do now?

"It's okay, I won't hurt you," he said next. *Yeah... they probably all say that at first.* It's how they reel their victims in.

He tapped again. "Please."

Why was he so desperate to speak to me? What possible reason could he have? Did he want to buy a plant? He'd been admiring the flowers I'd planted. *At night.* Why couldn't he wait until we were open?

I dared a peek at him, catching his gaze instantly. He rested his forehead against the glass, his breath misting the surface, as he seemed to breathe in slow pants. It was terrifying.

"What do you want?" I asked, just loudly enough that he'd hear me through the glass. My voice had been shakier than I'd wanted. He banged his head against the glass lightly, the sudden sharp noise making me jump.

"I have no fucking idea," he muttered, tapping the glass with his head again.

"*Fuck.*"

"We're closed," I said, unnecessarily, but with nothing else to say. He laughed, a short bark of laughter.

What should I do? He seemed to be in distress, but he was a stranger, and worse than that, he was *a man*. A big strong man. If I opened the door, I risked him hurting me, and I had no chance of fighting him off. He was even bigger than... No, I couldn't go there, not again.

"Come back when we're open," I said, my voice trembling.

"Will you talk to me then?" He asked, his eyes pleading with me. *No*, but I couldn't tell him that. I couldn't tell him yes either.

"I don't know."

He sighed, nodding as he pulled back from the glass.

"Yeah, okay." He backed up a few steps, running his hands through that dark blond hair. He stared at me for the longest moment, and then he nodded again, and turned away, his strides taking him out of sight.

I dropped to the floor, my legs shaking so much that they just wouldn't hold me anymore. Something about his voice had been calming, even though he had been clearly anything but. I was right not to let him in, because I couldn't be around any man who wasn't in control of himself. It was too dangerous, they all were.

When my breathing returned to normal, I grabbed my phone and keys, because I needed to go home. I needed to go and hide in my safe place for a while, thinking of puppies, and other cuddly things. I knew I wouldn't sleep, because it never happened until I reached that point of near exhaustion, when I couldn't fight it off any longer, and that's when the nightmares would come.

I closed and locked up the back door of the nursery, once I'd thoroughly checked for anyone outside. It was no way to live, but it was the only way to stay safe. I dashed the few steps to my car, my hand shaking, as I tried to control the key enough to get it in the damn lock.

Footsteps behind me made me gasp and turn, my back against the car. No no no. *It was him.*

He held his hands up, staying about a metre away.

"Please, don't be afraid of me, Mina. I won't hurt you. *I couldn't.*"

I held my hand in front of me, keys between my fingers, the way they'd taught me in the few self-defence classes I'd attended.

"I can't possibly know that. I don't even know you."

He sighed, lowering his hands.

"You never will, if you don't let me talk to you."

"Why?" I asked, my heart ready to beat right out of my chest. There was something endearing about him, while I still feared him, and all men, and I think that's all that stopped me running from him.

"I don't know. I... *fuck*... I don't know. I just really want to know you."

I shook my head, wishing there was room to back up more.

"I don't care what you want."

He snorted, shrugging a little.

"I got that already. Look... can you just give me a chance, please? I swear, I only want to get to know you. I'm a nice guy. Hell... I guess they all say that, huh? Ask Daisy. Ask her anything about me. We know each other through her husband, Ned. *I'm safe, Mina.*" I felt tears biting at my eyes, and blinked rapidly.

"I'm not." He sighed, running a hand through his hair.

"Don't you even want to know my name?"

I could feel my whole body trembling by now. He wasn't even close to me, but I was alone, at night, and he was the only person near me, and for some reason he didn't overlook me like everyone else. I'd worked so hard on becoming invisible, but he saw me.

My breaths started gasping out of me, and I felt my legs weaken. I gripped the car with my non key holding hand. No, please, I couldn't faint, not here. *Not alone with him.*

"Are you okay?" He asked with concern. He stepped closer, and I gasped.

"Please... don't... touch... me..."

I fell to my knees as the dizziness overtook me. *Don't pass out don't pass out don't pass out...*

When I blinked my eyes open again, I was propped up against the car, with a jacket draped over me. He was crouching near me, but backed up a few inches, when my eyes reached him.

"What..."

"You passed out, and I only stopped you hurting yourself, I promise. You're safe, Mina."

He looked devastated as he stared back at me. I swallowed hard.

"I... I don't know what to say."

"You could say thanks for stopping me braining myself on my car, or you know... *wow, I'm sorry I made you chin yourself, when you tried to stop me falling...*" He was laughing quietly, and I blinked at him dumbly.

"You chinned yourself?"

He laughed again, rubbing at his beardy jaw.

"Misjudged the distance, when I jumped forward to catch you."

I smiled, then caught myself.

"I'm sorry."

"As long as you're not hurt, Mina, it's all good."

I stared at him, scanning his features now that he was so much closer to me.

"Why do you care about that?" He was freaking me out, by appearing so caring and gentle, while I still saw him as a threat. It was so confusing.

"I... hell, I don't know how to answer that. Can I say again that I'm a nice guy?" He smiled at me, and my heart thudded in my chest. *No. Don't find him cute. Don't let your guard down.*

I glanced down at the jacket over me. It wasn't mine, and I knew that for two reasons. One, I was still wearing mine, and two, it smelled of male cologne. It was a soothing clean smell, with an earthiness to it. I found myself breathing deeper through my nose, so I could keep smelling it.

He cleared his throat. "I uh... thought you might be cold when you woke up." I glanced at him, and he looked embarrassed.

"I'm sorry, I had no idea what to do. It made sense at the time."

I nodded, still surprised that he seemed to care.

"It was the right thing to do. I do get cold when I get anxious."

He sighed softly. "You don't need to be anxious around me, but I don't expect you to take my word for it. I'll prove it to you, somehow."

I struggled to my feet, handing his jacket back to him, missing its warmth almost immediately.

"Thank you." He nodded, holding his jacket against his chest.

"I'd offer to drive you home, but I'm guessing that's not something you'd feel comfortable with."

I nodded. "Thank you for understanding, and for looking after me. Um… I'm sorry, I never did ask your name."

He grinned, backing up another step.

"*Asher*. Pleasure to meet you, Mina. You sure you're okay to drive?" I nodded.

"It's not my first panic attack, I'll be fine. It's only a short drive." Why did I tell him that? I should have pretended it's a long way away.

He stepped up close again and I gasped, pressing back against the car, watching warily as he crouched down, and picked something up.

"You'll need these." My car keys. *Crap.* I held out my hand, and he dropped them into it, making sure not to touch me.

"Thanks."

He stayed and watched me get in, lock the doors, buckle up, and drive away. When I glanced in my rear-view mirror, he was holding his jacket up to his face.

Asher

FUCK. FUCK FUCK FUCK! Talking to her was a mistake, and being near her was a mistake. And Jesus… looking after her, seeing her that vulnerable… *big fucking mistake*.

I just wanted her more now, and my wolf was practically fucking purring when I got closer to her, and come on, you're a wolf, dammit!

She's ours. He replied, chuffing a laugh in my head, the bastard.

I started walking home, taking one last delicious breath of her scent with me, and I had a fucking boner again. I was completely out of control over her. By the time I was home, the only thing I could do was go for a shower, and try to get rid of it myself.

What the fuck was I going to do? How could I be mated to a fucking human? And one who was terrified of me at that. I went to bed, completely unfulfilled by wanking myself off in the damn shower, and tried to go to sleep.

My jacket was in the corner of the room, and it still held her scent. It was calling to me, even from across the room. With a groan, I hopped out of bed, and grabbed it, burying my face in it, breathing her in.

I sighed heavily when my fucking cock bounced back up to attention. What the fuck? What the actual fucking fuck?! Tossing the jacket down, I threw myself back onto the bed, and took myself in hand again.

Was this my future now? Tossing myself off repeatedly, because just the thought of her, the scent of her, turned me into a fucking teenager again?

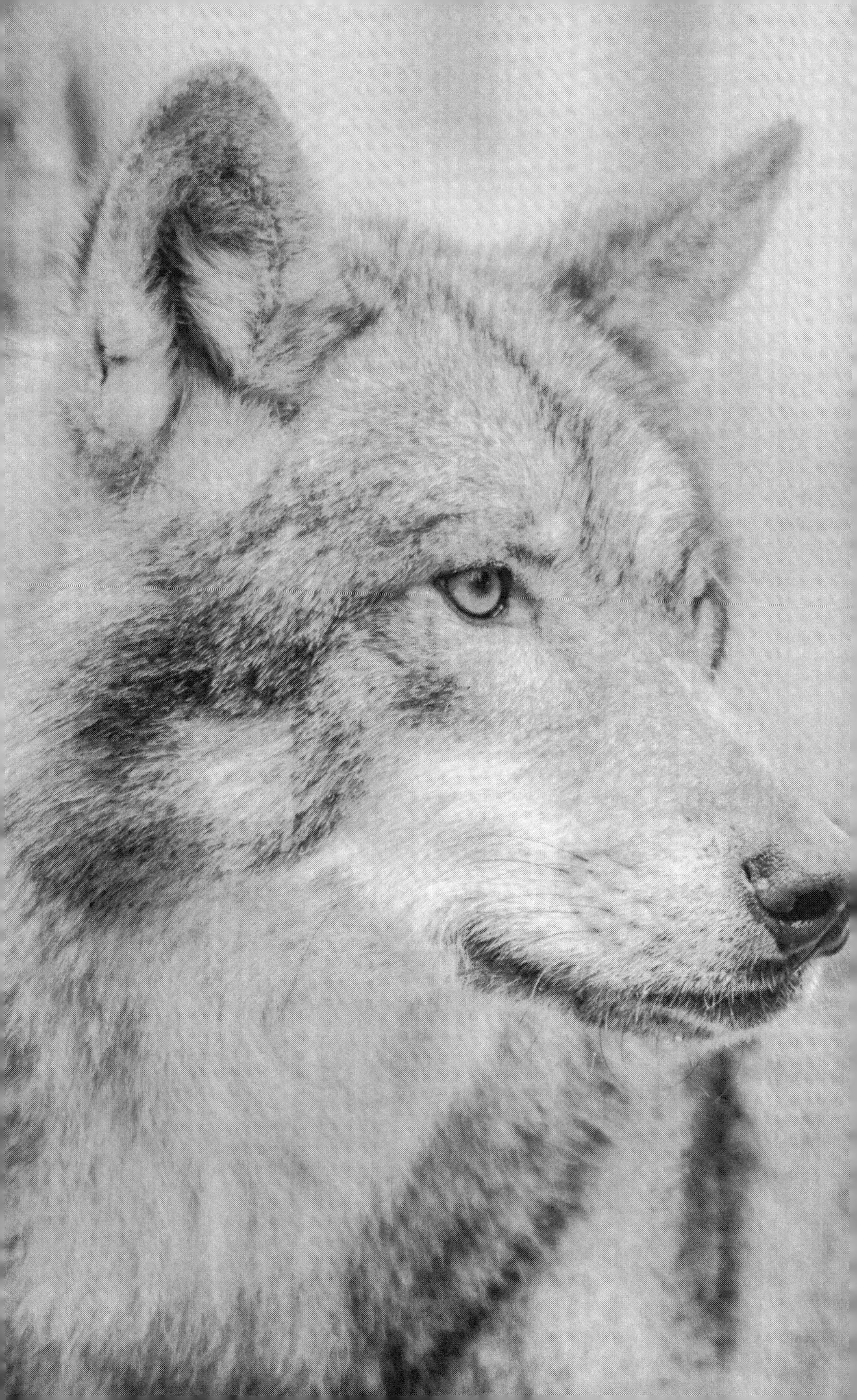

Chapter Six

Mina

I drove just as far as the first turn, then pulled over, because I needed a minute. I needed to breathe. I could still smell his cologne on me, and damn if it actually soothed me, rather than freaking me out.

I couldn't let myself trust him though. I wouldn't be that weak again, I couldn't. Trust led to betrayal, and pain, and I'd die before I'd let myself be in that place again.

The secondary reason for stopping was more of a countermeasure, because I had to make sure he hadn't followed me. He'd waited outside the nursery for me to leave, and that meant that he could just as easily follow me home.

There were no other cars out on the road, and nobody walking, so eventually, after about ten minutes, I started the car again, and headed home, pulling up onto my drive, and checking the street in both directions before getting out of the car. My keys were already in my hand, for quick entry.

It still amazed me that I'd been able to start leaving the house at night. My doctors had been impressed too. Apparently it showed some kind of improvement, or growth.

My therapy sessions mostly happened as video calls these days, since I'd moved out of town from my current therapist, and didn't have the courage to find a new one. I really liked Doc Phyllis.

She was sturdy, and unflappable, and she got me, she understood. She'd helped me more in the year since it had happened, than any other therapist. She'd been more than willing to keep up our sessions, even though the health service had long since stopped footing the bill. She'd promised me that other subsidies she received would cover it.

I was tempted to call her for help right now, but I realised it wasn't help I needed. It was someone to talk to. Just a person, a friend. What a shame I'd left the few I'd had, long ago, and far away.

My parents had moved to Spain a few years back, their retirement home purchased there, and I'd spent some time with them, before and after what happened. I truly had nobody to talk to now.

And this guy, *Asher*... suddenly he was on the scene, and wanted to get to know me? Why? He couldn't find me attractive, because I'd done everything I could, to make sure that I wouldn't appeal to anyone.

He seemed nice, but he was huge, and no guy that big could be safe. Even scarier, he was cute, if I'd even let myself consider how he looked, and I shouldn't.

He'd said... he'd said he wouldn't hurt me. He'd said he was safe. Had Daisy told him? Did he know why I'd fled here, with my tail between my legs, and a new name? How could she do that to me?

I'd trusted her with my darkest secret, and it wasn't hers to tell. I had to discuss it with her, but it was close to midnight, so it would have to wait until our hiking visit tomorrow.

I might end up awake all night, but I wouldn't disturb her sleep too.

Asher

I DREAMED ABOUT HER all fucking night. I dreamed of spreading her out beneath me, and licking every glorious inch of her body, pinching and teasing her nipples, and fucking her with my mouth, my fingers, and my cock. *Hard*. I woke up twice with a boner. Twice!

At this rate I was going to chafe the bastard, and I had the feeling he was still gonna want more. I groaned, glaring at the sun peering through the gap in the curtains. I was shattered, and I couldn't even remember what day it was.

I glanced at my phone. It was Friday, and that meant I had to work. I had a whole damn day to get through, and no chance of seeing her again, not that that was even the plan. I had to try and stay away from her, because she wasn't into me, in the sense that she'd rather run the other way.

I didn't even know if she got home safely last night. I wanted to check, but how do you do that, when you don't even know a person's last name, or number, or where they live? I could check the garden centre, but no... they were closed on Fridays.

There was only one thing left to try. Grabbing my phone, I texted Ned, asking for Daisy's number. He didn't argue, or question me, he just sent it back. I added it to the memory, then messaged her.

Me: *Daisy, it's Asher. Have you heard from Mina today?*

There was a long pause, and I sat there growling to myself, while she took an age to reply. I realised that I hadn't even remembered to use my title when I messaged her. This whole protocol thing just escaped me sometimes. Just when I was about to scream, my phone finally pinged.

Daisy: *Morning Alpha. Not yet but I'm on my way to meet her. What's up?*

Me: *Shop's closed, right?*

Daisy: *Yep, we're going out together. What's up?*

She wouldn't let up, I could tell. I groaned, and gave in.

Me: *I saw her last night, and she had an anxiety attack. She insisted on driving herself home.*

Daisy took a good few fucking minutes to reply, and they felt like hours. I was about ready to ring her, and demand an answer.

Daisy: *Shit. What happened to set her off? Did she go to the nursery? Is she okay? Why didn't you take her home? I'm nearly at her place now.*

Me: *I saw her when she locked up, and she freaked out. I stopped her hurting herself, and she left. She wouldn't let me drive her home. And stop texting me while you drive!*

Even I could see the irony in my statement as I hopped out of bed, and went for a shower. When I came back, there were two missed calls on my phone. *Daisy*.

I rang her back immediately.

"Finally," she said, laughing a little.

"I take it nothing's wrong then?" I blurted sharply, my heart thudding in my chest. *Just let her be okay, please.*

"Well, I mean, my Alpha demanded that I stop replying to his texts while I drive, so I thought I'd ring you, and just let you know that I have an app that types as I speak, so technically I don't text and drive. Ned would kill me if I even thought about it. Also, I'm just waiting for Mina to grab her stuff. She's fine. She's a bit quiet, but I'll talk to her about some stuff today, and see how she does."

"Shifter stuff?" What happened today would be vital, and I really hoped it wouldn't go badly wrong.

"Yeah, I mean, she needs to know about us before she sees you wolf out. She'll never trust you if not." I growled with frustration.

"Are you sure it's wise to take her somewhere to do that?"

She laughed again. "You think I should wolf out in her living room? I think that'd be a monumentally bad move. *This is her safe place, Alpha.*" Luckily she had her head in the game, because I was failing big time.

"You're right, neutral space is good. Don't be too far from escape for her though. I don't want her afraid, and feeling trapped."

Daisy giggled. "You've got it bad, Alpha." I cleared my throat pointedly.

"You'd do well to remember the *Alpha* part."

She giggled again. "I'm sorry, Alpha, I promise it won't happen again."

"Why don't I believe you?"

She laughed. "Gotta go, she's back." She ended the call, and I sighed heavily. In twenty-four hours, I'd gone from no women in my life, to two troublesome ones. What the fuck was I even doing?

When I hit the kitchen to grab breakfast, I saw Jase there already, eating his usual egg white omelette, with gluten-free bread.

"Morning, Alpha," he said quietly. I grabbed a few slices of bread, and shoved them into the toaster.

"How do you get through the morning on such a small breakfast?" I asked grumpily, as I tossed a few rashers of bacon in a pan, and grabbed some eggs.

He shrugged. "The joy of allergies, Alpha. Who knew that even we wolves could have food intolerances?"

"A well-kept secret, I'm sure." I focused on the art of cooking, beating the eggs, and tossing in some tabasco for a bit of a kick. Eventually I sat down across from him with my plate.

He looked longingly at my breakfast.

"God, that smells so good... I remember being able to eat stuff like that."

I stared at him, surprised. "You weren't always like this?" He shook his head morosely.

"I was badly injured in a fight with another wolf. Whatever damage was done internally left me unable to digest some things. Perks of being a wolf though, I survived when I should have died, so there's that."

I sighed. "I'm sorry, man, I had no idea."

"I joined the pack a long time after that happened. You didn't need to know, Alpha, because it doesn't exactly affect my ability to be your Beta." *Fair point.*

"So no egg yolks?"

He sighed heavily. "And no spices or hot sauces, and gluten-free stuff seems to agree with me better than standard stuff."

"Jesus... you can eat meat though, right?" I was horrified, because what would his life be if he couldn't? He was a wolf shifter, dammit! Meat was a staple of our diet!

"Fuck yeah. You just don't normally eat with any of us, so you haven't seen me chowing down on that."

I offered him a piece of bacon.

"Seriously?" He asked, looking shocked. I nodded, and he took it, biting almost half off in one go, and chewing it, his eyes closing as he ate.

"Oh god... that's so good... thanks."

"You should have made some for yourself. There's plenty, there's always plenty." He nodded.

"Yeah... I just got used to eating this boring shit each day."

I laughed at the expression on his face.

"Well, as your Alpha, I command you to eat more bacon." He snorted, bowing his head slightly.

"As you wish, Alpha. I live to serve."

I got up for coffee, and noticed he'd been drinking some, so I offered him a refill. He was staring at me shrewdly.

"What?"

"I... I don't know, you're just different." I sighed heavily.

"Oh Jesus, this again. I'm just a nice guy, is that so hard to believe?"

Jase pushed his empty plate aside.

"Alpha, I've known you barely a year, and in that time, we've spent only the necessary time together to do our work, and pack business. We don't eat together, and we don't hang out, aside from the occasional pint at lunch. You coming out to the bars last night was virtually unheard of. I'm not saying you're hiding from us or anything, but you don't really associate with us, outside of your duties."

I brought the coffees back to the table, with Jase muttering a thanks, as I slid his over to him.

"Really? I didn't even think of it, but then, I didn't plan to be Alpha. I thought dad would be doing this job forever. I mean, he was the tough one, and I'm only Alpha because of being born one. I'd never have been anyone's first choice." I cradled my mug in both hands, feeling a lot of weight on my shoulders.

Jase was shaking his head.

"You have a good command of your pack, and they respect you. That's pretty much the sign of a good Alpha, I just think you isolate yourself more than you need to. We're good people. We enjoy a laugh, a few beers, barbecues... *the ladies*... I know that last one is moot now, although last night..." He winked, and I laughed.

"Was it you or Derek who sent her after me?" He widened his eyes.

"No idea what you're talking about, Alpha. We just all got to hear you banging her up against the door. I think we were all pretty surprised it didn't come down, what with the battering it was getting." He sniggered, and I smirked because it was expected, even though I regretted every second of it. The wrongness of that moment, of that act, was heavy in my chest, like a ball of shame.

"Wasn't looking for an audience. Wasn't looking for anything, but she was hot." I shrugged like it was no big deal, but that couldn't be further from the truth.

Jase grinned knowingly. "Didn't scratch the itch though, did it?"

I gulped a mouthful of coffee.

"Not a fucking chance. Is this how it will be now? I struggled to even get it up for her, and she was fucking gorgeous. Am I just Mina's bitch now? I only have to think about her and... *oh fucking hell*."

I didn't have to say it, because he already knew. Jase snorted, holding up a hand.

"Maybe just stay seated until I leave, Alpha, and nobody ever has to know."

I laughed, feeling slightly unhinged at this point.

"I still don't even really believe in the whole mate thing. How can there be just one person destined for anyone? How is it that so many go through life never finding them? And as I say that, I realise that there are billions of people on this planet, so surely it's weirder that anyone ever does."

"I hope mine finds me soon, because I'm so done with the casual shagging. It's just... I see what Ned has and I'm enough of a pussy to say, I really want that too. We're around a long damn time. It's going to be lonely if I never find that."

I rested my head in my hands.

"I'm useless until I resolve this. I hope when you find yours, that she's a wolf, and willing to join you at this pack." He nodded, but looked unconcerned because wolf/human pairings were incredibly rare.

"I'm sorry yours is more complex than that, but you can still be happy... for however long she's with us."

"She's afraid of me, Jase. I don't see how this can ever be anything more than a stolen conversation in the night."

He glanced at me. "Whoa... you talked to her. You found her last night?"

"I was passing the garden place, and she was in there, but she wouldn't open the door to me. She was too afraid. I'm such an asshole that I waited out back for her." He gasped.

"What happened?"

I shrugged. "She pretty much rejected me, had some kind of anxiety attack, and passed out, and then she left."

"Jesus," Jase muttered. "Someone did her really wrong, you get that, right? Someone out there damaged her, maybe beyond repair."

I growled as I stood up, refilling my coffee, and leaning against the counter.

"Yeah, and I need to find out who, because their days are numbered."

Mina

DAISY DROVE US TO the hiking trail, and I was feeling really excited about getting out there. I'd slept well for the first night in months, and I couldn't imagine why.

Would I admit to myself that I slept with my jacket beside me, because it still faintly smelled of him? Nope, not going there. Did it soothe me, and calm me, so I slept really well? I had no idea, but I had my suspicions.

I was kitted up in my hiking boots, shorts, and t-shirt, with a flannel shirt over the top. I had water, and some snacks with me, so I was good to walk for miles. I was therefore surprised when Daisy stopped us, only a few minutes into our walk.

"Can we talk?" She asked abruptly, and I stared at her, nodding at the trail ahead.

"We can't walk while we do?"

She frowned. "I suppose, I just... it's important, so I didn't want to drag you out into the wilderness, in case you want to run."

I stopped, having taken barely two steps.

"Wait, run?"

She sighed, rolling her shoulders.

"You trust me, right?"

I was starting to wonder if that had been a mistake.

"Yes, why?" She groaned.

"You told me enough about your past to understand who you are. Why you are how you are, but, the thing is, I've never told you about me. Who I am. *What* I am. I feel like we shouldn't keep secrets. That's the only way trust works, right?"

I folded my arms, watching her closely as we started walking again.

"What can you possibly tell me that will make me distrust you now? I've worked for you for six months. You've always worked around my difficulties, and my anxieties. You've given me time and space when I've needed it. Hell, you've nursed me through about a dozen panic attacks. What could be so bad, that I would want to run from you?"

I really didn't want to know the answer, and I wanted to talk to her about Asher. If she told me something that made me run from her, I'd have nobody to talk to.

"I saw Asher last night," I blurted out, just as she opened her mouth to talk, and she laughed.

"Okay, babe, you go first."

I smiled, because looking back on last night, I realised just how miraculous it was.

"There's not much to tell. He was outside the nursery, and tried talking to me through the glass, but I wouldn't let him in, so he left. At least I thought he did, but when I locked up, he was waiting for me."

"Jesus, I told him to give you space." She was shaking her head, and I tilted my head at her.

"What else did you tell him? Does he know?"

She stopped walking, folding her arms.

"That's not my business, or my story to tell anyone. So no, he doesn't. I just told him to tread lightly. You know, give you a chance to decide if you want to talk to him, not just blunder in like well, you know, *a man.*"

"Yeah, they do that, I dimly recall. He didn't though, blunder, I mean. He wouldn't approach me. In fact, he only did that when I had a panic attack, and passed out, and even though he must have caught me, he made sure he wasn't touching me when I woke. He even covered me with his jacket, which he was embarrassed about, because he thought he didn't know what he was doing."

Daisy laughed. "I think his instincts are better than he realises."

I nodded, stepping over an exposed tree root.

"It was just what I needed. You know how icy cold I get."

She laughed and nodded.

"That's why there's a halogen heater in the nursery office now."

I stopped again and stared at her.

"You didn't always have that?" She blushed a little.

"I got it about a week after you started. It helps, right?"

Wow, she really did that for me? Maybe I wasn't as alone as I thought, because she kept showing me that she cared, and it felt good to know that, to have a friend. She was still staring at me, looking a little embarrassed, so I nodded.

"It's perfect, thank you."

"He was worried, you know, about you."

"Who?"

"Al... Asher. He was texting me this morning to check on you, because he can't." I felt my heart beat just a little faster. *No.* I shouldn't be excited by this. It couldn't be a good thing.

"You know him that well?"

She giggled. "Not really, no. Ned messaged me to say he'd asked him for my number this morning. Whether you want to trust him or not, he went to some lengths to check on you."

I frowned. "What did you tell him?"

"Well, after he told me off for texting and driving, which I so don't do, I rang him, and told him you seem fine. I told you, he's a good man."

I sighed. If only that could be possible. Somewhere deep inside me, I realised I wanted it to be true.

"So what did you want to tell me?" Daisy fell silent.

"Do you... uh... do you believe in the supernatural? Ghosts and stuff?" She looked nervous, and I stopped to stare at her.

"If you're about to tell me that you're a ghost, I'm going to have so many questions. Like how can you touch stuff, how can you drive, and oh god... so much more."

She laughed. "Nope, not where I'm going with this. I believe in some very different things though, so I'm interested in your beliefs, before I tell you more."

I shrugged, walking again.

"I don't know. I read paranormal stuff sometimes, for escape. Some of it seems like life would be more interesting if it were real."

Daisy hopped forward a few paces, and started walking backwards in front of me. How she avoided tripping, I had no idea.

"What kinds of things would make life more interesting?" She asked, and I stopped walking.

"You're going to trip if you keep walking like that," I replied, quirking an eyebrow when she laughed.

"Hardly. I'm way more surefooted than that."

"Is that what you're trying to tell me? That you're something supernatural? Something that has better reflexes than people do?"

She laughed and shook her head.

"First off, I'm still people, but yes, I'm also something different, which means that nature is my friend, and I generally don't fall over it."

I chewed my lip, staring at her, and wondering when our conversation stepped into the *Twilight Zone*.

"Like a vampire? Oh, no that's silly, because it's daylight, so what? I'm now starting to wonder if you're actually even sane."

She giggled. "I could show you what I am, but I don't want to scare you. You should know though that it's amazing, and magnificent, and you'd love it."

I backed up a step, my hands coming up in front of me.

"I, what do you mean, show me? You know you can't touch me."

"I don't need to. I just need to change form."

I gasped, one hand covering my mouth.

"Fuck, you're serious, aren't you? I thought you were messing with me, but... change form? What does that even mean? Is it scary? You know I freak out easily."

She nodded. "I know, and I promise it's not scary, at least, not to me, and I don't think it'll scare you. I'm not going to turn into a man, and I'm pretty sure they're the only thing that truly scares you." I realised she was right, and curiosity was really getting the best of me.

"What do I have to do?" I asked, not knowing what was coming, and unsure whether I needed to back up further or something.

She grinned widely. "Just hold my bag and watch. If you don't see this with your own eyes, you'll struggle to believe it."

I reached for her bag, which was fuller than mine was, and tossed it over my shoulder.

"Okay, I'm ready. *I think*." What the fuck was about to happen? Before yesterday, my life, my world, had been about one thing; surviving.

Hiding out here was my way to do that, and now it was all about avoiding the advances of a man, and whatever the fuck she was about to show me.

"Just don't be scared, okay? I won't hurt you, but if I approach you, don't run. It just means you can stroke me."

"What?" I gasped, as I watched her skin start to ripple, and sparkle, her clothing fading into a misty cloud of light, which dissipated seconds later, leaving in her place *a wolf*. A fucking wolf. Beautiful, and big, and with its large eyes focused on my face.

Her fur was a reddish brown, and there were lighter patches around her face. My legs trembled, and I dropped to my knees, as I stared at this beast who had previously been my only friend.

What the fuck.

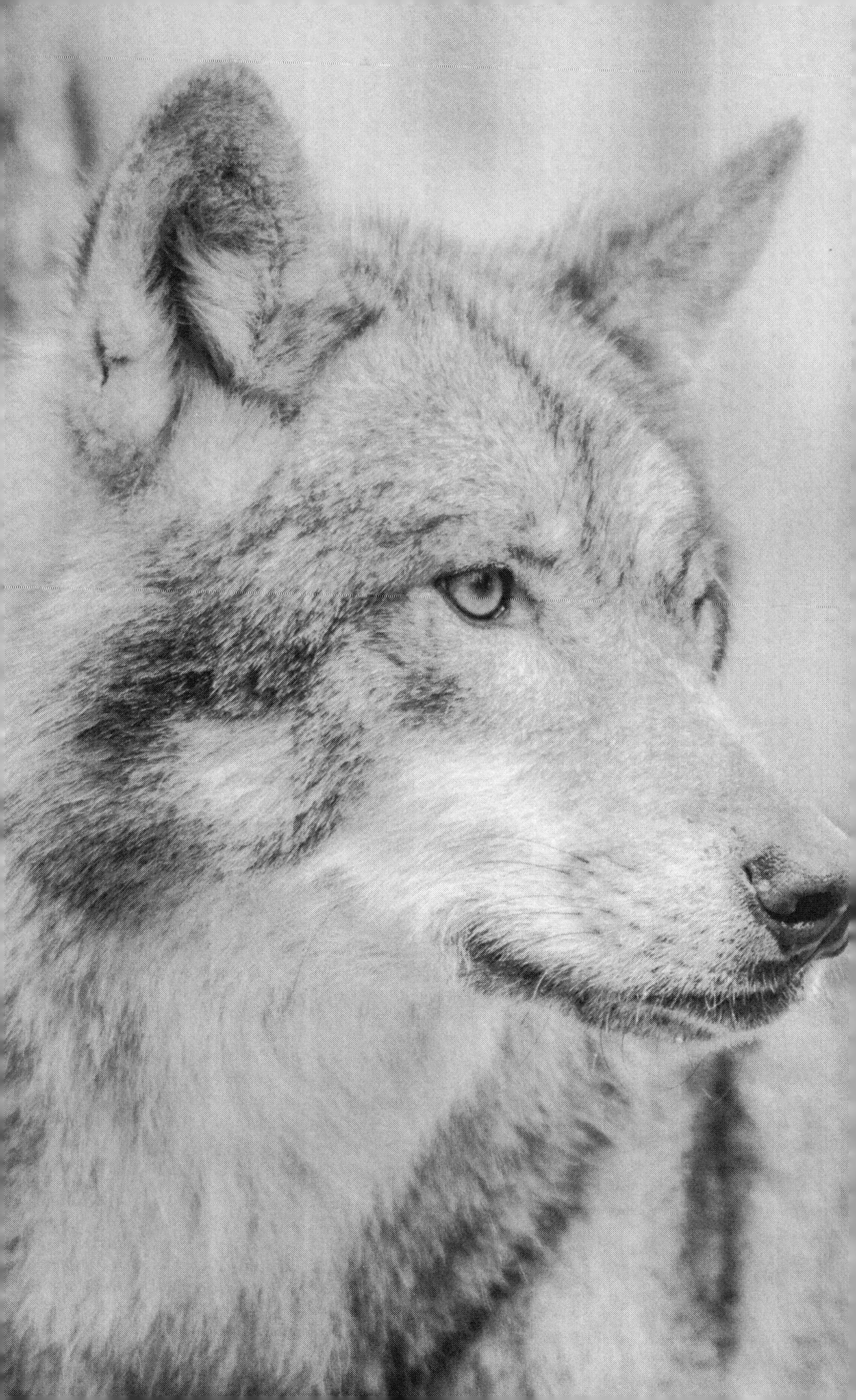

Chapter Seven

ASHER

Work was a fucking bitch. I mean, don't get me wrong, I'm shit hot with IT security stuff, coding, etc, and I could talk all day about it, most days.

Instead today, I fucked up, over and over, until I pretty much took myself outside for a good talking to. Why couldn't I concentrate on anything anymore? *She was destroying me, from the inside out.*

But then, it wasn't her personally doing this to me anyway, it was the fucking mate bond. Was there no way to refuse it?

There had to be, because our business wasn't small, but it wasn't big enough that I couldn't bring it to its fucking knees if I kept screwing up like this.

"Hey boss." Derek leaned against the wall beside me.

"Whatcha doin?" I sent a sideways glare at him.

"Getting out of the way, before I crash every fucking system on this side of the world."

He started laughing. "You're being a little hard on yourself there. It was just a few coding errors, they happen to us all."

I groaned, banging my head against the wall lightly, resting my head back against it.

"Not to me. Not before-"

"The girl?"

I rubbed a hand over my face.

"Jase told you?"

He snorted. "Boss, I might be a jackass, but even I can see you've been whipped. You can't help it. A mate bond is a real thing, but you thought someone somewhere made that shit up, right?"

I glared at him for the *whipped* comment, but then maybe he wasn't wrong.

"Yeah, I was pretty sure it wasn't real."

He laughed. "I've seen enough wolves lose their shit over their mate to know that it isn't. Think yourself lucky, boss. I was messing when I said what I said yesterday. If I find mine, I'm never gonna look at another woman. Sure, I love a shag as much as the next guy, but I'd just as happily do that with one woman for the rest of my days. Hopefully hers too."

I sagged against the wall.

"And if she's human?"

"That wouldn't exactly be her fault. It wouldn't be anyone's, would it? If she's human, I'll rock her fucking world, and look after her until her last days, and then I'll follow her into the abyss. Like I said; a mate is a mate, so be thankful you found yours. Some wolves go into the abyss, never having met theirs."

"She doesn't want to be anywhere near me, D."

He shrugged. "Humans can't feel the mate bond, so you're just gonna have to work for it. I mean, it's possible to reject your mate, but if you do, you don't get another one. That was your shot, and you blew it."

"Reject?" I stood up, stepping away from the wall.

"How do I do that?"

"Boss." He held his hands up. "Think it through. It's permanent, yeah? You reject that connection, and you'll never find someone who strengthens you the way the mate bond will. You'll never feel all the stuff that you're feeling right now, and I hear it gets better, the longer you're together. You really want to reject that? Just because it'll take some work?"

I grabbed the front of his shirt, pressing him against the wall, and he did his best not to fight back, although I could see the anger in his eyes, before he lowered them.

"You think I'm just pussying out, because it'll be hard work? What do you take me for? She's afraid of me, D. She's fucking terrified. Five minutes in my presence last night had her going into such a bad anxiety attack that she passed out. How the fuck is it fair to keep putting her through that?"

He stared at me, fighting the Alpha dominance I glared at him with.

"Passed out? What made her that afraid of you? What did you do to her?" He shoved me suddenly, and I was standing a few paces away, while he looked at me like he wanted to kill me. What the hell? He shouldn't be able to do that; *I'm his fucking Alpha*.

"What did I DO to her?" I snarled, clenching my fists tightly. I was about to punch his fucking lights out.

"Yeah, I said it. What the fuck did you do to a woman, to make her so scared that she loses fucking consciousness? You think that just because you're my Alpha, I won't kick your ass for it?"

Jase rushed up to us, stepping between us.

"Okay, that's it, calm down... whatever's happening here, it's all good."

"It's not anywhere near fucking good," I snapped, at the same time as Derek said.

"Get outta the way, before I clock you one."

Jase growled softly. "Seriously, I'm putting my fucking neck on the line here. Will you both please back up a few paces? Think about what's happening here, before we can't undo it."

I glared at him, but he was staring straight at Derek.

"What's your problem?" Derek snapped back.

"If you're planning to challenge your Alpha, this isn't the way to do it." Derek's face fell, as Jase's words finally sunk in.

"Say what?"

Jase groaned, and gestured to me.

"If you attack him, you're invoking a challenge to his leadership. One of you will have to die to end it. Is that what you want? What either of you fucking want?"

I backed up a step. *Fuck*. He was right, and what the hell was I doing, picking a fight with one of my supposedly most trusted friends. Jase had been right before too.

I hadn't taken the time to really connect with any of them. I'd kept them all at arm's length, trying to rule by disassociation. Was that why Derek hadn't struggled to challenge me, when I'd faced him down?

He sagged back against the wall, sighing heavily.

"Fuck, I'm sorry. I lose it when it comes to violence against women."

I glared angrily at him. "I get that, because I feel the same way. I could never mistreat a woman, any woman, let alone my own damn mate." He nodded, holding his hands up.

"I know. Sorry, this is my stuff, and I shouldn't be putting it on you."

I stared at Jase, who was nodding at me, trying to tell me something, but I had no idea what it was. He sighed, making further gestures.

"What?" I snapped finally.

He groaned, rolling his eyes.

"Why don't we go inside, and talk about it? Maybe if you confide in us, you'll feel better." He said that to Derek, and fuck me, he agreed.

We grabbed mugs of coffee, and sat around the kitchen table.

"So..." I prompted, and he nodded, nursing his coffee like a hit of something stronger. I stood up, grabbing a bottle of whiskey from the liquor cabinet, and topped each of us up with a tot. He nodded his thanks.

"A few years back, when I left Ireland... it wasn't for any reason I've ever told anyone. Truth was I lost the only person who mattered to me; my older sister. Uh, she married an abusive sack of shit." He looked drawn, and exhausted, just by those few words.

Oh. I saw my horror reflected on Jase's face.

"Jesus, I'm sorry, D," he said, and I nodded my agreement.

"They were only married a few years, but in that time, more than once, I begged her to leave him. Every time he put her in the hospital, I tried to get her to leave with me. Tried to make her come with me. Anywhere, I'd have gone anywhere with her."

"She was a wolf?" He nodded.

"And so was he. *Mate-bonded*." Oh. It was the first time I'd heard of an unsuccessful mate bond, and it was more horrifying than I could have imagined.

"What happened?" I asked, curiosity killing the proverbial cat.

He groaned, lowering his head.

"The fucker raped her. She called me for help, and I drove there as fast as I fucking could. She was finally ready to get out, and I raced all the way there, and..." He paused, taking a swig of whiskey directly from the bottle I'd placed beside him.

"She was dead. He'd strangled her. He'd raped her, and killed her, like she was nothing. Unimportant. Fuck, I lost my shit, I mean, *I really lost my shit.*"

I ran a hand over my face. This was not the story I'd expected, nothing like it. This was fucking heartbreaking.

"Jesus," I muttered.

"What happened, D?" Jase asked, his face serious.

Derek drank more whiskey. I should have just brought him a glass of that, rather than coffee. That was my mistake. I should already know him better than that.

"What do you think happened? I hunted that fucker down, and I killed him." He stared at us, daring us to disagree, or argue with his action. He wasn't getting that response from either of us.

"It was the only thing you could do." He stared at me, raising his eyebrows as he shared one last vital detail.

"He was our Alpha." *Oh shit.*

I stared at Jase for a second, and he looked as stunned as I felt.

"So, that made you the pack's Alpha," I pointed out, and Derek shrugged.

"Hell if I know. I left; left town, left the country. Went looking for somewhere to call home, now that mine was gone. She was the only family I had, and he killed her. I only wish I could have killed him more than once."

Jase reached over, and patted his shoulder awkwardly.

"You're home now."

He grinned weakly. "I'm guessing that's why I can resist your Alpha dominance though, boss."

I smirked. "You think?"

Jase looked between the two of us, his mouth dropping open as he realised the significance of that fact.

"Oh, I just thought he was being cocky."

"Nope, he doesn't submit like everyone else does, but I've ignored it because I like him. It turns out he can't submit, not if he's an Alpha himself. The real question is why you agree to be anything other than an Alpha yourself. You could have your own pack." So many things had fallen into place with his story, and I kinda wished they hadn't.

Derek shook his head.

"Nah, that's not my style. I didn't get to be Alpha by doing things the proper way. I just killed a raping bastard, and bosh... suddenly I'm Alpha? *I ran out on my pack.* Some would say that makes me the biggest shit there is, and I'm not sure I'd disagree."

"After what he did, they're lucky you only killed him," I said grimly, and he shrugged.

"Not usually my thing, but it turns out there is a motivator in me somewhere. That's why I freaked when you told me how she reacted, because I thought you'd given her a reason to be afraid. I'm sorry, that's my bad. I didn't think about who I'm talking to." He grinned, finally drinking some of the damn coffee. I nodded.

"I get that, and look, whether she ever wants anything to do with me or not, she's under my protection now, and that means you both get to share that honour. Nothing bad is ever going to happen to her again, are we clear? Not on my watch." They both nodded seriously.

Derek tried his trademark grin, a little weakly.

"Ah, you know I'm a sucker for a damsel in distress."

I glared at him. *"No fucking touching her."* He smirked.

"As if I'd try that."

I sighed sadly. "That was her rule to me, but I'm guessing it stands with any man, and I'll personally remove any male hand that touches her without her permission, *not that I plan to ever let anyone get close enough to try.*" Not least because she was fucking mine.

"Jesus, boss, god only knows what she's been through," Derek said quietly, and I nodded.

"I plan on finding out, and whoever was responsible is living on borrowed time."

Jase nodded, a grim smile on his face.

"What's her name, Alpha? I'll run some searches, and see what I can find out."

"Mina," I said and he groaned.

"That's all you've got?" I shrugged helplessly.

"She's not exactly forthcoming with information, but maybe there's a damn good reason for that. All I know is that she works for Daisy." He nodded, looking fiercely determined.

"Leave it with me."

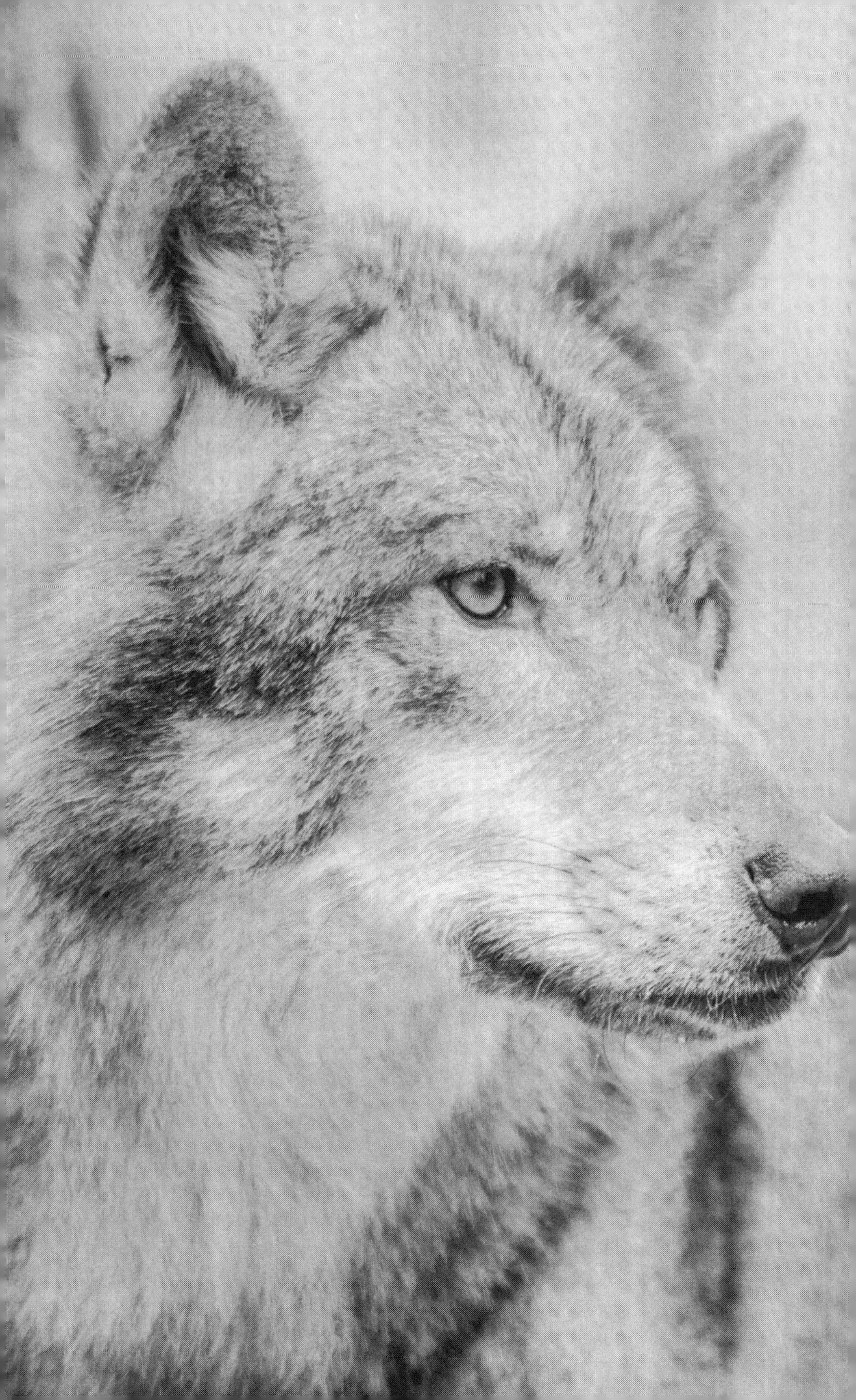

Chapter Eight

MINA

As the Daisy wolf approached me, I stayed completely still. She sniffed at me, and made a light chuffing sound, just like a big dog would, then she lowered her head and nudged at my hand. I couldn't help myself, lifting my hand and stroking it across her luscious coat.

It felt like silk, and within seconds, I had both hands on her back, stroking her, and taking from it a great sense of peace. Dogs had always made me feel calm. Was this why I'd gravitated towards her? Because subconsciously I could sense this side of her?

How could any person be evil, if they could become this amazing creature? I sighed with pleasure. It didn't feel weird to be stroking and scratching a friend's back, because right now she was an oversized dog in my eyes, *and oversized is right*. While kneeling down, I had to reach up to scratch her back, yet I felt no fear, because it was Daisy, right?

She made that chuffing noise again, and lifted her head, nodding at me, then she backed away again. When she was about a metre away, I saw the rippling start again, and the misty haze appeared, and then she stood before me. *Naked*. I gasped, and covered my eyes, and she laughed.

"I have clothes in my bag." I tossed the bag to her, still keeping my eyes averted.

"Oh come on, you weren't that shy when you were stroking my back." I laughed.

"It should have felt weird."

"It felt nice, and you were safe; you were calm. I could feel all of that, because as a wolf, I have a better feel of a person's emotions. I guess that's why dogs always know what their owner wants, right?" I laughed, peeking through my fingers, to make sure it was safe to uncover them.

"It's okay, I'm decent. Mostly." She was doing up her shorts, so I lowered my hand. Only now did I notice the tattered remains of her clothes on the ground.

I also realised that the clothes she'd turned up in were far crappier than the ones she wore now, and I wondered if that was on purpose.

"What?" She asked, glancing at the clothes.

"Oh right, yeah, I wore that crap because I knew it'd get shredded."

I nodded. "I figured as much. Wow, your clothing budget must be huge."

She laughed, tying her shirt at her waist.

"You'd be surprised. Mostly I just usually strip before I shift, but I didn't want to do that here though."

I glanced around us suddenly.

"My god, you're right. Someone could have seen you."

She shook her head, grinning.

"No, I mean I didn't want to strip in front of you, in case it freaked you out, and you ran before I could shift. I didn't want you to think I was hitting on you!"

I giggled, because it was a good call.

"I guess you had me pegged right. So, I have about a million questions."

She laughed, digging her water out of her bag and sipping it. She sat down on the ground, so I followed suit, finding a small raised stump to sit on. It wasn't comfortable, but it was less dusty than the ground.

"Does it hurt? It didn't look like it did?" She shook her head.

"It's mostly magical, so it's like phasing from one thing to another, rather than on TV where things break, and rebuild, and stuff. Thank god, because I'd hate having to do that. Shifting is a pleasurable feeling, actually, like stepping into a warm bath, when you're cold. I love doing it, and running like a wolf, especially with Ned, and other pack members, that's just heavenly."

I looked around us, suddenly worried again.

"Other pack members?" She gasped, covering her mouth.

"Shit, I didn't mean to mention the pack today. I wanted to ease you into it. It's a lot to take in, but you're annoyingly easy to talk to, probably because you mostly listen, and ask the right questions, rather than blathering on, you know, pretty much like I am right now."

I shook my head at her.

"Pack? As in, there are more wolves right here in town?"

She grinned easily. "There are wolves in all towns, all villages, all cities, everywhere. Each region is generally a separate pack, so we're in Wiltshire only. Our pack, I mean, we live here in town."

I felt a suspicion creeping in.

"Have I met any others?"

She glanced away, looking guilty.

"Maybe."

"Daisy?"

She shook her head at me.

"It's not up to me to out other wolves to you. If they want to show you, they will. The important thing for you to know, is that no wolf in this town will hurt you, and they won't threaten you. They don't do that to anyone, but especially not to you."

I didn't like the way that sounded.

"Why especially not me?" I was getting ready to get up and run.

"Mina, don't freak out. You're a friend of the pack, through me. I won't let anyone hurt you, and nobody would try."

"No other reason?"

She looked bemused.

"That's not enough?"

I sighed. Did I want to press more? No. I glanced around us again.

"Does shifting tire you out?"

She laughed, hopping to her feet in one graceful move.

"No! It's like an energy drink, rushing through me. Does that mean you want to start our hike?" I laughed, following her.

"Yeah, I mean, if you're okay with me peppering you with questions the whole time."

Her laugh drifted in the air, as she marched off ahead of me, and I followed.

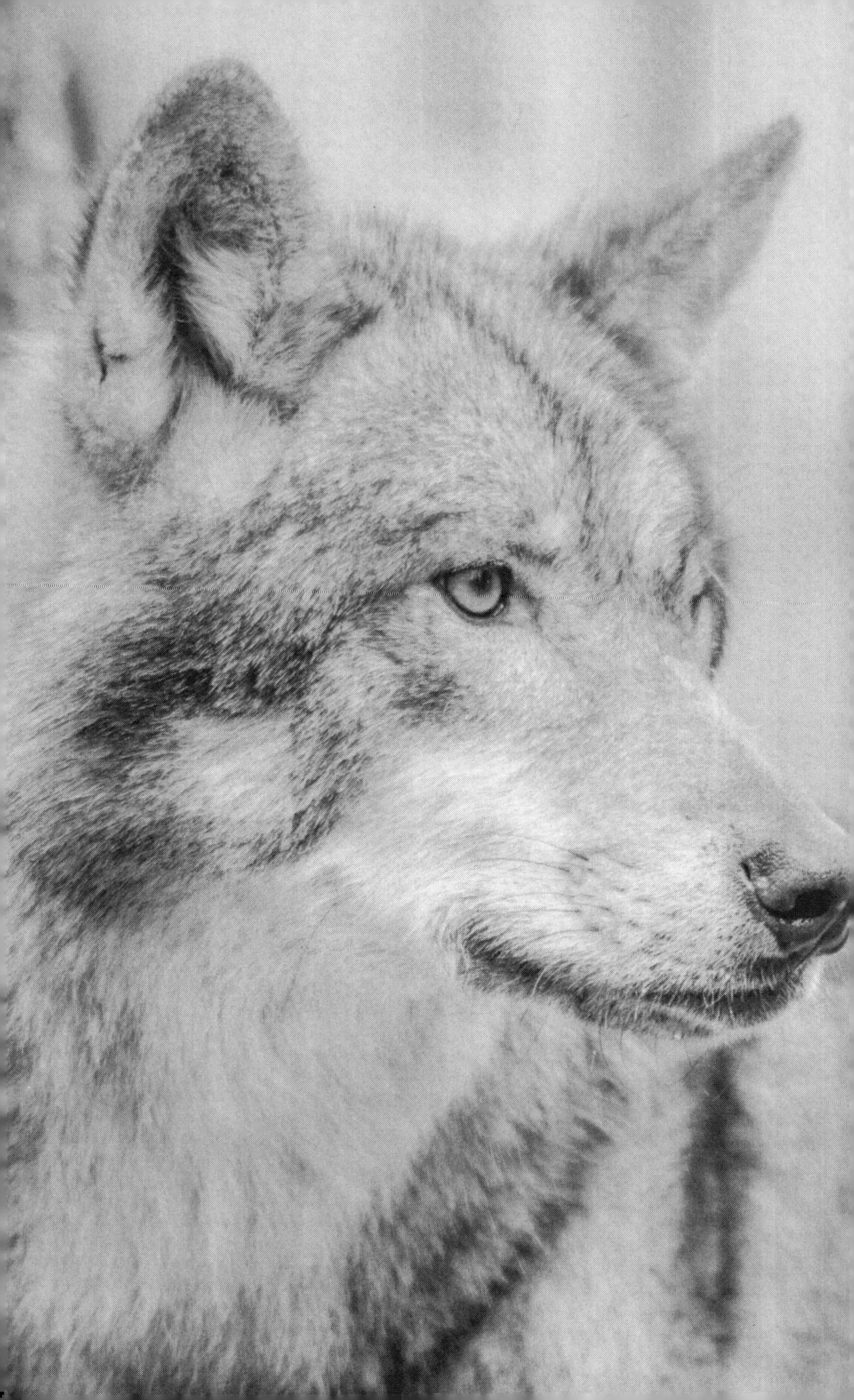

Chapter Nine

Asher

WHAT A FUCKING DAY. Not only did I get all kinds of shit laid on me, once I started actually talking to my pack members, but I was desperate to know how it had gone with Daisy and Mina. Did she show her the wolf? Did she freak? Did she run? Had she already left town, and Daisy didn't know how to tell me?

So far, Jase hadn't been able to find anything on Mina, in fact, it looked like she didn't even exist. That wasn't possible, but without her surname, and any sign of her in anything local at all, it was hard to tell. She wasn't listed anywhere. There had to be a good reason for that, and it was driving me fucking nuts trying to figure it out.

I knew she wouldn't tell me, at least not until she trusted me, and that might never happen. Especially if she'd already freaked out and run, at the sight of her first fucking wolf shifter.

Eventually I hit Daisy up with a text, because seriously, it's four-fucking-pm, and she hasn't updated me yet.

Me: *Any news yet?*

Daisy took longer than it seemed possible, for any person with a mobile phone in the 21st century, to reply to a text. I mean we're all glued to them, right? I was practically climbing the fucking walls by the time she replied.

Daisy: *We're still out. Don't worry. Will msg later.*

Dammit. I needed to know now. I didn't realise how on edge everything had made me, until I realised I'd kicked a hole in my wall. *Fuck.* I needed to cool down, and fast. Stomping to the bathroom, dropping clothes as I walked, I turned the fucker on cold, and stepped under the agonisingly cold spray.

Fuck. I swear I used to be normal and in control of myself, and now, thanks to one woman, I'm either attacking people or inanimate objects, wanking myself into oblivion, or resorting to cold showers.

As distasteful as it felt, the second I thought it, I wondered if I should head into town, and get myself blown again. Or, if I could remember to use a fucking condom, I could fuck someone, and hopefully get this out of my system for now. The mere thought made me want to vomit.

As I reached the bedroom, a towel around my waist, I noticed my phone blinking at me.

Daisy: *Just dropped her off, and no, I'm not driving yet. She's fine. Actually pretty cool with the wolf thing. Me that is. A pack? Other wolves? Not so much.*

Fuck. I can't stop saying that word, because everything is so messed up, it just comes out. *Fuck.*

Me: *Does she know about me?*

Daisy: *She suspects. I'm sure of it. She asked if she's met others, and all I'd admit to was maybe.*

Daisy: *I told her she's under pack protection because she's my friend.*

Me: *Good move, she is. I've briefed Jase and D, and they've cascaded that to the pack. She's got lots of eyes watching over her now.*

Daisy: *You need to tell her soon. Before she finds out some other way.*

Daisy: *Sorry to be so frank, Alpha. I just like her, and I think you'd be good for her. She needs to feel safe, and I think she couldn't be safer than with you.*

Me: *Thanks Daisy. I'm actually considering rejecting the mate bond.*

Why the fuck did I tell her that? I really wasn't. The second I sent the message; I knew it wasn't true. I could say it until I'm blue in the face, but I don't think I could go through with it, not unless she asked me to. I don't even know how it works. Maybe her rejection would be enough, but then she's not a wolf, so maybe the rules differ. Fuck, I needed to know more.

My phone was ringing, so I answered, without checking the screen.

"WHAT? Are you out of your mind?" Daisy screeched, then she checked herself.

"Ahem... I mean, Alpha, are you sure you want to do that?"

I laughed bitterly. "She's damaged by whatever happened to her. I want to think I'd be good for her, but I doubt that. If she's freaked out by the idea of a pack, she definitely can't be the mate of an Alpha, because I have no choice, but to be in one. I just think if she's resistant to the idea of knowing me, she's never going to give me a chance. If I can free her-"

"You wouldn't be, though. You'd only be freeing yourself. Rejecting the mate bond will only work on your side, because you're a wolf. She doesn't have that leading her, so look at it from her side. Ignore the state her soul is in, for a minute. She's just a girl, who until today, didn't know wolves existed, not our kind. She doesn't know about mates; she doesn't know about any of this. You're feeling a whole bunch of stuff for her, but she sees a man that she doesn't know yet. You can't make a judgement until you've both had a chance to get to know each other, and know if there's anything there. If she doesn't feel anything for you, then, yeah, maybe rejecting the bond would be best, *for you*. Until you know her better, you can't really make that decision. I personally think that you guys would be great together, if she can give you a chance, and you're willing to take it."

Wow. Does she ever breathe? I took a deep breath for her, letting it out slowly.

"I see."

She sighed. "Are you willing?"

"I'll consider it," I finally said, because I really couldn't commit to anything more at this point.

She sighed again. "For now, she's okay. She was actually really soothed by my wolf, so there may be something there. A kinship, or maybe just a love for big cuddly dogs, I don't know."

"I'm hardly a big cuddly dog." I said, affronted, and she laughed.

"You know what I mean. Mina doesn't touch people, but as soon as she touched me, and knew she could do so, she was running her hands over my hair, like it was a pleasure for her. It felt nice, and it was a huge deal for her."

I groaned, glancing down at the towel now tenting at the front. Fucking hell.

"Do you want me to go?" She asked suddenly. *I really shouldn't be on the phone to another man's wife, or mate, while I've got a raging fucking hard-on.*

"Uh, yeah... something's just come up." *Fuck.* She giggled.

"Night, Alpha." She was gone already. That chick hung up on me way too often. Does nobody respect their Alpha anymore?

And with that, I stomped back into the cold shower, my towel hitting the floor just before I stepped in.

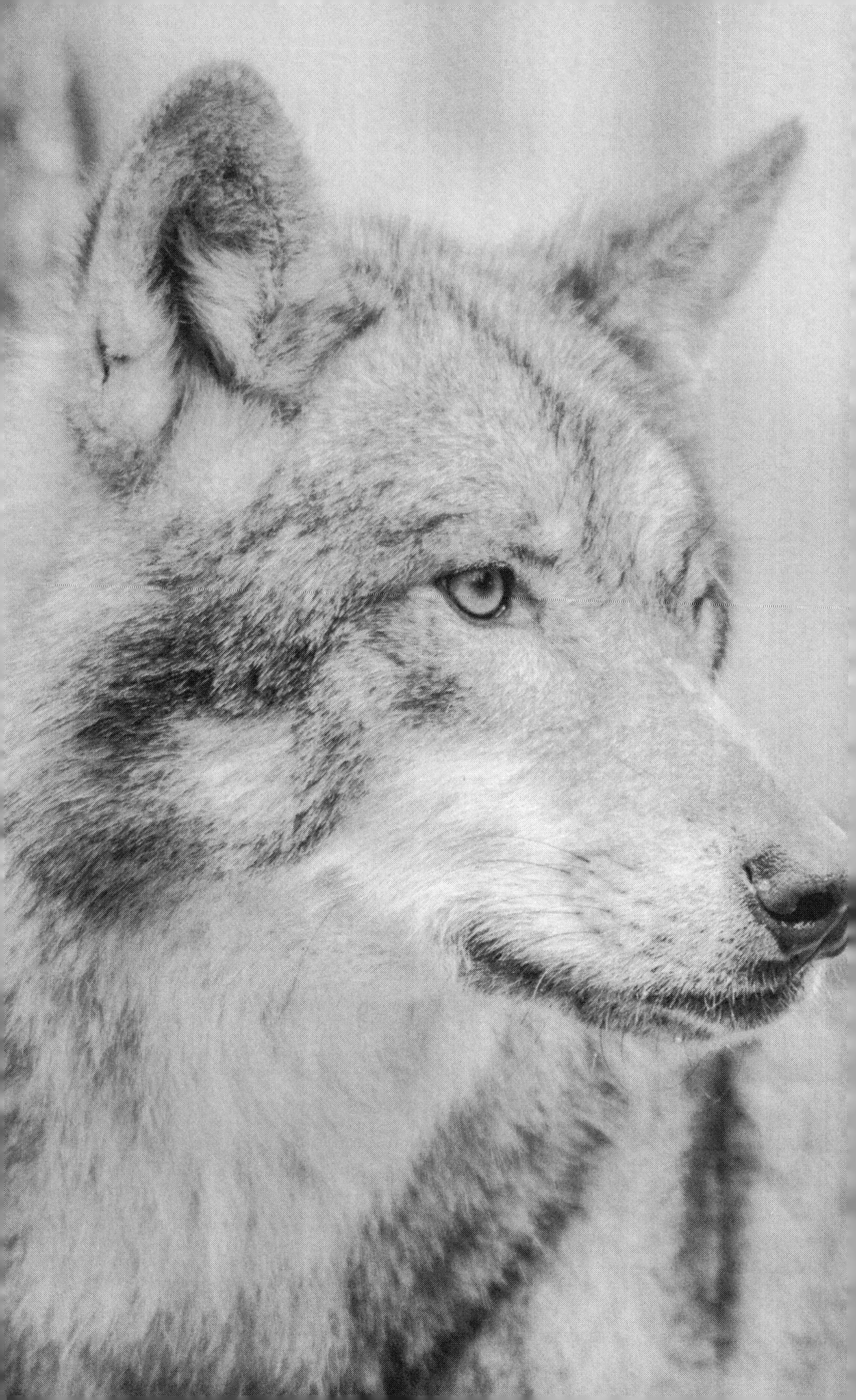

Chapter Ten

Mina

I WAS IN MY chair; *my safe place*. I was still stunned about wolves, shifters; they were actually real. I'd read books about them, of course. Hasn't everyone? Hasn't everyone read about Alpha wolves, and their dominant sides? I shuddered. That would be way too much man for me, not that I was ever considering one again.

But *Asher*; there was something about him. It made me think that I would consider talking to him, if I saw him again. I had a suspicion that maybe he might be a wolf too, and strangely, that didn't freak me out. I was pretty sure it should. The way I saw it, if a man had that gentle, calm animal inside him, could he really be bad on the outside?

I fell asleep in the chair, our hike having been a monster one, once Daisy was all beefed-up on shifter acid. My legs were going to kill tomorrow. I slept well, until I didn't.

"Grab her, hold her down." Arms were pressing me down, and I struggled, and cried, and begged.

"Stop please!"

"Hold her arms, dammit." I punched out, and tried to kick out, but he'd pinned me down pretty well. He pulled my skirt up, and my pants down, and had his bastard friend hold me still while he undid his pants.

"I'm gonna fucking enjoy this, bitch."

I woke up screaming. Not for the first time, and probably not for the last. Would it never go away? Would I never rest again?

Asher

I WAS GETTING USED to this shit by now. Sleep just wasn't going to be my thing anymore. Sure, the dreams about Mina were awesome, but all that happened was that I'd wake up with yet another fucking boner, and she wasn't even there for me to bury it in. In fact, I was pretty sure she never would be.

I wouldn't admit this to anyone else, but that was starting to dig a hole inside me. This hurt, that I was burying hour by hour. She was apparently my fated mate, my other half, and she didn't even want to talk to me, couldn't be alone with me. How could we ever be anything other than strangers?

I couldn't get her out of my head, and she barely knew I existed. Probably wished I didn't. Hell, I was halfway there myself. I'd been getting by okay, not great, but okay. I may not have chosen to be Alpha, but I was doing my damn best. Finding out that I had an actual fucking Alpha, as my Delta, was a bigger shock than I'd realised.

Since my wolf had found out, he'd been prowling in my head, frustrated, because he felt like another Alpha in my pack was a challenge, in and of itself, and I couldn't really disagree with him.

Derek said he was fine submitting to me, but let's be honest here. *He doesn't submit, and he never will.* Was that going to be a problem later? Should I try and find a way to force it? And if I did, would I break who he was, because he was truly an Alpha? Maybe even more of one than I am.

I growled, kicking back the blankets. Fuck this. If I can't sleep, I'll go for a run. Cold showers weren't working any better than taking care of business myself, so it was time to go run this shit off.

I ran for miles. I didn't plan to, but once I was in wolf form, I could move fast, and while out running along my favourite hiking trail, or alongside it because that was all grass, and far more pleasant, what happened, but I picked up her fucking scent. *Up here.*

Here, where I was supposed to be in my own territory. Where I should have been safe from all things human, and Mina. Damn Daisy, she must have brought her here to show her, and it was reckless of her. If Mina had panicked and decided to run, she could have encountered another wolf, who wouldn't have known who she was. *Jesus.* The thought alone scared the hell out of me.

They all knew her rule now, but they didn't then. If they'd found her here, and tried to manhandle their intruder to their Alpha, *me*, we'd have had two problems. One, that they'd have been touching her, and two, they'd have been fucking touching my mate!

Plus, of course, she didn't even know I was a wolf yet. Daisy did say she thought she suspected, though. Could that be a good thing? I wasn't so sure. *Fuck.* I needed to think about something else; anything else.

Back at the pack house, I went to the fridge for some juice, and dropped some ice in. I leaned against the fridge to drink it. The house was silent, but then it was dark, and probably still hours from being light.

"Jesus... you're up too?" A sleepy voice murmured, and a half-naked Jase strolled into the room.

I moved away from the fridge, since he was making a beeline for it.

"Yeah, what's your excuse?"

He snorted. "Weird dreams, I dunno. Something woke me up, and now I'm thirsty. You're sweating. Been for a run?"

I nodded. "Can't seem to sleep through the night lately, so I thought a run might tire me out a bit."

"Did it help?"

I dumped the glass in the dishwasher, and turned to walk out.

"Ask me again tomorrow."

I went back to bed, after a quick visit to the shower, because as he'd so rightly pointed out, I was sweaty as hell.

Would I get any sleep now? *Only fucking time would tell.*

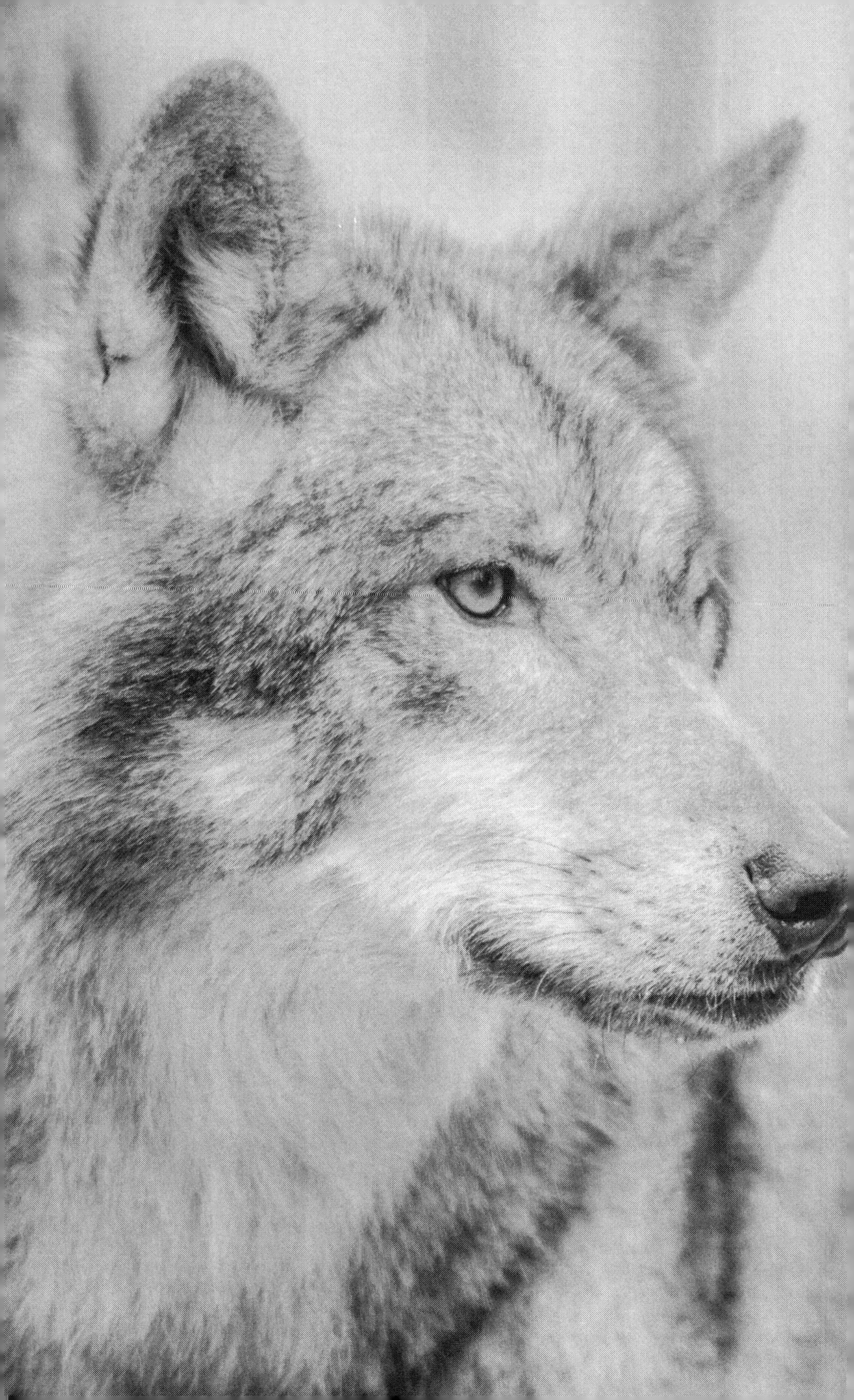

Chapter Eleven

Mina

I couldn't sleep after that horrible dream earlier this evening, and it wasn't fair. All that therapy, and it could all feel like it had been undone by one nightmare. Why couldn't I move past it? Of course, some had told me that was likely impossible, but I couldn't let myself believe that. If I did, I'd have no reason to carry on.

But then was I even really living now? Or was I just marking the days, by going to work and going home again? I had one friend. *One*. And she turned out to be a fucking wolf, and I had one man showing an interest, and I was terrified of him. I didn't want to be, but as the dream continuously proved, I had awful taste in men, and could never trust one again.

I briefly wished that I had Asher's number, and that sounds weird because it really is. I was afraid of him, and I didn't want to see him, but I felt like he'd understand, if I called him because I was scared to sleep. I don't even know why I thought that.

My knowledge of him came from that one meeting, and during that time, I was briefly unconscious, because I was so afraid of him, and what's scarier than a man? Being unconscious around one. I couldn't risk that again. I picked up my phone to text Daisy, because she'd understand.

As I hovered over her name to send a text, I glanced at the clock. It was 3am! Oh my god, that would be so unfair to message her now, because I'd wake her, and probably her husband too. I swiped the screen to close the texting app, putting the phone down, and then I realised it was making a sound. Oh god no!

I ended the accidental call, and put the phone on the floor, sitting beside it, with my back against my bed. I was such a fucking idiot. I prayed I hadn't just woken her and her husband. I was worried about a text waking them, and instead I'd phoned her damn phone.

I slapped my forehead, which hurt, but wasn't really enough retribution for me, because my phone started ringing then.

I answered it immediately.

"I'm so sorry, I didn't mean to wake you."

I heard someone clear their throat, and it wasn't Daisy. I pulled the phone away from my ear. *Unknown number*. No!

I ended the call, my heart thudding in my chest. Who the hell had just called me? Had they found me? They shouldn't be out yet, right? I picked up my phone again, checking my calendar. No. Not yet. It rang again, and I dropped it. Oh god oh god oh god. It was an unknown number again.

I rejected the call, then heard the ping of a text moments later.

Daisy: *Answer the phone, babe. It's okay.*

I frowned, because it hadn't sounded like her on the phone. It had sounded like a man, but she would've only known about the call if it was her, right?

It rang again, and my hand trembled as I reached down for it. I took a deep breath, and swiped the screen to answer.

"Don't hang up again, please," a voice said, too fast, the words almost running into each other.

"Huh?"

"I said, please don't hang up. *It's me, Asher*." I trembled again. His voice sounded so warm and sexy over the phone, but didn't it sound like that in real life too? I hadn't noticed because I was too busy losing my shit when we met.

"Mina? Are you okay?"

I took another breath.

"Uh, yeah, hi Asher... how did you get my number?"

He laughed lightly. "Daisy called, said you needed help, and gave me your number."

"Oh hell, did she really? I accidentally phoned her, that's all. I was messing with my phone" I lied through my teeth, but he wouldn't be able to tell, right?

"At 3am? Trust me, if you're messing with your phone at 3am, something's wrong." He sounded wide awake too.

"She woke you to tell you I was awake?" He laughed again, and I realised I liked the sound of it.

"I was awake too. Not long been for a run." I snorted, because that was crazier than me being awake and messing with my phone.

"You go for runs at 3am?"

"Well, when I'm too wide awake to sleep... yeah, I go for runs. What else can I do at 3am?"

I wanted to say that he could talk to me, but I couldn't say it out loud. The words were trapped inside me. I couldn't encourage him, and I shouldn't be awake at this time, any more than he should. I'd paused too long, so he spoke to fill the awkward silence.

"Why are you awake so late, Mina? You need your rest."

He sounded like a caring friend, or a boyfriend, and damn, I needed someone who cared, even just for a little while.

"A nightmare," I whispered finally, and he sighed heavily.

"Bad enough that you can't go back to sleep?"

"*Bad enough that I can't go to bed*. It was this evening, when I fell asleep in a chair."

I heard rustling, and he grunted a little.

"Sorry, just sitting up. So, I'm guessing a nightmare bad enough to make you want to stay awake all night, is about as bad as they get. Is it... is it a flashback to something?"

I gasped, feeling tears gathering in my eyes. How could he know that?

"Mina? Hey, it's okay, you can talk to me. I'm here. I'm not going anywhere, and I'm sure as hell not going to sleep while you need someone. Please."

I brushed the tears away as they rolled down my cheeks, a sniffle escaping, and his breath seemed to catch in his throat.

"Are you crying? Jesus, how bad was it?" I made a whimpering noise, which really didn't answer his question at all, but it was all I had.

"Fuck, I wish I could come to you and hold you, and make you feel safe. This is fucking killing me." I fell silent, trying to work out his meaning, while I tried to get myself back under control.

"What do you mean?" I finally asked, and he snorted.

"Nah, that's my shit. Look, I don't know what your bad dream was about, and you don't have to tell me a damn thing, but if you want to talk, about anything, or I don't know, watch the sun fucking rise, with me on the phone with you, I'm down. Just say the word."

What? I cleared my throat.

"Uh, you'd stay on the phone all night with me?"

He laughed again.

"Is that really so hard to believe?"

I stood up, going to the window, and peeking outside. It was still dark as hell, of course. Sunrise would be another three or four hours away, maybe.

"Men don't generally do things like that, without an ulterior motive of some kind, so what's yours?" I asked bluntly, and he sucked in a breath.

"Wow, you don't hold back, do you? I'm not used to that. Uh if you feel better about it, you could overcharge me for a plant, next time I visit."

I laughed. "You know that's not what I mean." He chuckled, a low, dark sound, that actually made long forgotten parts of me tingle for a few seconds.

"I honestly don't want anything from you in return. I'm awake, you're awake, I just thought we could be awake together. If you'd rather sleep, I can say goodnight, and go talk to myself for four hours. It wouldn't be the first time."

I giggled, and then mentally slapped my forehead again.

"Are..."

I couldn't ask that! Something horrific had just occurred to me, and I didn't want to ask the question, because knowing would make it worse. Wouldn't it?

"Mina? What did you want to ask me?" His voice was firm, telling me he would ask again if I didn't reply, so I sighed and forced the words out.

"Are you naked right now, because I'm not talking to a naked guy on the phone. You could be touching yourself."

He burst out laughing.

"You're quite right, a lesser man would be, but I'm wearing lounge pants. Is that better?"

I sighed, feeling conflicted all of a sudden. It wasn't, not really, but at least I knew he wasn't being a perv about me in his bed, even though I still didn't think that anyone would ever feel that way about me. Not ever again, and that's exactly how I wanted it, because they shouldn't.

Asher

WAS I NAKED? WHAT the actual fuck?

As if my cock hadn't already sprung to attention at the sound of her voice, now it was trying to make a tent out of my bedding. I hoped that my laugh had covered my discomfort, as I glanced down at my naked self, because who the fuck wears clothes in bed?

"You're quite right, a lesser man would be, but I'm wearing lounge pants. Is that better?" She sighed. Was that a good sign?

"I guess so. I'm sorry, that was a really inappropriate thing to ask you." I laughed again. She was adorable when she was trying to be the absolute opposite.

"Nah, it's only inappropriate if I ask *you* that sort of question, and don't worry, I'm not planning on it. It's not my business." I really fucking wanted to know, but it was too soon. My cock was trying to reach new heights just at the thought of her being naked right now.

She sighed again, and was it relief? Was it frustration? Was she bored? Did she want me to go? Why did I feel like a fucking kid, trying to ask a girl out on a date for the first time?

"Mina?"

"Yes, I'm here. I'm sorry, I'm just not used to being on the phone."

Oh. "You don't have long chats on the phone with friends, or family?"

She was quiet for a moment. "There's only Daisy, and my parents live overseas."

"You have nobody else to talk to, Mina?" Jesus, how can she be alone like this? I banged my head back against the headboard.

She sniffled a little. Jesus, had I made her cry again?

"Don't cry, Mina. Hey, you have me now, okay? Any time you need to talk, about anything, you ring this number, so make sure you save it. It's my mobile, and I always have it with me. Well, except in the shower, but you know... I'll always call you back, if I have a missed call."

She sniffled again. "Why are you being so nice to me? I've been nothing but a bitch to you."

Damn, I wished I was there with her. I could hold her, and set her fucking straight about everything. Jesus, everything in me was aching to touch her, and it was the one thing she might never let me do.

"Asher?" She made me realise that I'd gone quiet on her this time.

"Sorry, thought I heard something," I lied, hating lying to her, but not wanting her to know what I was thinking.

"Do you need to go?" She asked quietly. Did she want me to? It was the last thing I wanted.

"Nah, it was nothing, and don't be silly, you've been perfectly polite to me, definitely never a bitch. So, tell me something about you, I don't care what. Something big or small. Real or, you know... not... keep me guessing. *Just talk to me.*" I knew I'd do anything to prolong this time together, albeit as remote as a phone call was.

She sighed. "I don't know what to talk about. Um, I moved here about six months ago from... uh... I really don't want to say where. Is that okay?"

Fuck no. "Yes, of course. Just tell me what you're comfortable sharing." I really wanted to kill whoever had fucked her up so badly, and I had a feeling I'd only find that out by knowing where she came from.

"Uh... I met Daisy when I went shopping for plants for my little garden. We got on really well, and she offered me a job. I work there three days a week, because it's the most she can afford, and I love it. I love working with plants and flowers. They're pure, and beautiful, and they harm nobody. They just grow, and live, and make us happy. If only..."

Damn... could she be any sweeter?

"If only what?" I banged my head against the headboard again. Jesus, I almost called her 'baby'. I almost fucking responded like she was my girl, and she wasn't.

"I was going to say, if only people were like that, but they aren't. I'm sorry, I'm not easy to talk to, I know, not that I ever really used to be anyway." She sighed heavily.

"And I thought this was going really well! Am I dreaming?"

She laughed. "Well, if it seems okay to you, maybe I'll just carry on telling you bugger all, since I seem to be getting away with it."

I chuckled, enjoying her laugh. Every time she did that, I felt the ice melt, just a tiny bit.

"I wouldn't call it bugger all. You told me what you love, and that's a big deal. Want to hear what I love?"

She went quiet.

"Okay," she said carefully, and I grinned at her caution.

"Coffee."

"Oh!" She giggled. "Yes, *coffee is life*. I drink way too much coffee."

"And are you hardcore, as in espressos, or at the very least, a black coffee, or do you like them frothy and fluffy?"

She giggled again. "Somewhere in the middle. White coffee is fine, but a latte is always better. How about you?"

I found myself craving one right now, and I knew I'd need one or twelve to get me through the next day, or I guess, today.

"It changes, depending on my mood. Usually black with two sugars, but sometimes I'll go really nuts and allow a little froth."

She laughed. "Is that for when you've been a good boy, or bad? Oh god... Ignore me... *god*..." She was gasping, and sounded panicked.

I sat up from the headboard, my hand damn near crushing the phone.

"Mina? Hey, come on, breathe, *breathe*. It's okay, baby, just listen to my voice. I'm here, you're safe, and whatever just freaked you out is gone, okay?"

She was gasping more slowly now, and groaned.

"I'm sorry, I'm such a mess now. I was normal once, and I miss that so much."

I started to breathe properly now too, knowing she was coming back to me.

"It's okay, you can't help whatever happened to you, but you can grow in time, and you have friends to help you. I'm counting myself in that category, just so you know, I can be very helpful."

If she'd seen my face, she'd know how to take that statement, but over the phone, did it sound threatening or overly flirty? I didn't mean it that way, but to a brutalised woman, how did it sound? How did anything I said sound to her?

She giggled, thank god she fucking giggled.

"Do you call all your friends 'baby'?" My heart practically thudded to a stop.

"Huh?"

"You called me 'baby'." I shook my head. No, did I?

"Are you sure? I think I'd remember that."

She laughed softly. "I promise you. You said; 'it's okay, baby'. I heard it loud and clear."

"Jesus, I'm sorry, I didn't mean to overstep or anything." Damn, I had to be more careful. I slumped back down against the headboard, mentally spanking myself.

"It's okay, they never called me that." She fell suddenly silent, then cursed, and the phone went dead. What the fuck. *What the actual fuck!*

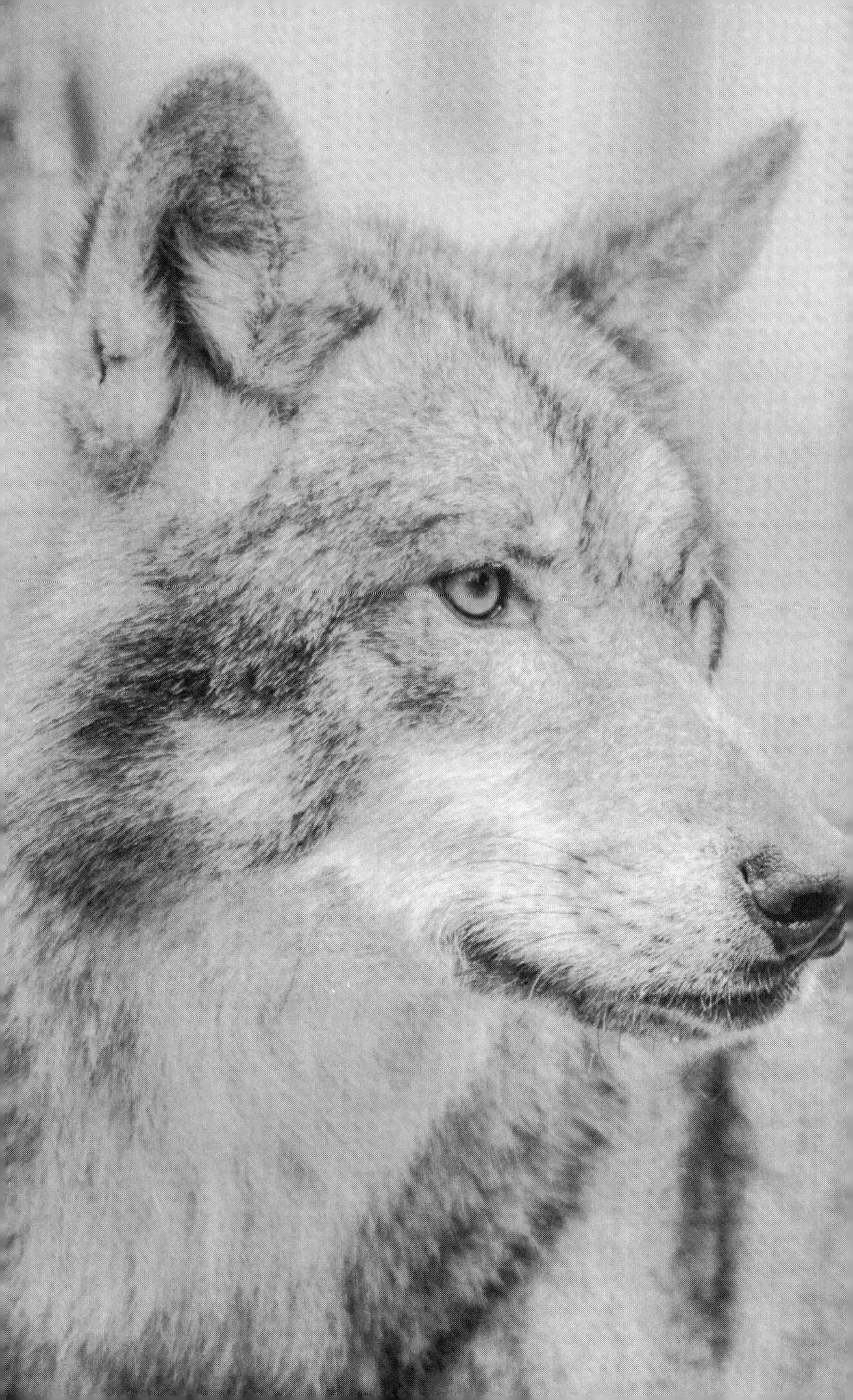

Chapter Twelve

Asher

I TRIED RINGING HER back but her phone was off, or it just wasn't connecting for some reason. It wasn't even ringing once, I was just getting standard voicemail, not even her voice. I left a message asking her to call me, but I couldn't leave it at that though.

Panic threatened to overwhelm me, because I couldn't be sure something bad hadn't happened to her. The need to protect her, to save her, was all I knew now, so I rang Daisy.

"Ugh, what time is it?" She muttered; her voice thick with sleep.

"I don't care. What's her address?" I snapped at her without meaning to.

"Wha... what?"

Then I heard Ned's voice. "What's up this time? Has something happened?"

"It's the Alpha," she said to him, and he groaned.

"Fuck! Whatever it is, just bloody give it to him, so we can get some sleep." He sounded pissed. *Well, join the fucking club, man.*

"I can't betray her trust like that, Alpha," she protested quietly, despite what Ned had just said.

I growled, long and dangerous, fury and frustration practically filling the air around me.

"Are you refusing a request from your Alpha, Daisy?"

"Fuck!" She was breathing fast, panicking along with me at last.

"Can I try calling her first? Please? To ask her permission?"

"She freaked out, and switched her phone off, or at least I hope that's what it was. Either that or someone was there." We were wasting precious time; every second could be vital. I was already out of bed, and I needed that damn address.

"Shit. They found her?"

They. That was the second time I'd heard that word in as many minutes, and it was enough to have me rushing around the room, grabbing clothes.

"The. Address. Now," I snapped, adding as much anger into my tone as I could. This shouldn't be taking so fucking long.

"Can't I go there instead?" She begged.

"She'll freak out and hate both of us."

"Shall I turn up on your doorstep, Daisy? I'll get what I want, one way or another. Do you really want me to wake Ned up again, at this hour?"

She groaned, because her husband was her weakness, and I was a total bastard for exploiting that fact.

Finally she rattled off the address, finishing our call with a comment about beating me there. *Like fuck*. I dressed in just a pair of sweatpants, tucked extra clothes in a pack, and ran.

Outside the pack house, I shifted, picking up the bag in my teeth, and then I ran. I was so much faster as a wolf, especially since there were fields between where she lived, and where I was. It was much faster than by road, so Daisy would probably do the same.

I shifted back in an alley between two houses, and dressed in the spare clothes. Tossing the empty pack over my shoulder, I stepped out onto the street, and headed up past two houses, toward Mina's address.

A sudden moment of uncertainty stopped my feet, because if I went to her door now, she'd never trust me. *Fuck*.

A fully-dressed Daisy grabbed my arm, having done exactly what I did, as I suspected.

"You're right to stop, Alpha, I get it, I do. I'd do anything for Ned too, but I'm here now. I'll go in and sit with her. *Please*, if she knows you're here, she'll never trust either one of us again." Hours of hard work would be out the window, and I was desperate not to break the small connection we'd started to build between us.

I felt my shoulders slump as I nodded, my wolf growling softly in my head. He didn't understand why we weren't already in there with her, but Daisy was right dammit. This would only scare her more.

"Okay, but I'm staying. I'll be out of sight, but you ask her if I can have her address, and if she says yes, text me, and I'll come in. Oh, and if I hear a single fucking scream, you're not keeping me out." I fixed her with a glare, making it clear that I meant business.

She nodded, waving me away, while I gritted my teeth at her impudence. I forced myself to indulge her, before Mina happened to look out of the window, and make the whole point moot.

I hid back down in the alley where we'd shifted back, and I watched from the shadows, as Daisy pounded on the door, and waited, then pounded again. *Fuck me, if she didn't answer in the next minute...*

The door opened, and Daisy disappeared inside. An edgy-looking Mina peered outside then, looking up and down the street, before she went back inside, and the door slammed.

As I crept closer, I heard several locks being slammed into place, then I sat down with my back to her neighbour's wall, and waited.

Mina

DAISY WAS AT MY door at 4.30am! Why? She wasn't going away so I let her in, checking outside for anyone loitering about.

Even though the call had been from Asher, I'd still not been able to shake the fear that they'd found me, and then I went and said too much to him. Somehow he'd started breaking through my defences, when it shouldn't have been possible.

"What happened? Are you okay?"

I stared at her dumbly. "What?"

"Al... Asher told me that you rang off, and he couldn't reach you. He was frantic, so he asked me to check on you." She looked tired, but worried, as she paced my living room.

I couldn't believe what she was saying. It made no sense.

"Wow, he really has some power over you. I can't imagine many men could make someone else's wife get out of bed to go and run errands for them."

She ignored my comment.

"He knows you're my friend, dummy, and he knows you needed me. So talk, and for god's sake, put a damn pot of coffee on. I'm exhausted."

I laughed. In a few short moments, she had already made me feel safe again, and of course, who wouldn't be safe with a wolf shifter on their side? I set a pot of coffee percolating, and returned to her.

"You know, first off, he demanded your address." She was carefully watching my response to that bombshell.

"What?" I gasped, my hand going to my chest, because my heart was pounding in my chest again.

"Please... no... you can't tell him." I'd have to move again, and I really didn't think I had the strength for that.

Her face fell. "You talked to him for over an hour, and don't want him to know your address? Hasn't he proven what a good guy he is? He keeps checking on you, and dragging me out of bed to look after you. A dickhead wouldn't do that. *Okay, some people could be called dickheads for waking a girl when she needs her beauty sleep, but whatever.* He knows how much I care about you, and he likes you, Mina, he cares too."

I sat back, my breathing easing a little. Thank god she hadn't sent him here, because I really would have to move out of my house, and run. Again.

"He doesn't know me, Daisy, so how can he like me?" I almost folded my arms, but it seemed childish, so I refrained, tilting my head to try and listen for the coffee percolator.

"It's not ready yet," she said with a grin. "And he likes you because you're you. He can see what you try so hard to hide. You can trust him, you know. I do, with my life."

"How do you know the coffee isn't ready?" I focused on that, because the other part was too weird to even think about. She trusts him with her life?

She laughed. "My hearing is a little sharper than a human's. Wolf genes, remember?"

"That doesn't seem fair, or maybe it is... that means you can pour the coffee when it's ready... you know, since you'll know before me." I smirked at her, and she folded her arms, pouting at me, and yes it really was childish, but she still made me smile.

"Nice try, babe, but I'm your guest. That means you wait on me, see?"

"But guests are usually invited."

"How rude! I came running to your aid, in the early hours of the goddamn morning, on a work night, no less, and this is the attitude I get. *Charming*." She was joking, even giggling as she spoke, but I suddenly felt like a prize bitch, because she was right. She'd gone out of her way to check on me, hadn't she?

"You're right, I'll go make it." I stood up, but she held up a hand.

"Still not ready. Um, one more minute, I reckon."

I shook my head at her, heading into the kitchen to see that she was pretty much right. As I grabbed two mugs, the light suddenly turned green, and I was actually jealous of her advanced senses. If I'd had those senses and abilities, I'd never have become the victim I was.

I brought our coffees back to the living room, and went straight to my safe place chair.

"Did he tell you what we talked about?" I asked her. She sipped her coffee, which made me wonder if wolves didn't burn their mouths either. Mine was definitely too hot, but then I also didn't have as much milk in mine as she likes in hers.

"Nope, he just said you were getting on great, and then you panicked and ended the call, and your phone seemed to be off. He was worried someone broke in, or something." She leaned back on the sofa, getting comfy.

I chewed my lip, mulling over her words, but it came back to the same question.

"Why does he care?"

Daisy groaned dramatically, rolling her eyes at me.

"Oh my god, do we have to keep going over this?"

"Yes, because you never answer."

"*So ask him.* Honestly, I don't know what goes on in his head. I just know he's interested in getting to know you better, and really wants to protect you from anything bad."

I glared at her, feeling like things suddenly clicked in my mind.

"Is he your Alpha?"

She gasped, nearly spilling her coffee.

"I..."

"Yeah, that's what I thought. That's why he can demand that you jump out of bed, and come here. That's why he gets you to give him my number, and stuff. *Fuck.* So he's the boss-man, and somehow he wants to know me? Does that mean that you're all going to start interfering in my life, and never let me be?"

I was leaning forward in my chair by now, my anger propelling me. I couldn't be powerless again, I just couldn't.

Daisy looked like I'd punched her.

"What? You think... you think we're friends because of him?"

I hadn't, but now I was wondering exactly that.

"Please don't let that be why, you're my only damn friend!"

She looked pissed off, rather than upset now.

"How could you think that? We've known each other six months! And in that time you've only just met him now, and suddenly you think it was all a ruse? I wouldn't do that, and he wouldn't do that, but more fucking importantly, *I* wouldn't do that!" She was definitely pissed, and my anger faded away, leaving guilt behind like a bitter aftertaste.

"I'm sorry, Daisy, that was wrong of me to say. I don't know why I'm so bitchy these days. I think I've gone so long with nobody in my life, that I'm struggling to even be a real person anymore." She quieted, and relaxed in her seat.

"You'd better not be calling me nobody, Miss Bitchy." She smirked, as she lifted her coffee back to her lips.

"Jesus, why am I picking on everyone today? I'm sorry, you know it's not like me. It's just... *he makes me forget.*" I pulled back into my chair, my cocoon, wanting that freedom from my fear. From my mind.

"Forget what happened?" Her face was so hopeful, and I hated having to wipe that expression from her face.

"No, he makes me forget that I don't want to tell him."

"*You never really told me.* You said you were attacked, and that you have anxiety attacks, and had to see therapists, and who could blame you? But if you want to talk about it, I'll listen, and I won't judge, and I'll never breathe a word to anyone. Hell, all I know is your name. I don't even know where you lived before." Daisy slipped her shoes off, and pulled her feet up under her.

"I can't tell anyone. I... I can't risk them finding me." I felt edgy and dirty, just thinking about it.

"You always say 'they' rather than just 'him'. I hate to ask, but does that mean what I think it means?" I couldn't look her in the eye, couldn't see the look on her face. Did I really want to tell her this? She said she wouldn't judge, but she'd still look at me differently.

"Mina, it's fine, and you're safe here. I'm your friend, and if talking helps you, and I'm sure it is what they recommend, then do it. The more I know, the better I can help with the Alpha's advances."

My heart thudded painfully.

"*Advances?*"

She groaned, shaking her head slowly.

"You know what I mean."

"*He wants sex?*" My hands shook, and coffee spilled onto my lap, but I didn't care. I'd drink what was left; the remnants, just like me. No longer a full drink, and no longer a complete person. No longer capable of coping with anything, let alone the advances of a man.

"I'm not mentioning sex, and neither is he, but I can see that's a big problem for you," she replied gently.

"*Rape,*" I said. Just one word that said so damn much. I desperately hoped it would be enough, because I didn't want to tell her more.

Her face fell, and tears pooled in her eyes.

"Jesus, you were raped, by more than one man."

I nodded, tears rolling down my cheeks.

"Please don't tell anyone. I'm so ashamed, I could die."

"*Why the fuck are you ashamed?* You didn't choose that! Nobody would choose that! Did they catch the bastards?" She looked ready to get up and fight for me.

I nodded again. "They're in prison, well... for another week or so, at least. I've marked the day on the calendar so I'll be ready. If I don't feel safe here, I'll make a run before that date. It's harder for them to find me that way. If I keep moving, I can stay out of their reach. They said they'd come after me, Daisy."

"You're safest here, Mina. You have no idea just how safe."

I stared at her, pushing down the tingle of hope her words created.

"What does that mean?"

She shrugged, leaning forward in her seat.

"What can it hurt now? You already know he's the Alpha. He has the entire pack watching out for you now. I wasn't kidding before, he has them all on protection detail. They're not stalking you or anything, but they're all around us, and they're keeping their noses to the ground for any threats to your safety. Anyone scaring you will get taken down hard, and they'll have to answer to him."

I looked down at my less than half of a coffee.

"He really did that?"

Maybe I'd misjudged him, but then I'd thought Teddy to be a good guy, and look how that had turned out.

"He would do anything to protect you, Mina."

"But why? I'm not a member of his pack. I'm nobody to him." *I couldn't be, could I? I was just a damaged human woman. No use to anyone.*

"You're not nobody to me, or him. We both like you, and care about you, so will you please stop rejecting any kindness that comes your way, and suck it up? Before you lost your shit on the phone, was it helping? Talking to him?" I nodded slowly.

"He talks me through it when I panic. Of course, he accidentally called me 'baby' in the process, but maybe it was just an endearment any guy would use when he's trying to talk a nutjob out of freaking out."

She was laughing with glee.

"Oh my god, he called you 'baby'! He's so not getting away with that."

"If he's your Alpha, why don't you treat him like it?"

She tilted her head. "In what way?"

"I don't know, doesn't he like, dominate all his wolves into serving him, or some shit like that?"

"Wow you have a lot to learn about wolves, and our hierarchy. We choose to submit to him as our Alpha, but we're not dominated. We're protected, and we work together, to keep each other safe, and happy. How could that be a bad thing?"

When she said it like that, it almost sounded like a good thing, maybe even a great thing. Perhaps I did want their protection after all.

"How do wolf shifters feel about rapists?" I asked idly, and her grin quirked at me.

"We prefer them to be *dead* rapists."

"Good."

She chewed her lip, her face serious again.

"So if the Alpha asks for your address again..."

I took a leap. "It's okay."

"Oh, thank god." She sent a text on her phone, and not even a minute later, there was a banging on the door.

"What the..."

She shrugged, smiling at me.

"Sorry babe. Alpha's orders."

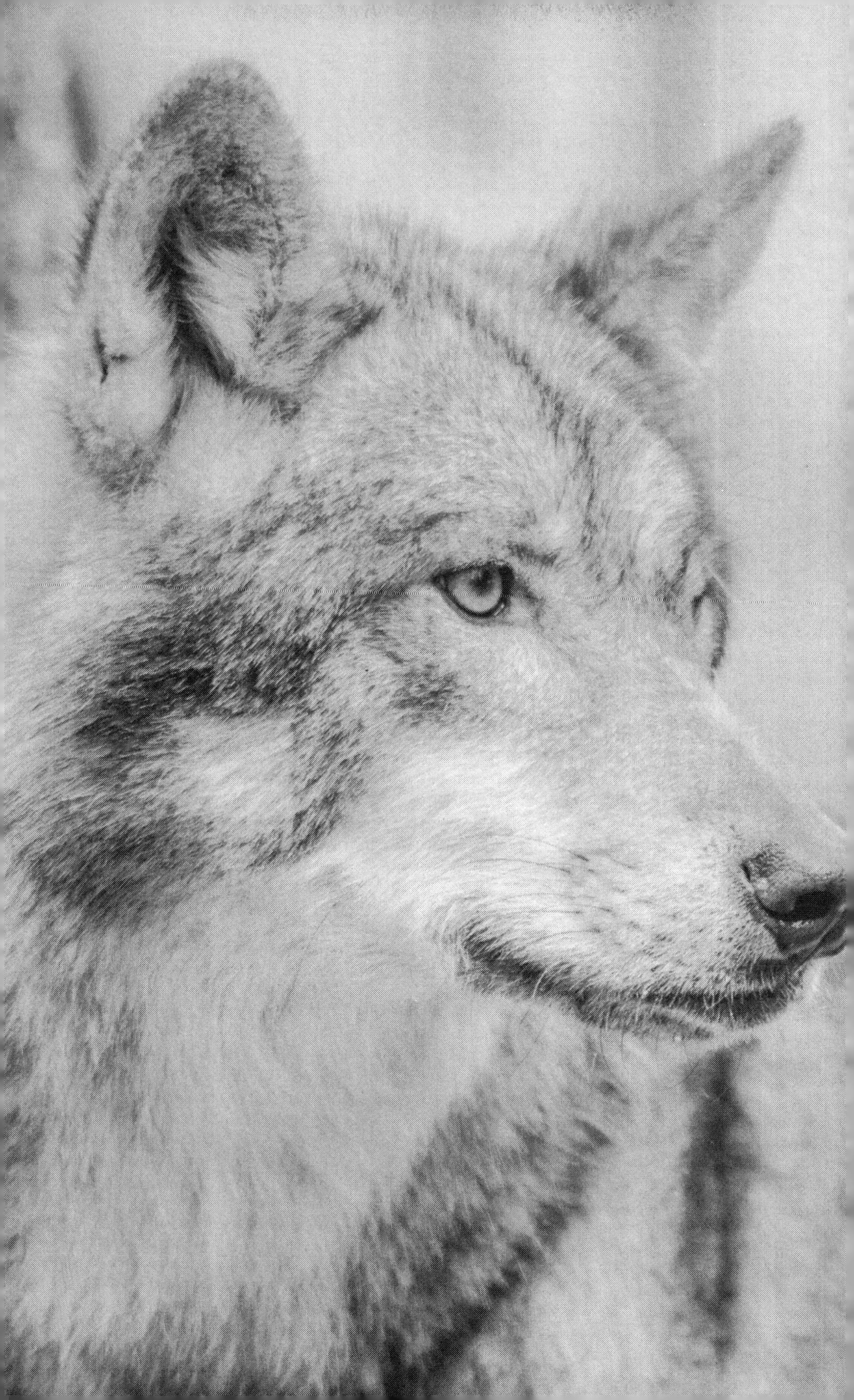

Chapter Thirteen

Mina

She went and let him in, or at least, she tried. When neither came in from the door, I looked out into the hallway, to see what the holdup was.

"It's not your house to let me into, Daisy. I'll only come in if Mina says it's okay. *To. My. Face.*"

I'd never seen him being so forceful, and it was unnerving, but Daisy just giggled, instead of cowering before him like I imagined.

"Mina, can he come in?"

I shrugged at her, chewing my lip nervously.

"Verbally," he said in a clipped tone, and I groaned.

"Fine. Yes, he can come in."

"*To. Me*," he said sharply.

"Oh, for fuck's sake! Yes, Alpha, you can come in," I snapped, glaring at him. He turned his glare on Daisy, before he stepped into the house.

"*You told her?*"

"Oh, come on, I guessed. What other man in the world can demand a girl get out of bed, and dash across town at 4am, to check on a friend?" I marched back into the kitchen, and made a coffee; black, with two sugars, and when Asher walked in, I passed it to him, then stepped back.

"My 'no touching' rule still applies," I warned him.

"Wouldn't think of trying," he said primly, sitting on the sofa Daisy had vacated, but I noticed that she was still standing.

"You can sit down too, you know," I told her, marvelling at the fact that my house was so full right now, and she smiled.

"Well, I could but, I mean, do you want me to? Or should I get out, and leave you guys to talk? I promise he won't do a damn thing, but talk. He's honourable that way." Asher shot another glare at her, and she groaned.

"I was being nice!"

"Yeah, and I'll be nice when I wake you again at this time tomorrow then."

"Fuck." He nodded at her.

"I'm happy for you to leave if Mina is. It's not my house."

I stared at him, and big and burly as he was, he exuded something that made me feel strangely safe. I nodded at her, and she left fast, but the second the door closed and I met his eyes, I stopped breathing.

"Mina?" He started to move out of his seat, his coffee already on the floor beside the sofa.

"*No*," I choked out, waving a hand at him, while I fought to breathe. Why was I alone in my house with a strange man? What kind of an idiot was I?

Asher

IF I THOUGHT NOT being with her was bad, this? Seeing her freaking out, and not being able to at least hold her fucking hand, *that was the worst of all*.

I prayed she'd told Daisy something that would help me find the asshole who did this... although on the phone, she said *they*, didn't she? They? They'd all pay, no matter how many of them there fucking were.

"Would it help if I called you 'baby' again?" I asked, trying a grin. She snorted, and her breathing eased just a touch.

"Maybe," she gasped out, and I nodded, dropping to my knees a few feet away. My hands were up, but not touching, just reaching out to her.

"Shhhh... Look at me, baby, you're safe... you're home, and you're safe. I'm not going to hurt you. I promise you I'll never hurt you."

She was watching me, and hell, I was lost, just so fucking lost. I was on my knees before someone else. *I'm a fucking Alpha, and I'm the one on my knees.*

Women usually ended up on theirs, with my cock in their mouth, and not anything like this, but *this woman*, I just wanted to find every crack in her soul and smooth it over, make her whole again.

"Do you need more coffee?" I asked unexpectedly, because as I scrutinised her, I noticed she'd spilled hers on herself. She looked down, and snorted again.

"Oh that was earlier. Daisy scared me."

"What did she do? I could wake her early for a week?" She smiled, and shook her head.

"Please don't. She gets really cranky at work, when she doesn't sleep."

Her smile suited her, lighting her up from the inside. I smiled back at her, edging just a tiny bit closer, keeping my eyes on hers. I wouldn't touch, not without her permission, but my wolf was growling in my head. He wanted to soothe her, and I really thought we could, if she could just give us a chance.

"She told you what I am, yes?" I asked her, keeping her gaze. She nodded, then shook her head with a frown.

"No, she refused to tell me about anyone but her, but I guessed. I guessed from how she does what you tell her. I mean, she's stubborn as hell, normally." I laughed out loud, because she wasn't wrong.

"Yeah, that she is. I haven't known her very long, but already she's given me more grey hairs than I thought possible."

She giggled. "How long have you known her?"

"Only since she married Ned, so about eight months, but truth be told, we only really met properly and talked to each other that first day I saw you." Honesty was key, so I had to hide nothing from her. Her eyes widened.

"So you didn't make her be my friend?"

I frowned at her.

"Why the hell would I do that? She's known you how long? I only sm... I only saw you for the first time on Thursday."

"I don't understand why you care about me," she said in a small voice, and damn if I didn't want to drag her out of that fucking chair she'd cocooned herself in, and spend hours pleasuring every inch of her body, until she couldn't breathe without moaning my name.

"You know what an Alpha is, don't you? As in not just from your talk with Daisy."

She blushed, looking away.

"I've read stuff."

"About wolves?"

"Shifters, but only because they were free, and I needed something to read, and I didn't reread any parts at all, and... *why are you grinning at me like that?"* She was still blushing, and it was so fucking sexy.

"You read chick books about sexy half-naked wolf shifters, and now you think you understand what we are," I smiled, so she wouldn't take offence.

"One book, because it was free, and it was hot, yes... but I did get one thing from it that I liked." I was hoping she'd get more from me than that, but I let it slide. She wasn't ready for me to come out with any innuendos, they'd only scare her. I ached to creep closer to her now that she was relaxing, but I stayed in place.

"And that was?"

"That each wolf has a mate, like one other wolf for them, and they can sense them, or smell them, when they're close enough, but that was one book. I doubt it's even right." I grinned widely at her.

"Actually, before two days ago, I'd have said it was just a book written by someone with a very vivid imagination."

"And now?" She seemed to be holding her breath for my answer, so I shrugged and decided to keep being honest with her, even if it might scare her right now. She had a right to know, didn't she?

"Now I'm here in your living room at nearly 5am, and I don't even care that I've barely slept since that day, without dreaming about you."

She gasped, her hand going to her chest, and I reached for her then stopped. Fuck! I couldn't take this hands-off shit, I needed to comfort her.

"You think I'm..."

"My mate, yes. Well, no actually, 'think' isn't the right word, I *know*." She was trembling all over. *Please let that be a good thing. Don't let her freak out, don't let her take fear instead of comfort from my words.*

"Are you okay?" I asked finally, when she stayed silent.

"I can't be your mate, because I'm not a wolf, am I?" I shook my head, and her face fell, just a little. *Interesting*.

"You know, just because my wolf has chosen you, it doesn't mean you chose me. I do get that. I can force myself to walk away and leave you alone, if that's what you want, and before you ask, my pack will still protect you with their lives. It's not an 'only if' situation. As I said on the phone, no ulterior motives. If you don't want anything to do with me, that's your right. *Your body, your choice*."

She whimpered, and tears sprang from her eyes. Her fist pressed against her mouth, and the tears rolled down her cheeks. Her sadness and pain was fucking killing me.

"Mina, baby, please, talk to me. I'm here, I'm right fucking here, at your feet where I belong. Just tell me what you need." I edged closer, my arms practically burning with the desperate urge to hold her, and protect her. To ease her, and comfort her.

She stared at me, still crying silently.

"I have... no idea..." she gasped out.

"Can I hold you?" I asked, trying to appear as unthreatening as possible, as if I could even hurt a hair on her head anyway.

She shook her head, but it was a slow shake, like she wasn't quite sure. That was a good sign, but reluctantly I stayed where I was, too far away from her. Always too far.

"You might find comfort in it. I'm told I'm quite soothing."

She made a hiccupy kind of noise, and shook her head again. Okay, it was going to take time to break down these damn walls of hers.

"Would my wolf be more soothing for you?" She stared at me, wide-eyed.

"You'd shift right now?" I nodded, because I knew he was desperate to be near her, just like I was.

"For you, I'd do anything. If you'd rather have my wolf here tonight, I'm fine with that. It'll stop him bitching at me in my head, anyway."

"Is he mad at me?" She asked in a tiny voice.

"Oh god, no, baby, no. *He's mad at me*, for making you cry, for pushing you to talk to me. And for not taking you in my arms, and making you feel safe. I promise you I won't do that, until you're ready."

She nodded at me, whispering her thanks.

"I should warn you, Mina, he won't listen to the 'no touching' rule."

She frowned, almost physically retracting in her chair.

"Wait, all I mean by that is that he'll insist on curling up at your feet, or on your bed with you, and he'll need to be touching you, even just his head on your feet. He needs to be touching you right now, as I do. He just wants to soothe you." I was watching her closely, and trying to keep my wolf back, until she consented.

She finally nodded, holding up her hand as she stood up.

"I'll get into bed, then... you... he... can join me. Do you promise to stay a wolf until I'm awake again? I don't think I could handle waking up next to a man." I clenched my fists and nodded.

"At some point, when you tell me what happened to you, I'm going to make whoever hurt you pay for it with their pathetic miserable life. I won't be gentle, or forgiving, and they will beg me for their life, and I'll leave them in pieces."

I was practically growling the words at her, but instead of scaring her, they seemed to strengthen her, because she nodded at me.

"I'd like to watch that happen." Well, check out Miss Vengeance over there. She'll get anything she fucking needs, I'll make sure of it.

She pushed the door almost closed, and then called out when she was safely in bed. I dropped my clothes, realising that I would have nothing to wear tomorrow otherwise, and then shifted, relishing the warm sensual bliss of the shift.

Padding across the floor, I nudged her door open, and watched her eyes grow really fucking wide. Hell, should I have warned her that male wolves were larger than females? Or that Alpha wolves tended to be even bigger than most other males? *Shit.*

I lowered my head at her, and watched from the doorway, giving her a few moments until she felt safe. Finally she nodded and patted the bed, and I launched myself from the door, and landed on the bed with her.

Instantly I was nuzzling her hand, and she giggled, running her hands over my long dark hair. I leaned over her, running my tongue across her cheek, and making her giggle again.

Then I lowered myself beside her, resting my chin on her shoulder, my body pressed up against hers. She fell asleep within minutes, and I followed quickly behind.

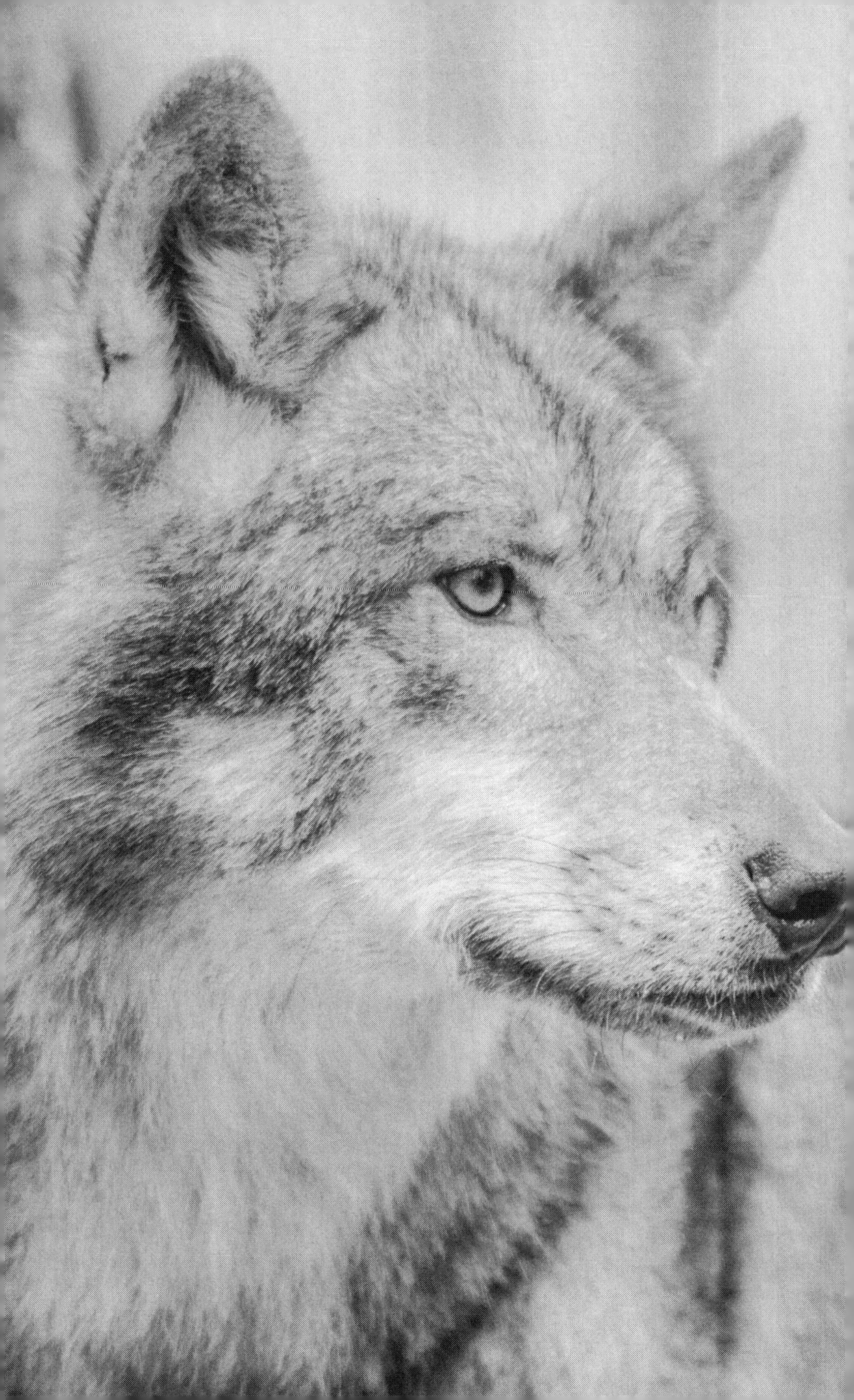

Chapter Fourteen

Mina

My alarm didn't go off, so I woke late, and that meant that wolf Asher also slept late. I hoped Daisy had too, even though the nursery was open on Saturdays. I didn't know if he works too, because we hadn't actually spoken much about him at all yet.

I risked a glance at him, and two huge wolf eyes stared back at me. How long had he been awake? I couldn't ask him, because he couldn't speak, or at least I didn't think he could.

"Been awake long?" I asked, smiling sleepily at him, and he nodded his huge head. Oh, of course, he could nod as a wolf.

"Bet you want coffee?" He did it again, his mouth lolling open, like a grin. I found myself smiling again.

"Turn away," I said, watching his huge wolf head turn, and look the other way. It was so strange that it made me giggle again. *Who was this person, and what had she done with the real me?*

I grabbed my robe, pulling it on over my pyjamas, and then slipped out of the room, to make a fresh pot of coffee. In the living room, I spotted clothing scattered on the floor, and I blinked. A man's clothing on the floor.

My heart seized in my chest for the briefest moment, before I remembered that he'd probably stripped off to shift, so he'd have clothes to go home in. Yes, that made sense, *so stop freaking the hell out.* I piled the clothes beside the door, so that I could take them back in, after I put the coffee on, otherwise we'd have to wait even longer for liquid sanity.

I'd slept great since I went to bed with a huge wolf dog protecting me, but he'd said that he hadn't slept in days. *Since we met.* Could I really be his mate? That couldn't be real, right? Because he's a wolf, but I'm not.

Did that mean he could turn me into one? I had no idea, but the thought of it appealed to me, purely because being a predator might stop me feeling like prey.

A sound behind me made me gasp and turn, just in time to see a naked man dashing across the room. I screamed, and he stopped instantly, as if frozen in motion. His bare ass was staring right at me, and I was trembling all over.

"Fuck! I didn't mean to scare you, I'm sorry. I was just looking for my clothes." His voice was tight, and a little gruff.

I pointed at the door, even though he couldn't see my hand.

"I piled them there for you, I was going to bring them in." My voice was surprisingly steady, considering the fact that it was the first time I'd seen a naked man since that night, in fact not even then, not really.

He didn't move, obviously not wanting to scare me even more, even though his head slowly turned to look for the clothes, and at the same time, his hands moved around to try and cover his ass from my gaze. It looked so comical that somehow, *somehow* it made me smile.

"It's okay, you can move," I said at last, and the tension dropped out of his body.

"Thank fuck. I was about to fall over," he said quietly, crab-walking to his clothes, so that he didn't flash me any other part of him, and I was grateful for that. He stared at the clothes for a moment, and I could tell he was wondering how the hell he'd pick them up, without uncovering himself.

"Want me to toss them through the door for you?" I asked, taking pity on him.

"Fuck yes, please." He disappeared into my bedroom, and my heart sped up. A naked man in my bedroom, that was a first for me. It didn't horrify me like I'd expected, and it really should.

He pushed the door almost closed, and I listened to him walk away from it, so I reached down to grab his clothes and lifted them, his cologne wafting up from them, making me sigh. I took a deeper breath of his scent, and realised how crazy that was, so I reached around the door with them, not wanting to actually throw them.

He did nothing for a moment, then I heard him walking towards me, and my knees weakened. I was seconds away from tossing them after all, when I felt him take them, and felt the briefest brush of his skin, as his hand skimmed past mine. I gasped, and pulled back.

"Sorry, Mina. I thought you were going to throw them." He called out.

"Yeah, it just… it didn't seem right to do that."

He laughed. "I'm not precious about my clothes, baby. It's just that I already shredded one set to come here last night, so these are all I have to go back home with. Of course, once I shift again, they're toast anyway."

"Then you'll be naked again, when you shift back?" Why was I so fixated on that fact?

He laughed again, suddenly approaching the door once more, and I backed away, afraid he'd get too close to me. Even as I moved, I wondered if it would really be so awful if he did.

"I'm always naked once I shift back, Mina. It's just that the pack don't give a shit about things like nakedness. It's all just a part of nature." The door opened slowly and he peered around it, checking where I was standing, before he walked back through, pulling it closed behind him.

"Don't worry, I'm keeping my distance. It's not like I was able to shower and brush my teeth, was it, so I won't risk killing you with my smell."

I sighed, and his head tilted.

"Is that a good sigh, or a bad one?"

"I'm not encouraging anything, but I do like the cologne you wear." I bit my lip, feeling like I shouldn't have shared that with him. It was too intimate.

His mouth quirked. *"Interesting."*

I turned away, feeling unnerved and out of my depth, and headed over to prep our coffee mugs.

"Why is it interesting?"

He followed me, staying a few feet away.

"Because I don't wear cologne."

Oh.

Asher

WELL, THAT WAS INTERESTING as hell. Did that mean that she was picking up a mate scent after all? Or did it just mean that she liked my manly smell? Either way, it was a win, as far as I was concerned.

A day ago she wouldn't be in the same room with me, and now I'd spent the night, albeit as a wolf, and she liked my smell.

She was fussing over coffees, embarrassed, or some shit.

"How does that make you feel?" I asked her at last, because her silence was actually starting to worry me.

She shot me a grin. "Are you my therapist now?" Oh wow, a joke, I liked this side of her.

"I can be anything you want, baby." Shit, that came off too flirty, but look, she didn't run. In fact, she snorted. It wasn't exactly a win, but I'd take it.

"It's good that you like how I smell, because I love the scent I get from you. It soaks into every pore of me. It makes me feel..." I trailed off, glancing down at my pants.

Nope, no spontaneous boner, and that was a damn good thing around her. Maybe that was why, or maybe it was just a proximity thing. In fact, everything had stopped hounding me, now that I was in a room with her. My mind was clear, and I felt normal again.

"Was that some kind of man gesture?" She asked, her arms folded. Oh fuck. I looked at her sheepishly.

"Would you prefer it to be?" She shook her head.

"Okay, I just wanted to make sure I wasn't sporting any... *you know*... morning, um..."

"I get it." She rescued me from actually saying it, but she frowned as she said it.

"But then, you'd know that because you just had your hands over it, when you were naked. And you just got dressed, so you would know."

Oh, double fuck. I hung my head. I was really fucked now, and not in the way I wanted to be.

"Does this scent I give off make you aroused?" She asked bluntly, and I stared at her, mouth open.

"You don't mince your words, do you?" She shrugged, finishing making the coffees.

"It *is* the only rational explanation for your behaviour."

"Is that how it was for the wolves in your books? Maybe I should read them, and get some pointers."

She glared at me then. "You don't get to joke about that right now, but no. They didn't dwell on that side of it. They were written from the woman's perspective."

Of course they fucking were, because heaven knows, nobody wants to know what the male character is thinking. *I felt objectified by every damn shifter book written from the woman's perspective in that moment.*

"Look, I just wanted to make sure that nothing down there was going to freak you out. I'm trying here, Mina, but understand this; my wolf wants you. *I want you*, and whether we like it or not, this bond that wants to connect us, it has my emotions fucked, like you wouldn't believe. To say that I've been fighting to stay, um… PG rather than X-rated, every minute since then, would be an understatement."

"Is that why you're here?"

I backed up as far as I could.

"I'm not trying to get you to do anything you don't want, Mina. *Am I pressuring you, in some way that I can't fucking see?*" She slammed the sugar bowl down.

"Stop getting snippy with me. I'm asking if you're only pursuing me because this mate bond you think you have is screwing with you. If so, is there a way to break it?"

Her words were like a punch to my stomach. I would have physically recoiled, if I wasn't already backed up against the counter. *Pain filled my chest, radiating throughout my body, as I realised that I was being rejected by my mate, by the one I was meant for.*

"What?" I choked out.

"Is that a no? Surely there's a way?" She asked, and I shook my head.

"*Fuck*, I never saw that coming. Last night definitely, but today, I thought... *fuck*. If that's what you want, I'll make it happen." I was walking already.

I couldn't stay, because I was so close to losing my shit, and I couldn't be here when that happened. My wolf was actually howling in my head, his pain burning through me. It was agonising, soul-destroying, heartbreaking.

I slammed the front door behind me, after fighting through all of those locks, and dammit, she didn't even follow me. She really meant what she said, her rejection of me.

I barely glanced around before I shifted right there in the fucking street and ran.

Mina

OF ALL THE TIMES to trip over my own bloody feet! I lost valuable seconds trying to chase Asher down, because the bastard could move pretty fast when he wanted.

The door was thankfully unlocked, although he'd closed it behind him, so I pulled it open and peered outside, checking the street in both directions. Empty, although tattered remains of clothing littered my path. Oh god.

My heart clenched in my chest, as I realised that he'd shifted and run. I gathered up the clothes, before anyone could spot them, and went back inside. I locked all of the locks and bolts, and then stumbled into the living room.

I tossed his ruined clothes on the sofa, and headed for my chair; my safe place. What had I done to him? I didn't even get a chance to finish what I was saying, and he was gone, before I could take it back. I reached for my phone to ring Daisy, then realised I had his number, but did he even have his phone right now?

I tried ringing it, and heard it ringing in my living room. Crap. He didn't have his phone. He said he'd always have it, but then I went and kicked him in the damn stomach, didn't I? Hurting him was the last thing I'd wanted. I rang Daisy instead.

"I need help!" I blurted, as soon as she answered.

"Where's the Alpha?" She replied, sounding worried.

"That's the problem. I said the wrong thing, and he left. He left, Daisy, and I couldn't even take it back, or explain what I meant, because he just left." I was frantic with worry. Worry for a man I hadn't even wanted to be near, or wanted to get to know, until he showed me his heart.

When he'd been around, it was almost too much, too close, but now? It was like he'd left a big hole in the wall, and the cold was coming in, and I was cold, too cold.

I couldn't breathe, and I dropped to my knees. My breaths were tiny gasps, and weren't doing anything to fuel my brain, or my body.

My limbs were tingling, and growing heavy, telling me I was running out of time. I choked out a last few words, before the darkness overwhelmed me.

"Find him, Daisy. *Stop him*. That's... the... pri...ority..."

Asher

RUNNING AS A WOLF normally did wonders for my soul, but this time it felt like it was shattered, broken, torn out. Did I expect it to feel like this? I thought she'd balk, of course. I thought she'd argue, and try to convince me I was wrong, but did I expect her to outright ask me to make it go away though?

Fuck no, even when I'd asked the guys about it, I hadn't been serious, not really. Not before I'd tried to make it work. It was crazy, really, because before I spent a few minutes with her, it was an easy thing to say. Even after sitting with her outside the garden place that night, when she lost it, I still felt like it would be better for us both, if we could do away with the whole thing.

The trouble was that I'd spent the night, and not in the way I wanted to, not in a way I ever would have for anyone but her. That had changed things for me, and for my wolf.

He was devastated at her rejection, and his despair was seeping into my bones, freezing me from the inside, even as my heart felt like it was on fire and burning away to ashes. Did I expect to feel this way after a few fucking hours around her? *Hell no.*

By the time I'd made it back to the pack house, I was exhausted. Not physically, but it was worse than that, because it was an internal thing. Could a soul be drained, and exhausted? I felt dead inside, numb. I ran a shaky hand through my damp hair.

"Boss? You been out all night? Ya tart," Derek said, opening the door as I approached. I tried to shoot him the expected grin, but I couldn't. I kept walking, and he moved fast, so I didn't brush my naked, sweaty body on him.

I grabbed a glass of water, knocking it back too fast, the chill just adding to the deadness I felt inside. With a roar, I turned, throwing the glass at the wall, smashing it and sending shards in all directions like tiny daggers.

"Boss?"

Derek stayed back, as I turned to look at him.

"Fuck, what happened? It's her, isn't it? She okay?"

I rubbed a hand over my face, trying to compose myself enough to speak.

"I'm going to shower. Get Jase. *We need to break the bond, now.*" The words destroyed me. I didn't want to be saying them. It didn't even sound like my voice.

He looked horrified, trying to follow me.

"Boss, you know that-"

"I know what you're going to say, but it's what she wants," I barked the words at him, the implication behind them being to back the fuck off and let me go, before I lose it.

I slammed my bedroom door, and headed for the shower. I turned the water on as hot as it would go. The pain would help, maybe even make everything external again. That I could cope with; punch me, stab me, whatever. I could fight that, but I can't fight this.

I stepped under the spray, hissing with pain when the water hit my cool flesh, like hot stabbing needles of glass. *Perfect*. I lowered my head, and let it rain down on me.

Mina

SHE DIDN'T LISTEN. SHE didn't fucking listen! I saw Daisy's car pulling up outside my house, and ran to the door, wrenching it open.

"What are you doing here? I said go to him! **Go to him**!" I was panicking, but not in the usual way for once.

My heart was racing, and I was scared. Full on scared, because I'd woken up on the floor, with the phone beside me, and the call having ended. I couldn't remember what had happened after I told her to go after Asher, but she clearly didn't even listen!

"Are you okay? You sounded like you just disappeared, and you couldn't breathe! It was freaking me out!" Daisy was running, as soon as she was out of her car.

I slammed the door behind me, my phone and his in my hand.

"He left his phone behind, so we can't phone and stop him."

Daisy stared at me. "Stop him doing what?" I glared at her, wondering why the hell she wouldn't listen to me.

"We need to go there now. Take me to his house please."

She folded her arms. "Are you out of your fucking mind? It's pack territory, Mina. We can't take non-pack members there. *It's forbidden*."

I let myself into her car, putting the seatbelt on, so she threw her hands up, and followed suit, getting back in and joining me.

"I can't take you there, Mina."

"Your Alpha thinks I'm his mate, so I think I get a pass." I pointed at the keys, sitting in the ignition, wanting her to start the car and get moving already. Why didn't she see the urgency?

"Mina, I can't. You need to tell me what's going on."

"Daisy, we need to stop him before he breaks the bond, please. Don't let him do this."

She stared at me in horror.

"Why does he want to do that? He was so keen to get to know you. What happened? When did he even leave? We may already be too late."

Oh god. What had I done? I clasped my trembling hands together.

"He left less than an hour ago, but I don't know exactly when. I was too busy freaking out."

She was staring at me, eyes wide with surprise.

"He stayed the night?"

That was all she was interested in? She needed to get moving dammit. The longer we waited, the more terrified I became that I'd destroyed everything before I gave it a chance.

"Daisy! What happens if he breaks the bond? Will I be able to feel anything?"

She stared at her phone, as if willing it to ring and be him. I showed her his phone.

"We can't reach him unless we go there."

She swiped the screen and pulled up a number.

"I'll ring the pack house, and see who's about."

Oh, I hadn't thought of that, but of course there would be a landline. She put the phone to her ear, with the number dialled.

"Uh... hey, it's Daisy. Uh... Ned's wife... Oh, you knew that... okay... listen, is the Alpha home yet?"

She looked nervous, and frustrated at the same time.

"I know it's not protocol for me to ring the damn pack house, but the alternative was bringing a human there. What was I to do?... *Yes*. Yes, she wants to come and see him... No... NO! Don't let him do that. Fuck... I know he's the Alpha. Fine, I'm bringing her, and I'm blaming you! Hello? Fucker!"

She ended the call and passed her phone to me.

"You talk to me while I drive, because I want to know everything." She started the car, and pulled away from the curb, fast enough that I was pressed back into my seat. Thank god. I prayed we wouldn't be too late.

"He talked to me for ages, my god, he was so patient and sweet. He, he couldn't stop me from panicking, so he offered to stay with me as his wolf."

"He showed you his wolf?" She seemed surprised, but I shrugged, maybe missing why it was a big deal to her.

"He slept on my bed, pressed up against me for the few hours we had left for sleeping. Wait, why isn't the nursery open?"

She shot me a frustrated glare.

"Because my one and only staff member rang me, freaking out, and demanded that I run errands for her!" I snorted. She was wearing her uniform, which I'd only just noticed.

"I didn't know what else to do."

"You just think if you're going to be shacked up with my Alpha, then you'll be the boss of me, well wrong, lady. You still work for me!" She giggled, and I almost joined her, before I remembered what was at stake.

"Why are we laughing? He's going to destroy everything!"

"Mina, why do you care?"

She steered out of town, and headed out into the country. Interesting, I'd never even asked where we were going.

"It'll hurt him, won't it?"

She nodded. "Wolves get one mate, if they're lucky, and some never find theirs. If he breaks the bond, he loses his only chance of true happiness, plus, of course, it could damage the pack."

I grabbed her sleeve.

"It'll hurt the pack too?" She glared at me, as she steered the car back on track.

"Can you try *not* to kill us in a car crash, please? I'm already pushing this piece of shit over her happy speed!" I put my hands back in my lap.

"I don't understand enough about the whole pack thing, and I don't even know for sure that I want to be mated to anyone. I mean, look at me, I'm a mess. I'm terrified of all men, even one who seems to want to look after me, and what if I can never give him what he wants?"

Daisy sighed, shaking her head.

"Willingness to try and talk to him, and see if it's there. That's all anyone can ask, and I get that's probably kind of selfish, after what you've been through, but look at it this way, if you fall for each other, and this works, you'll never be at risk of anything like what happened to you, ever again. You'll always be safe by his side, and he'll support you in anything, and everything. Wolves devote their lives to loving and caring for their mate. You'd be safe, and empowered. Trust me, it could be the best thing that happens to you, and to him. He will be stronger, and more powerful."

"But I'm not a wolf. Doesn't that mean I'll weaken him instead?" I wished I knew more, that I'd had more time to absorb all of this.

"Why would you think that?"

"Because I know so little about this stuff! Hey! This is the road to the hiking trail you showed me." I stared out of the window with sudden interest. Why were we here?

Daisy tutted at me.

"You think I'd take you anywhere other than pack territory to show you my wolf? I wanted to know that I'd be safe there." I stared at her incredulously.

"You took me into pack territory, when I knew nothing about any of it? And yet now you say you shouldn't?"

"Yeah, what's your point?" I shrugged, because I didn't really care about that.

All I cared about was stopping Asher, before it was too late.

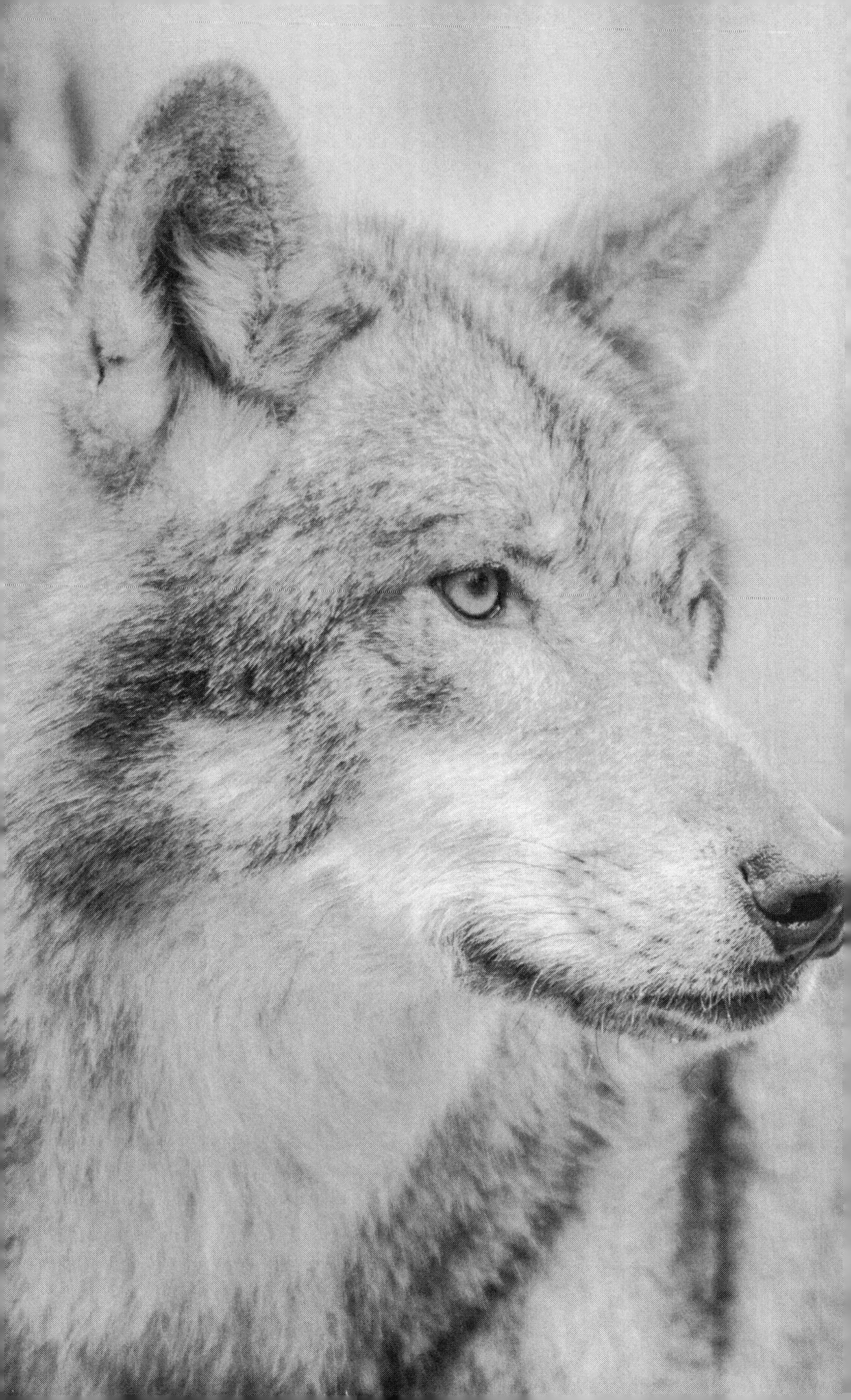

Chapter Fifteen

Asher

The first thing I did when I got out of the shower, which I'd stayed in for long enough that my skin actually felt burned, was look for my phone. It wasn't by the bed, and I stared for a long moment, too long, before I realised that I could only have left it in one place. *Mina's place.*

I had no clothes, and brought nothing back with me, so she had my phone. Of course, if I'd taken it, I'd have lost it when I shifted, so either way, I was fucked. I grabbed some jeans, and a t-shirt, and threw them on.

I didn't care what I was wearing, I didn't care that my wet hair was scruffy as fuck, my beard too. It wasn't like grooming was a priority right now, because nothing mattered anymore. I'd showered and brushed my teeth, and that was as far as it went. It was all I felt capable of.

I walked into the pack house kitchen, and saw Jase and Derek leaning over a laptop screen, reading something.

"Tell me you're ready," I barked at them. The phone rang, and Derek loped off to answer it, so I leaned over the laptop with Jase.

"Come on, man, what's taking so long?"

He stared at me, that serious look on his face; the one that told me he was about to give it to me straight.

"Alpha, please, if you do this, you won't get a second chance." He looked sad more than anything now, and I nodded, a heavy sigh leaching out of me.

"It's what she wants though, Jase, so what can I do? I can't force her to want this, I wouldn't even consider it."

"But you want this, right?" I shrugged, feigning something other than the chilling agony I felt inside.

"My needs aren't important here, so I'll stay unmated. Maybe hook up with a wolf bitch at some point, and marry her for babies. We don't all get the happy ending, but I still have a pack to run, so I have to get my priorities straight." God, my heart hurt just saying those words.

Derek seemed to be arguing with someone, even telling them off for calling the pack house. He actually used the word 'protocol'... could he even hear himself? He rang off, looking pissed off, and joined us back at the table.

"Uh, yeah, boss... I just need to check into one more thing, then I think we're all set. Why don't you grab something to eat, while we prepare."

Jase was staring at him, his face awash with confusion, then he suddenly nodded.

"Yeah, I'm almost set too. There's plenty there in the fridge, Alpha, although, you know, we could get the staff in to cook for you. They do get pretty put out that you insist on cooking for yourself."

I shrugged. "I like to cook. It calms me, and I need that right now." Crap, now I sounded as weak and pathetic as I felt.

"Get your shit in gear, boys. You have until I've eaten to be ready to end this." I marched to the fridge, pulling the door back to lean in, and did my best to ignore the angry whispers between the two of them.

My guess was that Derek wanted to do what I asked, and Jase was trying to delay things. If either of them disobeyed me, I'd have to deal with that as an Alpha. I sighed heavily.

When would this day just fuck off, and leave me alone? I wanted to curl in my bed and give in to the sorrow inside me.

I forced myself to dig out some ingredients, deciding on an omelette for something fast and easy. I couldn't really concentrate on anything more complex.

I focused on the task of chopping up ingredients, and beating eggs, every motion taking my full concentration, so that I could keep my mind off what was going to happen when I was done.

Fuck, it was like waiting to be marched to my execution. I felt like what we were about to do would actually kill me. Maybe that was how the mate bond worked. Go with it or die? I had no fucking idea, but I wasn't completely against that right now.

When I turned from the counter, waiting for the grill to finish off my breakfast, I realised that both of my wolves had buggered off somewhere else. As long as they were doing what I had commanded, they could do it on the goddamned shitter, for all I cared.

It was too quiet though, because I'd expected a flurry of activity. Surely this kind of process needed magic or witches. Oh fuck, if we needed witches, then we'd have to wait for them to be available.

I groaned, turning to check on my food, which was almost ready. I grated a little Italian cheese on top, and popped it back under the grill. It was really more of a frittata at this point, but it'd taste just as good, if I could even taste a damn thing. All of my senses felt dulled and useless to me.

When I turned back from the cooker, I was faced with four people. Jase, Derek, Daisy, and... her. *Mina*. She was here in the damn pack house. I stepped back, the shock pretty much slapping me in the face.

"What, why is she here?" I snapped, turning back around to turn the grill off, before I burned the place down. When I turned back, Mina still looked like she'd been slapped.

"I..."

I turned to the others.

"Does she need to be here for some ritual or process to kill the bond? If not, she goes. *Now*." I left the room, or at least I tried, *but a hand on my arm stopped me*. Warmth spread through me at her touch, and a gasp sounded from behind me.

As I turned to look into Mina's eyes, hers lifted from her hand on my arm, to look back at me. She couldn't believe she'd touched me, just like I couldn't. And hell, she wasn't moving away either. Her hand trembled, but she held on.

"*Mina?*" I choked out, emotion damn near overwhelming me at the thought of what it fucking took for her to do that.

"Please," she whispered, and I didn't want to move.

I didn't want to break that connection, because now that she and I were physically touching, I could fucking feel it. Warming me through, removing that chill that a murderously hot shower hadn't killed. It also went straight to my fucking cock, and I knew if she saw that, she'd freak out.

I just stayed perfectly still, staring at her, while she stared back at me. Finally I lifted my eyes from hers, checking for the others. If they were still here, I'd kill them all. We were alone.

I looked back at Mina, who was staring at her hand again, a strange expression on her face.

"I haven't touched anyone in so long, but it feels... nice," she whispered haltingly. My whole body trembled with the urge to pull her into my arms, and hold her, until she never had to worry about that again. My breath whooshed out of me, because I guess I'd been holding it in.

"Why did you come here?" I asked her, quietly, gently, because I may have been an asshole when she arrived, but this moment, *her touch*, just made all of that go away again.

She looked at me again, and her eyes were wide, almost stunned.

"You... *you left*..."

I nodded, a little anger creeping back in. I clenched my jaw on the torrent of words that suddenly wanted to spew out of me. She winced at the expression on my face, lowering her eyes for a moment.

"You're mad at me," she whispered, and I nodded, then shook my head.

"You rejected me, Mina. It hurts."

She shook her head.

"I never did that. I was just asking..."

I wanted to reach for her hand or place mine over hers, complete a connection with her, because it was too tenuous. I was desperate for more.

"You wanted to break the bond. I'm just trying to do what you wanted."

"No!" She snapped suddenly, pulling her hand away, and leaving a chill behind. *I felt bereft*. How the fuck could one woman's touch do all of that to me? I still couldn't let her see what her touch did to me. I gestured into the kitchen, and followed her back in.

I pulled the grill out, and plated up my breakfast. Her eyes fixed on the plate, and she bit her lip, so I chuckled, and passed her a knife and fork.

"Go for it. I'll make another." She didn't argue, tucking into my breakfast. What the fuck was even happening right now? I worked on another, making coffee for us both as I worked. She looked up with a smile as I placed one in front of her, so I was glad we'd talked coffee during our one phone call.

As if she thought of that too, she suddenly reached into the pouch pocket of her hoodie, and pulled out my phone.

She almost put it on the counter, then she changed her mind, and passed it to me. *To. Me.* I stared at it, then her, and then I reached out for it.

She placed it delicately on my hand, her nails brushing my skin as she did. Just that, and it was enough. For now, it was more than enough. She was trying.

"Thanks," I said, clearing my throat against the lump building up there. When did I turn into such a pussy?

Turning with a growled curse, I rescued my slightly overcooked frittata, and plated it up. I pulled up a stool beside her at the breakfast bar, and watched as she finished her food, waiting for mine to cool a little.

"That was delicious," she finally said, making me smile.

"Really?" She nodded, swiping a finger across the plate, and popping it in her mouth. I bit back a groan. She seriously had no idea how sexy she looked doing that. *My cock did though, the observant bastard.*

I looked down at my food, starting to tuck in, and she sighed.

"I haven't eaten that well in so long. I don't really cook, so I mostly eat ready meals, you know, whatever I can microwave. It's cheap, too."

I growled softly, because that shit was going to change. No woman of mine was going to eat like she's not worth a damn.

I sliced the side off of my frittata, the non-overcooked part, and slid it onto her plate. She looked up at me with a beaming smile.

"Really?"

I laughed, feeling like a fucking king.

"Eat it before I change my mind." She didn't wait, and man, I didn't realise how amazing it would feel to do these so-called 'little things' for her.

Feeding her, my god, I'd cook for her every day for the rest of her life if she asked, and I really fucking wanted her to.

When we'd both finished eating, and sat sipping our coffee, the silence started to feel less comfortable, and I couldn't bear it.

"So, you didn't want to break the bond?" I asked, praying that she'd say 'no' again.

She shook her head, and my breath left me.

"But you said-"

"What I did was ask you a simple question, Asher, and what *you* did was run, before I could finish. I was asking what's best for you, because I'm not sure this is it." Oh.

Well, talk about your crushing defeats. I was a mile tall a moment ago, and now I'm a fucking garden gnome.

"It is," I found myself saying, and even she looked surprised.

"How?"

"I think you were meant for me." *Sap of the year, that's me.* She smiled sadly.

"I'm damaged goods, Asher, beyond repair. You'd be chasing after someone who runs from you half the time." I tilted my head at her.

"And the other half?"

She grinned a little.

"She'll eat your cooking."

I laughed. "Listen, I'm not saying this would be easy for either of us. I mean, I'm a wolf, you're human. Although physically we're compatible, you'd find wolf life different, and maybe scary. You'd be absolutely safe here, always, but it's not like living as a human." She frowned at me.

"Living here? Is that what you're suggesting?" I bit down on the inside of my cheek, forcing myself to take a moment to think before I spoke.

"If we were mated, yes. I mean, I'd happily move you into a room of your own, any time you want. You'd be safe from everyone and everything here, I promise. We protect our own."

She focused on her coffee for a moment, and I hoped I'd made it correctly. She smiled after a few mouthfuls. Thank god. I was surprised by how much it mattered to me that I got it right.

"I'm not one of your own, but you're right, it's safe. I feel different here, less like a victim, even with so many big guys around. That would normally terrify me in itself." She must have been referring to Jase and Derek. She'd met no others yet, at least as far as I was aware.

"You should know, there are almost another fifty of them here," I warned her.

"Wolves?" Her eyes were wide.

"Men," I corrected her, and she looked down, blinking fast.

"Are they all good people? They don't hurt women?" Her voice was small again, like before, and I missed the more confident voice she'd been using with me.

I ached to lift her chin, to make her look at me, so she could see the truth in my words. Not touching her was agony.

"Mina, look at me, please," I finally said, and her eyes lifted reluctantly. She was chewing that lip again. *Fuck.*

"No man here would hurt any woman, and even more than that, none of them would hurt *my* woman. They would, in fact, throw themselves between you and any danger out there, and I say out there, because there is none here. Well, that's not entirely true, at some point another pack may challenge us, but they wouldn't win."

She gasped. "Is it dangerous, being Alpha?" She looked worried... about me?

I shrugged, trying to make a smaller deal of it.

"If an Alpha challenges me outright, I'd have no option, but to fight to the death. *Hey, don't look so freaked out.* I'm a scrappy bastard, trust me. I'm what they call a true Alpha, that means I was born to an Alpha, and was always meant to be one myself. If a non-Alpha wolf challenges an Alpha and wins, they become an Alpha in their place, but they don't become as strong as a born Alpha. It's more of a title thing."

"So any wolf could challenge you?" She looked more worried, rather than less.

Why did I bother trying to explain this shit now? I was apparently crap at it, probably because my heart wasn't really in it, not right now.

"They'd die if they did," I said firmly. She almost seemed to be leaning away from me now.

"Please don't be afraid of me, Mina, I'm no threat to you," I whispered.

Mina

IT WAS ALL SO confusing. He was so nice, and *oh my god he could cook, and it was delicious*. He fed me so much, I could burst, but then he started talking about this pack stuff, and it was all so violent, and it sounded tenuous, like anything could lead to other wolves attacking him.

How could this be his life, and how could it be safe, like he promised, when an attack could happen at any time?

"Talk to me, baby, I'm right here, and I want to hear how you feel." His voice was so calming, and soothing, that it made me feel safe. *And I touched him*, I actually willingly put my hand on him, and how did it feel? Warm, safe, peaceful, and normal, like I *should* be touching him.

I half wanted to do it again, and I was half terrified by that thought, because if I broke my one rule, and this soon after meeting him, how soon would it be before he was trying to get more from me.

"Mina, please." He was watching me, as I argued with myself. I chewed my lip.

"Truth?" My voice was a little hoarser than normal, so I cleared my throat, while he nodded.

"Always." I glanced away, then back to him, determined to meet his eyes.

"*It was nice,*" I finally managed, watching him frown.

"What was?"

My hands trembled, as I clasped them in my lap.

"*Touching you.*"

His face lit up. "Really?" I nodded, looking away, not wanting to see it on his face, his hope for more.

"Mina, you're hiding from me again," he said softly, and I shrugged.

"This is all so scary." He laughed softly, shaking his head.

"I'm not scary. I'm proud of you, though." I turned to look at him, shocked by his words.

"Why?"

He smiled, looking at my hands, as they came back up to clutch at my almost empty mug.

"I liked having you touch me. It's like you soothed my soul with one touch." I blinked at him.

"It felt good to you?"

He was laughing. "God, yes! Mina, if you had never been through what you'd been through, and you weren't afraid of me, *damn*, I'd have already shown you just how good... *hey, where are you going?*" I'd lurched away, hopping down from the stool, and backed up to the kitchen counter.

"Please," I whimpered. He rested his forehead in his palm for a moment, before staring back at me.

"Fuck, I'm sorry, I didn't mean to scare you. I'm trying to tell you that it feels right to touch me, because I'm meant for you. It's safe, because I will never hurt you, and Mina, this bit is the most fucking important of all. I will never, NEVER, demand anything from you, that you don't want to give, or that you don't feel safe doing. If you never touch me again, *fuck, it's going to hurt*, but that moment of trust between us, it was fucking everything to me."

"You swear a lot," I said finally, because his words were amazing, and beautiful, and perfect, but I needed time to process them.

He snorted. "Yeah, I've been told that before. Thing is, I think it got ten times worse a few days ago, when I found the woman of my fucking dreams."

I giggled. What was happening to me? Something about him was making me... more. More *me*. More human. More *woman*.

To distract myself, I focused on the first thing, other than his face, that I could. The words on his t-shirt. I stared at his chest for a few moments, and then I started laughing.

"Bikini Inspector?" He frowned, then looked down where I pointed, pulling the t-shirt away from his skin to read it.

"Fuck."

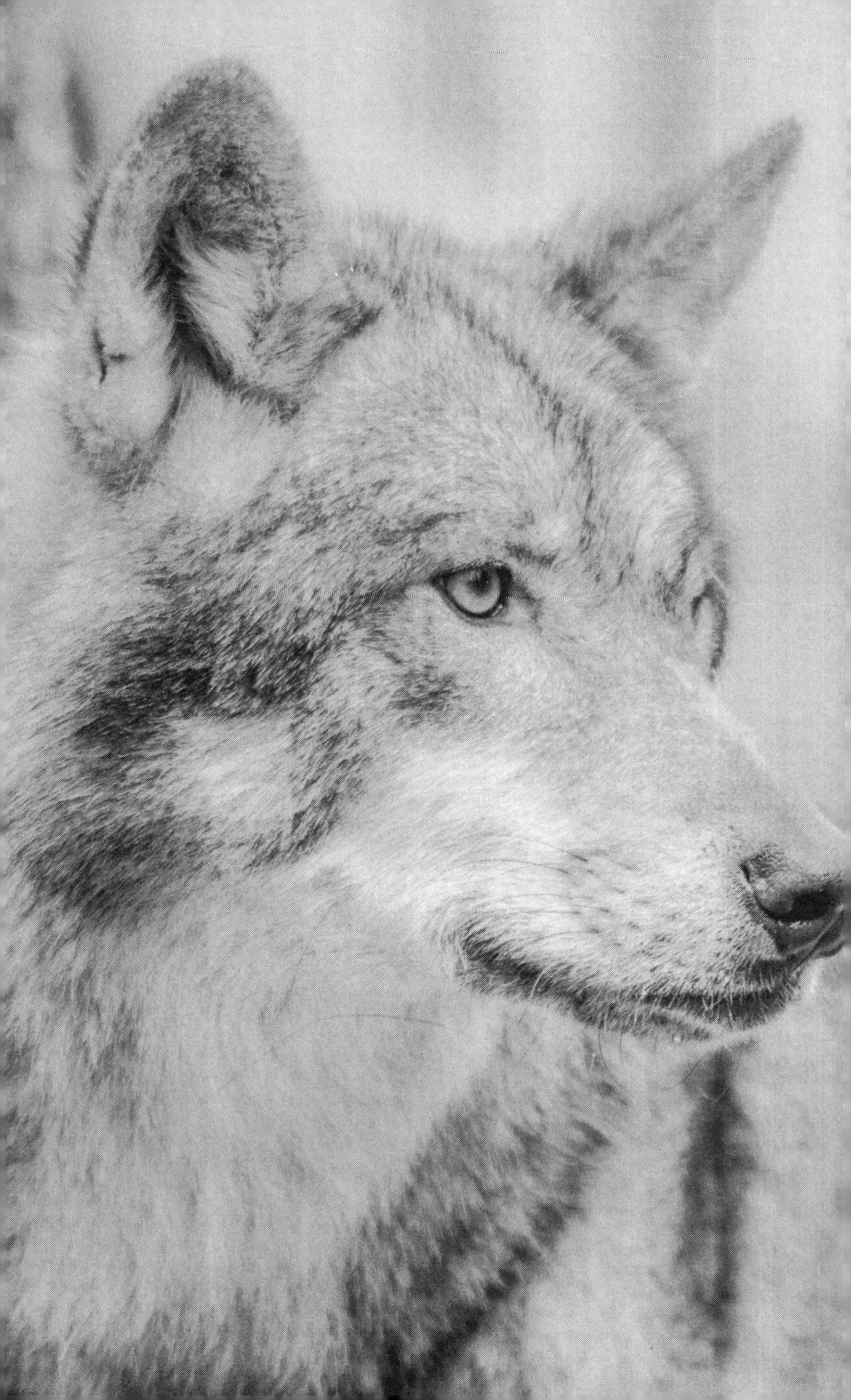

Chapter Sixteen

MINA

The expression on his face was so cute. Didn't he look at what he'd picked to wear this morning? He looked mortified.

"I'll change it," he said, standing up in a hurry.

"Why?" I was still grinning, and I liked how it felt. I hadn't smiled, or laughed, this much for more than a year.

"It's offensive, or I don't... *fuck*... why didn't I look before I put it on?" He groaned, pulling it off over his head, and tossing it across the room.

"There, that's better."

I was struck dumb, panic starting to tremble through me, but also there was something else. I didn't hate the sight of his chest; it was hairy, but then he had a full head of hair and a beard, so what did I expect?

It was muscular too; I could tell by the way it flexed when he moved. He'd stopped doing that though, he was frozen, statue-like, and staring at me.

"*Breathe, Mina.*"

I suddenly choked, and realised that I hadn't been breathing at all. I sucked in a few deep breaths, clenching my fists, while I waited for the panic to pass.

It was hard to breathe, and that was almost as scary as a half-naked man this close to me. *Alone.* I glanced around the room.

"Mina, you're safe. I'm so sorry. That was a dumb fuck thing to do. I was just embarrassed by the t-shirt, but I'll go put something else on." He stood up, glanced down, groaned and sat back down again.

"Or... you know, maybe you could just toss that one back over, and I'll wear it inside out."

He grinned, but he looked embarrassed, and I didn't understand. I glanced down, not seeing the problem, because he'd tucked himself back into that breakfast bar, like he was trying to become one with it.

"What's wrong?" I asked, when my breathing started to work properly again. He covered his face with one hand, sighing heavily.

"You don't want to know."

I frowned. "Worse than being alone with a half-naked man?"

He barked out a laugh, rubbing his face with both hands.

"Yes, way worse." *Oh.* I edged around the kitchen, keeping my distance from him, and retrieved the t-shirt.

He stayed still, facing away from me, so I took the opportunity that was screaming at me, and brought the shirt to my face, breathing in his scent. It seemed to soak into me, calming the panic, and the fear that always seemed to be present. I was so distracted by that feeling, that I didn't notice him watching me now.

"I think it's the mate bond that makes you feel comforted by my scent, just so you know," he said quietly. I looked at him, shocked and embarrassed at being caught.

"Oh... I was just..."

"*Enjoying how I smell*. Thank god that was clean on after a shower, that's all I can say." He grinned, and I tossed the t-shirt at him. I'd turned it back the right way first, and he quirked an eyebrow at it. I folded my arms and stared at him. At his face, only his face. *Dear god...*

"Now you *want* me to wear a t-shirt that says 'Bikini Inspector'?"

Asher

SHE WAS THE MOST confusing woman, but the challenge in her gaze right now, that did nothing to scare away the fucking boner I think I'm gonna be stuck with, until she personally did something about it.

I shrugged. "Fine, then I'm wearing it. On your head be it!" I pulled the shirt back on, and she almost looked disappointed, before she took a breath, and seemed to relax.

I could see she was conflicted, and that was good, right? She might still be afraid, but there was a little interest there too. I could work with a little. *Hell... I've got time, I'll spend however long it takes to gain her trust, and her love.*

"Hey, boss." Derek walked in and stopped in place, staring at me, then looking at Mina.

Just his eyes on her made me growl a soft warning, I couldn't help it. *Was it just because they were male eyes on her, or because they were Alpha male eyes?* He groaned, looking back at me.

"Easy there, I was just popping by to let you know we're all heading out for a run. You need anything before we... *did you seriously buy a t-shirt that says; 'Bikini Inspector'?*" I snorted, and Mina started giggling.

"Listen, asshole, it was a gift, okay? A dumb gag gift that I forgot about, until I blindly grabbed something to wear today. I'm a wolf, I tend to go through clothes. Now fuck off for your run, before I kick your ass." He laughed, waved at us both, and turned to leave.

Mina watched him go, a deep frown on her face. Was she afraid to be alone with me?

"Mina?"

She turned to me with wide eyes. "Yes?"

"You okay there?" She blinked a few times.

"Why did he just laugh when you told him off?"

I started laughing. "We were just having a laugh, baby, honestly. He's my Delta, although it turns out he's an Alpha, too. Remember how I told you that killing an Alpha can make the winner one too?"

She turned to glance back after him.

"He killed an Alpha? Doesn't that make him a danger to you then?" She looked worried, but not for him. *For me.*

I stood up, approaching her slowly, carefully.

"He chose to join my pack, to work for me. He's got my back, Mina, I promise."

She'd been watching me approach her, backing up to the wall as I did so. It felt a little like stalking her, even though I meant her no harm.

"I'm not going to hurt you."

She nodded rapidly. "I get that, but what you think of as hurting me, may not exactly mesh with what I think will hurt."

That made a shitload of sense, too much really.

"I'm not going to try anything untoward. I just want to be nearer to you."

She was trembling, and for the first time, I noticed that I was more than a foot taller than her, with her at maybe 5'6. Did she feel more afraid, because I towered over her a little?

"Do you want me to move away?" I asked softly. She blinked for a few moments, then shook her head, just a short jerky movement, but I smiled with relief.

"See? This is progress, Mina. You touched me earlier, and you surprised yourself as well, I know that. That was massive progress, and made me so proud of you. If it takes years, I'll work with you, to your limits and rules... just to be with you. Is that worth a try for you?"

I tilted my head, watching her wet her lips, pressing them together. I ached to lean closer and kiss those soft lips, but I fought the urge, forcing my eyes back up to hers.

"I..."

I nodded encouragingly.

"Go on, I'm listening." *Jesus god, talk to me, woman.*

"I was raped," she finally said, her words knifing me in the heart. My hand actually covered it, like I'd tried to soothe a wound, because it literally hurt like a bitch.

"What? Who, Mina? *Who did this to you?*" I knew I was barking at her, but I was trembling with anger. I wanted to tear the fucker limb from limb, slowly. He'd pay with his life for hurting her.

She was struggling to stay on her feet, her knees were trembling so much. I held out a hand to her, and she flinched. Okay, too soon.

I grabbed a low footstool from the other room, and brought it in, placing it beside her. She practically fell onto it, thanking me breathlessly as I crouched before her. Only a foot or so away, no more. She needed me beside her, whether she realised it or not.

"Talk to me, baby."

She blinked away tears, new ones replacing the fallen ones.

"His name was Teddy. I was... I've always been shy, you know? I might be twenty-eight, but I never had the courage to date. I hadn't... I dressed nice, but not provocative. I don't think..."

"The way you dressed is irrelevant. You didn't cause it."

"I did," she whimpered. My heart was thudding so hard in my chest, I began to wonder if it really had been stabbed. I rested my hands on my knees, although crouching wouldn't work for long.

Eventually, I got up and grabbed another damn footstool. I placed it opposite her and sat down again. We had so many fucking places to sit in this house. Why were we making a new one in the kitchen?

"Mina?" She looked up, not seeming to realise she'd fallen silent on me.

"Do you want to keep talking? You won't find any judgement here. Only support." I needed names, and I needed locations, and I needed them now. *Anyone involved in hurting her would die in agony.*

"Teddy kept badgering me to go out with him, and I kept saying no, not because I didn't like him, but because I was shy... afraid. Eventually, I gave in and agreed to a date. One. *God...*"

She sighed, clenching her hands into one big, twisted clump of fingers, and I itched to ease them and hold them, and do whatever the fuck she'd let me do, to comfort her. My wolf was practically screaming at me to hold her.

"He told me to dress nice, because he said he had a nice fancy dinner planned. I was actually excited when he picked me up. He told me I was pretty, and he... he liked my long hair." *Long hair.* I glanced at her short cropped blonde hair, and hated the sudden painful understanding of why it was that way.

"You're doing really well, baby, just keep telling me. I'm here, and you're safe." I needed to keep her on track. I hated making her talk... having to hear even a minute of this because it was agony for both of us, but I needed to know who hurt her. That was what I needed, so I could fix this for her, and make her feel safe again.

She glanced at me, her lips trembling.

"I trusted him." I nodded gravely.

"I know, and whatever he did, you have to know... that's not how normal men behave. What he did is not the norm."

She chewed her lip. "We drove to some park. It was almost dark, but he said he wanted to take a moonlight walk. It sounded romantic, and I was a dummy. I mean, I was a twenty-seven-year-old virgin. What the fuck did I know?!" She was angry, and that was good.

Fuck me, she was saying this only happened to her a year ago, *and she'd been a fucking virgin*.

"Still wasn't your fault, Mina... you can do this." Jesus, just let me hold a fucking hand. My fingers twitched in her direction, and I forced them back.

"He... he'd invited a friend... Travis... *Trav*... they..." She started doing that gasping thing, the thing she did when her breathing was failing. *Fuck*. I twitched in her direction again, and tucked my hands under my legs before I broke her damn rule.

Her head was down, her eyes hidden from me, and I ached to tilt her chin up, to look her in the eye, and tell her I'd keep her safe forever.

"Shhhh... Breathe, Mina... *you're so strong*. Look at you... look at where you are... you did that, despite them. You survived."

She lifted angry eyes to mine suddenly.

"Survived? Barely! Only fucking just, and I wish I hadn't. I wish every day that they'd been more efficient. See... when they finally finished taking turns raping me, they... they tried to kill me. I guess they really wanted to get away with it, because I was nothing more than a thing to them. *Something to screw, and discard when they were done*."

My wolf was howling with fury inside my head. He wanted blood, and he was gonna fucking get it, we'd bathe in their fucking blood.

"Baby... Mina, you're safe now, I promise."

She glared at me again.

"I'll never be safe, don't you see? They'll be out of prison soon, and they swore they'd find me, and finish what they failed to do. It terrifies me, but in some ways, I almost hope they do, because then at least it'd be over."

I snarled at her, my wolf shining through as he roared furiously in my head.

"Don't fucking talk like that. They're not going to find you; I'll make sure of it."

She was watching me, as I stood up to pace, kicking the damn stool across the room. I needed to do something to calm down before I scared her.

My wolf was almost forcing me to shift. He wanted to take action, and I could feel it starting, my skin starting to warm, as he began to ripple his way out. I fought against it. Not now. *Not like this.*

"No!" I snapped, trying to communicate with him, because he had to stay back. I needed to talk to her, and I couldn't do that as a fucking wolf.

"Asher?" Mina's voice was weak, quiet, *afraid*.

I turned to look at her, to apologise for scaring her, and lost my hold on my form. A second later, I was padding across the floor, my wolf heading straight for his mate. He desperately wanted to comfort her.

I tried to force him to shift back, but he was fighting me, dammit. Mina watched us approach, her eyes wide, hands out.

I felt my wolf pushing our head against her hands. It was strange, because normally, even though he was a separate entity, when I was in wolf form, I was still in control. He just relished the freedom to stretch and run. But today... yeah, he'd gone fucking rogue on me.

Please let me talk to her, I begged him. He sat in front of her, and she ran her hands over his, *our*, thick coat. It hurt that she'd so readily touch me in this form, but as a man, I was a monster to her. But after what she'd told me, who the fuck wouldn't be damaged beyond belief?

Maybe, like she said, beyond *repair*... but then, she'd rushed here to stop me breaking the bond. She'd put her hand on me, to stop me leaving. That had to mean *something*.

Did I have to keep pushing things to extremes for her to react? That wouldn't be fair to her, no matter how much I desperately wanted to feel her touching me again. *Me*, not the wolf.

Her story was horrific. She'd been a virgin, and those bastards had held her down and raped her, passing her around like a fucking possession.

They were lucky they were in jail right now, but the second they got out, they'd die. I'd make sure of that. I just needed the boys to get working on who they were, and how to isolate them so I could destroy them.

A thought occurred to me, and surprisingly, I'd never tried this before, but I was a wolf right now, and they were also wolves right now, and I was their fucking Alpha.

If it ever worked, it'd be right now, in this moment.

~ Jase? D?

I reached out to them with my mind. For long frustrating moments there was no response, and then I felt a wave of something. Shock, or maybe surprise, something like that anyway.

~ Boss?

Derek's response came back, instantly followed by a more respectful response from Jase.

~ I need you back here. I have more information on who hurt Mina. They raped her, and I want to know what prison they're at, and when they're being released. Now.

I felt more of that shock coming my way, along with pure horror and rage. Good. That was exactly how I wanted them to react, because she was one of us now.

~ On our way!

Derek's response came, with an affirmation from Jase, followed by a question.

~ Do you need Daisy back too? She's still with us.

I confirmed yes, and then they were heading back. Now I just needed to get the fuck out of wolf form. I growled, no, wait... *he did*... Mina's face fell, her eyes widened, and her hands left me in a hurry.

Great, now we'd scared her. What the fuck was going on? Why the hell couldn't I shift back?

~ Guys, we have another problem.

I sent that back out to both of them, feeling panicked and frustrated.

~ What's wrong, Alpha?

Yeah, what's wrong indeed?

~ I can't fucking shift back.

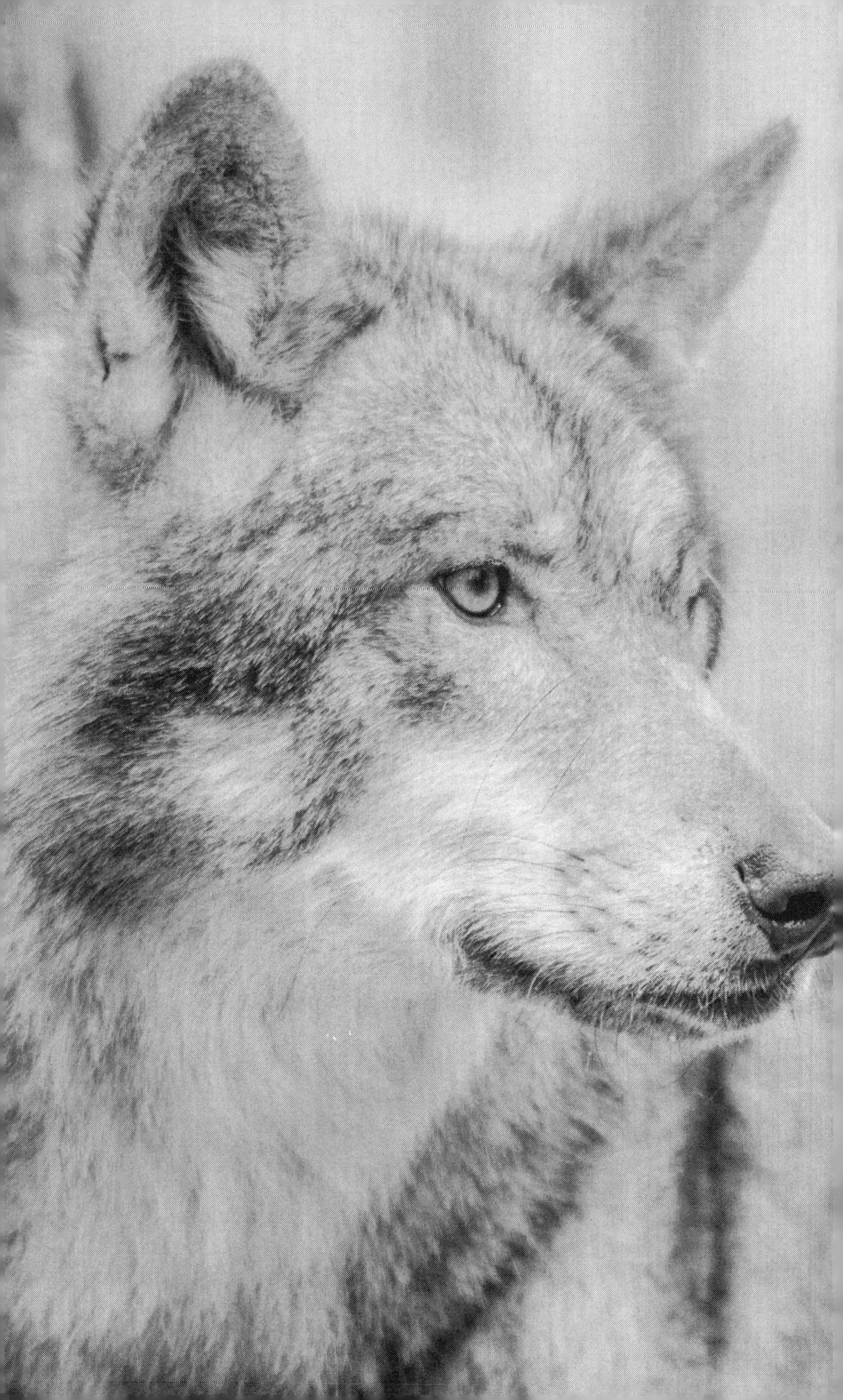

Chapter Seventeen

Mina

I DIDN'T KNOW WHY he'd growled at me like that, but suddenly he looked angry. Could a wolf really look angry, when he'd barely moved a millimetre? He'd actually shown me his teeth, and it was scary, because, well, he was a huge wolf.

He was just staring at me intensely no, and we were stuck this way, in a holding pattern. Both of us not moving, me through fear, and him... well, I had no idea what was going on with him.

There was suddenly noise elsewhere in the house, and a few shouts of 'we're back' echoed out. I let out a sigh of relief. That was faster than I'd expected because I thought they'd run for hours. Daisy rushed in, her clothes back on.

"Mina, sweetie, let's get you somewhere else for a bit, okay?" She stared warily at Asher, whose wolf growled again. She tilted her head at him, and nodded. Oh wow, was he communicating with her somehow?

She pulled me from the room just as his guys started heading in his direction, fully dressed, thank god. They both nodded to me as they passed us, and went into the kitchen, pulling the sliding double doors closed after them. There was some loud snarling, and shouting.

I suddenly realised that Daisy was still touching me, because she'd grabbed me and pulled me from the room. She was also staring at her hands, which she suddenly pulled back.

"Shit! I'm sorry, babe, I just wanted to get you out of there, fast. For your safety, I mean, but I won't do it again, I swear."

I stared at her, feeling a little numb and freaked out, but not by her.

"He growled at me." She nodded, staring at the kitchen doors.

"He's a bit out of sorts, that's all."

"Did he make you all come back?" She grinned at me, nodding once.

"You're pretty perceptive for someone who's new to all this stuff. How did you know?"

I pointed at the kitchen.

"In there, it looked like he was communicating with you, but in your head."

She nodded again. "It's an Alpha connection, he can choose to mind-speak with us, any of us in his pack, and he can also, it sounds weird, but he can group chat us. He could, if he chose to, speak to every wolf in this pack at the same time in his head, and he doesn't have to be a wolf to do it. Wow, he just never has until today."

This stuff just kept getting weirder.

"You're talking about telepathy?" She shrugged.

"Something like that, but I don't know how it all works. A lot of this stuff is magical, you know. Oh, I wonder if we can get one of the witches to come and talk to you. They'd explain it so much better."

"Witches? There are witches too?"

She nodded patiently.

"Yes, babe, just wolves and witches, that's the extent of magical or supernatural beings, don't worry. Everything else you hear of is a myth." So much was happening so fast, and it was pretty freaky stuff. I never imagined anything like this could be real.

"What just happened though? He was angry, and then he, it was like he was fighting against his wolf. I don't think he even wanted to shift right then."

Daisy nodded, gesturing to the sofa in the big sitting room we'd run into.

"Sit down, babe, and I'll tell you what I know."

I did what she asked.

"I'm glad it doesn't hurt," I said, and her frown told me I'd gone off script again.

"Uh, shifting, I mean. If it did, I'd imagine fighting it would be even more painful." She was nodding thoughtfully.

"Yeah, I think his wolf must have really wanted out. I think whatever you were telling him, he couldn't keep his wolf back."

I stared at the closed doors, wondering what was going on back there, because it had gone really quiet.

"Then he growled at me." I still couldn't believe it. It was like one minute he was enjoying my touch, and the next he was pissed at me for something. She was shaking her head.

"When he mindspoke to us, he was agitated. He said he was stuck as a wolf."

My head was starting to hurt. This was all too much.

"Stuck as a wolf?" I asked weakly.

She nodded. "You were sharing with him?" I still couldn't believe I'd told him everything.

"He was... he was so patient... so willing to listen to me. I told him more than I've told... well, even more than I've told some of the therapists, he makes me want to talk."

She nodded again. "Maybe it's that old Alpha charm. You did the right thing, telling him."

"Then why did he lose it at me?" He'd scared me, but I didn't want to say that out loud, to admit it to her or myself, because if I did, I'd have to question what was happening between us.

Daisy smiled gently.

"Oh babe, he didn't lose it *at you*. Don't you see? He's sworn to protect you, and you've just told him that he's too late. That he couldn't prevent the one thing he'd have died to protect you from. He's eaten up by it, and he wants revenge. His wolf took advantage of his conflicted emotions, and took his chance at freedom, to try and comfort you. They both know you feel safer with the wolf than the man."

I tried to absorb what she was saying. Was that what had happened?

"Should I go in there?"

She laughed then.

"Are you hoping to see him naked? Because if you do that, you'll probably get an eyeful." I gasped, covering my face with my hands. Of course, because he'd lost his clothes when he shifted. The t-shirt was destroyed; the one we'd laughed over. Why did that hurt? That one tiny thing, that probably isn't a thing to anyone else, but it was to us.

The doors suddenly opened, and three men stood there, their eyes on me. *He was a man again*. He was dressed, and he looked... what *was* that look on his face?

He approached me, dropping to his knees before me, while the others all gasped with shock. Was it a wolf *faux pas*, I wondered idly.

"What was your name, Mina, before you came here?" I stared at him silently, that question being the last one I'd ever expected to hear. Was it even safe to tell him? To tell any of them?

"What do you mean?" He sighed, looking at me with sad eyes.

"I know you weren't born Mina Masters, because you don't exist anywhere."

I lowered my shoulders, suddenly wanting so much to trust him, to give him what he needed from me.

"Mina Davison." He nodded, offering me a brief smile.

"Thank you. Boys?"

"On it, boss," the Irish one said, and they both left.

Asher glanced over at Daisy, who suddenly looked at her watch, and made an over-the-top exclamation.

"*Wow, is that the time?* Ned will be thinking I've got lost or something. I told him I'd only work a half day." She stood up, and I watched her nervously.

"Do... How do I..."

"*Mina*." Asher's voice was even, patient, and I turned back to him.

"I'll take you home whenever you want." Oh god. Could I even be alone in a car with a man, after a year of avoiding just that? Daisy made the decision for me, and left while we were talking. I was alone with him again.

I cleared my throat nervously.

"Are you... um..."

"Me again? Yeah, sorry about that. I gave my wolf a good talking to, and he'll behave better next time, I promise." He tried a grin, but I could see he was still too angry to pull it off. My hand twitched, and I stared at it in surprise, his eyes following mine.

"You wanted to touch me just then, didn't you?" He whispered, and I looked back at him, my eyes wide with shock.

"I think so."

"So do it, do whatever you need, when you need to. If you need to punch someone, you punch me. If you want to hold someone, or be held by someone, I'm right here. If you need distance, or space, I'll do it even if it kills me."

I chewed my lip as I looked at him.

"What if you want more?"

He grinned, a proper one this time.

"What do you mean 'if'? Mina, I understand, not what you went through... fuck, nobody should ever have to understand that the way you do. But I understand that you need to set the pace, set the rules, and trust that I won't do anything you're not ready for. Can I sit on the sofa with you?" I blinked at the sudden question, so unexpected amid what he was saying.

Oh... I glanced at the sofa. It was certainly big enough for three, and I was firmly placed at one end, so could it hurt?

I nodded, watching him slowly get up from the floor, and move over to sit on the sofa, but not at the other end, and not in the middle cushion. He sat in between the two, close enough to touch if I choose to. He rested an arm across the back, and turned towards me in the seat.

"Is this okay?" He asked, watching me closely. I chewed at my lip, watching him, wondering if I could cope with his proximity. I hissed in a breath when I bit too hard on my lip, and quickly released it.

His eyes were on my lip.

"Fuck... you need me to... uh, I could get something for the blood." I reached up, touching my lip, and finding a little blood on my finger when I pulled it away. I wiped my finger on my hoodie, which was feeling too warm now that we'd been inside so long, but I couldn't bear to take it off, to remove this protective layer. It was like my armour, and without it, there was one less thing in the way of hands touching me.

"It doesn't look so bad, baby, I think you'll live." I glanced at him again, surprised all over again by his proximity. I realised that it really wasn't scaring me. It was unnerving, because it was almost too much, but only almost.

I turned in the seat a little, because I felt safer if I didn't face away from him. He smiled, revealing another detail about him that I'd somehow missed before now; he had a lovely smile. It was wide, and genuine, and it warmed me inside. I found myself smiling back at him.

"I guess this isn't what you had in mind, when you realised that the mate thing was real, huh?" I tried being flippant, but I wasn't sure I was really pulling it off, and he was shaking his head.

"Well, I never expected to be happy about it, *but I am*." My fingers twitched again, and I glanced at his hand, which was rested on his knee. The other was behind me, on the back of the sofa. I was actually within touching distance for him, and yet he'd honoured what he said.

"You cut your hair because of them, didn't you?" He suddenly asked, and my hand went up to the back of my head.

It still felt weird to find no long tresses hanging down my back. The cropped texture of my hair was still strange to me, even after almost a year of keeping it short.

"Is it bad?" I asked him, wishing I hadn't wanted it all gone. I'd loved having long hair, although there was freedom in short hair. Not only was there nothing for an attacker to grab, but also showers took about ten minutes, and it dried in seconds.

He was smiling again.

"Why would it be bad? I just didn't realise you didn't always wear it like that. You know, until you told me... uh... what you told me." I nodded.

"They... used it... to hold me still. It was another part of me that was covered in them. It was tainted, but it was a part I could remove, and take control of."

His laugh was gone, and his face was stormy again.

"I'm sorry," I said, lowering my eyes.

His fingers touched under my chin lightly, nudging my head up. I gasped at the unexpected touch, and he pulled away fast.

"Shit, baby, I'm sorry. Just please don't hide from me, and don't ever, *ever* apologise for what they did to you, or how you react to it now, or how you did then. All of that is out of your control. What you can control is what happens when you're with me, and I'll never do anything to you that you don't want."

I glanced at his fingers, still hovering in the air after touching my chin, and he winced.

"Yeah, okay, you got me there. That hand is clearly not aware of how much trouble it's in. I... it was a reflex. I don't ever want you to hide from me, but... *fuck*... as I say that, I'm realising that maybe that's what you need. I'd be a bastard to sit here and say all this shit, and then instantly go against it, by insisting that you always look me in the eyes."

I giggled for a second.

"It's strange that I understood all of that, but I did. I don't hate you for the touch. It was brief, and it... it didn't scare me... but that has to be it for now. I'm... pretty much at all of my limits right now."

Asher

FUCK, SHE'S SO FUCKING strong, and she can't even see it. Did I mean to touch her? Well, yes, I do, I want to touch her every fucking where, but no, that wasn't planned. It was a moment of dumb reflex, and *she didn't freak*.

Did she feel how I felt when she touched me? Should I ask, or would that freak her out even more?

"How do you like to spend your time? What hobbies do you have? What keeps you calm? I'd like to try and learn who you are, not the damage, but the person. The person who might enjoy to read, and no, I don't mean *those* books, but maybe you draw, or paint... hell, maybe you like archery. I have no idea, and I want to know." She smiled, relaxing a little.

"Can you really see me with a bow and arrows?" I shifted on the sofa, begging my cock to stop twitching, before she noticed that our proximity was killing me; a slow painful death.

"Actually, yeah, you'd look pretty badass, whipping around the woods, taking down... uh... are you pro hunting, or against?"

She pulled a face. "I couldn't kill animals!"

"Right... so whipping around the woods, taking down bad guys then. There you go, you'd kick ass." I shot her a grin, relieved that she was giggling.

"I'm too weak for all of that. I used to enjoy crochet, but... well... I don't really do anything now."

"Crochet, I'm drawing a blank. Is it some kind of outdoor activity?" It didn't sound right, but I felt like my brain had gone on a damn sabbatical all of a sudden.

She giggled again. "Ha, not quite, no. It's making things with wool, and a hook, but I guess you could sit outdoors and do it."

"Ah, now I could definitely see you wielding a hook, merrily taking down bad guys."

"By crocheting them nice scarves and hats?"

Who knew she had a sense of humour, underneath all of that self-protection she'd built up?

"Do you enjoy movies? Music?" She shrugged.

"I used to. I used to like a lot of stuff, until a year ago. You know they got six months for what they did to me? Six fucking months. I can barely get through each day, and they get out soon, and can carry on with their lives. How is that even fair?"

It was like we'd opened the floodgates now, and she was willingly talking to me, *about them*.

"They won't be getting a happily ever after, Mina." She tilted her head as she stared back at me.

"What do you mean?"

"I mean, I'm taking care of it." And now, she was frowning.

"You're going to hurt them?"

I shook my head, because she just wasn't getting it, and she needed to understand.

"No, Mina, I'm going to kill them."

She gasped, her hands covering her mouth.

"No, you can't!"

See? That had me confused, because she must want them dead, *surely*. Surely to fucking god she must want them dead, gone, *fucking worm food*, because they soon would be.

"Why?" I finally asked, my voice a little rough.

"You'll get caught, and you'll probably get life! That's how the system works, you see. The bad guys get it easy, and the rest of us... we get royally fucked."

I stared at her in wonder, because I realised something vital in that moment. She saw me as the good guy, and she cared if I got caught. That was huge, it was more progress than I'd even imagined.

"Oh, nobody's gonna catch me, baby. I'll hunt them down, like a fucking wolf."

She bit her lip, then winced, and released it again. I moved my hand to rest on the seat between us, open palm facing up.

"I know that biting your lip is a coping mechanism, but while you can't do that, you can do whatever you like to my hand instead. You know... hold it... grip it, dig your nails in... *bite it...*" I offered her a little grin and she giggled again.

Jesus fuck, if my cock didn't stop trying to tear his way through my sweats, she was going to be running scared. I grabbed the cushion from the empty seat, and rested it on my lap, my other arm over it.

"You want me to bite your hand?" She was still giggling, and I shrugged, even as my entire body was saying fuck yes, please. *Bite me anywhere you fucking want.*

"Not about what I want, baby, it's about you. If it helps you, to have something to fiddle with, I'm right here. No assumptions, and no strings."

My cock was so fucking hard at the thought of her taking my hand, and putting it anywhere near her mouth. Yeah, I've got something she could fucking fiddle with alright, and I was a total fucking asshole for even thinking it.

~ *Boss?*

I'd left the mindspeak command open with the boys, so they could update me without disturbing us.

~ *Yes?*

Mina's hand suddenly rested on top of mine, and my whole body jerked with surprise. Her eyes darted up to my face, questioning, concerned, but I couldn't fight the smile already spreading cross my face.

She was touching me, and, *wow*, warmth started to spread through me, her touch waking every damn nerve ending in my body. Jesus fuck, if I didn't come in my fucking pants, I'd be amazed.

"Is this okay?" She asked, her hand trembling on top of mine. I nodded rapidly.

"More than okay, Mina."

She smiled again, looking back down at her hand on mine, and then she started fucking sliding it back and forth over my skin. Stroking my skin with hers, and I groaned, crushing that pillow harder against me. She stopped, her eyes on mine again.

"Are you okay?" She looked about ready to bolt, and the next few seconds would be crucial. I'd either say the right thing, and we'd progress, or I'd fuck up and we'd be back at square one. *A real fucking snakes and ladders moment.*

"Asher?" I decided to bite the bullet, and looked her in the eye.

"Baby, I love your touch like you wouldn't believe. I, uh... maybe like it a little too much..." Her face was blank for a moment, then her cheeks flushed bright red, and her hand pulled back, not fully away, just away from my skin.

I sucked in a few breaths, willing my fucking cock to behave. I was not gonna come in my fucking pants like a teenager, that would be humiliating as fuck.

"It turns you on?" She asked quietly, making me stare at her in surprise.

"Does that scare you?"

She shook her head. "If you were like them, you'd already have forced yourself on me. You've had plenty of opportunity to do so. I uh, I think I'm starting to trust you." Fuck me.

Thank fucking god. *Ladder it is.* I was so sure I'd fucked things up.

"I'm doing my best to hold back, but your touch runs through me, like... actually I don't know how to describe it. It's going right to the parts of me that you really don't want to be thinking about right now." She nodded, her eyes on our hands again.

"Is that how I'd feel... if you were the one touching me?"

My mouth dropped open. What the fuck?

"Do you want me to?"

~ Boss? Man, I don't think he can hear us.

~ Maybe they're fucking. We shouldn't interrupt that!

~ Shall I peek through the door?

~ Don't you fucking dare! Leave us.

I roared through our connection. I ended the connection before either could reply.

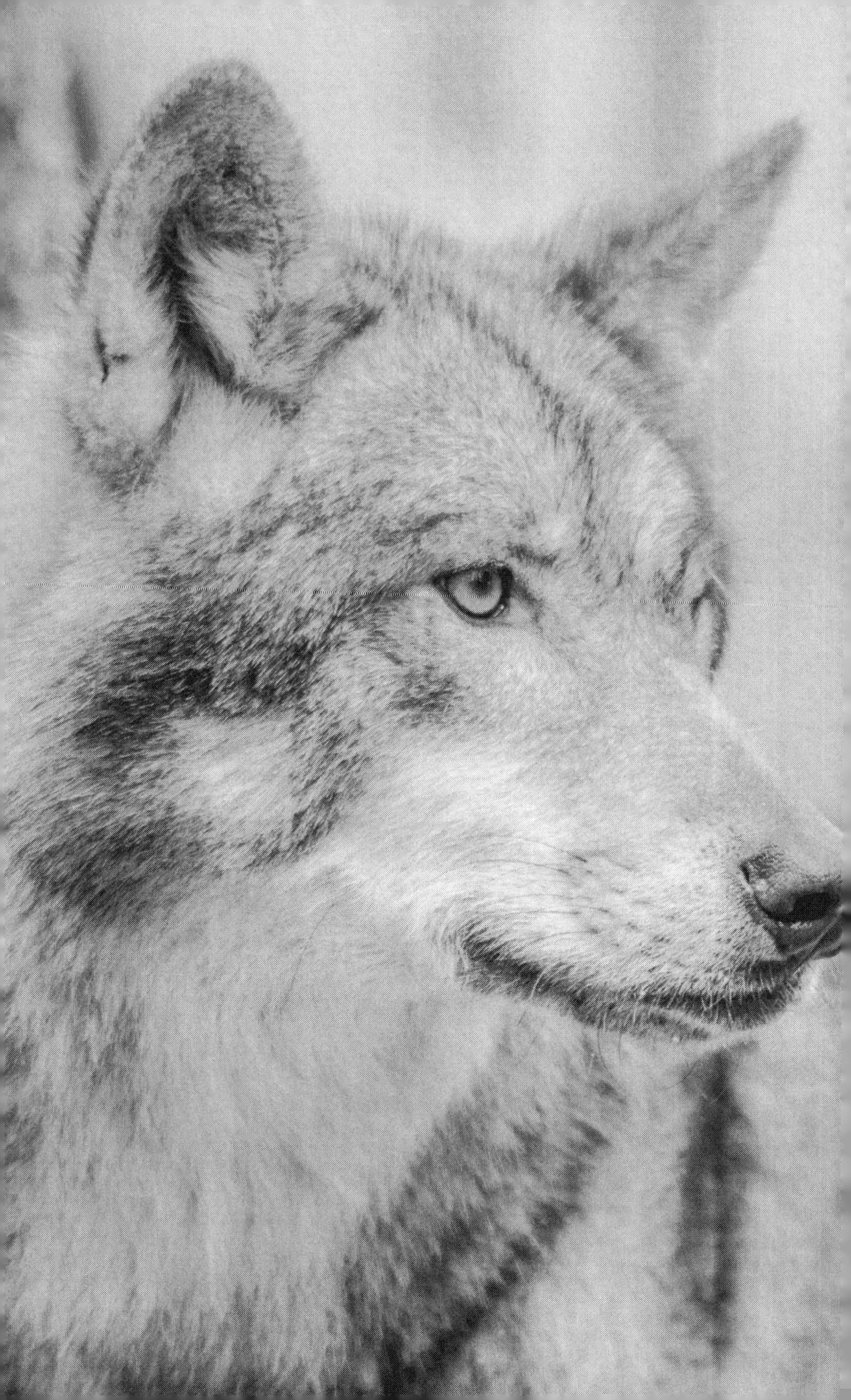

Chapter Eighteen

ASHER

She was staring at me, her eyes wide and nervous, but also, maybe curious.

"Your decision, baby. If you want, I can place my hand over yours, like you just did for me. You won't be trapped though. You'll be able to move if you need to. Perfectly safe, I promise."

She didn't stop staring at me, but her hand suddenly dropped onto the cushion between us, palm up, like mine had been.

"Is that a yes?" She nodded, but that wasn't enough for me.

"Can you say it for me?" She sighed softly.

"*Yes.*" I smiled at her, bursting with pride, suddenly feeling like she'd given me so much more.

I lifted my hand and moved it slowly in her direction, her eyes following it avidly. Her hand trembled, and I stopped.

"Too much?"

She shook her head. "*Mina?*"

"No, please, I want you to do this." Oh wow.

I lowered my hand over hers, stopping just above so she could feel the heat of my skin almost touching hers. She sucked in a breath, holding it, and then I lowered my hand those last few millimetres, and rested it on top of hers.

Her hand flinched beneath mine, and I raised it again instantly.

"No, Asher, it's okay. It's just… a lot…" She wanted to keep going, so I laid my hand over hers again.

Even though I was the one touching her, it still spread that warmth through me, but this time it was more like a sense of comfort. Of rightness, touching my mate made me feel right, complete. I really hoped it felt the same way for her. She was breathing slowly, and when she looked at me, her eyes were wide.

"It's... nice..." I laughed, widening my eyes at her.

"Just nice? Oh come on, Mina, throw a guy a bone!" She laughed softly.

"A guy who turns into a big dog jokes about throwing him a bone?"

I gave her my best hurt face, pouty lips and all.

"Big dog? *I'm a fucking Alpha wolf, baby.*" She giggled again, but she hadn't moved her hand, and she hadn't retreated from me yet.

I stared back down at our hands, taking a breath.

"Ready?"

She gasped, her hand twitching slightly beneath mine.

"Are you going to stop?" I winked at her, my lips quirking into a small grin.

"No, baby, I'm going to stroke you like you did me." She sucked in a shaky breath, and nodded. I quirked a brow at her, needing verbal consent, and she sighed.

"Yes, *please.*" Fuck yes!

I pressed my hand more firmly against hers, then slid it forward and back, hearing her breath catch in her throat. I stopped moving, and waited for her eyes to come back up to mine.

"Okay?"

She nodded, and followed up with.

"God, yes."

"I normally just answer to *Asher*, but that'll do." She giggled again, and then sighed, as I started to stroke my fingers over her palm, relishing the permission to touch her. I wanted more, so much more, but this was more than I'd ever expected, and it was everything.

Eventually, her hand flinched beneath mine, and I backed away. She'd had enough, finally reached her limit.

"Are you okay?" I asked, and she nodded.

"Yes, I mean, it's strange. It's downright scary, feeling anyone's skin against mine, after... but... it's you. *I know you won't hurt me, somehow I just know.*"

I felt like she was finally seeing me, seeing through her defences, enough to see the man before her. The man who'd die for her.

"I couldn't even if I wanted to, and I don't want to, I'd never want that. I'm so fucking glad you're feeling that way. The question is... what do you want to do now? It's getting late in the day, and I'm hungry again already, that's a wolf thing, by the way, and I really want to cook something amazing for you. Are you comfortable with that?"

Mina

HE WANTED TO COOK for me again? How could I say no to that? In the space of a day or so, he'd broken through several of my defences, and yet, somehow left me feeling stronger, instead of weaker, for it. He pointed to the kitchen, with a big smile on his face.

I nodded, and for once he didn't insist on a verbal response, and I understood the reason why. Every time he did that, it was in response to something that should be physically in my control, and every time I nodded instead of speaking, he pushed me to tell him, because it gave me a chance to say no.

It also proved to me that it was my decision, every damn time. He was making no assumptions; he was giving me my power back. Was that even a thing? It felt like it really was.

I stood up, and headed for the doors, then paused.

"What about the others?" He laughed, as he stepped past me, and slid the doors open.

"I told them to sod off."

I didn't remember him doing that, which meant he'd done the Alpha thing again, what did Daisy call it?

"You did that in your mind too?"

He was laughing, but he looked surprised.

"You don't miss a trick, do you? Yes, apparently as their Alpha I can do that, but I never tried before today. I hadn't really needed to before. It's quite effective. A bit intrusive though, when I leave the connection open, because they can still speak in my head, at the most inopportune of moments."

He was relaxed, and calm... a million miles away from the edgy, angry guy of earlier. Was this the real him, or had that been? Have I even met the real him yet?

"What'll ya have? We've got all sorts here. Steak... you like steak? Got some nice fillets... ah some of these freaking huge mushrooms... we could stuff these with... *what?*"

I was just staring at him as he planned dinner. How did someone even begin to know food this way, and enjoy it? I could barely get a microwave meal to taste like anything other than plastic.

"How do you know all this stuff?" I asked, stepping up closer, to peek in the fridge. I saw big red and green peppers, and pointed at them.

"The lady likes peppers?" I laughed.

"She does."

He grabbed them and set them on the counter.

"Then the lady gets peppers. You wanna pour us some coffee, while I get this started?" I followed his lead, and his directions to everything I needed to pour us both coffee, remembering that he liked his black with sugar.

As I watched him preparing food, I enjoyed his calm, and his comfort with the task at hand.

How could I be enjoying alone time with any man, and on top of that, how could I be enjoying the sight of this man, and the way he moved? *There was something seriously wrong with me.*

"Ready?" I shook myself out of my daze, to find dinner in front of me. The smells wafting up from my plate were almost as delicious as the scent of him.

My mouth was watering, and the look on his face, when I placed the first bite of succulent steak in my mouth and moaned softly, was one of pure satisfaction.

"Thank you," I said when I'd finished.

"For dinner?" He asked, smiling at me. I shook my head, then sighed.

"Yes, of course, but I mean for everything. For being so patient with me. I know it must be so damn frustrating for you, it is for me too. I can feel an attraction to you, which I never expected to feel for anyone ever, but I'm also not sure I could ever bear to be touched. You know the kind of touching I mean. I was... I was shy and introverted, and knew nothing about sex, and then..."

Asher growled, and I really liked his growls. They made a chill run down my spine, but again, it was a pleasant sensation.

"And then two bastards decided to use cruelty and brutality, to make sure you'd never risk getting close to anyone again, and I swear to god, *if you don't have a good fucking reason for interrupting us, I'm going to kick your scrawny ass all the way out of town!*"

He was standing by the time he'd finished his tirade, and I realised he was glaring, and jabbing a finger at someone behind me. Thank god for that!

I turned in my seat to see one of his wolf guys standing there, a morose look on his face.

"Sorry, boss, it's just, we've found some stuff out, and you need to know." He had a nice Irish accent, which I found quite pleasant to listen to, while his words made my stomach clench. It wasn't going to be anything nice, was it?

"And you thought *now* was the perfect time to blunder in, D?" Asher snapped.

"Alpha, time unfortunately seems to be of the essence, I'm afraid." The other one of his men stepped up. They looked quite similar in build, and both had brown hair, but their faces were very different.

Where the Irish guy was rugged, but had a tidy beard, the other guy was clean shaven, with very neatly cropped hair, and always seemed to be dressed for a business meeting. Both had dark eyes.

Asher's eyes, I'd noticed with delight, were a curious mix of blue and green, like they couldn't decide what colour to be. They were beautiful, intense, and expressive, but showed such warmth and kindness, at least when he looked at me.

"Should I go?" I asked, standing up to move away, but Asher's hand came down, stopping an inch from mine.

"No, please. Anything you two dickheads have to say, you can say in front of Mina."

"But, boss..." the Irish guy started.

"Did I stutter, D?" Asher was impressive when he was in Alpha mode. Strangely the others didn't seem fazed by his anger, but maybe that was just how they were with each other.

"Are they getting out early?" I asked suddenly, wondering if that was what all the urgency was about, because I knew Asher had them looking into my attackers.

They all looked at me, and the Irish one shook his head.

"No. No, love, that's not why we're in a rush. It's just that, well... *Jase will explain.*" Jase looked at him, his mouth dropping open.

"*Oh, thanks a fucki*... uh, yeah, so we found out that these two bastards, well, Mina wasn't their first."

Oh god. *Oh god*! I felt the room start to spin around me, and I felt chilled to the bone and too hot all at once. Asher stood as close as he could, without touching me.

"Mina, breathe. Come on, baby, breathe. You pass out, I'm gonna have to catch you. You know I can't do that without touching you."

I put both hands on the breakfast bar and leaned forward, breathing as slowly as I could. I could do this. How fucking embarrassing to do this right here in front of them all.

"Did you guys have to fucking do this to her now? Look at her!"

Asher

I WAS GOING TO kick their fucking asses, literally pound the crap out of them. Hours of fucking work it had taken, to get her to relax and start to trust me, and they'd just fucked it all up in mere seconds.

She didn't need to know about something like that, especially now, when she was trying to heal.

Why the hell did I insist on them telling me in front of her? Because I never expected them to say something like that.

"Alpha, you told us to look into them, and this is what we found. Now we can brief you in private, as is our preference, and our suggestion, or we can lay it all out for you now, together. You're the boss. *Just don't blame us for doing what you asked us to do.*"

Wow, Jase just sacked up big time. I nodded at him, grudgingly impressed.

"Okay, then you're going to tell us both, if Mina's okay with that?"

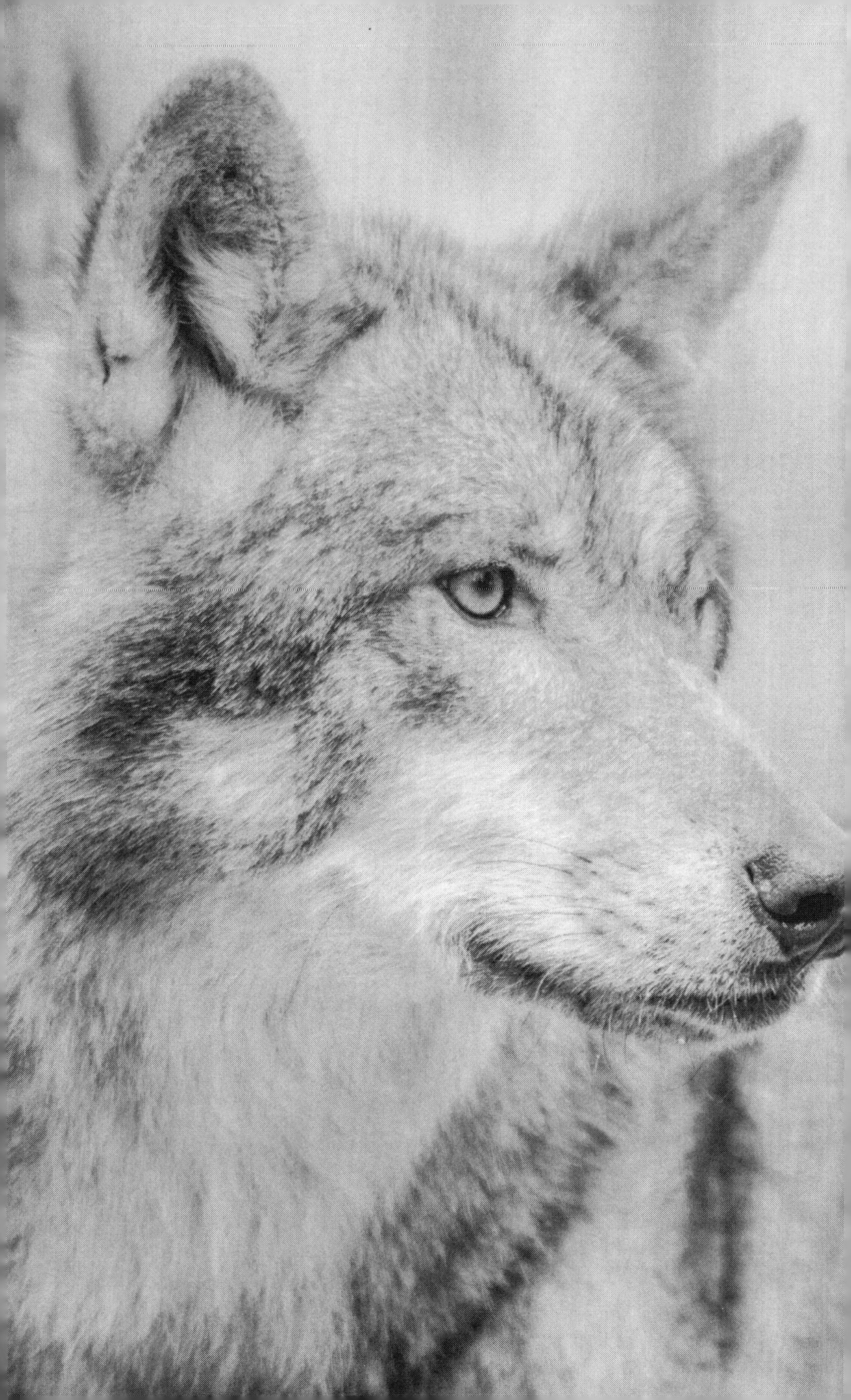

Chapter Nineteen

Mina

He leaned forward to look at me. He was closer than ever, and I noticed that he'd been creeping closer over time. Making me feel comfortable with him, and it seemed to be working.

Already my breathing was back to normal, and his closeness was actually, unbelievably, part of the reason.

I nodded, and he stood up. Without my permission, my hand reached back and caught his before he could move. He froze, and the room fell silent.

I looked back at him.

"Please, stay here with me."

He nodded, dropping onto the stool beside me, keeping his hand on the breakfast bar, so I could grip it. I was amazed that I could touch him, and not want to shower immediately, while crying, and scrubbing my skin raw. What was happening to me? He looked a bit shell-shocked himself.

"Proceed." He said quietly to the others. They had a folder, and they pushed dishes aside, and pulled printouts from the file.

They had found eight other rapes like mine, involving two men, a few even at the same damn park, and others in the local area. None of these women had wanted to go to court, so their cases went unresolved for them. They suffered hell, and survived it, and never got their justice. I could feel the tears running down my cheeks.

In some ways, I was angry. Angry that eight other women had to go through this, and if just one of them had come forward, maybe the others would have never gone through it, but... knowing what I knew now, about going through the whole investigation process, the soul-destroying gathering of the physical evidence, the endless talking with police, and lawyers, and counsellors, and then going to court, and having to face them, and talk about it.

Knowing all that, I could see why the hospital visits, and tests for all sexually transmitted infections were as far as they could face going. Why should it be down to any one of them to put a stop to these bastards?

They finished talking and the guys left, along with their ugly printouts of information that I wished I'd never seen. I'd tuned out of whatever they were planning, because I was too busy dwelling over the horror of another eight women going through what I did. Their pain, their devastation, their shame. Those two men were evil, and they had to pay.

Asher cleared his throat, and I turned to him, and then glanced down at my hand, still gripping his, still in awe of the fact that I'd felt safe enough to even touch him.

"Mina, you still with me here?" His voice was soft, not at all like the tone he used around the others, but the tone he only seemed to use with me. The voice you'd use when you're trying not to set off a reaction.

I swallowed, feeling off balance, because literally everything had changed within a few short days. I wasn't the same person I was on Thursday. It was only Saturday now, and I was in a strange man's house, and he knew where I lived.

More than that, we'd touched, most people would laugh at the awe I placed on such chaste moments, but put it in the perspective of a woman so brutalised by men, that her only experience of intimacy with a man was being forced into sex, over and over, and it was actually pretty fucking amazing.

Asher's hand moved in mine, and suddenly his fingers were closing around mine. His touch was light, but warm and soothing, and I didn't panic, and I didn't pull away.

I stared at our hands; we were holding fucking hands. *It was a miracle.*

Asher

I COULDN'T BELIEVE THAT I was holding her hand, and she hadn't done a runner on me. After the shit we'd just loaded on her, she was still sitting there, and she hadn't broken, and she was still fucking touching me. She didn't even lose her shit, when I turned her grip into us holding hands.

I was so fucking relieved that we hadn't lost all of that hard work and progress, with that stupid intrusion by the guys. They'd get an asskicking later, but for now, they had work to do. *Top priority*.

There were things to plan, before we could take the rapists out. We still needed to plan a place to do it; somewhere we could act without being caught, and we needed a way to draw them to wherever it would happen.

"I missed the planning, I'm sorry," she said at last. I shook my head at her.

"It's all good, nobody expects you to look at this emotionlessly. Even I can't, and I only know what you've told me. Fuck, Mina, you're amazing. Look at you, look at how you're literally growing by the hour. A few days ago, you couldn't even talk to me, and now..." I glanced down at our hands, still clutched together, and she nodded.

"It makes me feel stronger. *You do*. You make me feel braver. I didn't... I don't..."

"I know what you're thinking. You don't need me or any man to make you better than you are. I'm not doing this, baby, you are. I'm just waiting to catch you if you fall, and Mina, you could well fall at some point, but I'll be there, to catch you, to protect you, and to look after you, until you feel strong again."

She stared at me, looking a little dazed.

"What did you plan? I didn't hear any of it."

"You seem a little out of it. Are you sure you're okay?" She didn't seem to be taking in what was happening around her. She seemed distant, even as she let me hold onto her.

"You're sitting here calling me strong, and I'm disassociating. I'm trying to stay here, in the moment, but when things get too bad... sometimes I mentally back away."

I nodded, hating that we'd made her feel that way.

"What can I do to help?" She squeezed my hand.

"You're doing it. You're doing something nobody else has ever been able to. You're grounding me."

I squeezed her hand right back.

"Whatever you need. Would you like to rest? I can offer you one of the spare rooms here. They, uh, they all lock, so you'll be able to feel as safe as possible."

She lowered her eyes. "I have a safe place, at home, I mean. A chair. It sounds dumb, but it's one place where I can feel safe, and protected. It's nowhere near windows, and it's in a corner, where I can see in all directions." She looked embarrassed, but I got what she was saying.

"It's defensible." She nodded, finally meeting my eyes again.

"Okay, I say we take a walk around, and when you find a spot that looks or feels right, it's yours."

She shook her head.

"No, you're doing enough already." I shook my head, using our joined hands to pull her up from her stool, as I stood up.

"Nope, let's find this safe place for you. You need one here too." She looked surprised but a little less out of it. Maybe just the change of subject was helping her.

"Why?"

"Mina, I'm hoping you'll want to be here sometimes, maybe even a lot. You need to have somewhere to retreat to here, for when you need something you're not getting from me, or anyone here."

She nodded, and let me lead her around the pack house. We walked the lower floor, and nowhere was right. The damn place had far too many windows.

That's actually a wolf thing; we love the sun, and we love moonlight, so windows are a must. The more the fucking merrier, but that meant nothing covered the downstairs windows, because that was how we liked it.

The other problem with downstairs was that it was all communal space. Even though any wolf would know, on pain of death, that any spot designated for Mina was out of bounds, and so was she if she was in it, she didn't feel safe.

We headed onto the upper floor, and I pointed out two doors.

"That's Jase and D's rooms. I'm at the opposite end there." I pointed again.

"All of these other doors in between are spare rooms, all furnished and lockable. They were for any other pack members who needed to stay here, or if we needed them to. Mostly we like the place as empty as possible, and you know... if either of the three of us end up with offspring, they'll need rooms."

I shot her a grin, hoping she didn't take that as pressure from me. Instead she was looking from one door to the other.

"Can we start with the one closest to your room?" I liked the sound of that, so I led her in that direction. Our hands hadn't separated the whole damn time, but I knew I'd have to break the connection soon.

Nature was starting to call quite desperately, and I really didn't want to have to drag her into the bathroom with me. Not like that, anyway.

I let her push the door open, but her eyes fell on my door, as she did so. She wet her lips and forced her eyes onto the room we were in front of. It was nice, I mean, they're all nice, and pretty much identical. As the Alpha's suite, mine was bigger, and completely different in layout, but it was just a room.

"It's pretty," she commented, pulling me into the room with her. She wasn't making any effort to release my hand, and I wasn't going to make that happen. She turned around in the room, taking in the room layout, and checking each corner.

"I'd have the key?" She asked, and I pointed to the inner side of the door, to the key sitting in the lock.

"Only you."

She finally nodded, casting her eyes around again.

"This could work. I could rest here for a while before I go home." *Home.* No, I wanted her here always. This was her home now.

I forced myself to shrug like it wasn't the biggest fucking deal.

"Up to you, you could stay if you want. Lots of big dogs around here to keep you safe." She smiled again.

"So I hear. Uh, is that door an ensuite?" She pointed to the bathroom door, and I nodded.

"Thank god. I'm desperate for the loo." I laughed, squeezing her hand a little.

"Me too, but I was trying not to wuss out on you."

She giggled, and then she looked at our hands again. "I hate to let go." *Yes!*

"You can have it back any time you like," I offered, and she fucking nodded, with a smile on her face.

"I'd like that." Reluctantly, because she seemed to be incapable of it, I pulled my hand from her grasp, watching her react to the loss of my touch. She didn't like it, I could tell, and that shouldn't have felt as good as it did.

I nodded at the bathroom.

"I'll go and use mine, if you want to use this one? Lock the door after me, and I'll knock when I'm back." She nodded, then responded verbally, as she seemed to have realised I preferred it.

"Yes, I will."

As soon as I reached my room, I ran for the bathroom, barely making it. Fuck, any longer and I'd have made a hell of a fucking mess. Bladder empty, hands clean, I went back for her. I knocked and there was no response. What the hell?

I tried the door, and it was unlocked. Fuck. *I told her.* Lock the door, I said. I opened it as slowly as I could, giving her time, so I wouldn't scare her.

"Mina? Are you okay?" I peeked around the door. She was curled up in a ball on the bed, absolutely out like a light. She looked peaceful. *Relaxed.*

Man, everything in me made me want to go and fucking curl up around her, like a protective shield between her and the rest of the world. If she woke up beside me though, she could go off the rails.

In the end, I pulled the door closed, locked it, and then slid the key back under the door for her. I really hoped it wasn't a mistake.

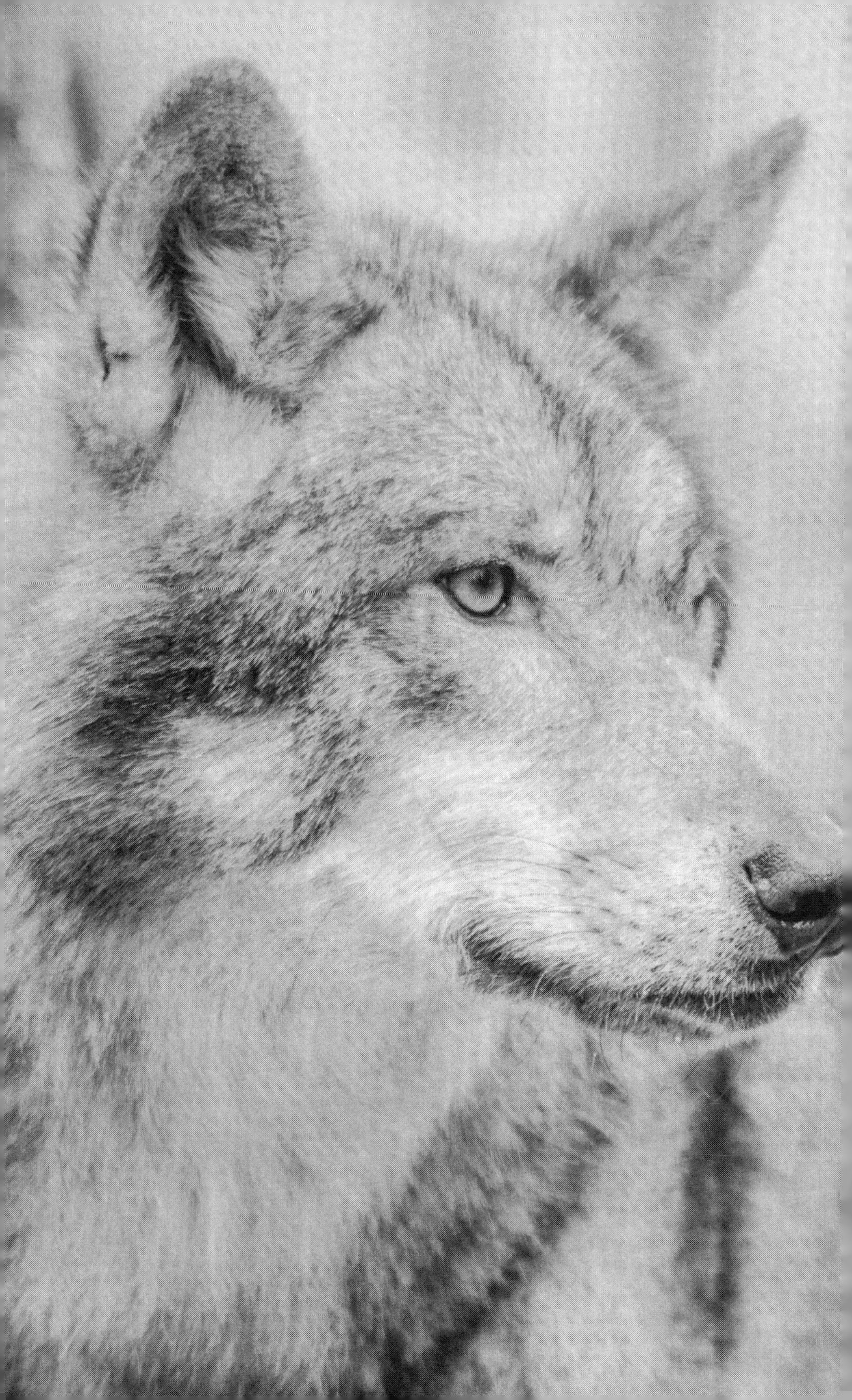

Chapter Twenty

ASHER

BACK DOWNSTAIRS I SUMMONED the guys.

"She's taken the room beside mine, and it's locked. Anyone goes near that fucking room, and they're gonna need new eyeballs, *and nuts*. Am I clear?" They were nodding at me like damn bobbleheads.

"Is it permanent, boss?" Derek asked, glancing at Jase.

"I hope it will be at some point, but not yet. She just needed to rest. It's been a fucking crazy night and day." I sat down, wrapping my hands around the biggest, strongest fucking coffee I could pour.

"Boss, she's warming to you. Any idiot can see that." Derek sat down too. Jase poured coffee for both of them, and joined us.

"Alpha, everything is under control here, nobody outside of this house knows anything about Mina, or what's been happening. This is all your business, until you decide to share it. In the meantime, everything is situation normal. You'll be able to focus on her one hundred percent."

I nodded, relief flooding me at his words.

"That's why you guys are my most trusted friends. I know you've got my back. I know I'm not the usual Alpha type, but we get the job done, and you know what? Mina has my time, she has all of it, until she no longer wants it."

"Boss, we've got plans in hand. We've got to fucking wait now, anyway, for them to get out. We still need a way to lure them, but I'm thinking we bring them out to pack territory, and finish them off here. Nobody will ever miss the fuckers."

See? This was why I loved D. Straight to the point, and absolutely spot on.

"It's a plan. Maybe we can even convince them she's moved here."

Jase grinned. "Hasn't she though? It's not exactly a lie." I shot him a glare.

"If you're suggesting for one minute that she's bait..."

He look horrified, holding his hand up.

"Alpha, I would never suggest that your mate would be any such thing. I'm merely pointing out that if she does move here, that's not exactly a lie."

"Just when exactly did you grow a set of balls, and why did nobody warn me?" I asked, shooting him a grin. He laughed.

"What can I say? I'm pretty sure I always had them, to be honest."

"Keep telling yourself that, man." Derek said, smirking at him.

My phone pinged then, sitting there on the breakfast bar where I'd obviously dumped it at some point.

Daisy: *Just checking in on Mina. Everything okay, Alpha?*

I was glad that Mina had such a good friend in Daisy. That was helping her to adjust to her new life, even though she didn't seem to realise how much had changed. She was no longer just Mina, the survivor hiding from her past alone. She was a friend, the mate to an Alpha wolf, and she was protected by fifty fucking wolves.

She would be moving in here. I just had to figure out how to convince her. Daisy could help me figure that out, I was pretty sure.

Me: *She's resting. Been a long day.*

Daisy: *At the pack house?*

Me: *She picked a room. I'll take her home when she's ready. Thank you for looking out for her.*

Daisy: *She was my friend first, Alpha ;-)*

I laughed. She was feisty, this one, but again that meant she was a good person to be around Mina. She'd keep her safe for me.

"She texts you?" Jase asked, watching me chuckle at my phone.

"Huh?"

"Mina?"

I shook my head. "Daisy checking in on her."

"Daisy texts you. Daisy? As in the wife of a committee member?" Jase frowned, and I glared at him.

"Nothing wrong with a member of the pack supporting their Alpha, Jase, or his mate."

He lowered his head.

"You got it. Just if Ned turns up, all pissed off, I'm letting him in." I laughed.

"Gotcha. Now, you got anything you need me to look at, before I go back to check on Mina?"

He shook his head, and sat back in his chair.

"Like I said, Alpha, it's all in hand. You look after your lady, and we've got your back."

I nodded, thanking them both as I got up. I needed to check on her again. I'd been away too long, although honestly even two minutes was too fucking long.

As I approached her room, I realised the door was open. My pace picked up, as I headed for the door, my heart speeding up. *No.* She was supposed to be safe here, and she wasn't in her room. The bed was still mussed up, but the space she'd curled up in was cool, so she'd moved some time ago.

I glanced at my closed door. *Surely not.* Still, it was the closest room, so I went there first. I quietly pulled the door open, and there she was.

Curled up on my bed, with her face on my pillow. *Fuuuck.* I bit back a groan, because my asshole body was too fucking glad to see her in my bed.

She belonged there; I knew that, but she didn't yet. She was asleep, so I didn't want to disturb her, but, damn, I just couldn't leave.

I quietly pushed the door closed, and headed across the room, to the sofa. I sat down, and watched her sleeping, and she went from peaceful to distressed so fast.

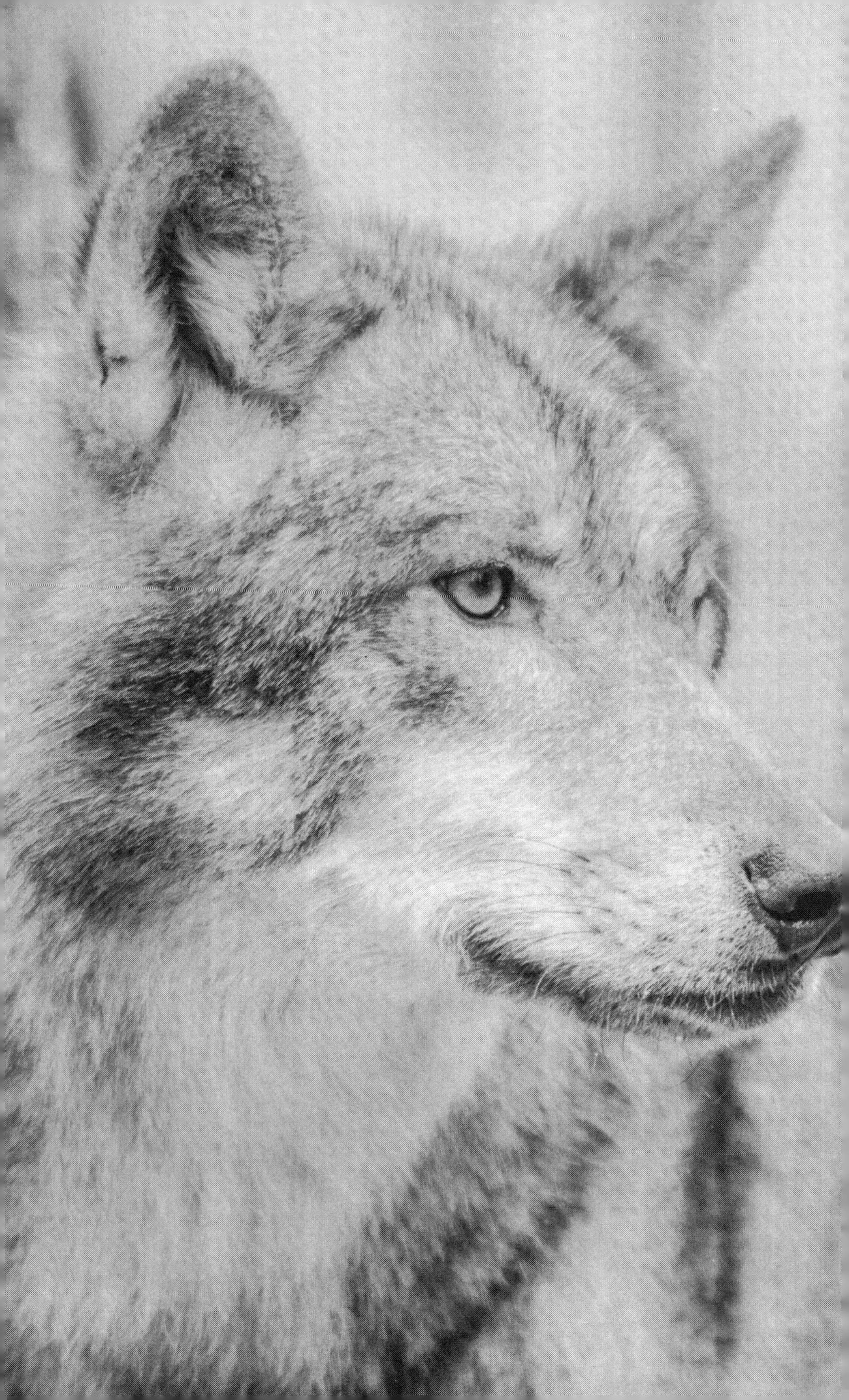

Chapter Twenty-One

Mina

"**H**OLD HER LEGS. Oh I'm going to fucking do things to you, bitch." Teddy was tearing at my clothes, and I screamed, I fought.

What was happening? The other guy, Trav, helped him hold me down, as he tore my underwear away. No... Please... I kept fighting, even as they brutally forced themselves on me, and then the stabbing began.

"Mina, it's okay, you're okay. You're safe. Wake up, baby." There were still hands on me, and I screamed as I fought them off.

"Stop. Stop please!"

He backed away, hands up.

"*Mina*. Baby, I'm not touching you. It's okay, please." It was Asher. He was safe, he was good, and he wasn't them. I tried to focus on my breathing, and he nodded, smiling.

"You've got this. You've got this. Shhhh." He started approaching again, watching me for a reaction. When I didn't panic, he sat on the bed.

His hands were still high, where I could see them, but I reached for him, and he offered one. I grabbed onto it with both hands, holding on tight. The fact that I wanted his hand to hang onto, after a year of letting nobody even close enough to touch, that still floored me.

Added to the fact that... yes, I was on a bed... and I was in the Alpha's bedroom, it was astounding. I was distracting myself, I knew that, but I needed to distance myself from the nightmare.

"Mina, I'm here. You're safe." He was edging closer, and stopped when I looked at him. I felt suddenly overwhelmed, prone, exposed, and he saw something change.

"What? I'm too close, right? I'll back up." I shook my head, and tried wriggling up to sit up.

"I could help, if you'll let me." I shook my head vehemently. I was already in his room, and in his bed. I couldn't let him put his hands on me too.

I released his hand, just long enough to push myself up, sitting against the headboard, and then I reached for it again. He was quick to put his hand back in reach.

"You don't know how much it kills me to not be able to wrap my arms around you, and hold you, and make you feel safe. I know it would be too much for you, but *fuck*... everything inside me is telling me to hold you." I could see it in his face, the truth to his words, and I nodded slowly.

"That's a normal reaction, for a normal person. I'm just sorry I'm not one." My heartbeat was back to normal, and that was with me being here, with him, touching him. It was so strange.

He was shaking his head.

"Stop apologising. The nightmare was bad, huh?" I nodded, looking around the room again, trying to put space between me and the memories.

"Mina? You're in the safest place you'll ever be; my room with me, in my pack territory. Trust me. There's not a fucking soul who can get in here, without everyone knowing, and they wouldn't get past the door."

I watched him as he tried so hard to make me feel protected and safe.

"I'm so out of my depth right now, Asher. I'm lost, and I don't know if I should be here. I don't know if I should be anywhere." He groaned, and ran a hand through his hair.

"Fuck! Look, this is exactly where you should be. *Right here with me*. We're destined for each other, remember? Here's the situation though, I really don't want you to leave. I know, it's not my decision, but... your house? That flimsy door, and a few locks? Multiple ground floor windows, *fuck*. I don't know that I can rest if you go back there." He looked exhausted. Was that my fault?

"I could stay." I didn't know where that came from, but there it was. I guess I felt safe enough here, that I didn't need to measure every damn response right now, and that felt really good.

Asher

DID SHE REALLY JUST fucking say that? I stared at her, my heart banging in my chest.

"You'll stay?" She nodded, her fingers rubbing gently at mine.

"A few days... I can't promise long term, Asher, I don't live that way. It's not worth planning for the future, because it's too easily destroyed." My heart was breaking for the way she'd had to live, because she'd had any hope for the future destroyed by those two monsters. Hell, getting rid of them wasn't going to fix her, maybe nothing would.

"We can take it a few days at a time," I said, hoping she couldn't tell how much it was against my nature to concede even that much. My wolf didn't like it, and I sure as hell didn't like it. She was home now, but how did I prove that to her?

She massaged my palm with her thumbs, not realising that every stroke against my skin was like a fucking wakeup call she really didn't want to be making. I cleared my throat, trying to focus on her.

"We need to pick up some of your things, is that okay?" She blinked, her mind miles away again.

"Hey, stay with me. Let me ground you again. What can I do?" She shrugged, and I stared at her, fighting the very real, very strong urge to drag her into my arms.

"Do you trust me?" She nodded, but her eyes were wary.

"Nothing scary, I promise." I moved my other hand over, pressing it over hers, as they held mine. She didn't pull away, and I didn't move. I just kept it there, holding her hands between mine. She looked at me.

"This isn't so scary."

"Oh you're just surprising me every fucking minute here, baby. Every time I think you're gonna bolt, you just step up, and show me what a fucking fighter you are. Can you see that? Can you see how strong you are?"

She shrugged. "I survive. It's all I know how to do. I'm broken, but I can still put one foot in front of the other. You don't want this." She was suddenly pulling away from me.

"Hey, what just happened here? We're good, right, and you trust me. You're safe with me, so what changed in that last minute, that I didn't see?" I couldn't let her retreat back into herself, not now.

"Mina, please, I'm doing my best here. Don't pull away." I reached for her again and she froze, staring at me like a rabbit in headlights. *What the fuck*. I glanced down at myself. Nope, nothing down there was misbehaving right now.

She was trembling.

"Ah hell, Mina, tell me what I can do to help."

She was breathing fast, and looked like death. I backed off, moving to the bathroom, and returned with a glass of water. I held it out, but her hands were trembling too much to hold onto it, so I edged closer.

"Take a sip, come on." I leaned the glass closer, pressing it to her lips, and tilted it when she opened up. After a few sips, I placed the glass by the bed.

"Talk to me, please."

She had some colour back in her cheeks at last.

"I don't know. I... I guess it's all catching up with me. I'm such a fucking mess." She lowered her face into her hands, and sat like that for a while. I was having to physically restrain myself from holding her.

Why the fuck couldn't I just hold her?

Mina

I HATED SHOWING SO much weakness, especially to him.

He was so powerful, and used to being around strong people, and then there's little old me. The pathetic excuse for a broken human, that he'd somehow magically been paired with. I imagined that he must be cursing that whole thing right about now.

He was sitting on the bed, watching me, waiting for some response. I just didn't have one. How could I not have one? I felt numb. I felt like too much had happened in too short a space of time. Too many hands had touched me today, and I'd touched people.

I looked at my hands, almost feeling the taint on my skin. I needed to feel clean again.

He was watching me closely.

"You need something... you need, fuck... *you want a shower?*" How could he always read what my mind was saying, even when I was struggling to get there myself.

"I'm sorry. It's not you, it's everything. It's today. It's a year ago. It's all now, and it's all over me, and I need to feel clean." He was nodding.

"It's okay, I get it. Don't worry, we can make this happen. I'll get some clothes and stuff for you, and you can shower in your... you know, uh, the room you chose. Great shower in there. What do you say?" I nodded, but I glanced at his bathroom, his shower. I didn't want to leave his room. Why was it that I was freaking out for being in here, but I also didn't want to leave?

He followed my gaze. "Yeah, my shower is good too, probably better. You want me to set you up in here?" I nodded.

"Is that okay?"

He was laughing. "Mina, I want you in every aspect of my life. Why the hell would I have a problem with you wanting to use the shower, or anything in my room? I'm hoping one day it'll be our room."

My heart was racing again. I wished I could be normal, and give him what he wanted. A real mate. Someone he could love, and touch, and one day make a home with.

I didn't think that was ever going to be me, but how would I tell him that? Could I even make him understand that?

He dutifully brought clothes for me. *His*. And he sent someone out to get my clothes for me. I'd have to manage a little while in his stuff, but I'd soon have my own. He brought me a couple of huge fluffy towels, and showed me where all of his products were, and how to use the shower, and then he left.

He closed the bathroom door, and promised to stay in the bedroom, but not to come in. I didn't want him further away than that. Even though I was afraid of being too close, I was just as afraid of being too far apart.

The shower helped, oh god, it really did. His products smelled amazing, and soothed me, since I'd picked up their individual scents on him, when he'd been near me.

His shower was incredibly soothing, the powerful needles of hot water pounding against my skin, and washing away all the invisible taint on my skin.

By the time I wrapped myself in those huge towels, and started to dry off, I felt more human than I had in a long time. I dressed in his clothes, finger combed my hair, and opened the bathroom door.

He was on the sofa, reading a book, but he immediately glanced up, and there was this look on his face. *That satisfied look was back.* What was it this time? Me being here? Wearing his clothes? Smelling of him? All of the above?

He closed the book and set it aside.

"Better?" I nodded as I stepped into the room and closed the door.

"Thanks. That was just what I needed."

He grinned, and pointed to a large holdall on the floor.

"Your things, milady. I didn't know what you'd need, so I sent Daisy." I breathed a huge sigh of relief.

She was the only one I could trust touching my stuff, plus that meant that I'd have underwear at last. I glanced back at my neat pile of discarded clothes.

"Leave those." I turned back to frown at him.

"I can wash them." He shook his head.

"We have people who look after stuff like that, so they'll sort out the laundry. They'll be back in your room when they're clean." I glanced back once more, then forced myself to walk away.

"Where will I sleep?" I asked suddenly, and he grinned.

"You mean other than the room you already chose?" I nodded, because I didn't feel like I could leave his room yet.

Wasn't that strange? This was his room. I couldn't kick him out, but I couldn't share his bed either. I'd never slept in a bed with a man. The mere thought horrified me.

He shook his head. "You're overthinking things again, Mina. Have I given you any reason not to feel safe with me?" I took a few steps closer.

"I'll take the sofa," I said, and he answered with a low growl.

"What?"

"No woman of mine is sleeping on a fucking sofa, while I'm in a bed. You get me? You get the bed, and I'll take the damn sofa." I'd made him mad, but it didn't scare me. He was mad on my behalf, and that wasn't so bad, right?

"That's not fair on you." He shook his head, holding up a hand.

"My place, my rules." I blinked. I hadn't thought of that. At my place, he'd said it was my place and my rules. Did that mean that while I was here, he could demand things of me?

He was shaking his head again.

"Dammit, that's not what I mean, Mina. I'm saying that it's my choice, and I'm sleeping on the fucking sofa. Okay? I'll get some bedding. Now the bed, I can get the sheets changed. They were fresh, and I've only slept in there once. In fact, I don't think I even slept. I talked to you, then I came to find you... but you don't have to sleep in it until it's refreshed."

I shrugged. "It's okay." He tilted his head at me.

"You just washed the day away, and now you want to sleep in my sheets?"

I smiled, just a little.

"The pillowcase smells of you. It's what soothed me earlier, when I couldn't sleep." His grin widened suddenly.

"You know what else smells like me?" Uh oh, I shook my head warily, and he laughed.

"Well, I was gonna say me, but I don't want to freak you out, so let's move on. You wanna check the bag, and grab whatever you need for the night?" *Yes*, I needed underwear. I couldn't be without it any longer, it was freaking me out. I just nodded though, and he seemed to get it.

"I'm going to fetch some bedding, so you sort out what you need. I'll knock when I come back, just in case you're not decent. Nothing to fear, remember?" I nodded, because I truly believed that now.

The more time I spent with him, the less I felt like evil was lurking just around the corner, and waiting to violate me again.

He left, and closed the door.

Asher

SHE WAS STAYING IN my fucking room, *in my fucking bed*. Was this even real? And worst of all, knowing she'd been naked in there? I'd been fighting my fucking cock for dominance.

I swear, I used to be in control of my body, but a few seconds around her, and it was like a separate fucking consciousness, and right now? I wasn't leaving just to help her out. I needed to get out of the way, before she saw what it did to me.

Seeing her in my bathroom, in my clothes, covered in the scent of me, that nearly did me in. She was so innocent, so pure. They took from her body, but her soul was still pure and young. It didn't know what beauty there was in our bodies, and what bliss came from two people coming together, not yet.

When we got to that stage, and I was now starting to think there was hope for that one day, she was going to lose her virginity the way she should have done before. In the arms of a man who loved her, and wanted to spend the entire night pleasuring her fucking body, until she couldn't breathe for screaming my name.

Now, the biggest problem I hadn't even broached with her yet, was how I'd manage to give up control in bed. I might have been doing okay with letting her make every decision for herself, for her sanity, but that's not how I normally roll when it comes to sex.

How would I tell her that I needed that control, that I had to be submitted to in order to get off? *Although, now I thought about it, was that even going to be a problem anymore, because my fucking cock didn't seem to be under my control any longer.*

If she hadn't been through what she'd been through, right now, I'd have her spread out on my bed, panting and begging for me to fuck her, because I'd already spent the last hour or so teasing and pleasuring every goddamn inch of her, and she'd be desperate for me.

She'd get what she needed, when I was good and fucking ready, and when I gave it to her, she'd take every damn thrust, because I demanded it.

And that was where the problem lay, because I'd been that man for so long. I was forty fucking years old, and now I had to play the opposite side, and let her decide how our sex life progressed? I was going to have to learn this shit all over again.

Still, there were some ideas occurring to me. If I made sure that every touch she agreed to was eminently blissful, she'd want more, right?

I grabbed the bedding and some more bath towels, and stood outside my own damn room, knocking on the door. She called out that it was safe, and I went in, dumping the bedding on the sofa I'd have to try and fucking sleep on, and dropped the towels in the bathroom.

"I'm gonna shower before I sleep, but before I do that, do you need anything from the kitchen? Food, drinks, anything?" She shook her head.

"The water will be fine. Asher?"

I stopped, with the bathroom door half closed, sticking my head out.

"Yeah?"

"Thank you." I grinned.

"Anything for you, baby." *And that's it; that's how I'm gonna roll, for as long as I can manage.*

I turned the shower onto cold before stepping in, praying I could send my damn boner back to the hell it came from, so I didn't have to jack off in here once more, and risk her hearing me this time.

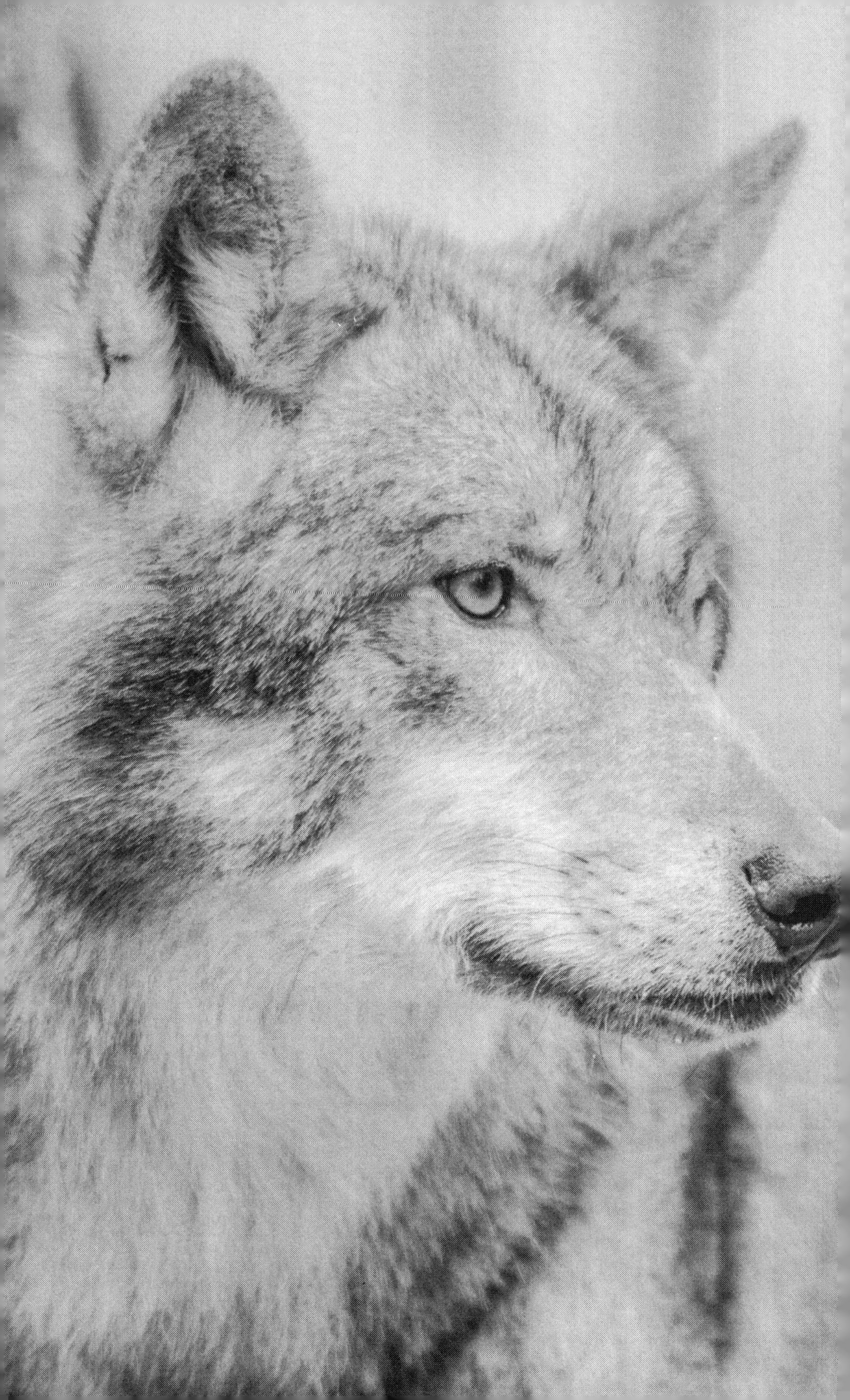

Chapter Twenty-Two

Mina

I WOKE IN A strange bed, and when I opened my eyes, and looked around, it was all strange. Everything was different. Where was I?

The room was laid out wrong, with the window in the wrong place. The bed smelled different, and oh, *there was a man in the room snoring lightly*. I scrambled up against the headboard, breathing fast and trembling.

It took me a few moments to remember the previous day, and everything that had happened, and that I was safe. Asher wasn't snoring anymore; he was watching me warily from the sofa. It was too small for such a huge man, and must have been incredibly uncomfortable. I should have been the one sleeping on it.

"Mina?" His voice was gruff, and full of sleep. I nodded, keeping my eyes on him.

"Baby, you're safe, remember? It's just me." He didn't move, how was he so good at knowing how to deal with all of my annoying freakouts?

"I... I'm sorry," I mumbled, and he groaned. He moved at last, pushing himself up from his crumpled position on the sofa, crunching his neck back and forth.

"The only thing about you that ever makes me mad, is how you think you have to apologise for everything. Nothing that happens because of them is your fault. Every time you say sorry, you're taking the blame." He seemed cranky, but as he stood up and stretched his back, groaning again as things crunched, I could tell why.

"You should have given me the sofa," I said, biting my lip when he turned to glare at me again.

"You know how I feel about that."

I nodded, because he'd been pretty clear.

"But I'm like half the size you are, so I'd fit on it. You don't." He shrugged, and groaned again.

"So I get backache and neckache for a few minutes when I wake up. It's hardly the end of the world." He approached the bed slowly, and sat on the end of it, tucking his leg under him so he could face me.

"Did you sleep okay?" I thought about that, and nodded.

"Actually I feel like I went to sleep faster than ever, and didn't wake once. No nightmares that I can recall either."

He nodded, shooting me a grin.

"You were flat out when I came out of the shower. You didn't even wake in the night, when I fell off that bloody thing."

I giggled. "You fell off the sofa?" He grinned again.

"Well, it's a fucking tiny, postage-stamp-sized bastard, so of course I did. I should really get a bigger one."

As I watched him glance back at the sofa, I felt incredibly guilty. He shouldn't have had to sleep on a sofa at all.

"I'll sleep in the other room tonight," I said, biting my lip, because it was the right thing to do, but I was surprised to realise that I didn't like the thought of it.

He shook his head. "Nah, it's all good. You'll sleep here, if that's where you feel safe and sleep well. Sleep is good, I mean, you feel better for it, don't you?" I nodded again.

"I just don't want to take over your bed."

He smirked. "I hope one day you'll be hogging the covers, and sticking cold feet on me in the night, so really, when you think about it, the bed's fair game anyway."

I was struck dumb, because how could he talk so easily about things like that?

I mean, obviously it was easy for someone who hadn't been attacked, but it still made me feel awkward. A very tiny part of me even liked the sound of it, but the rest of me was already wanting to back away.

"Mina, I say these things because they're true. They're what I really want, but it doesn't mean that I'd force the issue, if that's not what you want. I don't think you understand how a real man treats a woman.

It's not about using, and abusing, and tormenting; it's about loving, and protecting, and having fun. It's about waking up happy, because you're with the one you want to be with. Just waking up in the same room as you has me and my wolf pretty damn happy right now."

I chewed my lip, holding back so many words. If I told him that part of me liked the idea, it might make him push harder for it, and I knew I wasn't ready for that.

"You want to say something, don't you? You have a response, but you're afraid to share it." He always seemed to know.

"How do you always know stuff like that? Is it a wolf thing?" I asked, watching that grin appear again.

"It's written all over your face, Mina. Whether you want to admit to it or not, I can read you like a book."

I shook my head. It couldn't be that simple, it had to be some gift he had.

"Oh really? Shall I tell you what I think? I think you're starting to come around to the idea, that maybe you don't have to be alone forever. That maybe there's a future for you, a happy one, a safe one. One where you're loved, and honoured by a man, *this man*. I think you're afraid of that feeling, because I think you feel like it makes you vulnerable to being hurt again. I'm going to be really clear with you, Mina, you will NEVER be hurt again the way you were before. Even if you decide you don't want me, don't want to be here, I'll still make it my life's work to keep you safe. Even if I have to do that from a distance, and jack off in the fucking shower every night for some release."

I flinched from his words, from the mental image that popped into my mind. *It was too much.*

He held his hands up. "I'm just trying to make sure you understand me, Mina. I'm a man, not an asshole, not some monster who would hurt you. Just the opposite, but to lie to you about how much I want you to want me some day would be wrong. We're not about lies, because you can't rely on lies. You need truth, and you need certainty. You need routine and safe places, and peace, and I'll make sure you get all of that, whenever you need it. Now, I don't know about you, but I'm done with the sound of my voice for now, so either you talk, or we work out a morning routine you're comfortable with, and get on with our day."

He smiled, and waited, while I watched him watch me. Finally he sighed and pushed himself up, walking across the room to the dresser to sort out clothes for himself.

"Wait."

Asher

EVERY MUSCLE IN MY body froze, because she finally spoke. I turned to look at her, my hands holding a bundle of t-shirts, because I'd been making sure that I picked something more appropriate to wear today.

"Yeah?" I asked, anticipation eating me up from the inside. She nodded slowly, chewing at her lip.

"*You're right.*" Fuck me, really? I just tilted my head at her, waiting for her to continue.

She looked down, smoothing her hands over the silken bedding she'd slept in. Yeah, I liked my beds fucking blissfully kitted out, and I wasn't about to apologise for that.

"It... it makes me feel hope." She glanced up at me, as if she wanted to gauge my reaction to that one comment. I shoved the t-shirts back in the drawer, and walked back to the bed, sitting down.

I was only relieved that I had some pyjamas to wear last night, so she didn't wake up to me naked, which was how I preferred to sleep. I mean, okay... sweats and a t-shirt weren't really pyjamas, but they seemed to work, for the most part.

"Hope is good," I said finally, because she'd stalled again.

"I hold back what I'm feeling sometimes, because I worry that one little concession will make you feel like more will definitely follow, and I can't promise it will." *Wow, she was brutal with her honesty, but this was good.*

"That's fair. How about if I promise that I won't take anything for granted? If you say you like something, it doesn't mean you want more, or even that you'd like the same thing again."

She nodded, looking frustrated.

"I hate being like this. I hate that one minute I can have a conversation, and almost appear normal, and the next, I can't breathe, and everything feels dirty, and I'm nothing. *It's exhausting, but I can't seem to be a better person.*"

I growled softly. "Don't you go disparaging the woman in my bed now, Mina. My wolf doesn't like that, and neither do I."

Her eyes widened at me, and I shot her a grin.

"You're not deliberately being any kind of person. Every time you feel normal, enjoy it, and when you feel otherwise, just please trust me to support you. When you feel ready, and I really hope you will, I can help you through those scarier moments, by holding you in my arms, and showing you that nothing can break through to get to you. It sounds scary now, but maybe one day, it's that safety that you'll crave."

She chewed that damn lip again. *I was going to have to start a regime of punching my cock every time it twitched at her behaviours, and I was really hoping thoughts like that would make him behave.*

"Even now, that doesn't sound terrifying, but... what worries me is that I could become dependent on you. If you're the one who makes me feel safe, what's going to stop me from, I don't know... leeching off of you, when I need to feel safe? I need to learn to make myself feel safe, not the other way around." I grinned, feeling another wave of pride for the courage she still didn't realise she showed so often.

"You know, you can be quite logical, Mina. I think you should speak your mind more often, and hey, what do you think might help empower you that way? Do you... have you had any training in defending yourself? Any defensive moves, or offensive moves that you could use against an attacker?" She visibly shuddered in response to my question.

"They made me do some self-defence stuff after the wounds had healed, and I wanted to... but... it's hard for me to let anyone near me, to learn to defend against an attack." The thought of her having wounds that needed to heal was physically painful, and I couldn't help the growl that tore from my chest.

I'd seen a report on her injuries after her attack. When the guys showed us the details of the other attacks, they'd sneaked me a copy of it, so she wouldn't see. They'd raped her multiple times, causing all kinds of injury to her, and then they'd taken a fucking penknife and stabbed her a dozen times.

The tiny blade would have hurt like hell, and did some damage, but luckily didn't reach any major organs. She'd have scars, where the knife went in each time, but she shouldn't have any long-term health issues, not physically, anyway. She lost a lot of blood, but luckily she was O-positive, so thankfully it was a common blood group, and therefore easy to replenish.

Yeah, I took in the fucking details; two bastards had their hands, and their bodies, on my woman and *in my woman*, and they'd die for it. I wanted to make it last, to make them suffer.

"You look angry. Did I upset you?" She asked suddenly, and I rubbed a hand over my face. *Fuck.*

"Sorry, baby, just thinking things over. Would it help if I get Daisy to teach you some stuff, to help you fight? You trust her, and know she won't hurt you, right?" I really wanted to be the one showing her, but it'd be too much right now.

I wanted her to learn knife skills, and how to use whatever the fuck happened to be to hand. Daisy could do all of that, all pack members did regular training. We had to, because who knew when another Alpha would make a challenge against me?

She was nodding slowly.

"I could do that. I can. I *can* do that." Damn straight.

"Yeah you can, baby, I'll set it up. In the meantime, you keep that brain ticking over. Anything else you want or need, you just say. You're not going to need these skills, but I want you to know that you can protect yourself, for your own peace of mind. At least until you recognise that I'll make sure nobody will ever get close enough to even speak to you without your prior agreement."

She laughed, her face lighting up with delight.

"You sound like some warrior, who would march around, cutting people down as they approach."

"If the shoe fits, baby."

I decided that we were pushing it for sharing, so suggested she use the bathroom in here, and I took my shit with me to the room she'd previously chosen, and showered there. She had all her own toiletries now, her toothbrush, etc. and I had mine with me.

Once we were both showered, we went down to breakfast, and I whipped up a mountain of pancakes for the two of us, and Jase and Derek, who appeared mid-cook, and started drooling like the dogs they were.

We sat around the table, scoffing pancakes and syrup, and drinking coffee, and I couldn't help but feel so fucking satisfied by the way things were going. She'd stayed the night, in fact, we'd spent the last two nights together now. While neither of them had been the way I'd normally want, they were more valuable, because I knew how difficult they'd been for her.

Now she sat at our breakfast table, chatting with the guys, like she'd stepped out from under the cloud hovering over her. She laughed at something one of them said, and I tried to tune into what they were talking about. They were talking about what might happen on a Sunday in pack territory.

"Will you show me around?" She was looking at me, so I forced myself to focus back in on what was happening.

"Anything you want, baby," I said, finally, hoping I hadn't missed something vital in the conversation.

"*Oh, he's so whipped, man*," Derek muttered to Jase, who laughed.

"Leave the guy alone, he made pancakes. Alpha, these are fucking awesome. Uh... any more left?" He craned his neck, and Mina pushed the plate to him, with one left on there.

"You don't want it?" He asked her, watching her shake her head before he took it.

"What about me?" I said, half joking, but he just shrugged.

"You snooze, you lose, is the way I see it."

I was stunned. What the hell had happened to my previously formal, well-mannered Beta? Where was the dogged submission he always displayed? Was my Alpha power failing? Was he feeling a stronger Alpha pull from Derek now?

"What's up, boss?" Derek finally asked, telling me that I'd been staring at Jase for too long. I frowned.

"Am I missing something here?"

He glanced at Jase, who swallowed the last bite of pancake, and looked from him to me.

"It's me, isn't it?" He asked warily, and I shrugged.

"You tell me."

Mina was watching us warily.

"Did something happen?"

Derek finally groaned. "Look, Jase has undergone something of a personality transplant, or I don't know, sacked up a bit, and now he isn't sucking up to the boss, it's all starting to unravel. Honestly boss, I think he just removed the stick from up his ass."

Jase punched his arm. *"Shut up, dick.* Alpha, I'm sorry, I'm just... I've been repeatedly told that I'm too uptight, so I'm trying to loosen up a bit, but I'll watch myself in future."

Now I felt like an asshole. He truly had been told that a few times, but I'm guessing this time it had come from someone who mattered more to him, maybe a woman... *interesting*... in the end, I shot him a grin.

"Just keep it formal outside of the house, yeah?" He nodded once.

"Thanks, Alpha, it's hard to change, but it's actually quite fun without the stick I've apparently had up my ass for so long. Now if you'll both excuse me, I've got to go and get it, and then I'm going to twat Derek with it."

Mina was giggling, so I didn't bother telling him to curb the language. Hell, she'd heard worse from me by now.

They left, shoving each other and throwing insults, Mina started gathering up the plates, and I stopped her, narrowly missing touching her hand.

"What are you doing?" She glanced at me with a frown, like I was being completely dense.

"Loading the dishwasher?"

I pulled the plates from her hands.

"Like fuck. No woman of mine is cleaning up after those two assholes." She snorted, and grabbed another plate, so I snatched that too.

"So their Alpha is going to clean up after them?" She challenged, and I frowned. She had a point.

~ D, Jase, get the fuck back down here, and clean up your shit. If I find my mate cleaning up after you again, I'm going to kick your asses.

I felt guilt and shame coming back at me, but I closed the connection before they could respond.

As we were leaving the table after I'd loaded our dishes, they reappeared, gathering their plates up.

"Sorry boss," Derek muttered, while Jase lowered his head.

Mina let out a huff of frustration.

"It would have taken me less than two minutes, you know."

"You're not the fucking help, okay?"

"Is this normal for you?" She asked me, stopping in the living room, folding her arms, actually glaring at me.

I frowned, looking around to see what the hell I'd missed this time.

"Uh, is what normal?"

"This attitude about me wanting to tidy a few damn dishes? I can do things for myself, you know!" She looked pissed.

"I actually have lived alone for long enough to know how to do all of these things myself."

"Mina, I have no problem with you doing stuff for yourself, but you're not their maid. That was rude of them to leave the mess. They never did it before, and they're not starting it now." I raised my eyebrows, demonstrating that I could fold my arms too.

Mina

JUST WHEN I THOUGHT I was starting to understand him, he did something stubborn, and I realised that there were more layers of him that I had to learn.

He didn't want me cleaning up after his pack members, and guess what? Neither did I, but it was one time, and it wasn't a big deal, but he must have commanded them in their heads to come back and tidy up. What the hell was that even about?

That voice in the back of my head? The logical one, the one who disappeared for weeks at a time? She could see his side of things, because why the hell should I have to clean up after his housemates? It wasn't my job, and I wasn't their mother. Besides, he said they never did that before today. It was time to concede his point, so I let out a frustrated sigh and nodded.

"Okay, I get it. Just please don't stop me doing things, because you think I'm too weak or fragile to do them. I do laundry, I hoover up, I do all sorts of things. Hell, I changed a damn tyre on my car a month ago. It wasn't easy, but I did it. I'm not completely useless, Asher."

He approached, his hands out, before he groaned, and dropped them.

"That's not how I see you. I see you as my fucking queen. Why would I want you to feel like you have to do their dishes, or wash your own damn clothes, when what you really deserve is to enjoy life, and do things that make you happy?"

I felt my stubborn streak kick in despite my agreement with his point.

"What if washing dishes makes me happy? You really don't know me very well at all." I saw the irritation cross his face.

"Jesus, you didn't list it as a hobby, so I took a fucking leap, okay? Can we please move on from this? I thought you wanted a tour of the pack territory?"

I chewed my lip. I knew I was just being snippy because I suddenly felt like I was doing what he told me to, rather than what I wanted. But then there he was, trying to get me to go and do the thing I actually wanted to do.

"Sorry, apparently I can be a bit argumentative at times, or at least I used to." Were we both surprised that I was becoming so confident and outspoken? I certainly was, but he made me feel safe to speak my mind.

He grinned, the tension dropping from his shoulders.

"It turns out I enjoy a little verbal sparring with you, Mina, just beware, I give as good as I get."

"Let me go and grab my coat... I mean, unless you have coat collectors on staff?"

He facepalmed, barking out a laugh.

"I get it! I'm sorry, okay? Now get your ass moving. The pack territory is pretty big, so it'll take a couple of hours to show you around."

Wow. I couldn't wait to see it.

Once we were outside the pack house, and walking, I could see that there were many other buildings in the area. Not close, but over the course of a few miles out in all directions. It was pretty flat here, although there were hills along one side of the slightly more built-up area.

It looked like farms dotted around. Nobody would stand here and think that it looked like a specific community. They'd just assume it was a bunch of isolated farmhouses dotted around, with residents who didn't even know their neighbours.

I looked at Asher, in awe of the land around us.

"All of those houses in the distance, they're all pack members?" He nodded as I pointed.

"The land was a bunch of separate parcels, which were consolidated by the pack members as they bought them up, and overseen by the previous Alpha, my father. I'll tell you about him another time. For the moment, while we're in the best spot to oversee the area, I'll talk you through it."

He waved a hand at the hills. "This is almost the edge of the boundary of our land. There's a hiking trail all the way along there, which we use for running. It's private land, so there's no chance of random hikers or joggers."

"Is that where Daisy took me?" I guessed he'd know, even though he hadn't been there. He nodded, pointing the other way.

"And way off in the distance, you see the occasional flashes of light? That's cars on the motorway. Our land stretches almost that far."

Wow, that looked like it was several miles away.

"Really? It's huge."

"*That's what she said*," he said and laughed, then facepalmed.

"Sorry, schoolboy humour, but you grinned. Excellent." I shrugged. "The oldies can be goodies."

He pointed to some larger buildings in the distance, in the opposite direction. They looked bigger than all of the houses, including the pack house.

"Over there we've got the big hall, and other communal buildings, and the general store."

"You guys have your own store?" I couldn't believe this place!

"Where else would we get our essentials? Mac stocks pretty much most things, so it keeps us from having to head into town for things, unless we really want to."

"It's amazing. How could anyone not feel safe here? It's beautiful, and peaceful, and... it's a whole community... show me, show me!" I was overwhelmed with excitement, and Asher's face lit up.

"Really?"

I was practically bouncing on my toes.

"Please! I don't know that I want to meet everyone, but I just want to see it all." He laughed, looking like I'd just given him something wonderful.

He reached for my hand, then sighed.

"Sorry."

"Don't be." I reached my hand over, slipping it into his, feeling his warm fingers lightly wrap around mine.

"You sure?" I nodded, and squeezed his hand. I was getting to like how it felt to be connected with him in this way.

"Let's go." He smiled widely, and started moving, tugging me along with him.

We'd walked for miles. I was exhausted, and starting to flag, but I was determined not to show it. The territory really was massive; the farmhouses that looked so huge from a distance were not all huge farmhouses at all, but multiple smaller homes built into one field.

There were various businesses set up too; a metalworker and welder in one building, and a gardener, who was apparently responsible for many of the lovely gardens surrounding different houses. There was also a mechanic, and the general store. We went in when we got there, and I was grateful for a chance to sit down at last.

Mac, the owner, had a small coffee bar there, and used a big machine similar to the commercial coffee shops, although he swore at it a lot as he used it.

"He's only had that thing a month. *Swears it's more trouble than his wife.*" Asher had whispered to me. I liked Mac instantly, he was quick witted, chatty, and relaxed. Like Asher, he had a calming effect on me. Had I met him outside of the territory, and his business, I'd have been afraid of him.

We all judged people by their looks, whether we'd admit it or not. He was big, almost as big as Asher, with long hair tied back while he worked, and a long beard with a little grey creeping in.

He had so many tattoos, that it was hard to see his actual skin anywhere but on his face. He wore a t-shirt and an apron over that, which seemed to look wrong with the rest of his look, but as I said, something about him as I listened to them chatting, made me feel calm.

"Mina?" I blinked free of my thoughts, glancing at Asher.

"Coffee okay?" I sighed with pleasure, smiling at Mac.

"Heaven, thank you, and thanks, Mac."

He nodded his head at me, then turned to glare at the machine.

"Bloody thing cost a bundle, so if it doesn't pay its way, I'll kick its ass." I giggled at his antics.

"I could see me needing a daily fix, to be honest." Asher was grinning widely.

"You might end up seeing more of us, Mac. If the lady wants your coffee, she gets your coffee."

He laughed. "We do deliver, just so you know. Jake's pretty fast on his bike." He jerked a thumb at the young lad working behind the shop counter. For a pack territory shop, it was pretty busy.

I mentioned that to Asher as we left, and he pointed out that the shop frontage was on the main road.

"So they weren't all wolves in there?"

"Anyone passing by can use the store. He couldn't survive just with pack members as customers, but you know... we're trying to grow our numbers. It'd make us a little harder to challenge."

That sounded scary, but then all of this was new.

"How do you grow a pack?"

He grinned, winking at me.

"Can't you guess?"

"Children?" He laughed out loud.

"Well, they'll start with wives first, I hope." I glanced around us. We were walking back, and my trainers were rubbing at my feet. Why did I choose those, instead of my hiking boots?

"Nobody is married?" Asher reached for my hand, and I took it willingly. It almost felt natural to hold his hand as we walked. Me, who'd never let anyone touch me for more than a year, had willingly allowed him to take my hand, and held it most of the day. For some reason, his warmth gave me comfort, and it was kind of addictive.

"We have three guys who are mated, and married. Obviously, Daisy married into the pack from another, but yeah, the others have yet to find theirs. Mac is married, and Jake is their son. His wife is Ellie; she works at the store when she can, but she's an artist, so she spends a lot of time doing that too."

He knew them all so well. As we walked back past houses, he told me who lived there, as he had on the way down the other side, and when we walked past Daisy and Ned's house, he pointed it out. Their car wasn't there, which told me they'd probably gone out for the day.

Daisy only had Fridays and Sundays off, so it was their only chance, since she'd spent Friday with me, while Ned worked. I worked Wednesdays, Thursdays, and Saturdays at the nursery with her, although neither of us had ended up working yesterday in the end.

Asher suddenly pulled me to a stop.

"Mina, look at me."

I glanced at him in surprise. We were still pretty far away from the pack house.

"What is it?" I asked, seeing nobody around us.

"You're practically hobbling. Do you have a blister?" Jesus, he's too observant, this man. I shrugged, pretending my feet were stinging like a bitch.

"One or two, I think."

"For fuck's sake, why didn't you say? We could get someone to pick us up for the rest of the way. The roads run right through here, as you've seen."

I glanced down at my feet, which continued to throb even though we'd stopped. These damn trainers.

"I forgot to wear my hiking boots," I said sheepishly, watching him stare at my trainers.

"Why the hell didn't I check? God, I'm so sorry."

I pulled my hand away from him.

"It's not your place to check what I'm wearing on my feet. It's my responsibility, and I'm the one who messed up."

I saw Asher looking around for a solution.

"I mean, I could carry you, but that means touching you." I shuddered at the thought. While I didn't hate his touch, that would be too much too soon. He nodded morosely.

"Yeah, I know."

A car started heading towards us from the direction of the pack house. It pulled up, and Derek leaned his head out.

"Your chauffeur fucking awaits, boss."

I laughed, because he must have called him with his mind power thing. *Perfect.* Asher opened the back door for me, and I gratefully slid into the car. I expected him to go around and get in the front with Derek, but he gestured at me to slide along, and climbed in beside me instead.

"Oh great, now I really look like a fucking chauffeur." Derek grumbled, as he turned the car around, and headed back up the road to the pack house.

"That'll teach you to give me attitude," Asher said, sitting back in the car, and turning to smile at me. Being in the car, which I was now sitting alone in with two men, was starting to feel too much, too intimate. His smile dropped from his face.

"*Breathe, baby,*" he whispered. He rested his hand between us on the seat, and I grabbed it, like a life raft.

"Good girl, use my strength." He wrapped his fingers around mine. His hands were bigger than mine, so they enveloped my fingers easily, warmth flowing from him, into me.

Before I even had time to try and relax, we were back at the pack house, and Asher told me to stay while he got out, and came around to open the other door for me. When he offered a hand to me to help me out, I took it again. It was like an addiction, now that I'd touched his hand, I couldn't stop doing it again.

Every time I took his hand when he offered, he looked like he'd won a prize. Was this how it was supposed to be? Was this what other men were like? Kind, gentle, and soothing.

My only experience had been so horrific, that I'd never even spoken to any man I couldn't avoid since then. But then Asher walked into my life, and I felt like I was starting to rely on him, as much as I did on oxygen. He helped me hobble inside, and up to his room.

Upstairs, he guided me to the bed, and sat me down.

"Wait here." He disappeared into the bathroom, returning with a large bowl of water, and some other supplies.

He knelt at my feet, that same behaviour that had shocked his wolves so much yesterday. Looking up at me, he reached for my left trainer.

"Can I?" He wanted to remove my shoe? I nodded, and he focused on untying, and then loosening the trainer, before he eased it off my foot. He gently lowered my heel onto the floor, and glanced at me again.

"Can I just look after this for you, and you stop me if you're uncomfortable?" I nodded again, trusting him to not hurt me, and he quirked an eyebrow.

"Yes. *Please.*"

He grinned. "That's better, we like words, Mina. Okay, let's see what you've done to yourself. Oh Jesus..." He peeled the sock off carefully, his warm hand cupping my ankle. Again, his touch wasn't unpleasant, and it didn't make me flinch, or panic. It was actually comforting. He was frowning at my big toe though.

"Seems that it's the front of these bloody things that rubs. Your heel isn't blistered." I nodded, because I'd already known that from the pain.

"It burst, so it's gonna sting, but I want to soak it, okay?" I nodded again, and he lowered my foot gently into the warm water. There was a stinging pain at the front of my toe, which eased after a few seconds.

"Sorry." He reached for the other foot, and watching me for my reaction, he followed the same process, shoe untied, loosened, and slipped from my foot. Sock peeled carefully away, his hand cradling my ankle. Again he checked my foot over, a frown on his face.

"This one bled, so it must have been worse. Jesus, why didn't you tell me your feet were hurting this much?"

I shrugged, because I was used to not speaking up about things.

"It was bearable."

"I should have fucking driven us around the area," he was muttering to himself, as he lowered my right foot into the water, wincing when I hissed out in pain.

He muttered a curse word, and grabbed the fluffy towel he'd brought with him, lifting my left foot, and drying it gently. He treated the blister, covering it with a plaster, and carefully set my foot down on the carpet, then he did the same with the other foot. He disappeared with the bowl, and everything else and came back.

"Will you object if I ask you to put your feet up for a bit and rest them?" I shook my head, relieved at the suggestion. I'd definitely been stupid enough for today.

He offered a hand to help me up, and walked me to the side of the bed. When I sat back down, he reached for my legs, and as his hands touched me, I let out a panicked squeak, and he stopped.

"*Fuck*! This is so fucking hard. I want to look after you, and everything I do just freaks you out. Uh... you get comfortable, and I'll bring you a drink."

He left the room fast, and I moved up onto the bed, and lay back, fighting to get my breathing back down to a normal level. The hurt look on his face just then made me want to cry.

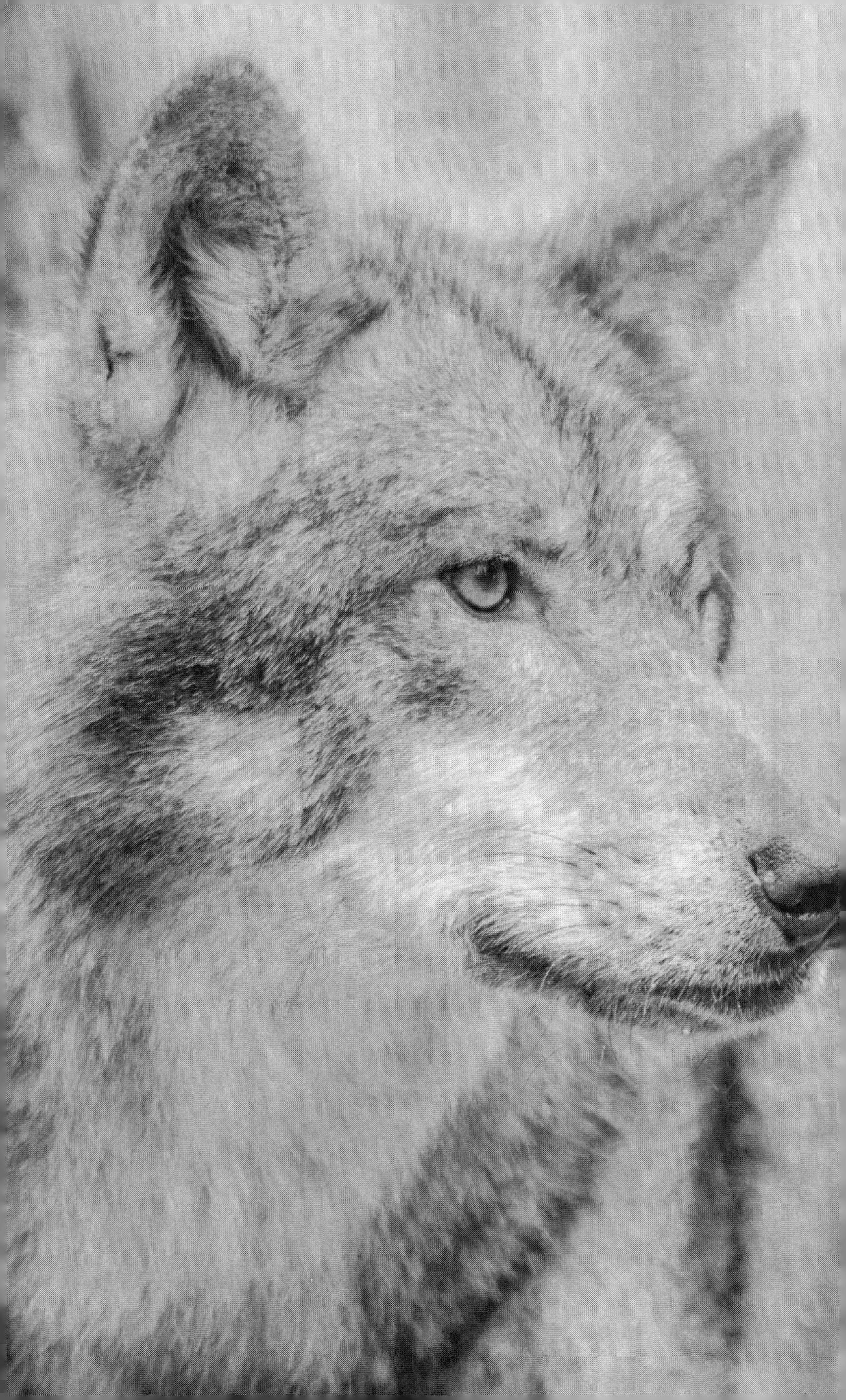

Chapter Twenty-Three

ASHER

I NEEDED TO PUNCH something, and that's why I left like a fucking pussy. How the hell could I be destined for someone who struggled to let me anywhere near her?

How the fuck was a man supposed to deal with his own woman being so afraid of him, that she squeals like a fucking kicked puppy, if he moves to touch her?

Why did I do it? Because I fucking forgot! Because today she's been braver, she'd allowed hand holding, and she didn't even flinch now, she just took my hand, like it was normal and nice, and what the fuck happened?

I stomped out of the pack house, marching around the back, needing a few moments to cool off, and if I bumped into anyone, they were going to take a few punches.

I leaned against the back wall, my head against the brick surface, taking deep breaths. My fists wouldn't unclench for the moment, so I let them be.

She'd handled me touching her feet like it was nothing strange, and yet I'd almost touched her knees, and she panicked, because of course she would. Feet; nothing could be further from the most vulnerable parts of her. Knees? That was halfway to the one fucking place she may never let me near.

Those two bastards had ruined her ability to even allow me to lift her onto a bed. I could have carried her home, if she'd just been able to allow me to lift her into my arms. How long could I keep holding back, and letting her push me away?

Everything inside me was saying hold her, protect her, love her, but her eyes and her reactions were saying that this may be as much as she can give. Was it enough?

I banged my head back against that wall a few times. What the fuck was I supposed to do?

My phone buzzed in my pocket, and I pulled it out, and checked it; Mina. Of course it was, because I'd stormed out like a prick.

Mina: *I'm sorry.*

Fuck.

Mina: *I know you won't hurt me. I panicked. It's my fault.*

See, that just made me even angrier. Why did she keep taking the blame for this, for any of it? If I could have been put in a room with even one of her attackers right now, I'd tear the spine from his pathetic body, and beat him to death with it, and I know that would be moot. He'd be dead already, and I doubted either of them had a fucking spine anyway.

Mina: *Please don't be angry with me. I'm trying.*

Jesus, I didn't want her taking this on as well. It wasn't her fault I was having a hissy fit, because I'd fucking forgotten not to touch her. I promised I wouldn't push her, and I'd failed her.

Me: *I'm not. Please don't apologise. I'll be back in a minute.*

I couldn't let her stew, just because I was losing my shit right now. None of this was her fault. She didn't ask for a single moment of what had happened to her, or for this fucking mate bond shit. She was just someone that these things were happening to, and that meant she reacted any way she could. Was it any wonder she was freaked out?

But then, wasn't I just as fucking freaked? I had no idea what I was doing with her, all I knew was that I wanted to protect her, but was I? Or was I making her worse?

And even if I knew that to be the case, was I in too deep to stop now? *Hell if I know.*

Mina

HE'D BEEN GONE TOO long. I'd hurt him, and I knew that. I could tell that after the day we'd had, and the touches I'd allowed, my reaction to that almost instinctive move of his to help me, had hurt him.

Did my acceptance of him really matter so much to him, that a moment of panic could cut him like that? He was a million times stronger than me.

Although I no longer worried about him overwhelming me, or overpowering me, I still couldn't see how anything I did could do such damage to him.

I wanted to text him again, but I don't want to harass him. Eventually I decided to go looking for him, and so it was that as I stood up, tentative on my sore feet, the door opened and he reappeared.

"Oh, you should be resting," he said gruffly, edging into the room, with two coffees in one hand, and a plate of toast in the other.

He shrugged when he saw me looking. "Uh, thought you might need fuel." He set the toast and a coffee by the bed, and moved away to sit on the sofa with his. I sat back down, lost for words. I'd hurt his feelings, and yet he'd gone and fetched food and a drink for me. Even after I'd upset him, he was still looking after me.

"Why?" I asked, finishing a slice of toast, and grabbing my coffee. He was cradling his drink in his hands, but didn't look at me.

"Why what?"

"Why do you look after me, when I can't help hurting you?" He lifted his eyes to mine, his face so sad compared to usual, when he smiled and laughed so much.

"You know why."

I didn't like that he'd sat across the room either. I didn't like the distance, almost as much as I couldn't bear the closeness yet.

"Why are you over there?" He groaned, and ran a hand through his hair. I was infuriating him, I could tell, but I just couldn't seem to stop doing it.

"What is this, twenty questions?"

"I can ask more if you like, I just don't understand why you stayed over there, when you normally sit here."

"Is there a 'normal' with us?" He asked, resting his coffee on his knee, while I wondered why it didn't burn him. Didn't wolves get burned? I really should have learned this stuff by now.

"Should I leave? This is your room, after all. I could go to the other one." He groaned.

"Look, I don't know what you want from me right now, Mina. I'm trying, I am. I want to look after you, and I'm doing my best, but... one minute you're pulling away, like I'm a monster, and the next you're complaining that I'm sitting too bloody far away. How can I possibly know the right thing to do?"

He had a point, but his words just made me angrier.

"Okay, I'll use my words," I snapped. "I prefer it when you sit over here with me."

He raised his eyebrows at my tone.

"I come over there, and I'm not sitting on the edge of the fucking bed, like a spare part." Oh, he was angry, but he was also right.

"It's your bed," I said grumpily.

He stood up, coffee in hand. "Fine, you're damn right it is." He marched across the room, around the other side of the bed, and climbed on, sitting against the headboard like I was.

He didn't get close, and the bed was huge, like a king size I think, so it wasn't too close. He sighed as he got comfy.

"I don't mean to keep you from your bed, you know, it's very comfy," I whispered, and he snorted.

"I put a lot of work into making it as fucking blissful as possible. We spend a large part of our lives sleeping, so it should be worthy of that."

I smiled. I liked that, and didn't it make perfect sense?

"I like soft bedding." He laughed.

"Yeah, it's a ridiculously expensive cotton silk blend, but I like how it feels on my skin."

I glanced at him. "On your... skin?"

He gave me a sidelong look.

"Well, I normally prefer to sleep without clothes, baby. It's freeing."

Oh. I looked away, not wanting to imagine him that way, not because I couldn't, or even because I didn't think he'd look good that way.

I'd seen his naked upper half, and it had been impressive; even a man-phobe like me could appreciate that. I just didn't know how I felt about that.

"Sometimes I feel like maybe you're not as repulsed by me as you think you should be." He said quietly, and I glanced at him, seeing his eyes on me. I clenched my fists, and unclenched them, just to distract me.

"I don't want to be, and I... I'm not... I'm just afraid." He nodded.

"You have no reason to be afraid of me, Mina, but I can understand why."

I was suddenly irrationally angry.

"How? How can you possibly understand? How can you understand what it's like to hate your own skin, because it's marked and scarred, and forever tainted by what they did? And to hate your insides, because they touched there too? And to hate your mind, for being so fucking stupid to not see what was coming, or have the sense to get out of it, or the strength? And to hate your heart, because despite all of that, despite the way you hate every fucking inch of yourself, your heart still beats a little faster when..." I trailed off, stunned, and humiliated by my outburst. I breathed hard, like I'd been running.

He was quiet, still, but finally he asked.

"When?"

Asher

I FELT LIKE I couldn't breathe, right along with her. What had she stopped herself saying?

"Mina, finish that sentence. *Now.*"

She glanced at me, the tone of my voice shocking her out of her misery. It wasn't Alpha dominance, not with her, but maybe I'd used enough of a stern note to corral her senses.

"When you're near me," she finally said, tears dripping from her eyes. *Fuck*.

I'd already dumped my coffee mug, so I turned to face her.

"*Please*." I found myself saying, and she stared at me with wide eyes.

"What?"

Oh fuck. *Fuck*... She's not going to want me to touch her, and I needed to. It was a burning urge practically taking over my entire body.

"Can I..."

I hung my head, because I was being a complete bastard. I couldn't keep pushing her to accept me, when she had to be the one to set the pace.

She was watching me, my struggle.

"What?" She asked again, and I shook my head. I couldn't do it.

"I should get out for a bit, maybe go for a run. I need to burn off some-"

"I want to know," she interrupted. I was already standing, anxious to get away, before I fucked this up irreparably.

"Asher, please."

I turned when I reached the door.

"I can't be here, and not touch you right now, I can't be fair to you. I'm not angry, I promise, not at you. I just need space to calm down."

For the second time in a day, I ran with my fucking tail between my legs, down the hallway, the stairs, and through the kitchen. Straight into Derek.

"Fuck, what's up, boss? Hey, wait up." He followed me as I surged out of the house, half out of my mind.

When I stripped, and shifted, he was doing the same, running with me as I left.

~ *Boss? Talk to me.*

What the fuck? I hadn't opened up to him, to let him mindspeak, but fuck, I was looking at another fucking Alpha, wasn't I? Whether he was in charge of this pack or not, he still had the power there to use.

~ *I'm losing my fucking mind.*

I finally told him, running faster, and charging up the hiking trail, letting my wolf stretch, and trying to burn off the anger flowing through me like fire.

~ *You're not getting away that easy. Look, nobody needs to know we had this chat. You have to talk to someone.*

Derek had caught up with me quite easily, too easily. I should have realised, long before he had to tell me. All the damn signs were there.

~ *I can't be with someone I can't even fucking touch. Everything in me wants to be touching her. All the time. She'd scream if I tried, and she should.*

I slowed down, letting myself enjoy the run a little more, now that I'd burned off a little of what fuelled me.

~ *A day ago she wasn't hanging onto your hand like she'd die without it. You're making progress, boss. She doesn't know that you know exactly what they did to her. Maybe that's eating you up more than you realise.*

And when did he become so fucking smart anyway? It was possible, I supposed.

I headed for the little stream I knew was up ahead, lowering my head down to lap at a few mouthfuls of icy cool water. Then I dropped down with a thud, resting my head on my front paws. I felt like a smacked dog.

~ *Boss, she's staying. For whatever reason, she's choosing to be at the house with you. She's had ample opportunity to leave, so what's keeping her here?* I growled softly.

~ *I think she feels something for me. She doesn't understand it, and neither do I. It could be nothing more than a self defence mechanism kicking in, telling her she's safer with me than not. Maybe she doesn't actually feel anything for me. Maybe she just likes feeling safe.*

Derek hopped into the spring, paddling in the water.

~ Is it so bad if that's how she starts out? The longer she's around, the more time you have to work on her.

I lifted my head, snarling in his direction.

~ She's not a fucking project. She's the woman I'm falling in love with. How would you feel?

He'd lifted his head at my statement, looking back at me from the water.

~ Love, eh? About time you admitted it. Just so you know, I think you were beaten to that realisation by at least three others.

His mouth dropped open, like he was laughing at me.

I growled at him again, my hackles rising. Rage was surging through me, needing to be released. If he pushed me much further, I was going to take him down, hard.

He hopped back up onto the bank, approaching me, watching me with his head tilted.

~ So... how far have you got so far, boss? Touched her tits yet?

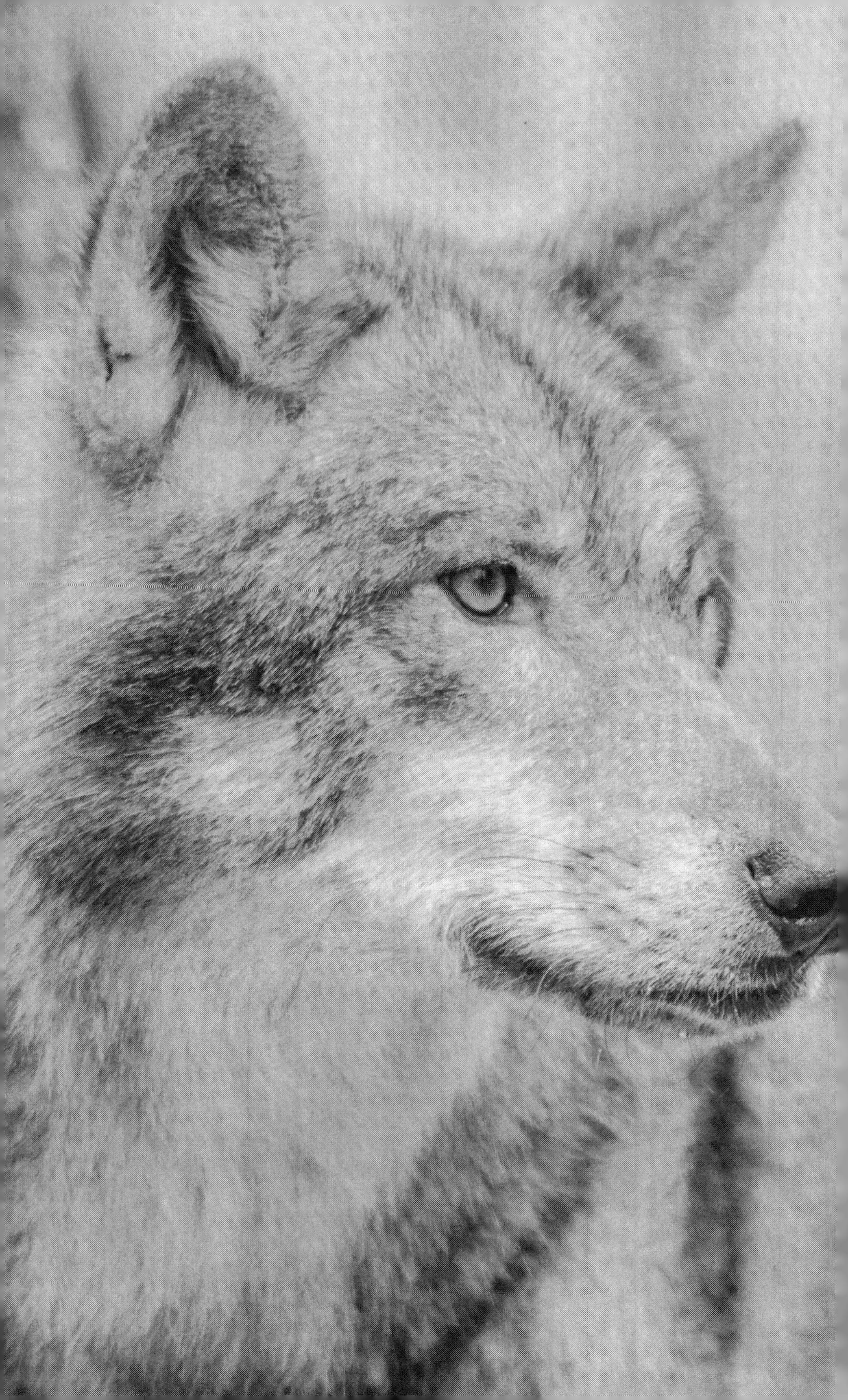

Chapter Twenty-Four

Asher

With a roar, I leapt at him, and knocked him down. What followed was a brutal dogfight that sick people would probably pay to watch.

By the time we'd finished trying to tear each other a new one, we backed away, both limping. His mouth fell open again, still laughing, the bastard.

~ You're welcome.

He said, as he started trotting back toward home. I sighed internally, and followed him. As we reached the pack house, I realised something. Mina was outside, and she was waiting for me, holding clothes in her arms.

I didn't know if they were my shredded ones, or others, but there was nothing strewn around. We both limped warily in her direction, and she stood up from the doorstep.

She looked from one of us to the other.

"My god, what happened? Are you okay?" We both just stared at her, and yet again, I wished I could speak to her in this form.

She fumbled with the clothes in her arms, suddenly revealing two bundles, a pair of sweats and a t-shirt in each hand.

Mina

NOW I WAS FACED with the two wolves, I felt stupid for deciding to wait out here. They both approached slowly, and they were both massive.

I could tell which one was Asher, not just because he was taller, and slightly broader, but because the other wolf was almost black. I had no idea who the other one was, but I held up both pairs of clothes regardless.

I'd found the shredded remains of two sets of clothes on the ground, so I figured Asher had gone running with one of his brothers.

"Sorry, I've got no idea who you are," I spoke to the black wolf. "But I thought you might want these."

He nodded his head, moving forward and gently taking them from me with his mouth. I had the craziest urge to stroke him as he moved past me, but even just lowering my hand a few millimetres wrenched an unholy growl from Asher.

I looked up, feeling nervous, and held up the clothes, as he started toward me. He was limping quite badly. The other one had been too, but he wasn't my problem.

It must have been either Derek or Jase, but I didn't care about them right now, I cared about Asher. Did wolf shifters heal fast, or should I be more worried about his injuries?

He had blood on his face, and his eye looked like it had been clawed at. He reached up for the clothes with his mouth, and I released them.

He stood still, staring at me, then he dropped the clothes on the floor, which confused me. Didn't he like the clothes?

Before I could say anything else, there was a rippling shimmering around him, and then a mistiness, and then he was there before me; naked and unashamed. I gasped, covering my eyes.

"*Mina.*" His voice was gruff, but I couldn't look at him.

"Mina, dammit," he snapped, and I uncovered my eyes; I couldn't help it, because his tone had shocked me. I didn't want to look anywhere except his face, but he'd grabbed the clothes, and was holding them in front of him, so I thankfully couldn't see anything too scary. He pointed to his eye.

"I think I cut my eye, is it bad? If so, I might need to get the doc to stitch it." I walked toward him, stopping close enough to take a look. I did my best to ignore the fact that his naked man parts were literally just a few inches away from me, but if he dropped the clothes, I'd scream.

"I... It looks like it's healing," I said with surprise. The cut seemed to have started to knit together, just since he'd shifted back. He grinned.

"Good, so can you stop looking so worried by our cuts and bruises? We heal pretty quickly if we're in good health." I smiled, relieved that he was okay, but I was also a little cranky about the nudity thing.

"You could have dressed before you asked me to check," I pointed out, and he smirked.

"Yeah, but I'm in a bastard kind of mood, even after handing Derek his ass."

I glanced back at the house, but the other wolf was long gone.

"That was Derek? What happened? You argued?"

He snorted, and I turned back, relieved to see he'd pulled the sweats on, and was half into the t-shirt.

"He can be a prick at times, but he knew I needed to blow off steam, so he provoked me." I looked at his arms, from his wrists to the sleeves of the t-shirt, and they looked unhurt. Wow, if he'd had injuries, they were already gone.

Asher

"MINA, I'M UNHURT. SHALL we go in?" I pointed at the house, and she hesitated.

"What if he's still naked?" I snorted, shaking my head.

"D will be back in his room by now, trust me, but I'll check if you like?" She nodded, so I asked him via Mindspeak.

~ You decent? We want to come in.

~ To my room?

I laughed at how his snarky tone sounded inside my head.

~ Nah, you stay there and finish jacking off. We don't want to see that.

I felt his amusement coming back at me, and I closed the connection again.

"He's in his room, baby. It's just you and me." She nodded again, and took my hand as we headed back inside. I squeezed hers as I tugged her through the door.

I wanted more, and it was agony. I just wanted to pull her against me, and put my lips on hers, and... she'd be horrified. She'd probably scream and run from me, because that'd definitely be too much for her too soon.

"Asher?" I blinked, looking at her after I turned to close the door. I fought to clear my mind of all the things I wanted to do to her, for her.

"*I want to try.*" What? I leaned back against the door, folding my arms, before I put my hands on her.

"What do you want to try?" I asked carefully. She'd better damn well use her words well. No more nods, no more shrugs, I needed exact details.

She spent a few moments, eyes darting around, before she answered. "I don't know." *Fuck.*

I groaned, banging my head back against the door.

"I need something from you, Mina. Guidelines, safety zones, warning zones, something. I can't just guess, or I could hurt you without meaning to." She made a frustrated sound.

"*I don't know, Asher*, I don't know where to start. Before I met you, I'd become used to nobody ever touching me at all, and now there's you... and all of a sudden, I'm not losing my mind at the thought of you touching me. And every time there's an opportunity to hold your hand, I need to, because it makes me feel closer to you. I need to feel closer to you. I feel like you make me stronger, and every minute I'm with you, I feel more... *just more*... I guess. I was weak, I was fragile. I never would have spoken this many words to anyone, even before what happened. You're bringing me out of myself."

I raised my eyebrows at her, my heart thudding in my chest. I'd never heard her say so many words in one go.

"These are all good things, Mina." She nodded, throwing her hands up, frustration filling the air around her.

"Yes, and now I'm impatient, because suddenly just holding your hand doesn't feel like it's enough anymore. And I don't mean for you, I mean for me, and that terrifies me, because what's next? How many more steps before we're naked, and you're wanting to be inside me, and that's when I might really lose it, because despite all of this, I'm damaged. *I'm broken.* I want to be fixed, but I'm afraid that I'd manage a few more steps, and then I'd be at a limit I can't move past, and if that happens, I've just strung you along, and... *Jesus*." She gasped in a choked breath.

"They... they said I'd been a tease... and I really don't want to be a tease." She started to cry, great heaving sobs that broke my heart.

It was agonising to see her in such pain, and be so powerless to help her. I pushed away from the door and approached her.

"If this is too much, just say stop, and I promise I will." I put a hand on her shoulder, and although she flinched, she didn't move or tell me no, so I pushed further. I slid that arm around her, and I pulled her against my chest.

I held her loosely, so she could pull away if she needed to, but instead? She just curled her arms up under her, and leaned into my chest, sobbing away, and letting me hold her.

Finally, because I'm a needy bastard, I brought the other arm around her too, and held her tight.

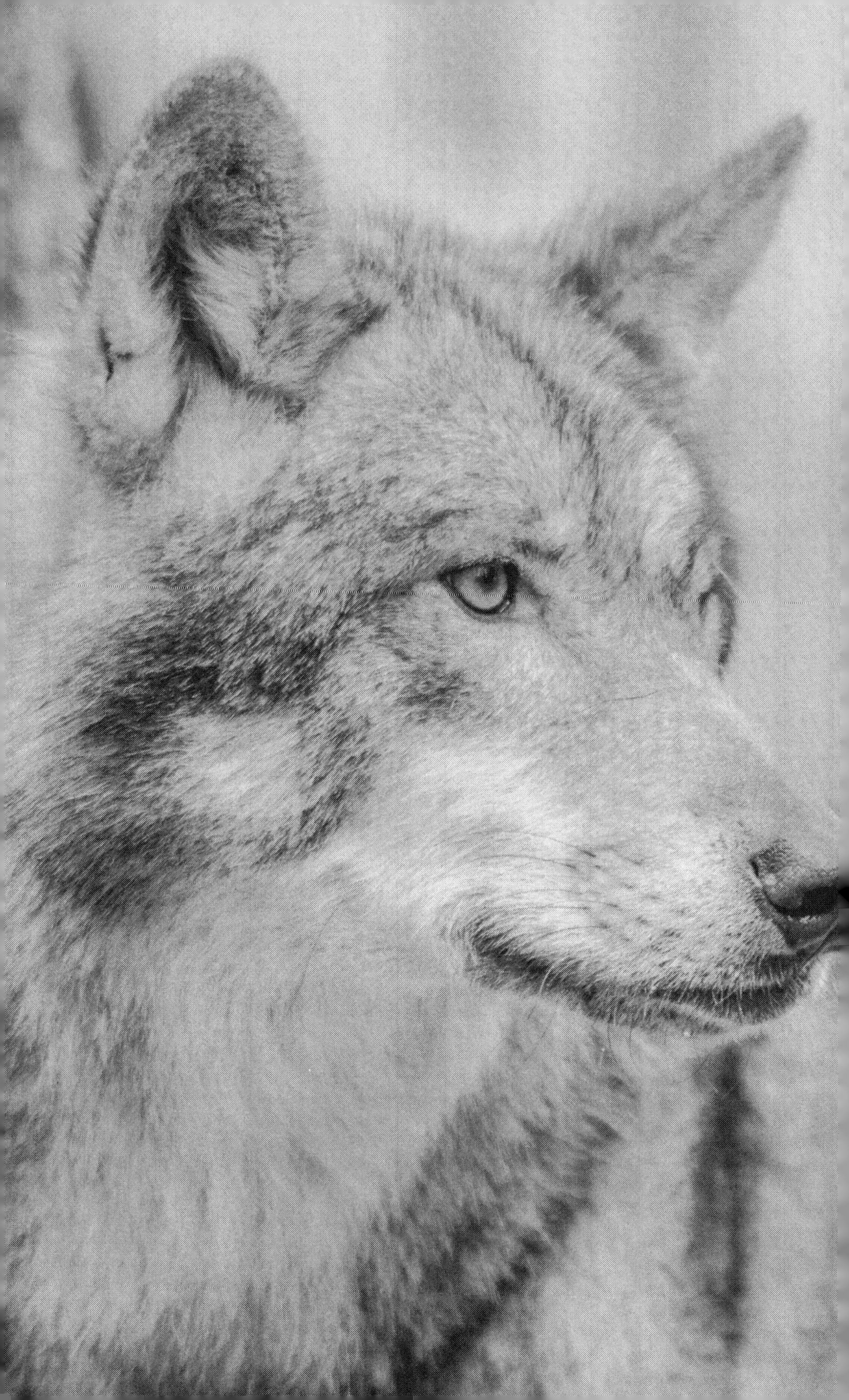

Chapter Twenty-Five

MINA

I WAS AMAZED. After what they did, being crushed against a huge man's chest, with his strong arms holding me there, well, it should be terrifying.

It should be making me scream, and fight, and run. But something about Asher's warmth, and the way I could feel him tempering his strength, so he didn't trap me, it soothed instead of scared.

I'd folded into his chest like a child, and he just went with it. His scent was almost overwhelming from this close. He smelled manly, and earthy, and there was just something about that whole scent that made me feel safe, protected, maybe even loved. We stayed like that for ages.

When I'd finally stopped crying, and could speak, I angled my head up to look at him. I didn't want him to break his hold, because I was terrified that if he did that, I'd be too scared to let him do this a second time. I didn't want to waste a single moment of it.

He was watching me closely.

"Okay?" He asked softly. I nodded, and he frowned.

"Yes," I whispered, and his face relaxed a little.

"You didn't stop me," he said sheepishly.

"I know. For some reason it's comforting, being held by you."

He snorted. *"Well, I've been trying to tell you that for days, but whatever, pretend it's your idea, that's cool."* I giggled. I really liked it when he joked, in fact, I liked most things he did actually.

Oh god, was this how it was supposed to feel? Finding that you like so many little things about a man, and then realise it's love? Was this love? How was I supposed to know if it happened?

I'd never been loved by a man before, and I'd certainly not loved one, apart from my dad, and that was the kind of love you grow up with, so how would I know?

Asher

NOW THAT WE WERE here, and I was finally holding her, I never wanted to let go. It felt incredible, and so inherently right, to be holding her, even soothing my wolf as nothing had before.

As ever, there was a fucking problem though. Now that she wasn't distressed, and she was relaxing, I was getting aroused by her closeness.

Like if this were a normal situation, without the past she'd had, I'd be backing her up against the wall, getting those damn pants off her, and I'd be fucking her hard, while she begged me for more. I groaned, and she frowned.

"Everything okay?" How the fuck did I answer that? *Yeah, of course, baby, just bear in mind that that thing about to poke you is not my fucking gun.* I needed to move, and fast, before she could feel it.

"Asher?" I swallowed hard, meeting her eyes again.

"Look, please don't freak out, and I hate to do this, but if we don't stop this now, you're going to be feeling another part of me very soon. I'm really trying to hold back, but... *fuck*... you're in my arms, and you smell amazing, and my body is as much of a bastard as I seem to be." She gasped, and I released her, letting her step back.

"I'm so fucking sorry," I said, backing away from her. She blinked a few times, then her eyes travelled down my body and... *fuck*... she looked right at it, and it twitched, because I knew she was fucking looking.

She gasped again, and I lifted my hands.

"I'm sorry. I'm only... a man... I don't... I didn't want to scare you, but now I have." I backed away some more, working my way around the furniture, and headed for the stairs.

"Help yourself to something in the kitchen. I'll go and uh, make myself decent." *I ran up the stairs, praying that I wouldn't bump into anyone else, and poke them in the fucking eye with it.*

From my door to the shower, clothes dropped off, until I reached the shower. Under the water, I took my cock in hand, and started pumping it.

I knew it wasn't going to go away from cold water, because it had barely worked last time, and this time she'd been pressed up against me. If she saw this right now though, it'd scare her off for good.

I rested my arm against the back wall, so I could focus my attention on my cock. Sliding my hand from the tip to my balls, back up again.

I started moving my hand faster, trying to get the job done, so I could put him back to bed for a while, and fuck... *it just wouldn't fucking work, it wasn't enough*.

I let go of my dick, pressing my other hand against the wall, head down, breathing hard. Fucking fuck! I just needed to blow my fucking load, and I'd be alright for a while, right? I let out a roar of total frustration.

"Are you okay?" Mina's voice called from the bedroom, *the fucking bedroom*. She was right in there, with the damn door open, and I was in here, trying to wank away my fucking need for her.

"Uh, what are you doing up here?" I called out, sounding more than a little rattled.

"I was worried." I laughed, a bitter barking sound.

"Don't worry, baby, it's not like I haven't done this before." What the fuck? I banged my forehead on the wall. *Idiot*.

"Can I help?" She asked next. What? My hand had just gripped my cock again when she asked that question, and it twitched in response. Her question had my mind in a million places all at once. This could not be fucking happening!

"Doesn't this freak you out?" I yelled desperately, and she was quiet for too fucking long.

"Yes, a little... but the fact that you're in there, rather than forcing it on me... it makes it less scary." *Interesting*, although not likely to help me out of my predicament.

"What if I asked you to touch it right now?" I asked crankily, because this was all kinds of fucked up, and my hard-on wasn't going away while she was so close.

If she gasped, I couldn't hear it over the water.

"Um... I, uh, no, I can't," she finally said. "But, will it help if I'm, I mean, does it help with me here, or should I go away?"

Her voice was closer, and I turned to look at the doorway. The glass shower cubicle was so fogged up that I couldn't see a damn thing, but she sounded close. Too fucking close. Fuck, fuck everything good in me, because I was about to push her again.

"Talk to me, baby, tell me how it felt to have my arms around you." I grasped my cock again. If she wanted to help, then I'd be the bastard I now knew I was, and I'd let her.

She cleared her throat. "Uh, it felt... warm... safe, you feel really strong, and powerful..."

Yes, fucking yes, finally my cock was responding when I stroked it, tingles of fucking pleasure working their way up my spine, and I felt my climax starting to build. Fuck me, at last.

"Yeah, baby, that's good, what else?" I groaned softly as my hand stroked and jerked my cock, each glide feeling like the touch of someone else. *Her*.

"You're so big compared to me, I mean, I feel like you could crush me-" As her words sank in, I caught a sudden change in her scent, and I let out a yell as I blew at last, my hand stopping and resting against the wall again, both holding me up for a moment, because fuck, *what was that?*

Pleasure was still rippling through me in diminishing tingles. I nearly fucking landed on my ass when I came, because it took practically every ounce of strength from my body, dimming the lights as my body shuddered through my release.

"Thank you, baby," I breathed, and she laughed.

"I'm glad I could help." She fell quiet, so I figured she'd moved back away from the door, and that was probably for the best, because I needed to compose myself after whatever the fuck had just happened. I showered, and turned off the water, reaching for a towel.

My hand patted the shelf outside the shower, moving in every damn direction. Oh crap, I'd used them for her feet earlier, hadn't I?

"Everything okay?" Jesus, her voice was still close after all. Had she watched me showering?

"Seems I'm missing a towel," I said finally, embarrassment flooding me.

"Oh, where do I find more." I directed her, and heard her hurry from the room. Could this day get any weirder? I heard her running back, and then a couple of big towels were pressed against my outstretched arm.

"Thanks, Mina, I won't be long." She took the hint this time, and left the room. What the fuck had just happened? She'd gone from terrified of being touched, to willingly being in the room while I was naked, jacking off in the fucking shower.

She'd actually wanted to help and, hell, if I'd ever doubted that we could get past her barriers, I didn't anymore. *She'd been alone in a room with me, while I was naked and aroused, and if that didn't scare her after what she'd been through, maybe there was hope for us both.*

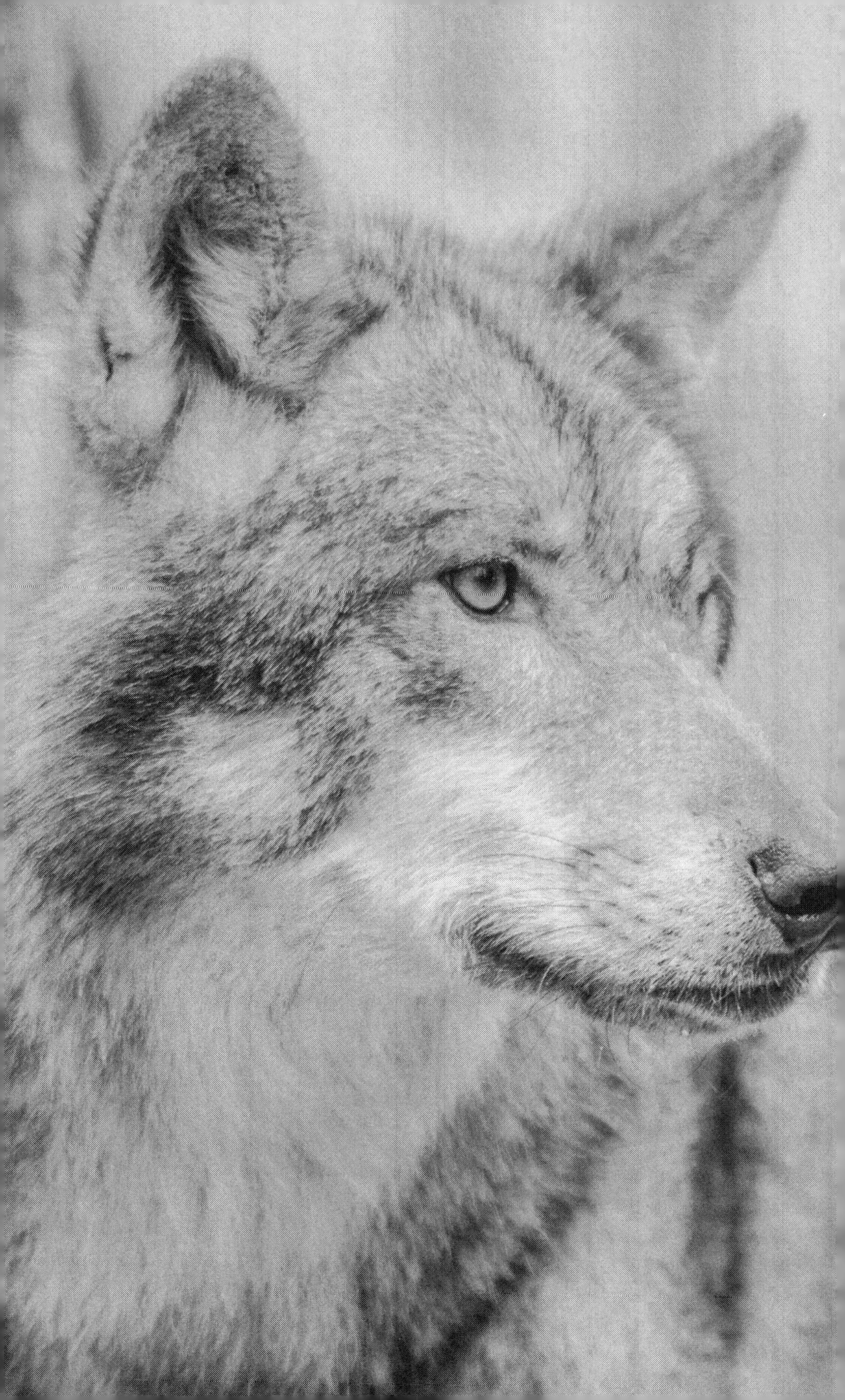

Chapter Twenty-Six

MINA

I DIDN'T KNOW WHAT even possessed me to follow him. When he'd warned me to back away, before he touched me with more of his body than I was ready for, I'd almost stayed in his arms anyway.

It wasn't because I was ready for that, I wasn't, definitely not. Maybe I never would be, but I'd felt so safe in his arms, warm, and protected, and... *it had felt right*.

It wasn't like being touched by *them*. It wasn't the wrong kind of touch, and maybe at last, it was the right hands. Maybe that was why each time we progressed a step, I didn't freak out like I always expected to.

When I reached the bedroom, saw the clothes on the floor, and heard the shower start up, I just couldn't leave. That part of my brain which still seemed to work like a real person's, it had pictured him doing that before, and... *that fascination*... sexual activity without pain or terror, or even having to touch each other, I just wanted to know it could be good.

I wanted to know that pleasure existed; that sex wasn't just about pain, and degradation, and hatred. When he yelled out, even I could tell that it wasn't a good sound, that something was wrong. I'd never seen a man do what he was doing, but it didn't sound like it was going well.

He'd sounded horrified that I was even in the room, and then something had changed. Suddenly my voice seemed to be helping him, and I really wanted to help him. After everything he kept doing for me, couldn't I do this one thing for him, and help him find some release?

The strange thing was how it felt to hear him pleasuring himself like that. The noises he made, they didn't scare me, and they didn't bring back bad memories.

Instead, they reached somewhere inside me. There were parts of me that I'd thought were dead forever, but something had happened in that bathroom.

I felt a warmth inside, a tingle I'd never felt before, and I felt a curious sensation between my legs, one of those parts of my body that I avoided like the plague.

I'd had to clench my thighs together, especially when he made that sound, the one that told me he'd reached it; *his climax*. The relief had been evident in his voice, and that tingle had remained. What was it?

I was confused, and puzzling it over, when his hand started comically blundering around for towels, and I had to go find some.

I sat on the bed, that curious sensation still there, just a light tingle, just a moistness that I'd never felt before. Don't get me wrong, I wasn't a child when I was raped, I was an adult, but one they'd call a late bloomer. I didn't go out partying and clubbing, and I didn't date.

I was just more interested in books, or crafts, than meeting boys. I'd never had that burning urge to explore my sexuality. There was probably a label for people like me, but that inexperience was exactly why I'd been naïve enough to go on a date with a guy I didn't know.

I didn't know what safety measures to take, because I didn't do this stuff, and I didn't have girlfriends who would talk to me about that stuff. I'd been happy in my little cocoon of hobbies, and chasteness, so I didn't tell anyone where I was going that night, because I just didn't know.

Women these days knew better than that. I'd had no sexual urges before the rape, and naturally, after what had happened, it was never going to happen, right? And yet, hearing Asher in the shower, hearing him make himself come, it was like it had opened a door I'd firmly locked.

It should have made me panic, but it didn't. There was something almost thrilling about that fact, because if my body still worked like it would have if not for the attack, then maybe there could be more.

"Uh, hi." Asher looked embarrassed as he stepped into the bedroom, and I blushed. He had a large towel around his waist, and his chest was bare, but he went straight to the dresser for clothes.

"Sorry, I didn't take any clothes in." I stared at his back, as he rummaged for clothes. There were a few scars, like old claw marks, across his left shoulder blade, and even more interesting to me, a tattoo. Across his unmarked shoulder blade, and partway down that side of his back, there was a beautiful wolf tattoo. It was only sketched across his skin in black ink, but it was stunning. I was amazed that I hadn't noticed it before, because he'd been naked in front of me before.

When he turned around, I was smiling.

"I can't believe I never noticed your tattoo before. It's beautiful." He frowned at me, tilting his head.

"I don't have a tattoo, Mina."

"Oh ha ha, very funny, I'm not blind. It's gorgeous." He tried peering over his shoulders.

"I don't have a... *what the fuck?*" He walked into the bathroom, and I got up to follow him. He was turning to try and see it better.

"I swear, I've never seen that before in my life." I could see that he was telling the truth. He really never had that tattoo a day ago, so I hadn't missed it, because it hadn't been there.

I watched him as he scrutinised it in the mirror, his head turned at an awkward angle.

"I wonder how it appeared. Does it hurt?" He laughed, but he was freaked out, I could tell. He was trying to smooth his fingers over it.

"It feels no different. I mean, it's slightly raised, like I can feel the edges, and the lines. I guess it's fairly appropriate, though, right?"

I nodded, stepping a little closer.

"Can I..." He looked at me.

"You want to touch it?" I nodded, and he shrugged, turning so I could reach. I stretched up my hand, pausing for a second before I ran my fingers over the intricate tattoo. Asher's back quivered, and he groaned softly, as I stroked my fingers over his skin.

I could feel the raised edges like he'd mentioned. It genuinely looked like a new tattoo, but how could it just appear like this?

"Uh... Mina? I never want to stop you touching me, but unless you want a repeat of the last twenty minutes, you might need to take a break." He shuddered, and I pulled away.

"Sorry."

He turned to face me, and I kept my eyes firmly on his face.

"Never be sorry, Mina. Your touch is something I never want to be without. I just think you've had your fill of my needs for tonight."

I giggled, feeling oddly carefree.

"Well, unless you stop liking my touch, I'm guessing that's something else I'd have to get used to." He blinked, casting his intense blue green eyes over me.

"You're... you're different. What changed?" I blushed furiously, literally feeling the heat blooming across my cheeks.

"Nothing."

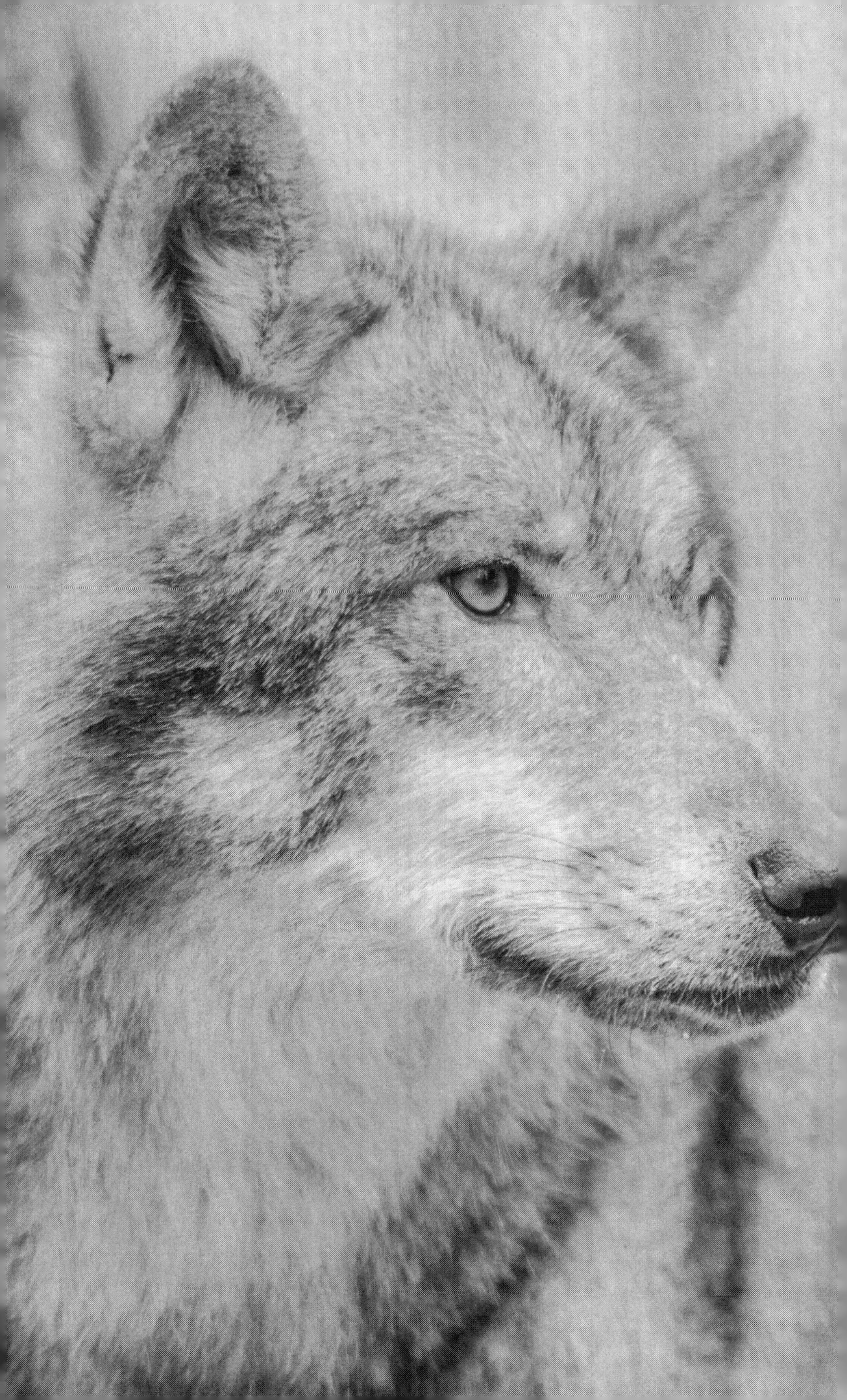

Chapter Twenty-Seven

Asher

Oh yeah, something had fucking changed for sure. She was blushing now? She didn't fucking blush before.

I advanced on her, watching as she backed up a fraction before she stopped, and held her ground. *Interesting.* Something was definitely changing in her, and I fucking loved it.

"How did it feel?" I asked her, and she blinked, confused.

"Kind of raised, like you said."

I shook my head, feeling a smirk on my face.

"How did it feel, being here when I was in the shower?" She blushed again, and it was sexy as fuck.

"Did you like knowing that my cock was hard because of you?"

She gasped, and looked away. Had I pushed her too far? I had a feeling her limits were shifting, and she seemed to respond better to me now when I pushed her a little.

"*Mina.*" She met my eyes again.

"Did you like it? Did it make you feel powerful? Knowing you can reduce me to such a desperate mess?" She chewed her lip, her cheeks scarlet.

"It's okay to say yes to that, Mina." She nodded, so I folded my arms, and stared at her.

"Okay, yes! Are you happy now? Yes, I liked knowing that. I liked hearing you... doing that, and... and knowing that my voice helped you get there."

There was something else; something she wasn't telling me. She didn't need to though, because I had a fucking nose, didn't I? She was *aroused*. Just like in the bathroom, she was fucking aroused.

If I wasn't careful, I'd be back in that shower in a few seconds, because her scent was intoxicating right now. I backed up, forcing myself to stop pushing her for now.

"Right, I guess we should eat." I walked away, leaving her standing there, blushing and awkward. It wasn't the right time to push her for more, but every fucking step away from her was agony.

We ate alone, because I told the boys if they showed while we were there, I'd put them on toilet duty, as if that was even a thing. I did leave them each a plate in the warmer though, before we went straight back to the bedroom.

I suggested we modify our sleeping arrangement, and she sort of closed up, her confidence melting away. Fuck, too much, or maybe I'd left things too long after she'd been opening up.

I held my hands up. "All I was going to suggest was that one of us takes the other room, Mina. I'm not pushing for *that*. Jesus, not a monster, remember?" She let out a ragged breath.

"I can sleep on the sofa." I folded my arms, glaring at her.

"I think we've already had that discussion, baby, I just can't sleep on it again tonight. I'm a little sore from the fight." I wasn't, but I was a bastard. I just didn't want to pretzel myself onto that fucking thing for another whole night.

She had a guilty look on her face, her eyes dropping from mine.

"I shouldn't have made you sleep on it last night."

"You didn't," I pointed out gently. "Look, it's not even time to sleep yet, so why don't we sit on the bed and chat for a while. I want you to feel like you can tell me anything."

Yes I did, and I really wanted her to tell me that it had turned her on, watching me jerk off in the shower, even though I knew I should leave it. For now, at least. I should let her get used to that feeling, and try to build on it, but, I had a feeling that the tattoo was part of the whole mate bond thing, and I didn't know if that appearance of the tattoo was a good thing or not.

Was it working? Was it a warning? My wolf seemed pretty content, so maybe it was just part of the process. I figured I'd check with the boys in the morning, because as a non-believer, I'd never even looked into it before. While we had a couple of mated wolves in the pack, I wasn't aware of whether they had these tattoos, but I'd never really looked, had I?

Once we sat down, we fell silent. I didn't know whether to keep pushing her on the earlier incident, or go back to safer topics, and give her a break. My knowledge on dealing with someone with serious anxiety was far too limited for my liking. I felt like I was failing her every time I blundered in with my pathetic attempts to talk to her, to interact with her.

"Do you have any other tattoos?" She suddenly asked, and I laughed.

"If you want to see the rest of my body, I'll happily show you, baby."

She giggled, rather than looking nervous.

"I'm just making conversation, because you seem distracted." I looked at her, turning to sit cross-legged, facing her.

"Do *you* have any tattoos?" I asked, raising an eyebrow. She shook her head, a sad sigh filling the air.

"I wanted one, you know, before... but now the thought of someone touching me, a stranger, it's just another thing I won't be able to do." I wanted, for the millionth time, to kill the bastards who destroyed everything she ever wanted. Waiting for that day was almost as agonising as her pain, and her fear.

"Maybe one day you'll feel ready. Maybe if I'm there, to lend my strength?" She shrugged, but she wasn't hiding from my eyes.

"Maybe. Maybe I'll only ever be able to bear you touching me. So if that's the case, maybe you should learn to tattoo."

I laughed, shaking my head at her. "Yeah, you don't want stick figures, but we'll shelve that idea for another day. Is there anything else you want to try?"

"Try?" She turned to face me, mirroring my position, and I nodded.

"Is this some way of getting me to let you touch me again?"

I grinned like the dog I was. *"Always."*

She laughed, and again I was stunned. What had changed in a day, that had opened her up in this way?

"What did you have in mind?" *The fuck?*

I quirked a brow, trying not to show my surprise.

"Okay, I'm guessing certain areas are off limits for a while yet, but so far I've touched your hands, your feet, your ankles, and I've had my arms around your shoulders and back. Is there anywhere you'd like me to touch you? Anywhere you want to feel my fingers caressing? Stroking? *Teasing?*"

She blushed, and I caught it again; the hint of a scent. *Arousal.* Yes, this was what we needed to build upon. If I could encourage her to feel that, then I could hopefully break down the other walls too. She deserved to be fucking worshipped, if I could just make her feel safe enough with me.

"Mina, I'm waiting for an answer," I prompted. Her eyes were darting around, and that usually meant she knew exactly what she wanted to say, but didn't know how, so I figured it was time to change things up.

"Okay, how about this? I'll give you my hand, and you put it where you want it."

She gasped, and then giggled. "Really?"

I shrugged. "I'm running out of ideas here, baby. If you put my hand where you want to feel my touch, we can go from there. Otherwise, I'm just going to risk picking somewhere at random, and you're going to have to wonder where."

She shook her head firmly. "No, that option is too scary." I grinned at that brief flash of fire in her eyes.

"That's what I thought." I wriggled a little closer, so that our knees were almost touching, because then my arm would be easier for her to move. I rested it on my knee.

"Do you want me to close my eyes?" She grinned and nodded.

I closed them instantly, because I'd do anything for her, even though I wanted to see her reaction as she let me touch her. Her fingers, when they suddenly landed on my wrist, made me jump, because she'd been more eager than I'd imagined.

I thought she'd delay for longer than half a damn second. She didn't pick up my hand though; instead she stroked my wrist, and slid her hand further up my arm. Her fingers trailed over my skin, and left tingles as they moved. I never wanted her to stop touching me.

"Fuck," I breathed, fighting to keep my eyes closed. Her hand halted, resting on my skin.

"Don't stop, please." She started moving again, and I could feel her leaning closer, so she could slide her hand further up, to my bicep. I tensed it, and she giggled, smoothing her hand around my upper arm.

"I can't believe how safe I feel this close to you, touching you." I sucked in a breath, as pleasure rippled through me, not for the first time.

"Might not say that in a minute," I murmured, and she stopped.

"Oh. Do you want me to stop?" *Fuck no, never.*

"Probably best right now." She pulled back, and I opened my eyes.

"Your touch drives me wild, Mina, I've never lied to you about that. I wasn't prepared for you to start touching me just then though. I thought you were going to put my hand on you."

She swallowed, casting her eyes over me.

"I was more interested in your body than mine." I smiled.

"I'm honoured, I really am, but you need to learn to love your body again, or maybe for the first time. I can help you with that, Mina, I can make every touch a pleasure. I could give you pleasure... like you did for me." The deliciously sweet scent of her arousal reached me again, even though she was shaking her head slowly.

"I can't." I watched her closely. Perhaps it was time for another gentle nudge.

"I think you want to, but that scares you."

She blinked. "I, no..."

I leaned my elbows on my knees.

"I think that you like the idea of feeling pleasure, Mina. I think that you like the idea of me giving you pleasure, like you gave me. I think you're just afraid of what comes next."

Her hands were trembling again, and I sighed, leaning back.

"This is too much. Jesus, I'm sorry. It's just... I know you liked watching me, and I know you felt something. Whether you'll admit to it or not, I know it aroused you, and you're enjoying touching me. Maybe because you think you might make it happen again. Just tell me what you want, and I'll do it, and if what you want is for me to fuck off and leave you in peace, I'll go as far as the bedroom next door. No further."

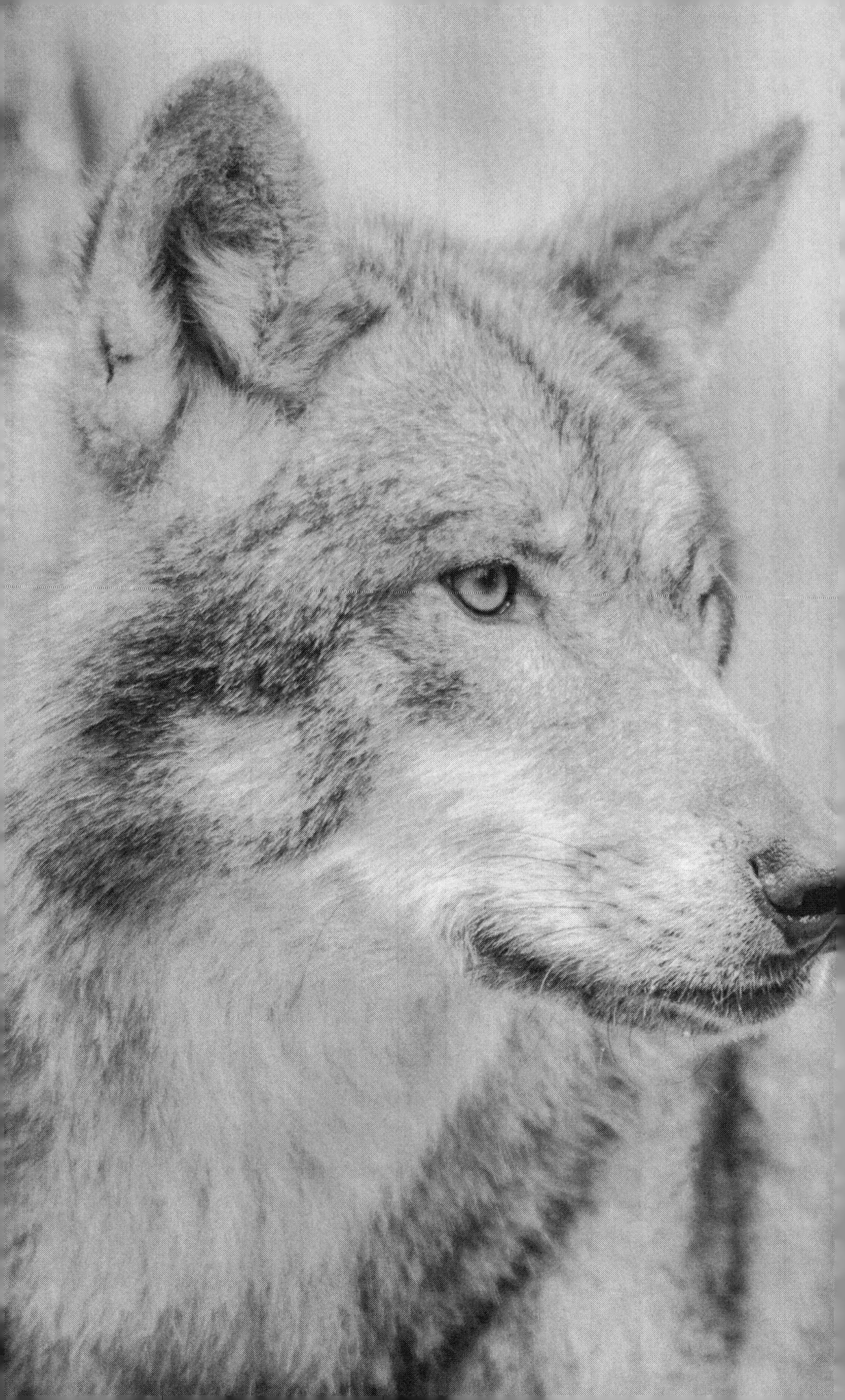

Chapter Twenty-Eight

MINA

I HAD ENJOYED TOUCHING him. His skin was warm, and smooth, and it made me feel calm, but also strong, powerful, and I wanted to keep doing it, but if it made him aroused, could I be brave enough to stay, or would I run?

I chewed at my lip. The damn thing was practically raw by now, so I released it, and Asher tutted.

"You gotta stop mauling that poor thing." He reached toward my face, and then caught himself, and I sighed.

"It's fine."

"It doesn't look fine. It's bleeding again." I shook my head slowly, gathering up my courage.

"I mean, you stopped yourself before you touched my face, but I want you to." He blinked, obviously not expecting that.

"You want me to." Suddenly it was all I wanted; his touch against my skin, even just a fleeting moment of it.

"Please."

He smiled, lifting his hand again, and brushing the backs of his fingers against my cheek, the lightest brush of skin on mine. I shivered, and he stopped.

"Too much?" I shook my head rapidly.

"It's nice."

He smiled again. "Good, because I never want you to be scared of me, or my touch, Mina. I want you to want it, need it, yearn for it. *I mean, begging is fine too, of course.*"

I started giggling, because he had a talent for making me laugh at intense times, and that helped so much. He was better at this stuff than he probably even realised.

He continued stroking my cheek, then trailed his fingers down the side of my face, to my neck. As his touch moved down my neck, I flinched, and he stopped again.

"Limit?" I nodded jerkily.

"Okay, moving on." He moved back to my cheek, then angled his hand to brush a thumb lightly across my lips. *Oh*.

He was watching me, catching every intake of breath, every tremble, waiting for me to break, and I didn't. Eventually he pulled back, and just stared at me.

"You're amazing, look at you."

Asher

I'D PUSHED THINGS FAR enough for tonight. We'd progressed miles in one day, and she was opening up like I never thought she would, but I needed to give her a break now.

I'd take the other room, and let her sleep, and tomorrow we could see how she felt when she woke up. She might wake up a different person, and we might have to go back a few steps, but I wouldn't know until then.

"I'm going to hit the sack, Mina. It's been a busy day," I said, pulling back, and moving up from the bed. Her eyes never left mine.

"Why?"

"Like I said, I'm tired. I should be working tomorrow, but... wait, do you work Mondays?" She shook her head. Good, neither would I. The way I'd been messing up on Friday, I was probably best away from work for a few days anyway. The guys said they had things under control, after all.

"Wait." I turned when I reached the door, and she was standing.

"You need something before I go?" She nodded, taking a tentative step closer.

"Do I have to guess what it is?" She stared at me, like she would have preferred me to guess, so she didn't have to voice what she wanted.

"Downstairs, when you put your arm around me... *that was nice.*"

I grinned widely, feeling like a fucking king.

"Baby wants a bedtime hug? Well, come on in then." I held out my arms, welcoming her to take the step and come to me, *and she fucking did*.

She stepped up and leaned against my chest, and I wrapped my arms around her, like I never wanted to let go.

Now, obviously, I was going to need yet another shower wank before I could sleep, but it was worth it, because *she came to me*. It was hard leaving but I did it, because, well, for obvious reasons, but also because she needed some space to absorb everything that had happened today.

Going into that other room was strange, because I'd never slept in any other room since becoming Alpha. I showered, jerked off while replaying our moments together in my head, and climbed into that bed. At least I could sleep naked for the night. Clothes had a tendency to bundle up when you move in bed, and it was fucking annoying.

Sleep didn't want to come though, and for ages I lay there, running through the day in my mind. So much had changed in such a short period of time, but I wasn't dumb enough, or arrogant enough, to think we'd keep up that pace, or that we wouldn't hit more bumps in the road.

I finally fell asleep, and so when someone knocked on the door, and woke me, I was initially fucking furious.

"What!" I may have barked at whoever was out there. Silence.

"Who's there?" I swear if that door hadn't started to open then, I'd have been over there, pulling it back to punch whoever was out there.

Mina poked her face into the room, and she looked upset.

"Did I wake you?" All of my anger faded in a split second, and I rubbed at my face groggily.

"Nope, I'm up."

"Liar." She stepped into the room, and I instantly noticed that she was wearing a t-shirt and some shorts. Well look at that, she had legs, and I could actually see them. She usually wore long trousers, so I was seeing them for the first damn time.

"What's wrong?" I asked her, and she lowered her eyes.

"Can I sleep here?" I was beyond confused at this point.

"You don't like my room?" She came closer.

"It's not that, I just... I don't... can't be alone right now." *Oh.* I sat up, gesturing her over, then held up my hand as I realised my mistake.

"Wait. *Shit.* You can't get in here with me."

She just stood there, blinking at me, looking lost and fucking confused.

"I thought, I..." *Fuck.*

"You're not getting it, baby. I didn't know you'd come in here, so I'm not wearing any clothes under this sheet. You don't want to be this close to a naked man, not yet."

Unbelievably, she wasn't freaking out.

"I could sleep on top of the covers." Who the hell was she?

"Mina, what's going on? You've been pretty adamant that you're not ready to share a bed, so talk to me."

She was standing right against the bed now, and I could see that her damn hands were shaking.

"You had a nightmare again." She nodded, tears filling her eyes.

"I can't be alone. Every time I wake up from one and I'm alone, I'm too scared to move for hours, because I don't know if it was real, and they're there in the shadows, waiting for me. Even in your room alone in the dark, I knew I wasn't safe. It took me nearly an hour to be brave enough to come and find you."

Fuck.

I reached for her, and then stopped again, even though she'd moved onto one knee on the bed.

"*I'm naked, Mina,*" I hissed desperately, and she shook her head.

"I don't care. Please, Asher, I need your arms."

I fell back and held my arms out, and she crawled up and into my arms. She sighed with relief when my arms locked around her, holding her against my chest. My poor girl was shivering.

"Cold?" She shook her head.

"Scared." I groaned, or was it a growl?

"I'm not going to do anything to you, baby."

She lifted her head to look at me.

"I know. I mean, I came to you because I was scared, and I knew you'd make me feel safe again."

Wow, I felt like she'd just given me everything.

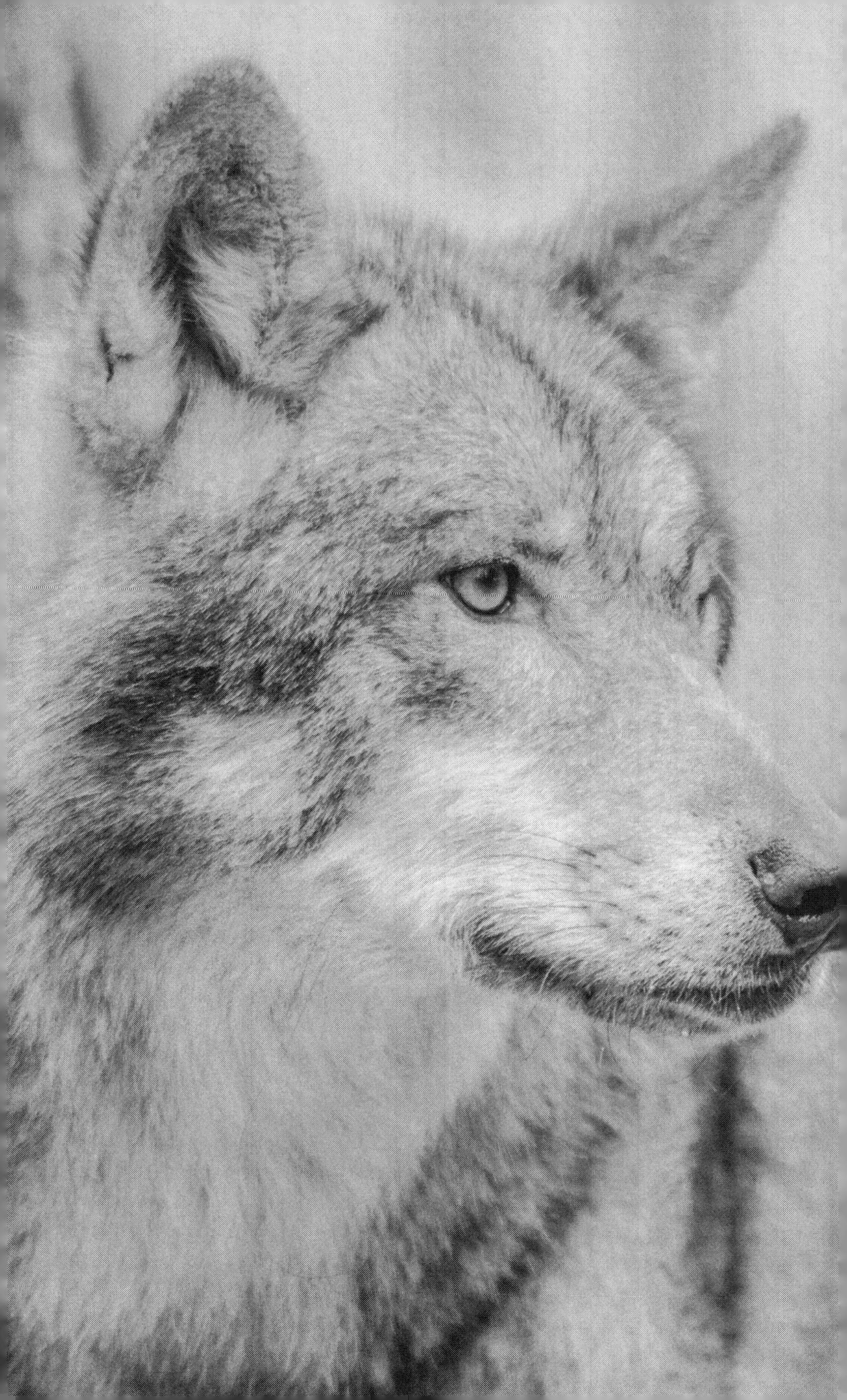

Chapter Twenty-Nine

MINA

I WOKE UP IN his arms, *Asher's arms*, and I didn't panic. We'd shifted in our sleep, so that he was draped slightly over me, but it felt right. *Safe.*

His face was just beside mine on the pillow, and with him asleep, I could admire him without him being awake, and anything meaning anything. He looked so peaceful when he slept. His lashes were long, and his hair, which just looked a dark blond from a distance, had streaks of several colours running through it; his beard too.

His lips were full and smiling as he slept. I lifted my eyes back to his, and they were open, after all. I gasped, and he just made shhhh sound, soothing my brief panic.

Neither of us moved, for maybe a minute or so, both unwilling to break the spell. Eventually I tried to extricate myself from his arms, at the same time that he tried to move them to free me, and the result was my hand brushing another part of him entirely.

He hissed in a breath and rolled fully onto his back, and when I glanced down, I could see the sheet tented over his waist. I'd brushed against it, against his hard... *thing*. I scrambled back, my eyes darting back up to see a guilty look on his face.

"I'm sorry."

I nodded rapidly. "I- I didn't mean to."

He snorted. "It happens most mornings, fuck... I didn't mean to scare you."

I'd pulled myself up to sit against the headboard, but I couldn't not look at it, and he was watching me as I stared.

"I understand if you need to get out." I looked at his face again, and he'd tucked his hands behind his head, looking perfectly at ease. Strangely, it helped me to feel a little calmer.

"Is it uncomfortable?" I asked, because I'd never had moments like this, or someone to talk to about it, not with what had happened.

He snorted again, grinning at me.

"Yeah, the longer it's like that, the more frustrating it becomes. I'll go shower though and hey presto... it'll hopefully be gone when I come back. You might want to avert your eyes when I get up though. I *am* nude, after all." I hadn't forgotten that fact, not for a moment, but I shook my head.

"You *want* to watch me walk across the room naked?" He looked stunned, and kind of proud.

I shook my head again, and he stared at me for a moment, eyebrows raising at me when I didn't respond.

"So what *do* you want, Mina?"

I didn't know how to put it into words. What was wrong with me, that I had this fascination with him, with his body? It should terrify me, because it could all turn so bad so quickly.

I twisted my hands together, staring at him, wanting him to pull it from my mind, like he seemed to do so often. *Don't make me say it, please...*

A slow grin crept across his face.

"Why don't I suggest things, and you nod if that's what you want?" I nodded, and he grinned wider.

"You want to watch me in the shower again?" I shook my head, and he grinned again.

"You want to touch it?" I shook my head vehemently this time, and he laughed.

"You want to watch me make myself come right here, right now?" There it was, but I hesitated, and he laughed.

"Mina?" I nodded, feeling my cheeks heating again.

"And now in words?" Dammit, he knew I couldn't.

"Mina, I want you to say yes to this, if you want me to do it."

I took a deep breath, and the word came out on the exhale.

"*Yes.*"

Asher

I HAD NO IDEA what fucking game she was playing, or if this was some kind of personal challenge for her, but it was on now.

Somewhere along the line, she'd turned a corner, and if this was what she wanted to see, she'd get a show alright. I just hoped it wouldn't scare her off.

Before I threw the sheet back, I gave her an out.

"If this gets too much, say stop, okay? I'll stop, and I'll go deal with it out there. Or, well, I'll at least pause long enough for you to run back to my room. Okay?" She nodded.

"*No*. No nodding, Mina, I want words. *Yes, Asher, I understand*," I prompted.

She swallowed hard.

"I... Yes, I understand. Please, Asher." I grinned with delight.

"I love it when you say *please*, baby."

I kept my eyes on her as I grabbed the sheet and tossed it aside, baring my naked, aroused body to her. Her gasp genuinely wasn't one of horror, in fact, I think it was excitement?

"Is it scary?" I asked her, and she nodded, and then groaned.

"A little. It's... it looks so big."

I grinned again. "Baby, you say all the right things. Okay, I want your eyes on me the whole time. If you can't look there, you look at my face, okay?" She sighed, but it was breathier than normal.

"Yes, I mean, okay."

Yes!

I wrapped my fist around my cock, palming it tightly and fuck, with her eyes on me, it felt like she was the one touching me. I couldn't hold back a groan of pure pleasure. She was watching avidly, that lip between her teeth again.

I slid my hand up my length, brushing my thumb across the tip, and then I started up a lazy tease of my own fucking cock, because I wanted to drag out this experience of her watching me jerk myself off.

This wasn't impersonal like in the shower, this was her sitting on the same fucking bed, a few feet away from my erect cock, and she wanted to watch me make myself come. *It was intimacy, pure and simple.*

Around the time that I switched from dragging it out, to full-on jerking my cock, I realised she'd leaned closer. I caught her gaze.

"Want to take over?" She gasped, but she shook her head. A few more strokes and I'd be there, I could feel I was getting ready to blow… what I didn't count on was her hand.

Suddenly her hand touched my shoulder, and she gripped it, her nails digging in, and *fuuuuck*, I came hard, jerking a few more times for good measure, as I coated my stomach with my cum, shuddering as pleasure blew through me in waves.

She was breathing hard, and that scent was back. Oh yeah, she enjoyed the show alright. She was still holding onto my shoulder, and damn, those nails were still digging into my skin, delicious bites of pain.

"Was that good, baby?" I asked softly, not wanting to spook her. Her eyes were wide when she finally looked me in the eye, her nails still digging deep.

"I feel strange." She was still breathing in little gasps, and that smell of her arousal was so strong, *fuck*, I just wanted to make her come as hard as I just did. Was she ready for that, though?

"Baby, you're turned on, and it's perfectly normal." She let out a shaky breath, hell they were all shaky breaths. *My baby was horny as fuck.*

"I don't… I haven't…"

I didn't want to move; in case I scared her away.

"Baby, it's exactly how you should feel, because you saw me experience pleasure, and now your body wants the same."

"No," she murmured, shaking her head slowly.

"*Yes*. That doesn't mean that you have to do anything, but if you want to know how it feels, I can help." She was trembling.

"I… I don't know…"

I rolled toward her a little more.

"Mina, I can make you come so hard, you'll see fucking stars, but I'd need to touch you, or I could show you how to make yourself come."

She was on the edge; I could see it. She wanted it, she wanted to feel something good, and fuck, didn't she deserve to?

I pushed myself up, seating myself against the headboard.

"Baby, you don't need to suffer. You can feel good too, it's how it should be." She had taken her hand back, but now it was pressed against her mouth.

"I... I can't," she mumbled, and I sighed, wishing I could just show her what she should have always known; pure blissful pleasure, gifted by the hands of the man she was meant for.

"You saw how good it made me feel, Mina, don't you want to feel that too?" She nodded, *she fucking nodded.*

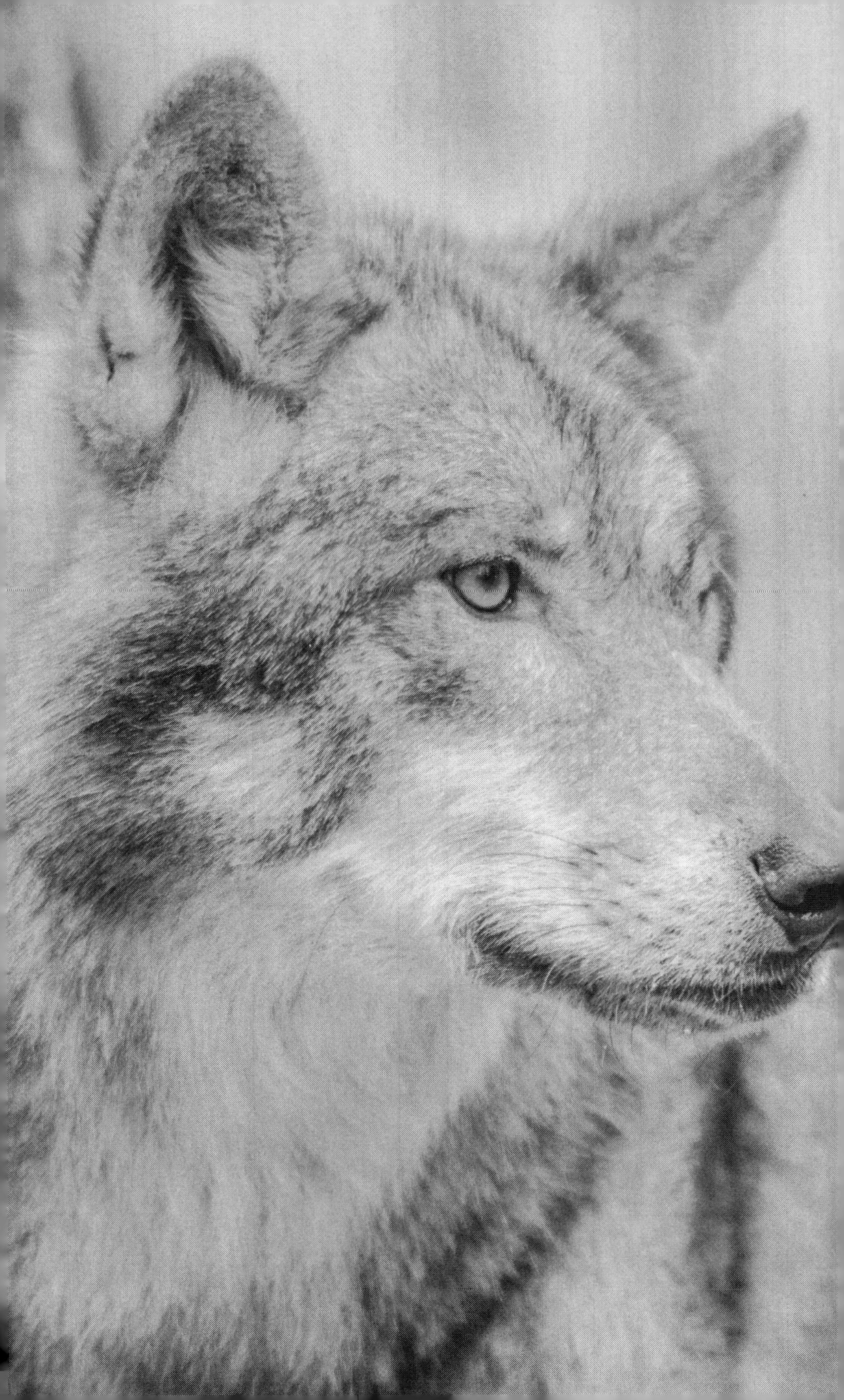

Chapter Thirty

MINA

He kept asking, and asking, and that feeling that I had before, it was back. That tingle, which started when he first started stroking his hand up and down, had intensified as I watched him speed up his movements, as his breathing had sped up too.

His back had tensed as he grew closer to that edge, and I couldn't help it. I crept closer, so entranced was I with his motions, and his pleasure, that I couldn't stop myself touching him, and when I tightened my hand on his shoulder, it went off!

It was like nothing I'd seen before; his back arched up off the bed, his head pressing back into the pillow, a blissful look on his face. It was... beautiful.

"Are you sure?" He was speaking to me again, and I looked at him, feeling like we were on the edge of something huge.

"It won't hurt?"

He shook his head, offering me a sad smile.

"It'll only feel good, I promise."

"How... what..." I had no idea what I was trying to ask him, but he smiled at my attempts.

"Just follow my lead, baby, will you feel safe if you lay down on the bed on your back?" My heart thudded in my chest, and I took a deep breath to calm myself, then I nodded. *I could do this, right?*

"Then do it," he said softly, and I moved almost on autopilot, laying back on the bed. My heart was beating faster, but that sensation... that arousal, he called it... that had intensified. He was watching my face, a gentle smile on his.

"Okay, we can do this one of two ways, Mina, your choice." I looked up at him, feeling a tingle just from the way he looked at me.

"I can use my fingers, *or my mouth*." I gasped. His mouth? His mouth, there? I shook my head fast, unable to even imagine that.

"No to both? Or just one? Words, Mina, please."

"F... fingers..."

"You don't want me to use my fingers?" I shuddered, shaking my head again.

"Please, your fingers... *not your mouth*..." He sighed, almost looking disappointed. Did he really want to put his mouth there?

"You got it, baby, do you want to push your shorts down, or should I?" He was kneeling beside me now, still naked, but it didn't scare me. Why didn't it scare me?

"Mina, baby, do it or ask me to. It's your choice, remember? Always your choice." Was I really brave enough to do this?

After what had happened, this... this was like exposing the one part of me that made me truly vulnerable again. Of course, they hadn't asked, they just took, but he kept asking. He was putting the decision in my hands, and that made it easier, somehow.

I nodded at him, and he frowned, so I reached down and grabbed the waist of my shorts, hesitating for a moment, steeling myself. I closed my eyes, and pushed them down, shimmying so they moved down to my thighs. He made a low growling noise, and my eyes popped open again.

He reached down, pushing them a little further, being careful not to touch my skin. Then he kept sliding them, until they were completely off, and I was naked from the waist down. *No!*

My breathing started to hitch, catching in my throat, and he looked at me, concern flooding those intense eyes of his.

"*Breathe*, this stops any time you want it to, Mina. Only pleasure, I promise." I didn't want it to stop, I really didn't.

I could feel a full panic attack was just there, like I was on the edge, but dammit, I wanted to feel what he'd felt. *That look of bliss on his face; I wanted that bliss, and couldn't I have that, just once?* He placed just a finger lightly on my knee, and my whole body jerked.

"It's okay, just relax." I breathed in and out, as slowly as I could, but now that I was exposed like this, I felt less safe. I felt prone, and vulnerable. He tutted, and I looked at him.

"I don't want you scrunched up like that, with your eyes squeezed shut, like I'm about to hurt you. This is supposed to be a good experience, but if you're truly not ready, Mina, we shouldn't push you." He looked serious, and worried, and suddenly the idea of him stopping caused me far more fear than the idea of being touched by him.

"Please, I need... I need to feel..." He chuckled in response.

"Oh, you're gonna feel." His finger trailed up my thigh, slow and deliberate, but his eyes were on my face every few seconds. Every now and then he'd stop, and raise his eyebrows, and I had to nod before he moved further.

He'd settled himself on his side, his head propped up on one arm, so he could watch me, and that put his head near mine. His finger reached the panic zone, and I made a noise, not one I'd heard from myself before. I wasn't even sure it *was* panic, at this point.

"Shhhh, you're safe, baby. This is where it gets really, really good." I fixed my eyes on him, trying not to freak out and stop him.

"Don't hurt me, please."

His eyes were sad. "I will never do that. Just relax, Mina, and enjoy the sensations. *Trust me.*"

His fingers settled in place, over the front of the forbidden area, and something zinged through me. I knew the names for all of my parts, but naming them made it all real, and scary.

His fingers moved, and it made me gasp. He chuckled, as his fingers started to massage, and tease, and my body started to tremble, and warm up. I could feel so many things all at once. His fingers slipped down, into the crease between my legs... that really forbidden spot, and my legs... *they moved*... they made room!?

He grinned widely, nodding at me.

"*Good girl*, see? Nothing to be afraid of, it's all good. I just have to see if I can bring a little moisture up here, so I don't make you sore." He slid his fingers in that crease, and I felt them slide, because there was wetness there. Was that a good thing? I looked at him to see his reaction.

"See? Your body wants this, and it knows what to do. This wetness here tells me you're ready, your body wants the pleasure, baby, so let's just see about sending you over that edge, shall we?"

His fingers moved again and circled, more easily now that there was moisture making his fingers slip and slide. My legs jerked and quivered, as warmth and urgency started to build up inside me. Asher kept circling and rubbing, pressing down, and then doing it all again, and my body was reacting to it.

I reached my hand down just to find something to grip, and ended up with a handful of the bedding. My body kept flexing and writhing involuntarily, and there were tingles starting to emanate throughout my body. It was exciting, and almost scary in its intensity, but I wanted more.

"Oh god..." I gasped, and he chuckled, a low, dark sound.

"Yeah, baby, ride that wave, and let my fingers get you there." He was leaning closer to me now, watching my face as I trembled and gasped, and pulled at the bedding in my hand.

Other noises had started coming out of me, my gasps now sounded more like whimpers, or moans. Ripples of something wonderful were tingling every nerve ending at each touch of his knowing fingers.

"Good... you're amazing, baby, let's get you to come now." My god, that wasn't even it yet? What the...

My body erupted, my back arching, as a garbled scream came out of me, and everything was set alight. Literally no part of my body missed out on this joyous feeling of pleasure and wellbeing crashing over me in waves. His fingers slowed down, lazily teasing me now.

His eyes were heavy looking, and he kept looking at my lips.

"How are you doing now?" He was grinning, and I stared at him, his face slightly hazy, while I gasped for air.

"I... I... wow..." I had no words. My body was still tingling when he pulled his fingers away, and I watched as he lifted them to his lips, and slipped them into his mouth. It shocked and confused me, even while my body still tingled with little tremors of residual pleasure. It was incredible, magical. Was that was it was supposed to be like?

"What are you doing?" I asked him, my voice mostly a whisper. As he released his fingers, he showed me a wide grin.

"Proving to myself that I was right."

"About what?"

"How fucking amazing you taste."

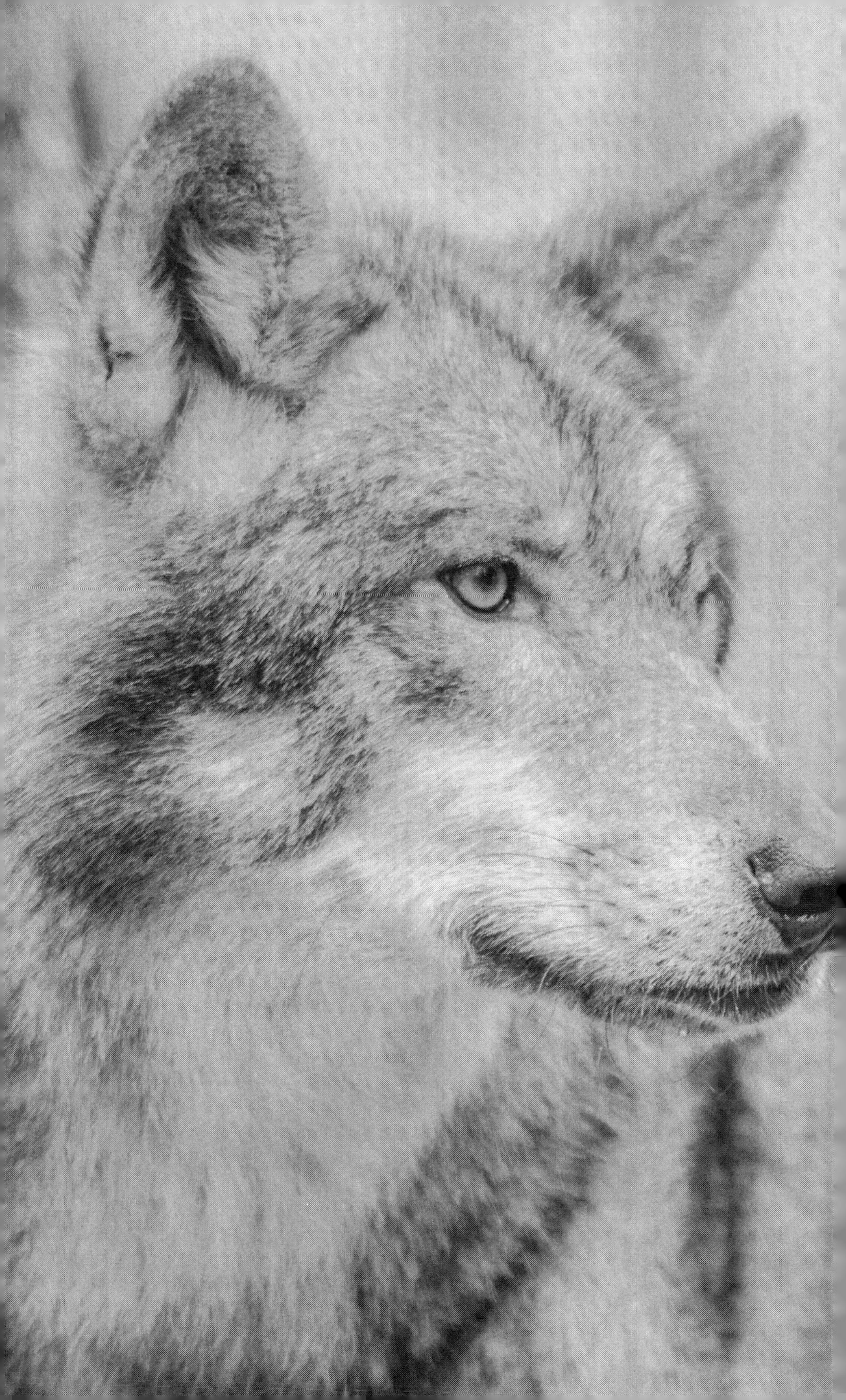

Chapter Thirty-One

ASHER

Amazing turned to crap, a few short seconds later. First she started to tremble, her breathing hitching, and gasping, and then she suddenly curled into a ball, facing away from me, sobs gushing out of her, like her heart was breaking. *What the fuck?*

I knew that touching her would be the wrong thing right now, so I pulled the sheet up and around her, giving her back that shield, between her nakedness and everything else.

I grabbed my sweats from beside the bed and slipped them on, hiding my cock from her, because I could sense the fear. She'd let go, and I think it had loosened her hold on all of the bad shit she'd been holding in. *Fuck.* I should have seen this coming. Did I just break her?

"*Mina.*" I moved around to crouch in front of her, at her side of the bed. Her eyes were squeezed closed as she sobbed, and I ached to hold her, to pull her into my lap and cradle her in my arms, until she felt safe again.

"Fuck, I'm so sorry," I said, at a loss for anything else to say, but she shook her head.

"Not... you..." she gasped out, her voice hiccupping a little.

I needed help, because I was close to losing my shit here. If I'd hurt her, if I'd pushed her too fast, I needed to fix it, or at least try.

~ D? You awake? I need help with Mina.

As soon as I thought the message to him, I asked myself two questions; why him? Okay, that was one, but my point was twofold; he wasn't my Beta, Jase should be my go-to, and more importantly, he was a fucking guy. Another guy.

~ Scratch that. Can you get Daisy here asap? Mina needs her.

~ On it, boss.

Of course, I could have just spoken directly to her, but this way followed protocol, and would be faster, because I needed to focus on Mina right now, and Daisy would have questions.

"Mina, I'm gonna get Daisy to come and see you, okay?" She opened her eyes, her tears soaking the pillow.

"Daisy?" I nodded, wishing I could do something to help her myself.

"What else can I do? Anything you want." She shook her head, fixing her teary eyes on me.

"Just don't go." Thank fuck for that.

"Wasn't planning on it. I need to get you some water though, but I'll only be in there." I pointed at the bathroom, and she nodded.

I made it as far as the sink and rested both hands on it, my head dropping, my back tense as fuck. What was I doing to her? She wasn't ready for all this.

She was raped a year ago, and I was trying to get her to let me touch her, and I was fucking jerking off in front of her, and... *I'm an asshole; that's what it is*. I wanted her, so I was pushing her too fast, because I was an impatient fucking ass.

I growled at my reflection.

"Yeah, you, you're an asshole. You gotta go easy on her. She's fragile. Now, get your cock under control, and man up." I rubbed my hand over my face, then tried to smooth my beard back down, because I suddenly looked like a fucking caveman.

I filled a glass with cold water, and went back to Mina. Banging at the door came only a few minutes later, when I still hadn't even coaxed her to sit up and drink.

"Yeah?" I called out, and Daisy came barrelling in.

"What? Mina? Oh god." She took in the room; Mina's distressed state, my half-naked self, I'm guessing, and Mina's pants on the floor.

"What did you do to her?" She practically screamed, stomping toward me with her finger in the air.

"You bastard!"

I stood up fast, facing her down, because I was her fucking Alpha, and she should be showing more respect. A low warning growl came from me, but she just stood there, and glared at me.

"What did you do, huh? Did you decide that surely she must be ready by now, and you jumped on her? Did it feel good, big man? Huh?"

I snarled then, and she backed up a step.

"What do you take me for? Of course I didn't fucking hurt her! I've been looking after her!" I roared.

She pointed at Mina's shorts on the floor.

"So you got her pants off because?"

I stared at them, figuring they must have been tossed on the floor, when I flipped the sheet over her.

I know I looked guilty when I looked back at Daisy, not because I'd done anything wrong, but because I knew how fucking bad it looked.

Mina

I FINALLY MANAGED TO yell the word, "Stop!", my first two tries having been barely more than a whisper. Asher and Daisy turned to look at me, and they were clearly both angry, but they shouldn't be.

"Please stop," I whispered, and Asher turned, dropping to his knees beside the bed.

"Shhh, it's okay, baby. *Breathe for me.*"

He was always telling me to breathe, always so patient, knowing when I needed time, or air. I looked at Daisy firmly.

"He didn't hurt me, he couldn't." I watched the torment on his face, hating that I'd hurt him. I'd lost it, and he'd taken the brunt of it on himself.

"*You didn't,*" I insisted again.

He nodded jerkily; his eyes dark and tortured.

"I need to bring you some food, or something. I need to look after you."

"Thank you." He smiled, a brief jerk of his lips, and then he was standing again, and heading for the door.

"Stay with her," he barked at Daisy, slamming the door behind him.

She instantly sat on the bed, reaching for my hand, and wow, I just let her take it. She looked stunned, staring down at my hand in hers.

"You... did you mean to do that?" I shrugged, still confused by everything myself.

"It seems easier now."

She sighed, squeezing my hand lightly.

"Did he hurt you?" I shook my head again.

"Honestly, he's uh, I didn't know a man could be so patient, and sweet. I thought they just take, and force, and I mean, I don't have experience to know, you know?" She looked confused.

"Did he undress you?" I pulled the sheet tighter around me.

"Only because I allowed it."

She growled softly. "The bastard shouldn't be touching you until you're ready." I pulled my hand back from her.

"I allowed it. I wanted to be touched," I said more firmly, sitting up with the bedding pulled tight against me.

"I need clothes..." Suddenly I really needed to put my armour back on. She nodded, seeming to understand that need.

"Want me to get them?" She headed for the dresser, and I stopped her.

"They're not in here." She frowned, as she looked back at me, jerking an empty drawer open.

"What?"

"They're in his... room." She turned to stare at me, her arms folded.

"He made you keep them there?"

I didn't understand why she could suddenly only see Asher as a bad guy. He was her Alpha, but then, he was only that because she'd moved here, from her own pack. Maybe she really didn't like him, after all.

"He didn't. Look, Daisy, I know you now seem to think he's not a good man, but he is. He gave me a choice of rooms, and I picked this one, but I couldn't rest here. His room, it smells of him, and it's soothing. It was me who insisted on staying there instead."

She came back to the bed with a robe she'd found on the bathroom door, which looked and smelled freshly laundered. She helped me into it.

"Did you let him convince you that you were ready for sex?" She suddenly asked bluntly, and I gasped, wrapping the robe tightly around me, as I tied the belt.

"What? No, of course not, I'm not, and he knows that." She raised an eyebrow.

"So why does it smell of sex in here? Something happened, and you were in pieces when I arrived. Tell me what I should think of him, when he's half-dressed and you're distraught, and I can fucking smell that he did something."

I sat back down on the bed, and patted it to get her to sit with me.

"It's embarrassing, but I'll tell you, because I don't want you misjudging him." She leaned back on her hands.

"Hit me."

I chewed my lip, feeling suddenly shy.

"I, when we, when *he* woke up... you know..."

"Morning wood; it's a thing," she said with a giggle, and I nodded, feeling myself smiling.

"He was going to get out of the room, and not let me see, but I wanted to." She darted a shocked look at me.

"Huh?"

"He sleeps naked, and I knew that when I sneaked in here last night, but I'd had a bad dream. I was afraid to be alone."

"So you slept in a bed with him, while he was naked?" I shook my head.

"I slept *on* the bed in my clothes. I just needed his arms around me." She was frowning deeply.

"You've really come a long way since I was last here. His arms?"

I shrugged. "It doesn't terrify me, his touch. In fact, I seem to crave it, and I don't understand why, but... it's nice. It makes me feel normal, like maybe there's still a person in here, and they didn't destroy me completely."

Daisy just looked sad.

"He gets that a lot around me, apparently. He keeps getting embarrassed, and wanting to hide it, so he doesn't scare me. I wanted to see him uh, oh god, I wanted to see him make himself come."

She gasped, looking scandalised, and then she laughed.

"Girl, check you out!"

"It was wow. It was-"

"Hot? Sexy? Kinda messy?"

"Yes, exactly! Well, of course you probably know all that, but it was new for me, though. *Pleasure*. Sex stuff without pain, or terror; I just didn't realise."

Daisy patted my hand, and then shook her head.

"It's so weird that you don't freak out when I touch you now. That one time I tried to help you at the nursery, you nearly crawled under a bench, and now..."

"I let him make me come too," I said in a rush, before I lost my nerve.

She was staring at me, open-mouthed.

"Say something," I finally said, because she just looked stunned. She blinked.

"Wow. I mean, wow! You let him touch you there?"

I nodded, finding that smile on my face again, because I still couldn't believe it myself. We'd jumped from light touches of my hands, and arms around me, straight to the most intimate place... the place I never thought anyone would touch again, definitely not with my permission. How had I even had the courage?

She frowned suddenly, her smile fading.

"So, why the tears? Oh no, was it not... good? I mean, looking at him, I imagine it would be damn good."

I giggled, even as I felt a niggle of jealousy at her words.

"I don't know what happened. One moment I was in bliss, feeling better than I'd ever felt, all kind of tingly and drained, and then I was crying. I don't... I wasn't upset, so I don't get it, but I scared him. Oh poor Asher, he was so worried he'd hurt me somehow." I rested my head in my hands. I'd ruined everything, when it had started out so damn good.

Daisy was staring at me knowingly.

"It's a release, babe." She tilted her head at me. "You get that, right? Orgasm is release, and it lets out all of the pent-up crap inside you. It's why we sleep better after, because we're not holding stuff in anymore. I mean, I'd be surprised if you didn't cry afterwards, with what you've got to let out. Hell, even I've cried after orgasming before. Scared the hell out of Ned, but it was intense, and wow, I didn't even know I was bottling up anything!"

My heart was starting to ease, that fear that I was ruined beyond repair.

"So I'm not broken?"

She laughed. "Girlfriend, the only thing broken is your confidence, but I don't think that'll be the case for much longer. Look how you're growing! Less than a week ago, you couldn't be touched, and spent most of your time alone. Now you're practically living with a man, and you're letting him touch you in all the best places. And believe me... there's better to come. So much."

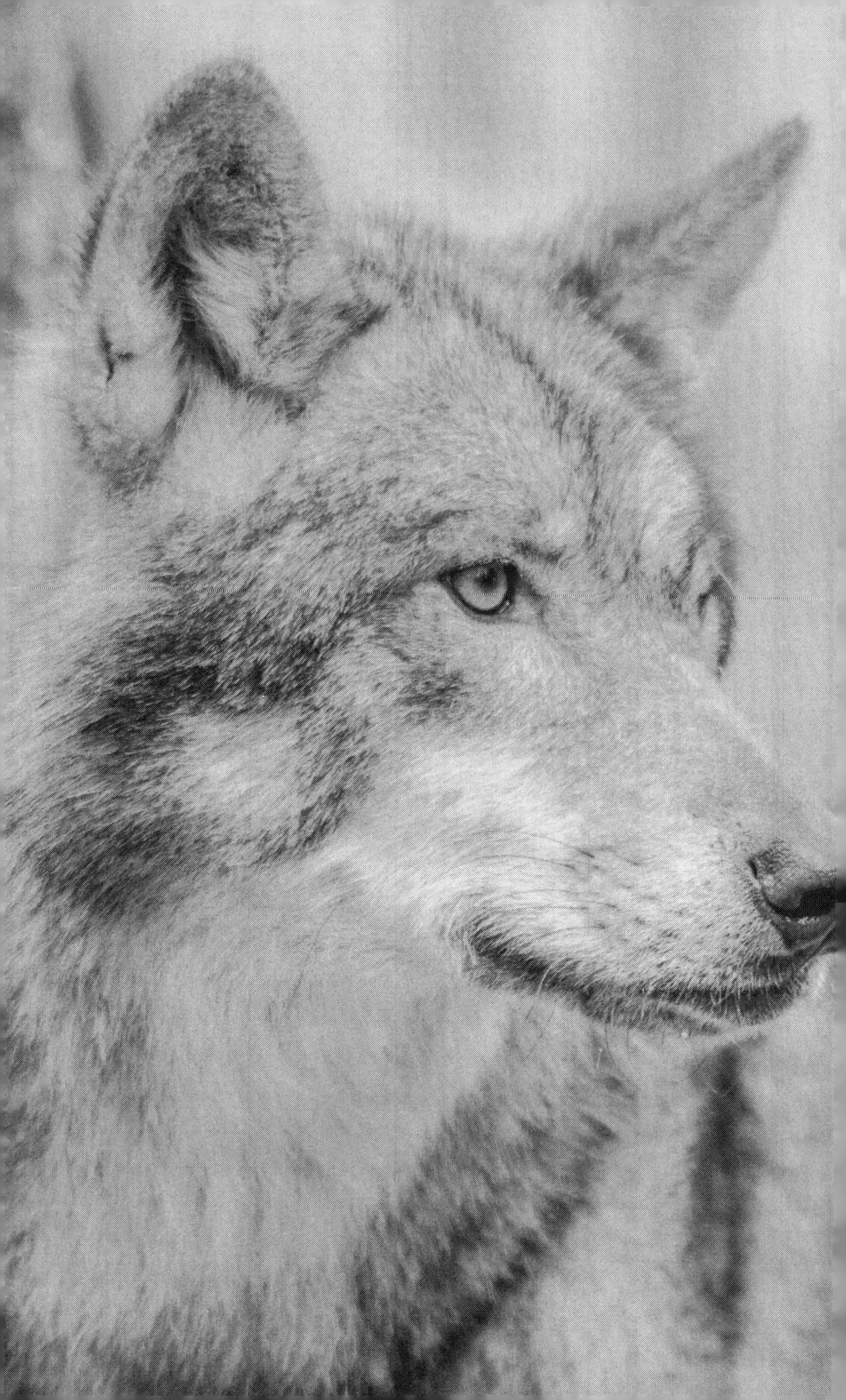

Chapter Thirty-Two

Asher

I SHOULD HAVE BEEN up there with her, but at the same time I want to cook for her, to bring her sustenance. I was so fucked up right now, I had no idea what was going on anymore. Was any of this natural, or were we just making a mess?

"Hey boss, you cooking for an army?" Derek asked, coming into the kitchen, where, yes... it looked exactly like I was cooking every fucking ingredient we had.

"Uh... I..." I had no words, so I just shrugged and carried on, jiggling a pan holding so much bacon, I was surprised it was even cooking. I'd made scrambled eggs, fried eggs, fucking poached eggs. There was toast, as well as sausages, mushrooms, fucking steak, and hash browns. It was all in warmers on the breakfast bar, because as fast as I finished something, I just started something else.

"What smells so... *oh, wow*... please say some of that's for us, Alpha," Jase said, appearing just after Derek. I shrugged.

"Go nuts. I need to take some up for the girls first though."

Jase stared at Derek, mouthing the word 'girls?', and Derek laughed.

"Daisy's upstairs with Mina."

"Oh. Okay, uh... morning ladies." His tone changed, and I turned to see Mina, with Daisy, both eyeing the food, and I groaned.

"I was going to bring you both some food."

They grabbed stools, staking their claim on seats at our table and I laughed, digging plates out of the oven, and sticking them on the counter.

"Fill your boots."

My wolves had the good sense to let Mina fill a plate first, followed by Daisy, and then they stepped up. I dumped bacon on each plate as they passed me, and then tossed the rest in with the sausages to keep warm.

Fuck me, I'd cooked enough for ten people. I rubbed my hands over my face, trying to shift the daze I was in. Cooking normally calmed me down, and balanced me out again.

Mina was up again, loading another plate with food, then she grabbed my arm, and towed me to a seat beside her, setting the plate in front of me. She nudged me to sit down, while everyone stared at her in disbelief.

She grabbed juice from the fridge, and a bunch of glasses, because I'd shown her where these things were yesterday, and sat back down. We all stuffed our faces, and drank juice, and they talked among themselves, while I just watched.

I was still out of sorts, and edgy. The day had started out so fucking amazing, and now I felt like I'd taken advantage of her, and she was just soldiering on, putting a brave face on it, while I'd joined the ranks of Teddy and Trav, as her abuser.

"Will you relax please?" She finally said sharply, drawing my attention, along with everyone else's.

"Huh?" I blinked, focusing on her at last. My plate was only half empty, because my appetite had disappeared right around the time I realised how I'd mistreated her.

"You cooked an amazing breakfast, and you're not even enjoying it," Mina admonished. "Do I have to do the airplane thing, and feed it to you?"

There were laughs from the others, but I just stared at her.

"You're not mad at me?"

She sighed heavily. "What could I possibly be angry about? You've given me only pleasure."

Derek groaned, and Jase facepalmed.

"TMI, lady."

She glanced at them, giggled once, and shrugged.

"I really don't think you wolves are as uptight as all that." Derek snorted.

"She's got us pretty well pegged already, and I'm enjoying this discussion as much as the next guy, but my real question is... *when the fuck did you get a tattoo, boss?*"

Jase slammed his hand on the table, making everyone jump.

"*Thank you!* I was freaking out trying to figure out how I'd missed that all this time!"

Mina looked at me, her eyes wide with wonder.

"It really did just appear." She leaned around me, to peer at the design and made a strange sound.

"What?" I tried to look, but it was fucking impossible.

"It's changed." *What?*

Everyone was staring at me. What the fuck was happening?

Derek handed Mina his phone so she could take a photo and show me, and I noticed he did it carefully too, sliding it across the counter to her.

She showed me the image, and she was right; it was more elaborate than before. It now covered more of my back, and looked almost like it was growing right out from within.

"Is this a mate bond thing?" I asked, and the boys just stared at me, but Daisy finally sighed.

"*Um, hello? Bonded fucking wolf over here, why don't you just ask me?*"

We all turned our eyes on her. I still hadn't decided what to do about her insubordination upstairs, but for now, I held that back because this was more important.

"Ned has one?"

She nodded. "It appeared overnight when we bonded, fully formed and covering most of his back, and wrapping around his sides. I'm guessing yours might be incomplete because your bond is forming more slowly. Maybe someone can check into that, because I only have our experience to draw on."

I stared at Daisy, wondering why the fuck I hadn't just asked her these questions before, or Ned, even. I knew him fairly well, as a committee member. Speaking of which, the committee meeting went poorly the other day, and I should really be doing something about that.

Jase poured coffee, and brought everything to the counter for self-service.

"Seems to me, I need to get back to the research about the mate thing. Maybe there's more to the bond than we realised."

"In what sense?" I asked him. Daisy was also curious.

"Wouldn't Ned and I know that by now?"

He shrugged, looking thoughtful.

"Maybe it's different when it's an Alpha and his mate."

I nodded. "That's not a bad shout. Uh, look... I know it's a workday, but I'm going to take a few days out, and get my head back in the game. I wasn't up to much Friday, and I have more important things to worry about right now. You guys have got it under control?" They were both nodding, but were also kind of stunned.

"Boss, you've never taken a day off since I've known you. It's probably about fucking time." I snorted.

"Like I said, I have something more important going on right now." I glanced at Mina, and she blushed.

Daisy cleared her throat.

"Okay well, I should get out there and open the nursery, you know, just in case someone in town has the burning urge to grow a border or something." Mina walked her out, and I just sat there staring at my coffee. This was turning into the weirdest week of my life.

Jase had disappeared at the same time as the girls.

"You alright, boss?" Derek asked, and I sighed heavily.

"I feel pretty much turned inside out at the moment, but it gets better, right?" He snorted, shrugging his shoulders.

"Well, my understanding is, once you're whipped, you're whipped, but yeah it must do."

I shot him a glare. "Daisy was rude to me earlier too, full-on in-my-face insubordination." Derek frowned.

"What did you do?"

"I didn't *do* anything!" I snapped, and then realised he was asking what action I'd taken for her behaviour.

"Sorry, I'm a bit defensive today, it seems. I didn't do anything, but I feel like my Alpha status is diminishing by the day. Can an Alpha just suddenly not be one anymore?"

He frowned again. "You think your pull over your wolves is weakening? Boss, that's not good."

I scowled at him, slamming my coffee mug down.

"Gee, ya think?" He got up, and leaned on the table.

"I'll look into this. *Privately*. I'm not bringing Jase in. Let him deal with the mate bond, and I'll see what I can find out. Maybe it's nothing, but nobody else needs to know until we know more." I nodded, appreciating his support.

Idly, I even wondered if it could be his Alpha overshadowing mine, but that was crazy, because he wasn't born to it like me. That should make me the more powerful, but did I feel that way right now?

Mina

DAISY HAD SAID SOMETHING interesting when I walked her out, about the wolf tattoo, and I wondered if she could be right. When I reached the kitchen, Asher was alone, and he looked tired, frustrated, worried, maybe even angry.

In fact, he looked like I normally felt. Had my improvement caused some kind of decline in him? He noticed me watching him from the doorway.

"Hey," he finally said, turning his focus back to his coffee. I approached, noticing his mug was empty, so I took it and returned it, full and steaming. I sat down beside him.

"I'm sorry." He growled softly at my words.

"Baby, you can't keep apologising for everything that happens in life. None of it is your fault."

I put my hand on his arm, feeling his muscles tense under my touch. *Did he not like it?* I pulled away again.

"Did I do something wrong?" I could feel uncertainty returning with a vengeance, just when I'd started to feel almost in control of myself, and like I could actually function like a normal person.

Asher stared at me. "You did everything right, you hear me? I'm just, I don't know, tired, I guess." I tried putting my hand back on his arm, and he stared at it.

"You're getting pretty good at that, Mina, I love your hands on me."

I sighed, stroking my hand over his bicep.

"I never thought I'd willingly touch a man, but something about you makes me want to."

He smiled, the first proper one I'd seen, since before it all went wrong upstairs.

"I like that you want to, and hey, *I'm a giver*. You touch me whenever you want, wherever you want." His smirk made me giggle.

"That's very generous of you."

He nodded his head.

"Like I said."

I stared at him for a few more moments.

"I'd like to take a shower, and then, I don't know. What do you feel like doing? What would help rejuvenate you?"

His eyes briefly flickered over me, before he turned his head, grinning slightly.

"Sometimes I run, as a wolf." *Oh.* I lowered my eyes.

"I could wait for you here, or... I don't know... should I go home?"

His eyes came back to mine fast, his grin gone.

"*No.*"

I pulled my hand back. "No?"

He sighed, running a hand over his face, smoothing his beard almost obsessively.

"I was thinking, if your feet are okay, you could come with me." Was he insane?

"Walk with your wolf? I can't keep up if you run." He snorted.

"We'll take a blanket, then you can sit and watch me run."

I shrugged, because the main thing was not being away from him yet. I went up for a shower, taking his bathroom in his room, because it had begun to feel more and more like mine, than my own house ever had.

After I showered, I wrapped a huge towel around me, and moved to the mirror. It was fogged up, so I smoothed my hand across the surface, clearing it enough to see.

Taking a deep breath, I turned my body, to try and peer at my own back, and screamed.

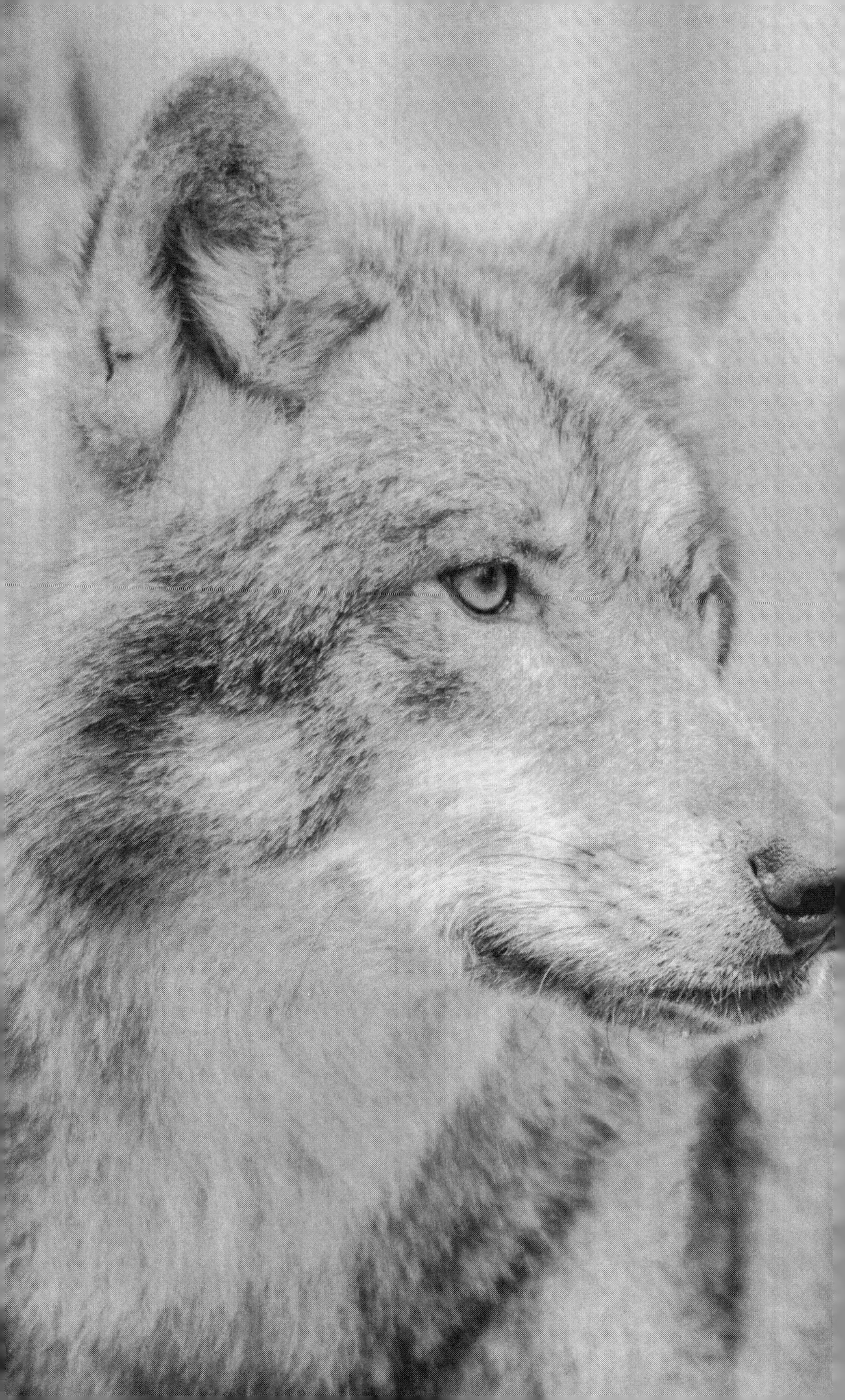

Chapter Thirty-Three

ASHER

I SWEAR, I'VE NEVER left a shower so fucking fast in my life. I was in the spare room, because there was a little lady in mine, but I ran naked and dripping wet from that room to mine, throwing the door open and racing to the bathroom door. I threw that open too, and she stared at me wide-eyed.

I cast my eyes around the room, but there was nobody else in the room. Nobody to defend her against.

"Mina?"

She was breathing a little fast.

"I'm sorry, that was so stupid. It just... it freaked me out."

I looked around again.

"What did?"

She turned, showing me her back.

"This." *What the fuck?*

"Boss? Everything okay?" Derek was at the bedroom door, and I hurriedly blocked the bathroom doorway, so he wouldn't see her, even wrapped in a towel.

"Yes, thanks, D. All fine."

"*Mina screamed,*" he insisted, and she groaned.

"I'm sorry, Derek, I just scared myself. It's fine. Thank you, though." She tried to peek out through the door, but I was in the way.

"Yeah, no problem. I'm gonna get out of here, so I don't have to keep looking at my Alpha's junk. You guys carry on." He closed the door after him.

I liked his unflappable nature. Maybe he would have been a better Alpha than me. I turned back to Mina.

"Let me see again? Out here, in the light?" She followed me out of the bathroom, and turned in front of the window.

It was light and barely there, but there was something... a pair of eyes, looking almost like a really old tattoo, faded by time and sunshine. My fingers hovered over them.

I could see why she screamed. Who would expect to see eyes staring at them from their own skin? They looked like they could be wolf eyes. Would she get a tattoo as well? I hadn't thought to ask Daisy, foolishly assuming it was a male only thing.

"Is it... is it like yours?" Mina finally asked, and I sighed because I had no idea.

"They could be the eyes of a wolf, Mina, I don't know. Does it hurt?" She shook her head. "Can I?" She simply nodded, and I blinked. She amazed me every damn minute of the day.

I lightly ran my fingers over the eyes, finding them slightly raised like mine, but not as much, more like a slight change in texture.

She shivered at my touch, and like the bastard I seemed to be, I didn't stop, brushing my thumb over them. I leaned closer, taking a deep breath and inhaling her, like a drug.

Before I could stop myself, I was pressing my lips against the tattoo, and she flinched, still trembling. She didn't move though so I kept doing it, running my lips over her shoulder and back, light kisses, sneaky tastes of this woman I suddenly realised I loved.

Her breathing had changed, and so had her scent. Good, this *should* arouse her, it should make her feel.

"Asher?" Her voice was barely a whisper, shaky, and I could feel her legs were unsteady.

"Yes, baby?" I asked, my lips still pressed against her skin, not stopping my exploration of her skin.

"Why do I only have eyes?" Oh. I didn't expect a question, not really. I thought she'd tell me to stop, or ask me to move away. If she didn't say no, I wouldn't stop, I couldn't.

I put my hands on her upper arms, moving slowly, again making it easy for her to pull away. She flinched, but didn't panic, didn't move. Or was she frozen in terror?

"Mina?"

"Yes?" She gasped.

"You doing okay?" She nodded, fast, jerky movements, but she clearly wasn't. I sighed, blowing out a breath over her skin, as I moved, feeling her shiver.

Taking one last look at the tattoo, I released her, then grabbed her again, making her whimper with surprise. I hadn't meant to touch her again, but...

"It's darker," I said, amazed that it had changed again, just since we'd been aware of it.

She gasped. "Is it? I want to see!" I laughed, looking around for my phone, eventually finding it on the corner of my bed. I hadn't even looked for it until now, because I didn't normally need it when I was in the pack house.

I took a picture, and held the phone up for her to see. She gasped again, looking fascinated.

"They look more defined now, don't they?" I nodded.

"I don't know exactly what's happening, but it seems that the closer we get, the more intense the tattoos become. I'm guessing if and when we bond fully, they'll be complete."

She stared at me warily.

"How *do* we bond fully?"

I glanced down, realising I was still naked, although my skin had started to dry off. She didn't seem to notice, so I ignored it, amazed that my cock had stayed under control while I was so close to her, with her so barely covered up.

"Mina, sit down." She visibly gulped, and sat down, about a foot away, and I really tried not to let it bother me. It didn't feel right after the closeness of moments ago.

"Baby, bonding is what happens when we give ourselves over to each other completely. I don't know when you'd even be ready for such a thing."

She pulled at the towel, because it wasn't quite covering both knees, so I got up and grabbed another towel, handing it to her. She draped it over her legs, a grateful look on her face. She still seemed unconcerned by my nudity, and that suited me, because I really didn't want that to frighten her.

"It's more than sex?" She asked quietly, bringing me back on track. I shrugged, surprised to even be having this conversation with her.

"Sex pretty much *is* how we bond, but sex right now is a bigger deal than it would be for most couples in this situation. If I lay you down right now, and tried to bond with you, I'd be no better than them." She shuddered, but she was shaking her head vigorously.

"No, you're nothing like them! I see that now, I think I saw it from the start, to be honest. How... how much... um..."

"We'd have to make love, Mina. *I'd have to be inside you, pleasuring you with my cock.* We'd both have to come, you see, it's not about dabbling in little sex acts here and there. The normal way it goes is, two wolves scent each other and come together, and fuck their brains out all night and by the next morning, it's done; they're mated. There's no preamble, that much I know, that much I've heard. If we bond, and at this point, it's still looking like an 'if', we've got a long way to go before you'll ever let me near you in that way." She was trembling just from talking about this shit, her hands twisting at each other.

"What if... what if I can't?" She asked finally, and I tilted her chin up to pull her attention from those hands.

"Mina, right now, what matters is that you're safe, and protected. I don't want or need to take anything from you. If you can't ever complete the bond with me, then it doesn't happen. If it does, then it does. It's not just about what you went through, though, the difficulty is that as a human, you don't feel the pull of the bond the way we do. You don't scent a stranger from a few metres away, and just know. You don't have that burning desire inside you, telling you to find them, and be with them.

At most, you might feel attracted, or... *I don't know*... even just safe, and you're trying to build on that. Bonding only happens if we both want it, and we're both sure. You can't un-bond if you change your mind."

She was chewing her damn lip again.

"Am I stopping you from finding a proper mate?" Why was there nothing to throw or punch in this fucking room? She was making me angry, because she just couldn't see her worth. She didn't value a single thing about herself.

"Mina, you ARE a proper mate. You ARE enough for me, but if nothing else comes from this, but you believing in yourself, then it worked. Maybe that's the purpose of it, to help you grow again, and live. Maybe I'm surplus to requirements, just a tool to help fix you, but I don't give a shit. I'm in it for as long as you'll put up with my grumpy ass."

She giggled, suddenly looking lighter and less troubled.

"I don't want to talk anymore. Let's go run!"

Mina

HE DIDN'T THINK I could run, didn't know that I'd worked hard on getting fit enough that I could outrun the next attacker. My pace was pretty good, I mean, don't get me wrong, he could leave me standing in a heartbeat, but he didn't.

Sometimes he'd loop around and run back to me, but it was fun regardless. It was nice, and so safe here on the pack's hiking trail. I wished I could turn into a wolf like him, though, it looked so freeing, and blissful.

Our earlier conversation had been intense and pretty scary, leaving me with a lot to think about, but to be honest, I still found the tattoo exciting. If I ended up with one, I'd be overjoyed. A tattoo, without a stranger having to touch me, or put their hands on my skin. How perfect would that be?

And Asher, I mean, how could I even begin to put into words just how amazing he'd been? I felt like a different person already, *because of him*.

In just a few days, it was like he'd changed my entire perspective on people, and it felt like the sun had come out, when I'd previously lived in the dark.

I'd spent so long hating myself, and hiding from the world and the evil finding me again, that I hadn't been living. Looking back on my entire life, I could only picture darkness, as if the sun had never been out before.

Every moment that I looked back on with Asher was bathed in sunlight, and peace, and I hoped, prayed, that maybe I could complete the bond with him.

How amazing would it feel to be linked to him forever? Even if I couldn't live as long as him, because my assumption was that their lifespan must be different to mine, I could spend as much of it as possible with him.

What were the implications for his pack though, if we did? I had no idea, because I didn't know about any of that stuff, and hadn't sat down with anyone and asked.

Daisy had said the mate bond strengthened the wolves, but was that only if it happened with another wolf? What if mating with a human made him weaker instead?

I felt Asher's wolf tugging at my backpack, abruptly stopping me in my tracks. The pack had caused enough of a disagreement as it was, so why was he trying to take it now?

I turned to look at him, and he seemed to roll his eyes. He jerked his huge head in the direction of a small path, leading away from the trail. Oh, I didn't even notice that.

"We're going that way?" He nodded and started trotting in that direction, stopping every few paces, to make sure I was following him. We slipped between the trees, and through a light wooded area, and then it opened up into a small dell.

It wasn't a field, it was a small area of grass, among the trees, hidden from the world, and with a small stream running along one side.

I gasped with delight, looking around me. The sun beamed into this area, and the water glittered in the bright light.

"Wow…" I breathed, stunned by this beautiful little hidden treasure.

"Perfect, huh?" Asher asked from behind me, making me jump. I didn't know he'd shifted back, but I kept my eyes facing forward as he pulled the pack from my back, and slipped his sweatpants out and on.

Then he lifted out the blanket, and spread it on the ground in the shade of a huge weeping willow tree.

"Where are we?" I asked, sitting down when he gestured. He joined me, taking care not to crowd me.

"Pack land, the little bit that sits on this end of the trail. Nobody knows this is here, and it's nowhere near the road, so nobody is likely to find it."

I sighed, leaning back on my elbows.

"I wish I could paint, because I'd sit here for hours trying to capture this, and I think I'd still fail to do it justice."

He laughed, mirroring my position.

"Photos don't do it justice either, I've tried. You just have to be here to see it with your own eyes. I thought it could be our place, you know, a retreat."

Could he have been any more perfect?

"I'd like that. I'm happiest when I'm surrounded by nature. I could see me curling up with a book here all day actually." He snorted.

"Well, I think I'd object to that, eventually."

He rummaged in the bag, pulling out a bottle of water, which he passed to me.

"*Hydrate.*"

"I packed the water, so *you* hydrate." I pointed to the bag, and the other bottle that I knew was inside, and he let me hear a soft growl.

"I still don't like you carrying everything."

I grabbed the bag. "A blanket, your pants, two bottles of water, oh and a few chocolate bars. It's hardly going to break my back, is it?"

His eyes had narrowed at me.

"Dammit, Asher, what?"

"*Chocolate? You brought chocolate?*" I laughed, handing him a bar, which he tore open instantly.

"Want some?" I shook my head, so he broke off a few squares, and popped them in his mouth.

We sat in comfortable silence for a while. Birds were singing around us, and I could pick out certain specific songs.

I wasn't a bird expert or anything, but I'd found nature particularly soothing during my convalescence at the hospital. I'd be outside in my wheelchair, beside the same lovely old lady, who would point them out, and tell me things about them.

I knew I could recognise the sound of a robin out there right now, singing such a beautiful song. I sighed, and lay down on the blanket, staring up at the sky through the long leafy branches.

Eventually Asher lay down beside me, his bare chest now catching the sun, as it made its way across the dell. I think we both dozed for a bit, because it felt safe and private here and we finally relaxed.

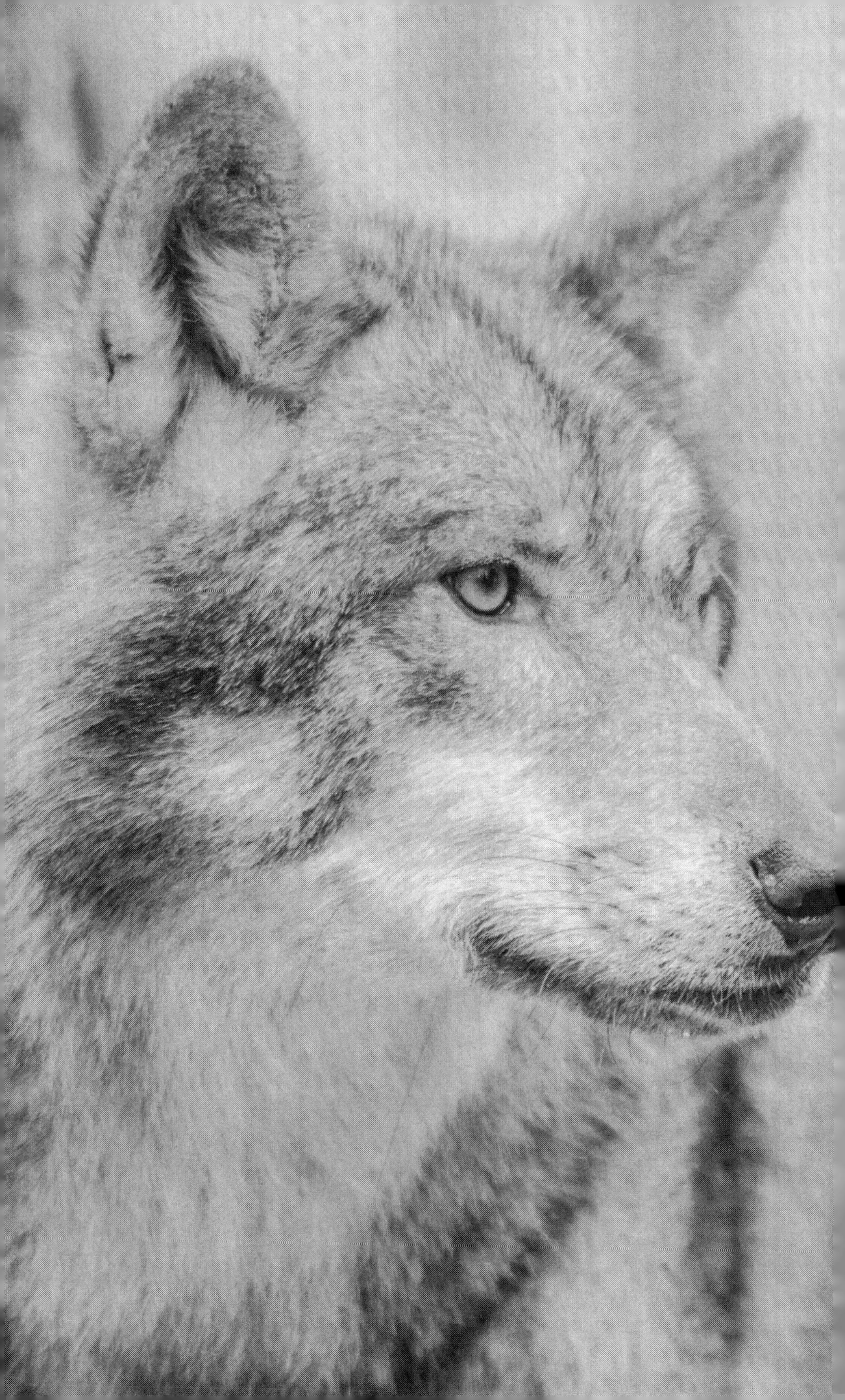

Chapter Thirty-Four

ASHER

She'd fallen asleep, and it felt pretty fucking good that she felt that relaxed out here, alone with me. I carefully rolled onto my side, to watch her as she slept.

I wasn't trying to be creepy, I just liked seeing her face so peaceful and serene.

She smiled in her sleep, and that felt great too, because she couldn't be having a bad dream, if her lips were smiling. I let my eyes travel over her from head to toe, taking in every glorious detail.

Her blonde hair, so tightly cropped, looked velvety and soft, and I ached to see it longer, so I could run my hands through it. Her lashes were long, resting against her cheeks, which had pinkened a little, as the sun started to move across her body.

I'd have to wake her soon before she burned, but I'd give her a few more minutes of peace. Her lips were full and so fucking kissable, that if she had permitted it I'd probably spend half the fucking day kissing her.

Her face was almost heart shaped, her neck narrow and elegant, and her stature was small, petite, but clearly in pretty good shape. When she'd started running and I'd had to catch her up, I was amazed and so fucking proud. She liked to run? *Brilliant.*

I figured I knew why, but still, it was good for her, keeping her fit and strong. Her breasts were perfect, I could tell, even though I hadn't seen them yet.

I couldn't wait to touch them, taste them, use them to make her unravel like she had this morning. I knew that there would be scars from her stab-wounds, but I'd make her forget every last fucking one of them.

Making her come this morning made me feel like a fucking king. The way she came apart, those gasps, and moans, wow, I hadn't realised how breathtaking she'd look. Her reaction after, I figured it wouldn't be the only time her release brought that shit to the surface, but I'd be ready next time. I'd hold her, and ease her through it, if she'd let me.

"Asher?" I lifted my eyes back to her face, feeling guilty for being caught ogling her.

"Hey, I was just going to wake you."

She stared at me sleepily.

"I'm sorry I fell asleep like that, it was rude."

I gestured around us. "Showing me how safe you feel with me is not being rude, Mina. I'm glad that you feel so relaxed here."

She smiled, something she was doing more and more.

"It's almost magical here, I mean, I've never felt such peace inside."

I reached out to touch her lips, stopping about an inch away, but she didn't move. "Yes," was all she said, but it was the way she said it. *She was permitting my touch.*

I smiled back at her, watching hers move once more, before I lowered my fingers to brush them over her lips. It was the lightest of touches, but she sucked in a breath, her lips parting slightly. *Fuck.* I wet my lips, desperate to taste hers.

"Ever been kissed, Mina?" I asked, my voice a little more guttural than I'd expected. She shook her head a little.

"Did... did *they* try?" I asked, my voice cracking a little, and she shook her head again. *Thank fuck they didn't ruin that for her.*

"Want to try?" I finally asked her, shooting her an attempt at a casual grin, as I brushed my fingers over her lips again. Her eyes widened a little.

"I... like a French kiss, you mean?" I groaned softly, as my cock twitched. *Not now, dammit.*

I did my best to try and shrug carelessly.

"Anything, a peck, or more. Your decision, Mina, as always." She looked away, her eyes darting around nervously.

"Would you be holding me down?"

"What? No, of course not. *Jesus.*" Now she looked embarrassed.

"I'm sorry."

"Dammit, Mina, stop apologising for not knowing how this stuff is supposed to be. How the fuck would you know, if you've not had the chance? Now, hear me on this, the only time I want to hear you apologise is if you accidentally punch me, or I guess, if you deliberately punch me. I mean, that's the sort of stuff to apologise for, not being unsure of yourself, or embarrassed, or even afraid."

She was giggling again, thank fuck, so I grinned at her.

"Now, about this kiss." She frowned again.

"A peck?"

I nodded, because it was a fucking start.

"Is this okay?" I gestured to her position on her back, in case she wanted to sit up, and she nodded. Fuck me, I mean seriously, fuck me. She just kept saying yes to things, and hell, I was going to take every fucking opportunity she presented me with.

I leaned closer, taking a breath, finding it almost as shaky as one of hers. This was a big moment for her, *for both of us.* It had to go well.

Her eyes watched my approach, a wariness in them that I hated to see, so I stopped, millimetres from her lips.

"I need words, Mina." I felt her lips move.

"Yes."

I pressed my lips against hers, and felt her relax suddenly, her lips parting slightly. It took all I had not to thrust my tongue in there, and kiss the fuck out of her, because I knew it would be too much.

When I pulled back, she looked disappointed, but I'm fucked if I knew why. Didn't she like it, or was it that she wanted more? I stayed close, my hand bracing me, between us.

Staring her in the eyes, I pushed it, like the bastard I'd become.

"More?" She nodded, breathing faster, and I grinned.

"If it gets too much, just push me back. I'll move, I promise." She nodded, and I growled softly.

"Yes... I mean, yes, I will."

I lowered to her lips again, covering hers with mine, then I felt her lips moving beneath mine. She was kissing me back. When she seemed to grow more confident in returning my kiss, I started to tease.

My tongue traced her lower lip, before I sucked it lightly. She gasped, a light moan following, as I did it again. Her heart was racing, and I could smell that whiff of arousal again, so I kept pushing.

Her gasp had opened her up to me, so I took advantage, my tongue plunging in as I started to kiss her hard. She moved, and her hands flinched, she was kissing me back, but seemed at a loss.

I pulled back, just enough to look her in the eyes, they were wide, and she was breathing hard.

"You good, baby?" She nodded, pressing her lips together, moistening them.

"More," she whispered. Fuck yeah, there's going to be more.

Before I did anything more though, I grabbed one of those twitchy hands of hers, and placed it on the back of my head, and she instantly gripped at my hair. *Oh, fuck yeah...*

I growled softly, before I lowered my lips to hers again, and went straight back in with my tongue, hers stroking mine as she responded.

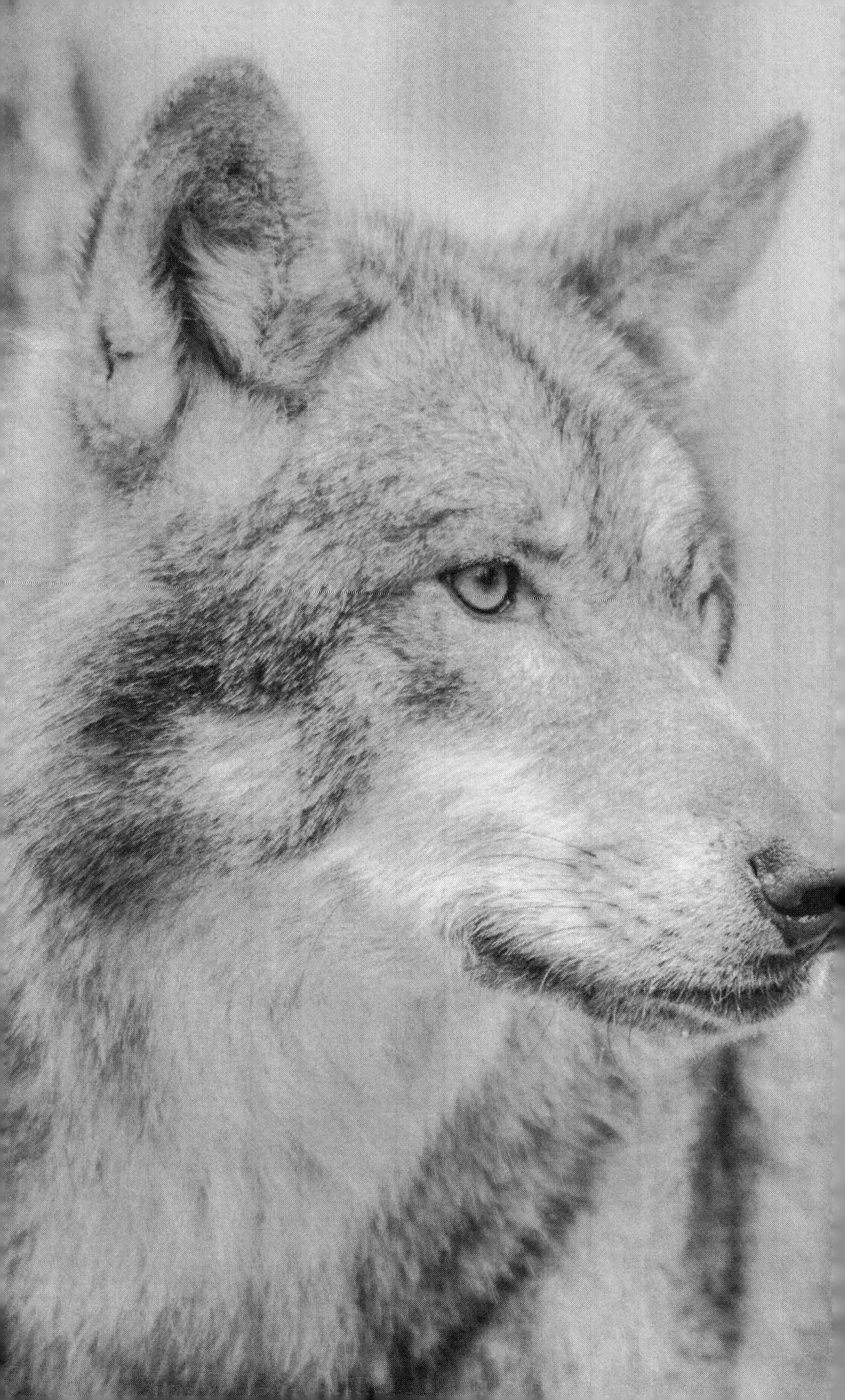

Chapter Thirty-Five

MINA

I COULDN'T BELIEVE IT was happening, and more than that, I couldn't believe how amazing it felt. It was scary and it was close, but it was so good because it was him.

His tongue kept thrusting into my mouth, and that tingle was back, and I clenched my fingers in his hair, so soft, and thick.

He groaned, pushing in harder, kissing me deeper, and suddenly I couldn't breathe. It was too much, *he was everywhere*. He was going to hold me down and hurt me, and I wouldn't be able to get away, because he'd overpower me.

He seemed to notice the instant things changed, and he pulled back, his eyes fixing on mine.

"Hey, what's going on, Mina? You're safe, baby. What's this?" I shook my head, feeling like I needed to run, but also knowing I'd probably faint if I tried. He nodded, seeming to sense my fear.

"I'm going to back up slowly, baby, you're fine, okay? You're safe." I nodded, trying to breathe, clenching my fists to try and breathe through it.

"Ow... okay, okay, Mina...Ow." He teased my fingers out of his hair. *Oh*. He left his fingers in my grip, and I hung onto them like a lifeline, while I tried to get air into my lungs.

"I'm sorry, baby, that was too much, and that's on me. *Breathe*. Shhhh, you're safe, listen to the birds singing, look at the tree moving in the wind. Smell that sweet smell? I think it's those blue flowers over there. It's bloody strong if you ask me, but I guess if you're a nature person, you probably like that." His words were helping.

As he jabbered away, and kept moving my focus to the beauty around me, I felt my panic starting to ease away, the peace returning. I let him help me sit up, and I looked around me.

"Hyacinths," I breathed, and he stared at me.

"That's what made you panic?"

I laughed. Oh... I could laugh again. I had air again.

"The flowers you mentioned, over there." I pointed.

"Ohhhh, okay, that makes a hell of a lot more sense." He looked relieved, and a bit confused. It was pretty adorable, really.

I glanced at his mouth, and his lips. They had felt so good, until everything became too much.

"I was really enjoying the kissing," I finally said, because although I wanted to apologise, he'd been right the many times he'd told me off for it. I shouldn't have to apologise for how I felt. I knew I'd do it again, but not this time.

I took deep breaths of that sweet smelling air, and risked a glance at him. He was watching me with a smile.

"*I'm so proud of you.*" He reached up to stroke my cheek, and I actually leaned into it. I didn't flinch, or panic, I welcomed it.

"I want to try that again soon," I said, putting my hand over his, holding it to my cheek.

Asher grinned, running his tongue over his lower lip.

"I look forward to it, baby." He pulled me to my feet, and folded up the blanket, tucking it back in the bag. He straightened up and looked at me, swirling his finger in a downward circle. I stared at him, wondering what the hell he was getting at.

"It means; *turn around, if you don't want to see my junk.*" I giggled, and turned around, hearing clothing rustling as he stripped again. He tucked the trousers into the pack, and zipped it up with everything inside, and then fell silent, and eventually I dared a peek.

His wolf sat there waiting for me, the pack strap in his mouth. I laughed.

"Why didn't you tell me?" I reached for the pack, and he growled.

"Oh come on, I can carry it." He growled again, and turned to head back up to the path, turning back now and then, just to make sure I was following.

Just before we disappeared into the trees again, I turned and looked back at our beautiful hideaway. The sun had moved away, and it had cooled as it grew shaded, but it was still breath-taking.

I followed Asher the wolf back to the pack house, but inside, there was unexpected activity. There were several men there that I didn't know, chatting with Derek and Jase, and I faltered in the doorway.

Asher strode past me a moment later, his sweats back on. *He put himself, very deliberately, between the men and me.*

"What's up?" He asked abruptly, as they all fell silent, all staring at me. He turned to look at me too.

"Close the door, Mina, you can go upstairs if you prefer." I shook my head, moving to shut the door.

"Who's this, Alpha?" One of the guys asked. He was huge, bigger and wider built than any other wolf in the room, and I shrank away from the boom of his voice.

Asher growled softly.

"This is my mate, Mina. You'll all stay back, if you know what's good for you."

The men exchanged surprised looks. They'd obviously heard of me, but I figured this was the first time he'd called me his mate, in that way, in front of any of his pack.

"Nice to meet you, Mina," another one said, and they all chimed in, while I waved at them a little awkwardly, and said hi.

"Now, can you tell me what the fuck is going on?" Asher snapped, turning his glare on Jase. He gulped, and stood up from the chair he was in.

"Uh, we've got some news... uh..." He glanced at me, then back at Asher.

"You want to go to the war-room?" That sounded bad, and I found myself grabbing at Asher's hand.

Asher groaned, rubbing the other hand over his face.

"Fuck me, who is it?"

They were muttering among themselves, so Jase continued.

"It's just a rumour at the moment, but it's the Somerset pack. Their Alpha might be planning a challenge of sorts."

My stomach rolled, and I tightened my grip on Asher's hand, suddenly needing his strength before I panicked. He squeezed my hand right back.

"It's okay, baby."

He nodded at Jase to continue.

"It's not a challenge yet, Alpha, more of a hint that it's being considered. Neil banged one of... I mean, he was on a date with one of their female wolves last night, and she suggested that 'when our packs merge' they'll be able to see more of each other."

I felt Asher's arm tense up, and then he let out a breath.

"*Fuck*. Okay, Neil, you seeing her again?" He nodded.

"Yeah, of course. She's a good... *I mean, she's nice*. I'm seeing her again tomorrow night."

Asher nodded. "Pump her for information, there's a good boy." They all laughed.

"Anything else?" They were all shrugging.

"Great, we'll reconvene after your date, and see what more we know. In the meantime, Jase, D, get your ears to the ground, and find out what you can." He turned to the huge guy.

"Ned, talk to Mac about having our defences ready. If it's an Alpha challenge, that's on me, but on the off-chance they try a pack assault, I want everyone ready to defend their home."

My heart was thudding heavily. *That was Ned?* Daisy's Ned? The huge scary guy? He had a scar across one of his cheeks, and his hands were as big as my head, or at least it seemed that way.

He was terrifying. I suddenly wanted to run, because the room was too full of men, big men. *It wasn't safe*.

Asher pulled on my hand, like he could sense my fear.

"It's okay, baby, you're safe. Nobody in here would do anything other than protect you, right guys?" They were all nodding and agreeing.

"Great work, now sod off, will you? I want to feed my lady." They all started moving, some nudging and joking as they went. Some even called out a goodbye to me as they passed.

Finally it was just us, well, and Derek and Jase, and they both looked edgy.

"Got info, boss," Derek said, and Jase frowned at him.

"I thought I was going to tell him."

Asher sighed. "Come on, guys, out with it." I could practically feel his patience wearing thin.

Jase nodded. "Okay, so the mate bond. Apparently the tattoo *is* a sign that it's working. The fact that yours is growing slowly is probably due to the pace you're taking things, but it should continue to fill in, and spread, until it covers your back, and Mina, you'll get one too."

We both nodded.

"*I have eyes*." I piped up, and he looked confused.

"Uh, of course you do…"

I giggled. "I mean a tattoo, but just of eyes."

His face cleared, and he laughed.

"*Oh*. Okay, that makes more sense. I mean, yours might be developing at a different rate because you're human. There isn't much lore on that, because it's not that common, but I'll keep reading up. The closer you guys get, the more yours should develop too." I nodded, because I really didn't hate the sound of that, and Asher chuckled beside me.

"*I'll just have to get more handsy*," he murmured, and I giggled, while Derek and Jase just exchanged wide eyed stares.

"D?" Derek glanced at Jase, then me.

"Uh, yeah, that's about it, I suppose." Jase frowned deeply, tilting his head at Derek.

"No, that's everything. I didn't miss anything; you know info gathering is kind of my thing."

Asher groaned, running a hand through his hair.

"D's looking into something else for me. D, you might as well tell us all."

Derek looked concerned.

"You sure, boss?" Asher nodded. What was this about?

"Fine, it's your call. Okay, so it's possible that the delay with your mate bond is reducing your Alpha power over your pack. It should go back to normal, once you bond fully." *Oh.* Jase looked horrified, looking from one of them to the other, while Asher just looked sheepish.

"You didn't want me to know?" Jase sounded wounded.

Asher just shrugged. "On the off chance that I'm losing my Alpha mojo, that puts you in the frame. I don't have a descendent yet, so I wanted to be sure it was reversible, before we mentioned it."

Jase threw his hands in the air.

"You've got us both researching different parts of the same fucking thing! We could have found more faster if we'd worked together, instead of against each other. Dammit, Asher!"

I stared at Asher, wide-eyed, and then saw Jase turn to him too, shocked.

"I'm sorry, I... Jesus fuck... you're right. Wait, *Alpha me*."

Asher laughed, and I stared at them all in turn. What did that even mean?

Asher advanced on Jase, his body tense, and his face suddenly scarily serious. He glowered at Jase, and I'd have folded under that intense threat, but Jase just frowned.

"*Fuck*, you weren't kidding. I should be on my fucking knees under the force of that power, but I can barely feel it. This can't leave this room. You're more vulnerable to a challenge right now, than ever. We're all weakened by this."

"You think I don't fucking know that, Jase?" Asher snapped, and Jase nodded.

"Yeah, of course, I just mean, well, can we speed up the mate thing? It's getting super dangerous now, for everyone."

My heart was racing as guilt started weighing heavily on me. This was because of me. *This was my fault.* Asher squeezed my hand.

"Hey, stop that. Whatever you're doing, just pack it in, right now. This is the life of an Alpha, Mina, and we'll sort it. Jase, don't put this on her. She's doing her best, we both are."

Derek laughed, showing his usual carefree side.

"We've been through worse. I do think, though, boss, we need to keep the rest of the pack away from you until we fix this. If any of them realise your power over them is weakened, you could just as easily face a challenge from within the pack."

Asher nodded. "Okay, boys, thank you. I'm probably gonna cook something up now, so I'll try to leave you both a plate, but if not, you're on your own."

"Thanks, Alpha," Jase said as he left, and Derek nodded at us, before he followed.

I felt so guilty, because if I'd been a normal woman, we'd have bonded already and Asher wouldn't be in danger. I had to try and put aside all of my stupid fears, so we could... *oh god*... have sex.

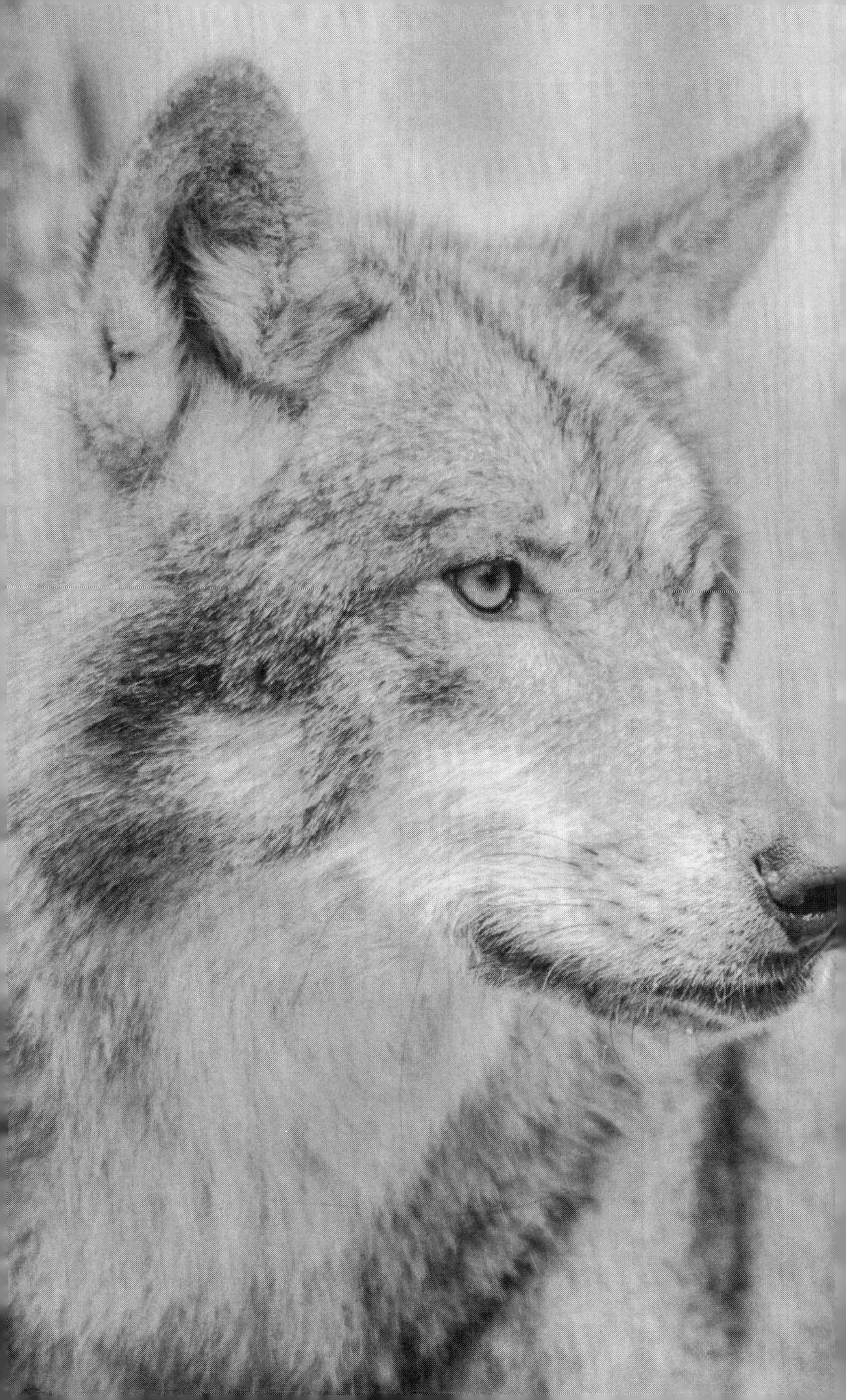

Chapter Thirty-Six

Asher

It was killing me that she was blaming herself. I could see it, hell, I could practically feel it coming off her in waves. I dragged her to the sofa and pushed her down, crouching in front of her.

"*Mina*, look at me." I put just enough command in my tone that it shocked her out of her daze, and she met my eyes. I grabbed those trembling hands, and held them in mine.

"This. Is. Not. Your. Fault." She lowered her eyes.

"*No*, stop that. You don't have to hide from me. Dammit, Mina, you have enough shit to try and get through. Leave this for me to worry about."

She stared at me then, her eyes watering.

"I thought we were making progress, but it's not enough. It's taking too long, and it's hurting you. I can't be the reason you or your pack are in danger. I need to try harder."

I let out a heavy sigh.

"Baby, you're doing amazingly, but we don't have to achieve everything at once. You didn't ask for any of this, and look how well you're doing. You don't need more pressure on top of this. It has to be at your pace."

She suddenly lunged at me, her lips slamming against mine, and her hands in my hair, gripping it in handfuls.

Her tongue swept into my mouth, and I gave in and went with it, because like I said, *bastard*. My arms locked tight around her, and I took control of the kiss, leaning into her as I did.

My balance was going, with me being crouched in front of her, and eventually I fell against her, my weight pressing her back against the sofa, but she just kept kissing me.

She was really fucking good at it, but suddenly something wasn't right. I forced myself to pull back, and look at her, although her hands didn't fucking loosen in my hair.

She was breathing hard, with her eyes tightly shut, and her body had frozen. Tense. *Afraid*.

I took stock of our position; I'd trapped her against the sofa with my body, my weight crushing her so she couldn't move. *Fuck*.

I started pulling back, eventually reaching up to tease those fingers back out of my hair. They stayed clawed up, and she was breathing really shallow breaths.

"Mina? Fucking hell." I swept her up into my arms and carried her upstairs, taking her straight to my room.

I set her on the bed, letting the safe place she'd chosen work its magic. She curled up in a ball, hugging my pillow against her, burying her face in it.

She muttered something to herself, over and over. I had no idea what it was, but I stayed back, I had to let her find her control again, because touching her would do nothing to help her right now.

We sat in the dark for a damn hour, before she finally seemed to come out of her shell again.

"Asher?" She whispered.

"Yeah." I was sitting on the floor against the wall by the door. Close enough in case she needed me, but fucking far enough away that I couldn't touch her, because it was getting harder and harder to keep my fucking hands off her.

"If I say something, do you promise not to get mad at me?" Her voice was tiny, and broken, and I sighed, rocking my head back against the wall.

"Yeah, of course."

She sighed. "I'm sorry." *Fuck*.

"Jesus."

"*You promised*." She was quick to point that out, and I laughed, despite myself.

"Yeah, I fucking did, didn't I?"

Mina

HE SOUNDED EXHAUSTED, AND I could see it, day by day, how I was destroying him. I thought this mate bond business to be an unfair burden on me at first, but now I could see the truth. My side wasn't the problem.

The problem was that he was being weakened by my inability to accept him as my mate, and that was hurting his entire pack. And while we stayed in this precarious limbo situation, it was wearing him down, and killing that spark in him that made him so vibrant, and alive.

"You could get me drunk," I half joked, watching him lift his head to stare furiously at me.

"That's a fucking horrible idea."

I frowned, feeling like his response had been a little extreme.

"You don't get it, do you?" He asked quietly, and I shrugged, hugging his pillow to me.

"If we get you drunk, you're not consenting to anything. We're just lowering your inhibitions, so you'll be less likely to refuse me. That's not too far from rape itself."

I shuddered. Why hadn't I seen that? Because my desperation to fix this for him, was taking over everything else, even my good sense.

"There has to be a way," I insisted, and he shrugged.

"I don't think it needs to be rushed, Mina. We met for the first time on Thursday, and it's only Monday now. In terms of dating, we're moving pretty damn fast."

I groaned. "But the longer it takes, the more dangerous it is for you. I can't be the reason you get hurt, or you lose your pack!"

Asher pushed himself up from the floor, and approached the bed, sitting down close to me. I didn't move, because I didn't feel unsafe.

"I want you to focus on one thing, and one thing only." I stared glumly at him.

"What?"

He grinned. "What you want, what you need. If you want me to touch you, want me to kiss you, I'll oblige. If you need pleasure, need to come, I'll get you there. If you want to try something new, you tell me. *But you need to tell me.* Don't just stare at me, and pray I can read your mind, because I can't. I'm guessing my ass off every time you do it, and I'm going to get it wrong."

I felt a wave of warmth at his words, at his earnest expression, and the way he treated me every moment.

"*I think I'm falling in love with you.*"

His face lit up, a huge grin creeping across it.

"See? That's more important than anything else going on here. Mina, I feel the same, and I want this bond with you, because I want to be with you, not because of anything pack related. So I want you to look at it like that." He leaned closer.

"There are so many amazing experiences waiting for you, so much pleasure. I look forward to walking you through every stage. It's a journey, Mina, and you should enjoy every part of it, not try and rush to the destination before you're ready. That'll only do you more harm."

I sat up, feeling a surge of courage from his words.

"Fine, then show me something. Anything we haven't already done, or experienced together." He grinned easily, almost like he'd expected this response.

"Okay, okay, I can see you're going to be stubborn, so here's what we're going to do. I'm going to take off all my clothes, and you're going to put your hands anywhere you like." *Oh my god.*

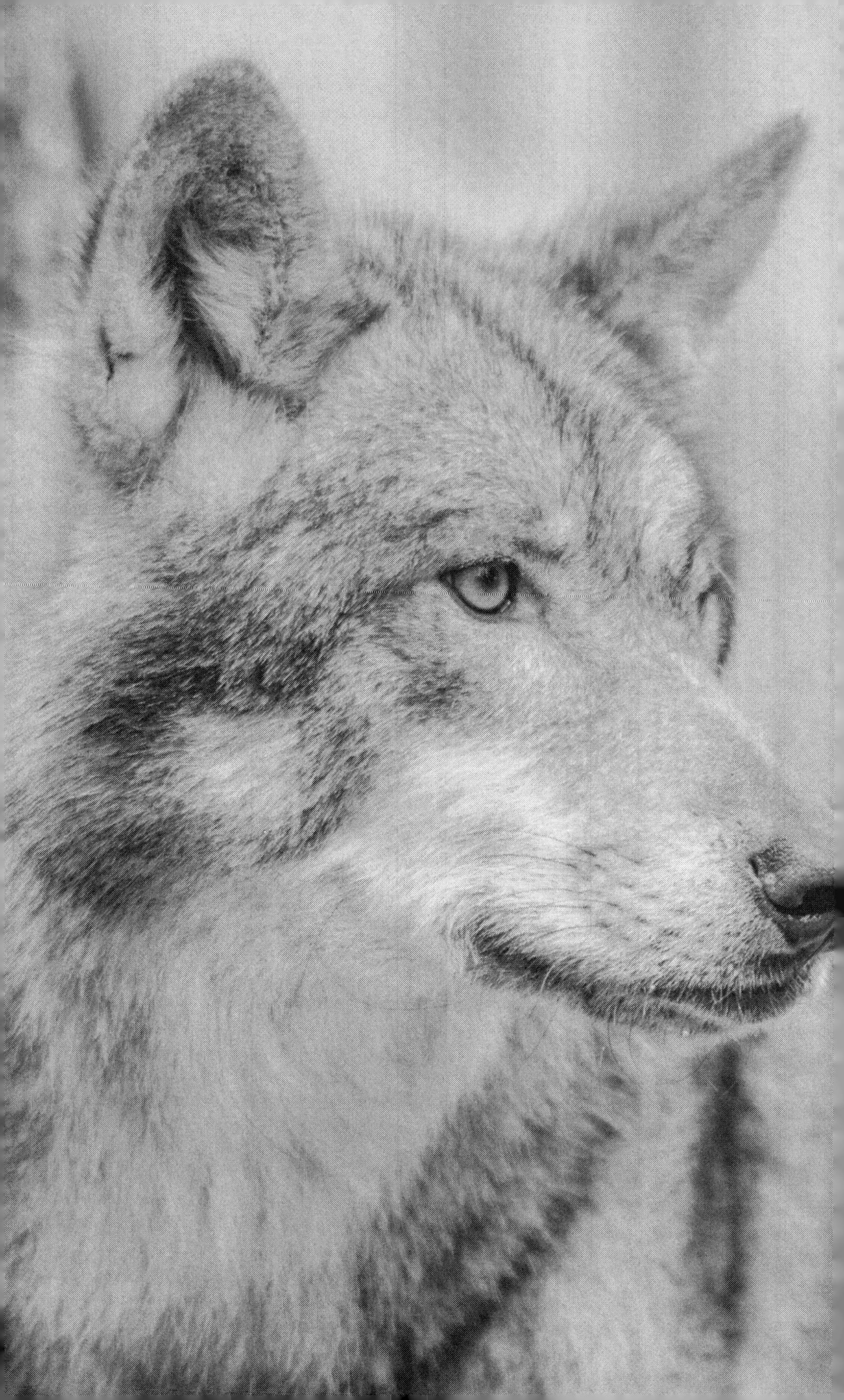

Chapter Thirty-Seven

ASHER

I HAD NO FUCKING clue what I was doing, or what was the right approach. What was the best way to not scare the shit out of her?

We had a few more days before those bastards got out of prison, and when they did, she was going to watch me shred them for her. Until then, we had to 'baby steps' this shit, and see where we go. She wasn't running anymore, she was determined to see it through, and I could work with that.

I shoved my sweats down, and stepped out of them. The beauty of being so underdressed, was how quickly I could go 'au naturel'. I walked around the bed, and lay down on my front, with my head turned to face her.

She looked surprised, and I know it's because she expected me to wave my dick in her face, and expect her to go straight there, but that wasn't what I wanted. I wanted her to *want* to go there.

"I... you just want me to touch you?" She asked tentatively, her eyes travelling over my body. I deliberately tensed my ass when her eyes landed there, and she grinned.

"Yes, baby, I want your fucking hands everywhere. You choose where, but be adventurous... you just might even enjoy it."

She chewed her lip. "I... I'm going to start with the tattoo." I figured she would, it was a safe starter, after all. I closed my eyes, doing my best to appear at rest.

"Go nuts, baby, I'm just gonna chill here, while you explore."

She didn't move at first, and I was starting to rethink the idea when her fingers suddenly grazed across my shoulders, and then they became braver.

I hissed in a breath as she trailed her nails across my skin, not hard enough to scratch, but enough that it felt fucking amazing.

If she kept that up, I really would be waving my cock in her face by the time I rolled over. Her hand slipped down to the small of my back, resting there for a moment, then she stopped. Not brave enough to touch my butt cheeks yet, I guess.

She returned to the tattoo, or at least where I figured it was, and as she brushed her fingers over it again, she suddenly gasped.

"*It shimmered*." I opened my eyes.

"Please tell me I don't have some girly, glittery shit going on back there."

She giggled, but she looked fucking delighted.

"No, it's when I touch it, it reacts to me." I sighed, aching to feel her stroking me again.

"Then by all means, keep stroking it, because it feels awesome, and FYI, your nails? I really like that too, baby." Her nails dug in for a moment, and then eased away.

"Yep, just like that, even harder if you like. Fair warning, though, it *is* turning me on, but then your touch always does."

She was quiet, but her hand never stopped.

"Both hands, Mina, please." She adjusted her position, sitting closer, and then her other hand stroked my back too. Both of her fucking hands on me was almost too much, but the confidence she'd gained, in just a day or so, was incredible.

As one of her hands approached my butt, I clenched again, making her giggle. She only made it as far as the top of one butt cheek, but it was progress, and I was so fucking proud of her.

She turned then, and looked at me, and I winked at her.

"Ready for the front, baby?" She trembled, and then nodded.

I stared at her. "Be warned though, that was fucking hot. You're probably going to see what you saw this morning." Her gaze faltered for a second, and then she nodded again.

"What did I say before?" She looked confused.

"Huh?"

"I'm not moving until you tell me with words, Mina." She sighed, tilting her head.

"What if I say no?"

"Then you have to stroke my butt."

She laughed. "Fine, you win. Oh, wait, before you turn over."

"Yeah, you're going for my ass. I knew you would, baby, it's so pert, right?" She was giggling, but her hand instead ran through my hair, for once not twisting up like a pretzel and staying there until I pry it loose. Then she pulled back.

"Okay, time to turn over."

I flipped over, getting comfortable on my back with my hands tucked behind my head, so they weren't tempted to explore her at the same time. She chewed her lip.

"This is scarier," she said quietly, and I nodded.

"That's why we started with my back. No part of me is ever going to hurt you, though, and it's your choice. Only put your hands where you're comfortable putting them. Now, I have some ideas, but I'll try to keep my trap shut. Be warned though, my cock is already at half mast, and it's going to move, and grow bigger and harder, and you're going to find that freaky. Don't panic, okay, I'm not going to make you touch it."

She'd already fixed her eyes there, and her hands trembled as she twisted them together. I pulled one hand out from behind my head and tucked my fingers under her chin, turning her to look at me.

"Start up here, baby. Don't ever be afraid of me."

She nodded, so I put my hand back, allowing her a silent response this time.

She leaned over to look at my face.

"I'm going to start here."

"All yours, baby."

Her fingers started with my lips, trailing so lightly across them, I could barely feel her touch. Then she stroked my beard, even cheekily tugging the end of it, and making me laugh.

Her fingers returned to my lips, stroking more firmly. It made me smile, and then while she traced my lips for the second time, I kissed her finger, and she stopped. Then she smiled, and did it again.

From there, her hands both went to my chest. Now I was a hairy guy, so there was a fair amount of chest hair, and she threaded her fingers through it, as she stroked my skin.

It was heavenly, her hands on me, her fingers exploring my body. I could feel how hard I was getting, just from this tentative treatment of hers, but I relished every second of it.

How I longed to spread her out on the bed, and bury myself balls deep, fucking her into a blissfully exhausted and satisfied coma.

If it happened eventually, I'd probably have a hard time not blowing my load straight away. Clearly I needed to get my control back, before I let her down.

Her fingertips circled my nipples, and I moaned, feeling my cock jerk again. Her eyes went to it, every damn time it moved. She almost seemed amused by the way it responded to her touch.

"Do you want to touch it? No pressure, but if you do, be prepared for a stronger reaction from me."

She stopped her teasing of my nipples, thank fuck, and looked at me.

"Why?"

"Seriously? Your hand on my cock? Uh, that would probably cause what you saw this morning, only a hell of a lot sooner." She bit her lip, glancing at it again.

"Mina, I'm not saying you have to." She groaned, her nails digging into my chest.

"I know, but I *do* have to."

I sat up, pushing her hands away.

"No, you don't, I'm being serious."

She let out a frustrated huff. "It's about learning to feel safe around you, so I can have sex with you. How can I do that if I can't even touch that part of you."

I raised an eyebrow. "What part?" Her brow creased.

"That part."

"Words, Mina. *What is that part of me?*"

She blushed.

"I can't."

I growled, reaching down and wrapping my hand around it.

"My cock. Say it, *cock*."

She lowered her head, and I stroked it hard, wrenching a guttural moan from myself. I knew it'd make her look up again.

"Mina, *now*."

She blushed again.

"Cock! *Your cock*. Are you happy now?"

I grinned widely. "It's a start." I let go and rolled back again, hands behind my head.

It was so fucking hard not to just finish myself off there and then, but I was really hoping she'd at least touch it.

Mina

HE KEPT SAYING THAT I didn't have to touch it, but I could see he didn't mean it. *He wanted me to*. It was all he wanted, and it freaked me out, because it was the part of the body that could be used as a real weapon against a woman, and I'd been there.

Could I touch it? His *weapon*. He made me call it by its name, or the name he uses, anyway, but there are so many.

"Mina, are you done?"

I glared at him.

"Stop rushing me, Asher."

His eyebrows raised at my tone. *Good*. He told me to take my time, and then he was getting cranky because I was doing what he asked.

I clenched my right hand, the nearest hand to his lower half, and released it again. I glanced at him, then looked back at it. *I can do this*.

I reached out, and although my hand was still shaking, I stroked one finger from just below the tip, to the base. His whole body jerked when I touched him, and a moan rumbled from his chest. His cock felt warm to the touch, and silky smooth.

It didn't look like a weapon, and the way he reacted when I touched it, made me feel like I was the one with the power, and not him. *If it could be used as a weapon, right now, I would be the one wielding it.*

I wrapped my hand around it, and he practically jerked off the bed.

"*FUCK!*"

I glanced at him, and could see he was tensed up, his arms pressed against the sides of his face, the pillow crushed against the back of his head.

"Jesus, Mina, you nearly made me come with one touch." He was breathing hard, and suddenly I felt strong and brave. I could touch a man's... cock... after what they did to me, and if I could do that, who knew what else I could do?

He stared at me desperately.

"Are you... you know if it goes off, it'll get messy." I nodded, swallowing hard.

"Mina," he said sharply, and I stared at him.

"Yes. I get it."

"Be really sure. If you're not ready for that to happen with your hands on it, I suggest you back off now, because I'm closer than I fucking should be right now."

His frustration added to my sense of power. I could make this amazingly strong man come undone, with my touch.

Did I ever think I'd be in this situation? The balance of power between us had truly shifted, or had it always been this way?

"How do I... *do* what you did?"

Asher was staring at me, and I couldn't read his expression. Was it desperation? Confusion? Pride?

"You really want to try?" I nodded, and then forced myself to voice it for him.

"Yes, please, Asher." He groaned, and I saw a shudder run throughout his body.

"I'll walk you through it."

He put his hand over mine, and guided me, stroking up and back down again, his body trembling with the effort he was clearly making to hold back.

His hips flexed up at my hand each time I moved it down, and then he pulled back, and left me to carry on. I kept moving my hand, and sped up when he suddenly gasped out the word 'faster', and then it jerked, and spurted his warm juices all over my hand, some hitting his stomach.

He was panting, his hand clenching a handful of the bedding, and he glanced at me, his eyes looking a little glazed.

"Thank you, baby, that was fucking amazing." I pulled my hand away, looking at the sticky mess and wondering why I didn't feel dirty, or have that desperate urge to wash the last few minutes away.

Asher saw me looking, and hopped up, returning with a warm wet flannel, which he used to clean up my hand, and then his stomach. He tossed it in the general direction of the bathroom and lay back down, turning on his side to look at me.

"How are you doing?" He asked, and I stared at him, feeling a little overwhelmed.

"Okay, I think. It's not so scary seeing you without clothes now."

"That's good, because I like being naked. I think I'm really going to like being naked around you."

I looked away, because I could already see the next problem.

He'd want to see me naked, and I wasn't sure I could let him do that. To wear absolutely nothing in front of him, to let him see the ugliness of my scars, the damage they did to my flesh. *He wouldn't want me anymore if he saw.*

Asher

SHE JUST FUCKING CLOSED up on me again. We were doing so well, and then something changed. Did I say something wrong, or was she going back into her head, to hide from me again?

"Mina? Talk to me." She shook her head, getting up from the bed, and going to her bag. She grabbed some clothes.

"I'd like to change for bed."

What the fuck was going on? I stood up and straightened the bed, which had been changed while we'd been out today, but now looked like it had been slept in already.

"Mina, wait." She stopped at the bathroom door, her hand on the handle, her head down.

"I can't."

What... what was this? I followed her, unable to stay away.

"Stop, please don't run from me. What's going on? Did that push you over the edge? You didn't have to do it."

She shook her head. "Please just let me go and change." I put my hand on the door like a bastard, stopping her from pulling it open.

"*Please*, Asher."

"Why?" She gave me the good old side-eye, before looking at the door again.

"I don't know what you're asking me."

I pulled the clothes from her hands.

"I want to know what just happened that you're suddenly running from me, and you're going to tell me, dammit."

She rested her forehead against the door.

"Please, I just need a few minutes. *Please, Asher*."

I backed off as she requested, I just walked away and let her disappear. Grabbing my sweats, I stepped into them, and left the room.

While she showered, I whipped up something for us to eat. There were a lot of breakfast foods left over, and in the fridge, so I made them into sandwiches, and fried them, with cheese on. A good high calorie dinner.

I took a big tray up, with both plates, and two cups of tea, because I thought tea might calm her more than coffee would.

Back upstairs, I found her already sitting on the bed, wearing a t-shirt and long trousers, not even shorts, but trousers. We'd gone back a step, and I didn't understand why.

I placed the tray on the bed for her, lifting my own plate and drink away, taking those over to the sofa. I'd give her space until she felt safe again.

"Thank you," she muttered, picking up the huge sandwich, and inspecting it.

"Is it okay?"

She smiled. "It smells amazing." She took a huge bite and nodded, moaning a little. I followed suit, and we sat in silence while we ate. After, as we sipped our tea, her sitting back against my headboard, and me on the fucking sofa, she spoke.

"I'm sorry I shut you out."

I shrugged, trying to pretend that it hadn't hurt so much when she did.

"No, really, I know it was unfair." I sighed, running a hand through my hair.

"Look, I don't expect you to tell me everything. I know this is a fucking huge amount of shit for such a short space of time. Just please, don't hide from me. If you want space from me, just tell me. If you don't want me touching you anymore, tell me. I'm not a complete bastard, you know."

She sighed heavily, pressing her head back against the headboard.

"I'm afraid, Asher, of what comes next."

I leaned forward, my hands on my knees.

"And what comes next, Mina?" Did she really think I was going to throw her down on the bed and fuck her, now that she'd touched my cock? Did she really think I'd do that to her?

There was so much more she needed to be comfortable with, before I was ever going to put us that close together.

"It's... you're going to want me to show you more. Of me, and it's, fuck... you won't... it's not pretty, okay? I'm not. When they attacked me, they stabbed me. I'm..." She trailed off, breathing a little fast.

"You have scars," I prompted gently, and she looked at me again.

"Yes, I'm hideous. Marked forever by them."

Fuck. I ran a hand through my hair again.

"That's how you feel?"

"How else? I can't... I can't even look at myself in a mirror. I wish that tattoo would form over the front of me, and cover them, but it still won't make my body not be ugly. I'm sorry, Asher, this is so much worse for you than me. Why would you be destined for someone as damaged as me?"

What the hell could I say to that? How could I show her that she was already beautiful to me?

"Mina, Jesus, I don't think it's anywhere near as bad as you think. You don't look at yourself with my eyes." She was shaking her head.

"You're wrong. You'll be repulsed, and I don't want you to be repulsed by me."

I stood up, trying not to scare her, but I was literally just seconds away from grabbing her, and shaking her, to try and get her to see sense.

"Mina, don't be ridiculous. Scars are scars; I've got some, and you saw Ned, he has a bad one, and that's on his face. He can't hide that, but did it stop Daisy from seeing him for who he is? *No.* I can see past what they did to you, physically and emotionally, so please don't judge me without giving me a chance."

She lurched up from the bed, her face angry now.

"Really? You're so fucking sure, are you?" She pushed down her trousers, stepping out of them.

"Mina, come on, don't do something you can't undo."

"Screw that! I mean, we're supposed to learn about each other, aren't we? So let's fucking learn just how repulsive and disgusting my body is. Let me show you their handiwork, and you can tell me if you can even still look at me after you've seen this!"

She pulled her t-shirt over her head and threw it aside, and then she stood there, her chest heaving, and her fists clenched, wearing just her underwear. No bra. I could finally see those fucking nipples, and I was right, they were glorious.

I crossed the room, casting my eyes over every delicious inch of her body. *Fuck me.* I dropped to my knees in front of her.

"Baby…" She started gasping in huge breaths, huge sobbing breaths.

You could see every fucking mark those bastards had left on her. Small, puckered scars, haphazardly scattered across her chest and stomach, a dozen of them, and yet, all I could see was those fucking nipples, that pale smooth skin, the curve of each breast. The way they moved when she gasped for air.

She was crying, gasping, wrenching, broken sobs.

"Baby, you're beautiful, hey, come on, come here." I took her hands and pulled her closer, and she dropped to her knees, letting me pull her into my arms, practically wailing with despair.

I was terrified. Had I finally broken her? She didn't even flinch as I pulled her against my chest, bare skin to bare skin at last, and wrapped my arms tight around her.

"*I'm ugly,*" she whispered, and I shook my head, pressing her face to my chest, tucking her head under my chin.

"No, baby, you're fucking gorgeous. *I promise.*"

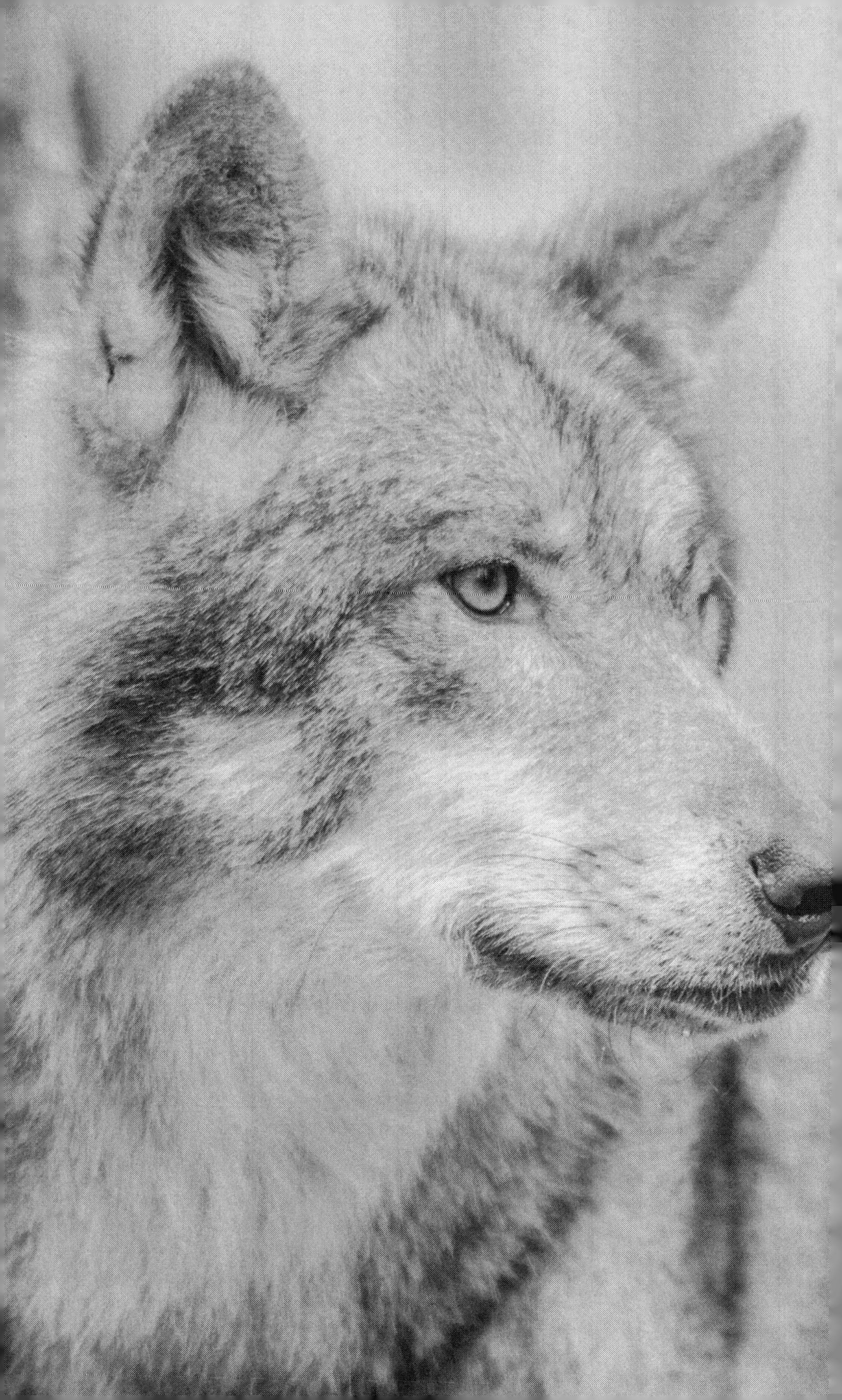

Chapter Thirty-Eight

MINA

I FELT SO SAFE, wrapped in his arms with his warmth surrounding me, even though I could feel him against my bare skin, and I'd been so sure that would terrify me.

He kept stroking my back, and telling me he found me beautiful, and loved my body, and I just took solace in the cocoon of comfort he provided.

"Mina?" He was talking to me again.

"Mmm?"

"You're beautiful."

I sighed, because he was doing it again. He cleared his throat, his arms tightening for a second.

"Mina." His tone was sharper this time.

"Please don't make me move," was all I said, and he fell silent for a few moments, but eventually he chuckled.

"Baby, I don't want to scare you, but being pressed against your hot body is going to be a problem soon."

"Why?" I whispered, still not wanting to pull away.

Now that I'd crashed through so many of my personal barriers, I knew it would feel like a loss to pull away, and would I even have the courage to let him hold me like this again? Or would I lose my nerve?

"Because now you're not upset, I'm getting aroused by the feel of your sweet body against mine. I'm sorry, I'm a bastard." I groaned and opened my eyes.

"Yes."

"Oh, thanks. So I'm a bastard then?" He was laughing, so I relaxed, pulling back just enough to look up at him. He looked like he'd cried with me, his eyes red and a little wet too.

"No, you're really not," I said, and he brought one arm up, brushing my cheek with his thumb, brushing away the last of my tears.

"How are you not repulsed by me?" I finally asked, putting my fears back between us again. He loosened his hold, just enough to let me lean back a touch, to see him more easily.

"Your scars are part of you, Mina. They're not ugly, just like no other part of you is. If you want, you can lay back on the bed, and I'll show you just how beautiful you are. I'll put my lips on every one of those tiny scars, and I'll pleasure your body, until you're screaming my name, and waking the guys down the hall." I trembled in his hold, the tingle in my body at his words, surprising me as always.

"I'm not sure I'm ready for that." He nodded.

"I completely agree, but what you are ready for is sleep. So we're going to get in that bed together, exactly as we are now, and we're going to sleep. And you can snuggle with me, or you can curl up in a ball and not touch me, but we're both going to be there together, okay?" I nodded, stunned by the realisation that I was pretty sure I could do that now. He stared at me, not moving.

"Bloody hell, yes, okay." He snorted, but he looked delighted every time I snapped at him.

"I'm sorry if my attempts to empower you are frustrating, Mina. I'm simply making sure that you tell me what you want, so I don't make any assumptions. Now if you need to pee, go do it, then get in bed, and you'll have to sleep on the left side tonight, I'm afraid."

I stared at him, then the bed.

"You prefer the other?"

"I prefer whichever side puts me between you and anyone else, yeah."

Asher

WE WOKE UP, PRESSED together in the bed, her bare fucking chest pressed against mine. I bit back a groan, as I felt her breaths against my skin, slow, even breaths. Yep, she was still asleep, *on me.*

I took the opportunity to relish the feel of our bodies together, before she woke up and reality crashed down on her, as it seemed to do, particularly early in the day.

We were so close to completing the bond, I could feel it. Another day of her as she was yesterday, and we'd get there.

That was if the morning wood I was sporting right now didn't scare the crap out of her when she woke. She had no idea how close her fucking hand was to it right now. A few inches down, and she'd be touching him. *Fuck.*

For the millionth time, I had to fight the urge to roll her over, and spread those sexy legs, and slide him deep inside her, fucking her senseless.

I wished she could be able to do that. In that one moment, I wished for her to be different, and I hated myself for it.

"Does it do that every morning?" Her sleepy voice asked, and I started to laugh.

"How long have you been awake?"

She lifted her head to look at me.

"A few seconds, and it was the first thing I saw when I opened my eyes." *It was pretty hard to miss, I guess.*

I grinned at her. "I'm all man, baby. He does that a lot, especially around you." She slid her hand across my chest, up to just below my nipple, and my hand stopped her progress.

"Baby, I love your fingers on me, but you need to know how close you are to getting fucked right now. I'm barely hanging on, you start teasing me with those things, and I'm gonna want to be inside you." Her eyes had darkened at the word 'teasing', but she didn't look afraid.

"What if I think I'm ready and we start, and then I panic, and want you to stop?" She asked quietly. I tightened my hand around hers, rubbing my thumb against her palm.

"Stop means stop, Mina, and no means no. *Every damn time.* Anything you say that tells me you don't want that, and I back off. You think I'll be like them, but they were *animals*. They wanted a one-night thing, and no consequences. I want the rest of our lives, and fucktons of consequences. You hogging the bed, nagging me for leaving wet towels on the floor, demanding my cock when you want it, because it'll be yours, and maybe, just maybe, babies one day *if* that's what you want too. Why would I risk hurting you if I don't ever want this to end?"

She was staring at my chest, mulling over my words.

"So if I said I wanted to try right now, and then we had to stop, you wouldn't hate me?"

I sighed, while my entire body went into fucking party mode.

"Baby, I could never hate you, but I don't want to push you if you're not ready either. We have time, I promise."

She groaned, pressing her forehead against my chest, her breaths coming a little faster.

"If we don't push, I might never be."

I nodded after a moment.

"Okay, but first, I have to go and try to pee without it hitting the ceiling, and since I don't want to hit you with morning breath for your first time, I'm gonna brush my teeth too." She nodded, and I reluctantly slithered out of bed.

"It won't be, though," she said quietly as I crossed the room, and I knew exactly what she was saying, and it was bullshit.

"They don't count, because they took from you, and you didn't permit that. I'm going to *give*, I'm going to make your real first time so fucking mind-blowing, you'll forget your own name." She giggled.

"I do that sometimes anyway... the fake one, I mean."

I grinned at her, and disappeared into the bathroom before I said anything that shifted her out of the playful mood she was in.

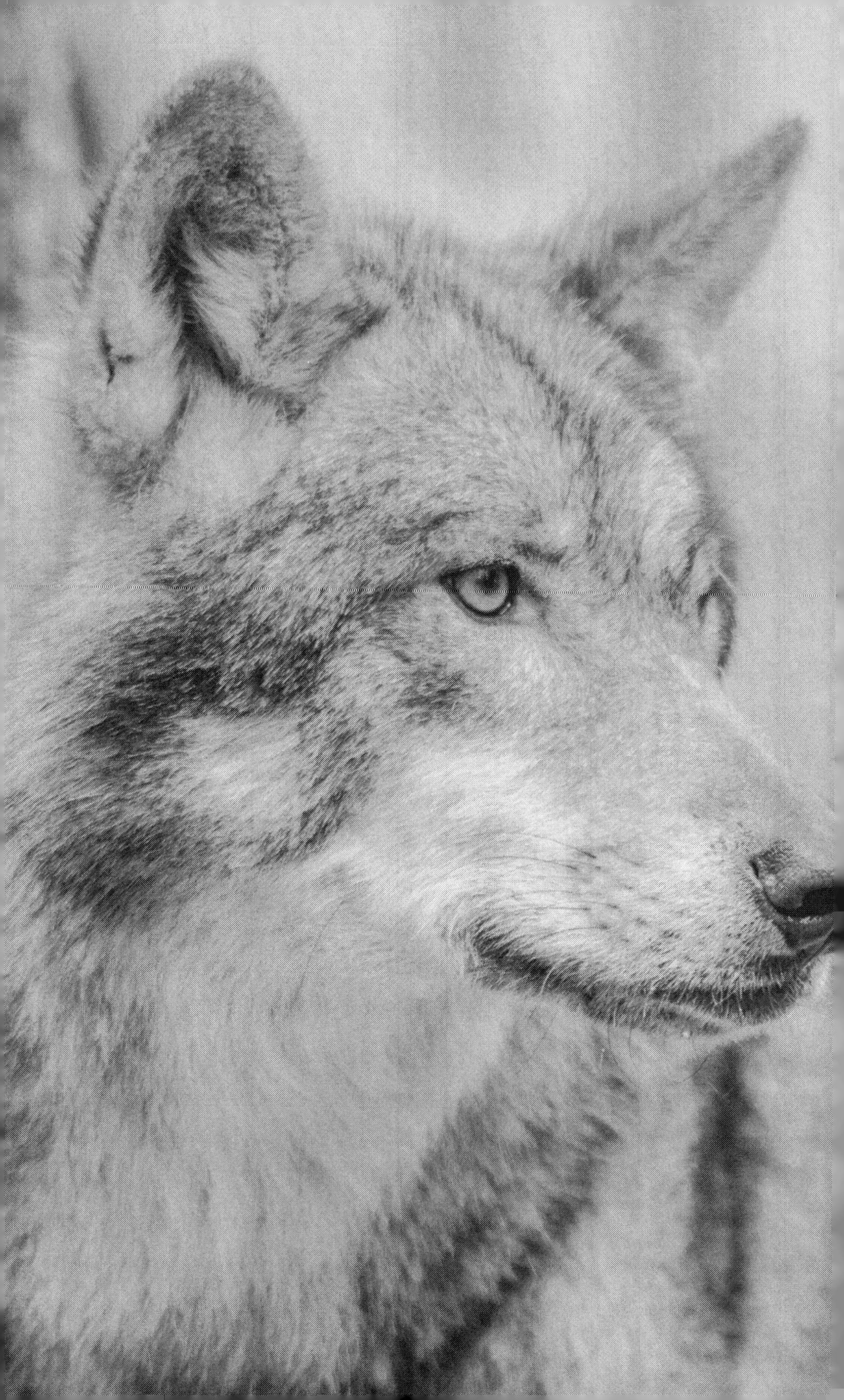

Chapter Thirty-Nine

Mina

I FELL FORWARD INTO the warm space he'd left when he moved. Did I really just say that, that I wanted to try now? Was I out of my mind?

I buried my face in his pillow, breathing in that scent that I now knew was entirely him, and not even a little from a bottle. It soothed its way through me, taking a little of the tension from my body.

How would he do it? Would he pin me down like they did? Hold me, so I can't move, or escape? Would I panic? Would I scream? Would it hurt? Worse... would I even have the courage to say no, or would I just lay there and let him, because he needed it, and I was supposed to give it to him?

By the time he returned, I was practically curled up in his space, with my face buried in his pillow. I heard him chuckle, and I froze. I didn't mean to, I just knew it was about to happen, and I was afraid. *Terrified*.

He heaved a heavy sigh as he approached.

"Baby, you're not ready, and that's okay." I angled my head to look at him.

"I want to be." He crouched by the bed, since I'd taken up most of it.

"I don't want you to try before you are. If I scare you, if you become afraid of me, you'll never want to be with me, and I don't think I can be without you now. I need you with me, and if that means I spend an inordinate amount of time jacking off in the shower, then so be it." I giggled, despite everything. He could be crude, but somehow he always added enough humour, to take the sting out of it.

I rolled over, making room for him. I still couldn't believe I was topless, and I slept pressed up against him all night. I felt so safe, and yeah, loved, pulled so tight against him, his warm skin against mine. I stared at his face as he sat beside me, a sad smile on his face.

I looked at his lips, remembering how they felt when he kissed me, how his beard tickled my skin on the approach, and how it felt to have his lips on my back and shoulder, when he inspected my burgeoning tattoo. I felt that light tingle between my legs again, and I saw his nose twitch, then a grin started to spread across his face.

"What are you thinking about, Miss Masters? I'm hoping it's positively filthy." I giggled again, and he tilted his head.

"How about this? You give me permission to make you come again today, no sex, but I get to choose how? You can stop me at any time, but I get to touch you wherever, and however, I want?"

My heart thudded in my chest, and that sensation of arousal increased. Why did it increase? His grin was wide as he watched me.

"Oh yeah, I think you like the sound of that, and I hate to make you admit it out loud, but if you want the pleasure that you know I can give you, just say yes. Remember, 'no' at any point means I stop. *Immediately.*"

Oh my god, I wanted to, I really did. I wanted to be normal and real, like a proper woman, and just his words were making that squirmy feeling inside, so much more intense. I knew he could give me pleasure, but could I give him free rein over my body? What would he do?

"Ah ah ah, don't go disappearing into your head, Mina, yes or no?" I chewed my lip, pressing my legs together, because that feeling was stronger now.

"What... what will you do to me?" He winked.

"All good things, baby, I promise. Just be open to letting me try, and remember the power is all with you, okay?"

I nodded, and he frowned.

"Sex is off the table. Anything else to avoid? Anything you know will definitely scare you?"

I nodded immediately.

"Don't trap me, or pin me down." He sighed sadly.

"Of course, done. Anything else?" Was there? I didn't know what he could be planning, so how could I know?

I shook my head, and he reached for the sheet, but stopped to stare at me.

"I need consent, Mina."

I took a breath, oh god. "Ye... Yes." He laughed softly, his eyes lighting up.

"Good girl." Why did that feel so good when he said it? Like a shiny medal on my chest, for all to see? I think it gave me some of his strength every damn time he said it.

He pulled the sheet back slowly, revealing me to him a little at a time. His eyes travelled all over me, and I flinched, moving my hands to cover my scars.

"No, Mina, don't hide any part of this beautiful body from me. I want it all."

My hands seemed to move away on their own. I could feel my breathing speeding up, as he trailed his eyes across my skin, stopping at my breasts, and moving further down.

"I'm going to get these pants off you, okay?" I met his eyes as he leaned down over me, his hands reaching for them. I nodded, and his smile was quick again. The approval in his eyes made me feel brave.

He hooked his fingers in the waistband and pulled them down my legs, and I even lifted my hips to help him. Feeling him bare me to him was both exhilarating, and terrifying.

I felt gooseflesh cover me for a few seconds, before I adjusted to the temperature in the room. He let out a sigh, tossing my underwear over his shoulder.

"Beautiful."

I could feel my body trembling lightly under his gaze. Not knowing what was coming was almost unbearable. What if he'd lied? What if he decided to have sex with me, while I was open and trusting him?

"Don't fear me, Mina, never fear me." He leaned over me, breathing in deeply, a low growl seeping out of him. He lowered his face over my stomach, his beard tickling for the briefest second, before his lips touched down, to the left of my belly button, right on top of one of my scars.

I knew where they were by memory. I hadn't looked in so long, but I didn't need to, because I knew. Sometimes it still felt like they hurt, where the knife had cut in, over and over.

"Mina, don't go there... whatever bad place you're on the verge of, just step away and come back to me." How did he know? Had I tensed up? I lifted my hands, and they were clenched tightly. I let out a breath, and another, forcing myself to unlock.

"*Good girl*." There it was again, helping me to let out another breath, further unclenching my body.

His lips touched down again in the same place. His tongue circled the area, and I twitched under the sensation. He laughed softly.

Pressing his hands either side of my body to brace himself, he worked his way across my stomach, kissing, and then circling each scar with his tongue, covering them with him. Leaving me feeling his touch, rather than the ugliness of each one.

As he approached my chest, I felt another tingle of desire, and gasped. His eyes flicked to mine.

"Yes, baby, it's about to get so much better." The next scars were on my left breast, and I saw his eyes zero in on them. There were more of the wounds here than on my stomach, so I guess they'd really hated my breasts.

"Mina," he snapped, and I focused on him.

"That's better. Stay with me and enjoy this, it's for you."

He kissed the next scar, just to the side of my left nipple. As he trailed his tongue around it, his breath washed over my nipple, and I quivered, a gasp whooshing out of me.

My back arched a little, and he did that low chuckle again. He blew air over my nipple again, and this time it was a full body shudder.

"Oh god..." I murmured, and he chuckled again.

"Still just me, baby."

When his tongue flicked my nipple, I nearly came up off the bed, and then his lips closed around it, sucking it into his mouth, and a long moan came out of me.

My hands. My hands were on autopilot. No longer clenching and unclenching at my sides, they came up to burrow into his hair, holding him in place, as he rubbed my nipple with his tongue.

The tremors that were running through me were intense, and I couldn't stay still. When he pulled back, looking at me through heavy eyes, I bit my lip, having a million words, and wanting to keep them all in, so he'd carry on.

He blew a breath over my damp nipple, and it wrenched another gasp out of me. I had no idea it could feel this way, and I wanted more of this delicious sensation.

"You're so fucking responsive, Mina, I just want to do this for hours." I trembled at the idea of that. How could he want to keep making me feel this way, and not want the same in return?

Why didn't he just want to take his own pleasure, and then be done with me? Like they did.

Without meaning to, I tensed again at the thought, and he growled, sucking my other nipple into his mouth suddenly, making me yelp with surprise. My hands pulled at his hair, as my body writhed beneath his touch. I couldn't stay still, my entire body was alight, and it wanted more.

"M... More..." I whimpered, before I could stop myself. He laughed, freeing my nipple, and staring at me again.

"Demanding, baby, I like it." He paid the same attention to every other scar on my chest, before he started to work his way down again, but what was he doing? He'd done those ones, and I wanted him playing with my nipples again. I'd never felt anything like that before.

My hands tightened in his hair, as he moved below my belly button. Moving there... the place I still couldn't let myself think about, or even think the name of.

Giving it a name gave it power that I couldn't let it have, because it had destroyed my life. It was what they'd wanted. What they'd hurt me for.

"Relax, baby, you're about to scream my name for the neighbours to hear." I didn't understand. I pulled at his hair again, and he laughed, reaching up to loosen my fingers.

His hands travelled down the outside of my thighs, and I felt my body trembling again. He was going *there*.

"No," I whispered, and he stopped. He lifted his hands and looked at me.

"No?"

I covered my face. "I don't know..."

He sighed, and I felt him move, and his mouth suddenly locked around a nipple again. It wrenched a garbled moan out of me, and my back arched again as pleasure rippled through me.

When he pulled back, he stared at me, my hands now under my chin, clenched together.

"What I want to do, Mina, will feel ten times better than that. A million, in fact. You said more, well, that's more, right?" I nodded, suddenly desperate for him to do whatever it was, because I wanted more.

He raised his eyebrows, waiting for me to say it.

"I'm sorry, yes, please. I panicked, I'm sorry."

"Stop fucking apologising, Mina. You're so much braver than you realise. Now, shall I continue? I really want to taste you again." I shivered, and nodded.

"Yes, please..."

"*Good girl*," he whispered, breathing the words against my stomach as he moved back down my body again. He'd been careful not to put his weight over me, or cover too much of me at any time, and it helped. He looked at me again.

"Bend your knees, Mina. Pull your legs up to make room for me." I did it, because it was easy to follow instructions. He didn't demand, but he asked firmly, and I consented with my actions.

It was easier than making the decisions from scratch. I was just responding to his requests, but when I'd said no, *he'd stopped*, just like he promised. Until he realised that I didn't know what I was saying in that moment.

He grinned, and moved to kneel in front of my legs, then he leaned closer, and my legs... I moved them apart for him, like my body knew what was coming and wanted it, while my brain was still at 'what the fuck is going on?'.

"Good, so good, and your smell? You're so fucking turned on, I can smell it, baby. It's beautiful. Delicious." He blew a cool breath down my left thigh, and my hips jerked, *on their own*. He chuckled.

He moved, adjusting his position, pushing my legs wide, to let his shoulders come in closer, his face lowering to between my legs. Another of those breaths on me down there made me gasp, and jerk.

I felt a finger trail between my folds, finding them slick with my desire. He groaned, and I lifted my head, to see his finger in his mouth.

"Delicious," he said, shooting me a wicked grin as he pulled his finger back out, and lowered his face to me.

That first swipe of his tongue just against my clit, oh my god, *my clit*. Words... they were coming back at me with a vengeance, and I couldn't deny them any longer.

That first flick of his tongue made my whole body flex, wrenching a choked gasp from me. He chuckled again, pressing his hands to my hips, to hold me still. Next, his tongue swept along the seam, slipping between the folds, and my fists came back to his hair.

He groaned, swiping his tongue across me again. My legs were still bent, held in place by his arms, but it didn't make me feel trapped, although my legs were shuddering uncontrollably.

I couldn't focus on anything but the swiping and teasing of his tongue. He went back to my clit, flicking at it, sucking it into his mouth, while I breathed mostly in short, sharp pants, and my vision seemed to go spotty.

"You taste so fucking good, baby, I just wanna eat you all day," he murmured, before he plunged his tongue between my folds again, licking deep into me.

My body erupted, a yell coming out of me as my back bowed up from the bed, and my fingers tugged harder on his hair. He chuckled softly, but he kept thrusting his tongue over and over, while I made strange high-pitched noises, and jerked with each thrust, as my body coiled, and heated, and writhed.

By the time he sucked my clit into his mouth again, I was screaming, my body on fire, every part of me feeling like it had tensed and then released, while I practically thrust my hips into his face.

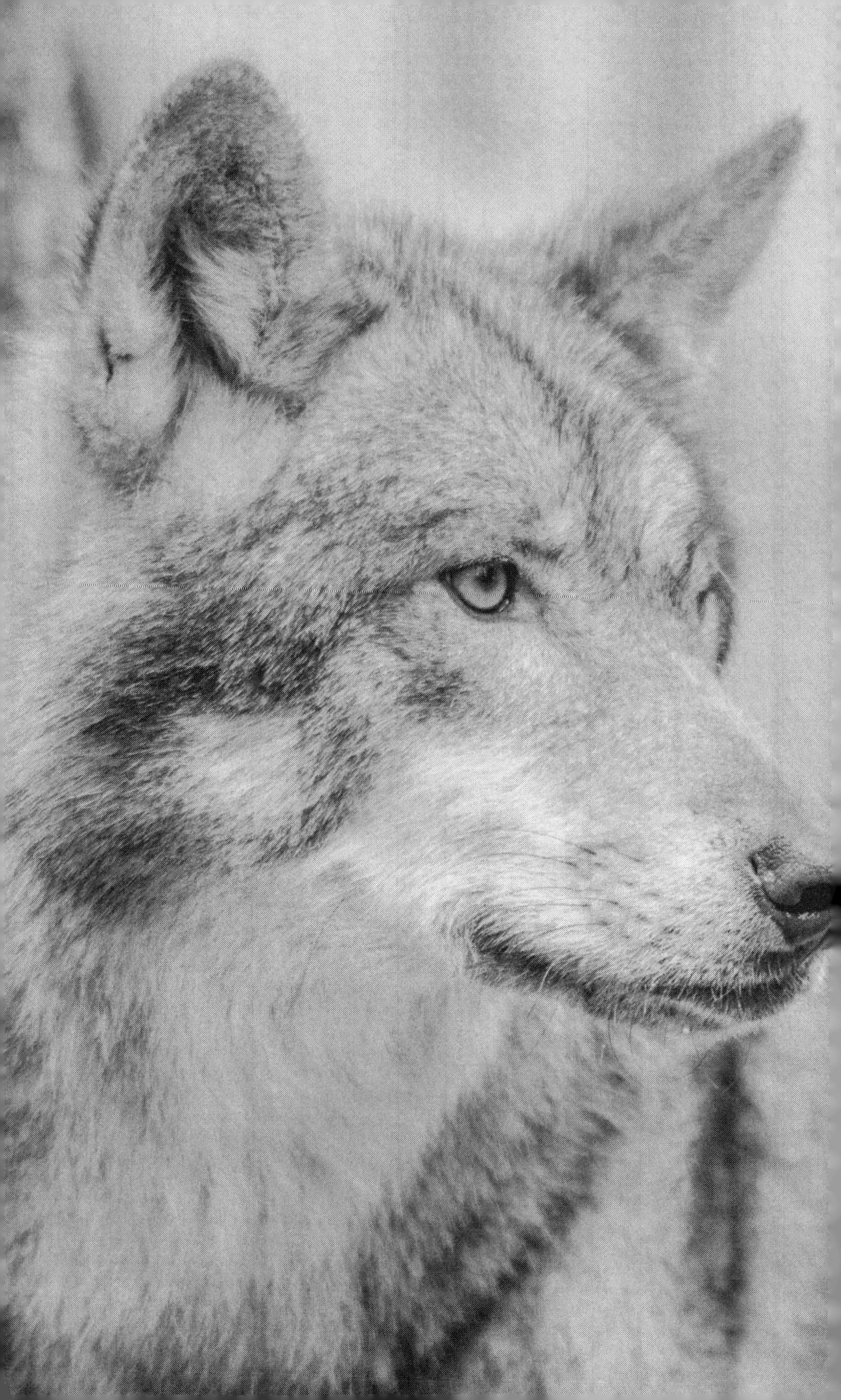

Chapter Forty

ASHER

Fuck. Me. As I lifted my head, still relishing her taste on my tongue, I took a long look at her, my mate. Her gaze was fixed on the ceiling, and her breaths were hard and heavy, practically wheezes.

When I finally released her legs, they just slid down on the bed, like she had no strength to hold them up anymore. *I knew I'd given her a fucking bone shaker of an orgasm.*

I'd felt it building and tried to keep her at that edge for a while, so she'd really blow when she came. I licked my lips, sitting back on my haunches.

Was I feeling a little satisfied? Well, yeah, fucking right I was, because *look at her*. She was practically catatonic; she'd come so hard.

I moved over to lay beside her, resting my head on my arm. I trailed a finger down her cheek, and she blinked slowly, finally turning to look at me. She seemed dazed, like she couldn't even see me properly, and then her lips twitched into a smile.

"Hi," she whispered.

"Hi yourself. You okay?" She sighed out a deeper breath.

"A bit dizzy."

I grinned proudly, feeling like a fucking Alpha again for the first time in days.

"As it should be. Was it what you expected?" Her eyes narrowed, and she let out a shaky breath.

"That? Never..." She was still blinking slowly, and I didn't want to pull her from that feeling just yet. She was finally relaxed, finally completely at peace, and I wanted it to last forever.

Her voice was hoarse from that scream though, that fucking scream. I rolled off the bed, and returned with a glass of water for her. She stared longingly at it, and I laughed.

"You'll have to sit up, baby, I can't pour it into your mouth." I cheekily quirked an eyebrow.

"Well, I guess you could suck it off my fingers..." She blinked, staring at me dumbly. I lifted my fingers, holding them over the glass.

"Shall I?" She shook her head, groaning softly as she tried to push herself up.

"Help me." I set the glass aside, and offered a hand so she could try and pull herself up to sit against the headboard.

She felt cold to the touch, so I pulled the sheet up for her, covering up those fucking gorgeous tits, so she could warm up.

I passed her the water, keeping my hand there when her hand seemed to twitch at first, like she couldn't hold it. She took several deep swallows.

"Thank you." She passed it back, and I took a few gulps myself.

"So..." I stared at her, running the back of my finger over her pink cheek again; she was embarrassed for some reason.

"Did you enjoy being tongue-fucked?" I asked bluntly, shocking her out of her embarrassment. She glared at me, and then saw my smile.

"Is it always like that?"

I shrugged one shoulder.

"I mean, normally I'd have finger-fucked you at the same time, but I didn't know if you'd be ready for that. They'd go deeper inside you." She was still staring at me, and I actually felt a little light-headed as I looked at her.

The last fifteen minutes were replaying in my mind like the most beautiful and filthy movie reel. We were so fucking close; the bond was in reach, and I wanted it more every minute. Wanted her more.

"I haven't told you everything about the mating process," I blurted out, then groaned, practically facepalming. I'd meant to hold this back until she felt closer to being ready, but I just didn't want to lie, or hide anything from her now.

That fucking wariness was back in her eyes, the look that I'd managed to chase away for so long.

"More than sex?" She asked, her voice a little frustrated. *Join the club, baby, I'm just as fucking frustrated.*

I took a breath, and said it, knowing it'd scare her.

"I have to mark you." She physically recoiled from me, her face twisting with panic.

"Mark me? *Why?*" I cursed, wishing I could undo this fucking conversation.

"It's not like I created this stuff. I'm just a slave to it, just like we all are." She folded her arms, glaring at me.

"Get back to the part where you have to add another fucking scar to this body of mine. Go on, what is it? A knife to the heart? You have to scar me elsewhere? All over? Don't get shy on me now. *Apparently my body exists just for men to leave their fucking marks all over it.*"

Wow. She was really angry, and I wished I'd held it back longer now. In the throes of passion, she may have taken to it differently, as part of the pleasure, rather than as an addition to her war wounds, which was exactly how she'd chosen to see it.

"Jesus, Mina, don't say it like that. If you were a wolf, you'd have to mark me too. It's just how it works." Again, I wanted to take back the last two minutes, go back to the way things were. I reached for her, but she just kept glaring at me.

"Turn away." I frowned.

"I don't under-"

"Don't look at me."

I sighed, turning away.

"This isn't going to make it any easier."

She was moving; getting out of bed, and dragging the top sheet with her. She made it to her holdall, which was still on my floor, and looped it awkwardly over her arm.

Then she marched from the room, slamming the door loudly. I dropped my head into my hands. What the fuck had I just done?

Derek's voice in my head added to the frustration.

~ Boss, we've got a problem. We need you downstairs now.

Fuck me, I wasn't sure what was worse; being interrupted right now, when I needed to do something to fix this, or the fact that he could initiate mindspeak with me.

I wanted to punch him, and in fact, I was pretty sure I would.

Mina

I WAS SHAKING BY the time I slammed the door on the room I'd chosen so few nights ago. I threw my bag down, and started pulling clothes out, and throwing them on. I frantically glanced around for anything of mine that needed to go back in the bag.

I noticed my clothes from the other night, neatly folded on the bed, which had also been made. The laundry gnomes had been around. I shoved them into my bag too, and froze on the spot when I heard Asher storming from his room.

I waited for him to storm in here too, but he didn't, he went straight past. *Oh.* Was I disappointed? Did I want him to fight for me?

As soon as he'd gone, I checked the hallway, then ran to his room to gather up anything of mine I could see. I loaded my arms with my discarded t-shirt and trousers, and some other clothes, shoes, and my toiletries from his bathroom.

My toothbrush sat beside his, and it cut a hole in my heart to split them up when I still felt they belonged together, just like I thought we did.

I crammed it all back in my bag, and spotted my phone by the bed. That went into my pocket, and then I looped the bag over my shoulder.

I made my way through the house as quietly as I could, but when I reached the living room, I noticed the kitchen doors pulled tightly closed, and there were voices on the other side.

Despite myself, I crept closer. *I knew them all well enough now to recognise their voices, but their conversation filled me with horror.*

"Boss, you're not listening. I'm not trying to be a prick here." That was definitely Derek, then there was an angry growl, followed by Asher's voice.

"It doesn't matter."

Jase piped up next. "Alpha, at the risk of getting my head punched in too, this isn't any of our fault. We're merely telling you what the lore is saying."

There was another roar of frustration from Asher.

"I know."

"Boss, you're putting us all at risk. This isn't how it's supposed to go, and you fucking know that."

"Alpha, you heard what he said. The bond isn't working how it's supposed to, and instead of strengthening you, it's weakening you. *Another day of this malfunctioning attempt at a bond, and you won't even be an Alpha any longer.*" Oh god!

Something crashed against something else, and I jumped, hopping away from the door, but it didn't open. Their voices were quieter now, so I had to press closer.

"... ending the bond is the only way. To save you, to save all of us." That sounded like Jase, and he spoke haltingly, sounding nervous.

"I can't. *I love her.*" Asher's voice was gruff, almost defeated.

"Boss, the longer you stay in this limbo, between bonded and not, the more she's draining from you. Every tiny fucking step you guys take, it's pulling power from you, and it's going to her. She's probably more of an Alpha right now than you are. I'm telling you, it's *toxic*, and you need to cut it off now, before she destroys you."

I clasped both hands over my mouth, so I couldn't gasp out loud, as I backed away from the door. I turned and once I'd sneaked out of the house, I ran.

The only thing I could think of was to run to Daisy's house. It was the nearest friendly place I could think of, and I needed help getting out of here, to get far away.

Maybe once I was far enough away, maybe it would help. If not, he'd have to break the bond, by whatever means necessary.

It took me a few minutes of solid running to get there. My phone buzzed in my pocket, and I ignored it. I finally reached the door Asher had pointed out as Daisy and Ned's, and I balled up a fist, banging on it over and over. I needed her to let me in before he came looking for me.

I was freaking out by this point, feeling like I'd been chased down the hill, like he was right behind me, ready to snatch me and drag me back there, regardless of the risk to him. I couldn't breathe, and tears were running down my face.

When the door was wrenched open, it wasn't Daisy standing there, but Ned; big, scary, angry Ned. I squeaked, and jumped back from the door.

"No."

He took one look at me, stepped outside looking around, and then he shoved me in the house, slamming the door behind us.

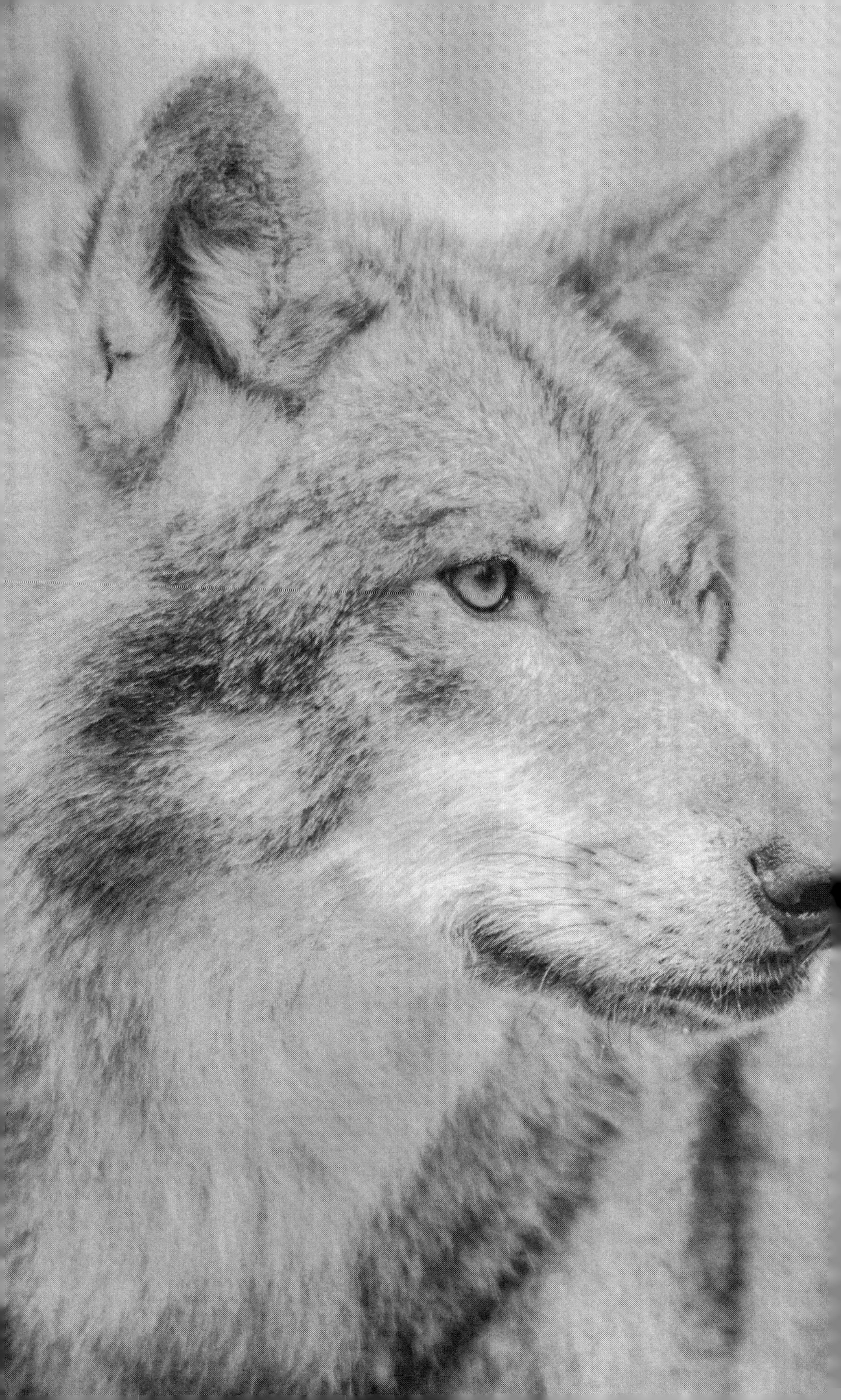

Chapter Forty-One

MINA

I ALMOST FELL AS I frantically backed away from him.

"I'm Daisy's friend," I said hurriedly, my hands out in front of me. He just shook his head at me.

"You think I don't know who you are?"

His voice was so strong, it practically boomed, filling the room.

"Is Daisy here?"

He laughed. "It's a work day, Mina. She's at work." I facepalmed.

I couldn't remember what day it was, because I'd lost all semblance of normality, being cocooned here in Asher's world. I covered my face, feeling the panic starting to overwhelm me again, and Ned cleared his throat.

"You want to sit down?" I peeked at him, and he was gesturing to the sofa in the room to my left. I walked there on shaky legs, dropping my bag beside me.

He sat across from me in a big recliner, which he seemed to dwarf with his body mass. He was truly terrifying.

"What did he do to you?" He asked softly, and I stared at him in surprise at his words, his *tone*.

"What? Who?"

He rubbed a hand over his buzzcut hair, looking uncomfortable.

"The Alpha, has he hurt you?" His voice sounded more concerned than angry now, and I shook my head.

"So why the hell did I just condemn myself to death?"

I blinked at him.

"I don't understa-"

"I just touched the Alpha's mate. He's going to tear my fucking arms off for that." I shook my head.

"No, he won't do that."

Ned folded his arms, the way big men do, where they tuck their hands under their armpits with their thumbs out.

"It's how it works, love, because you're his. My hands were on you, and from what I hear, that was a big enough fuck up as it is, because of who you are, putting aside all the Alpha stuff for a minute."

"You're not as scary as I thought," I blurted out, and then sighed. "God, I'm sorry, that was thoughtless."

He laughed, shrugging his huge shoulders.

"I'm used to it, don't worry. It's one of a few reasons that I work from home these days." I glanced around me, expecting to see a desk or paperwork or something.

"I'm keeping you from your work. I should go."

He shook his head.

"Nah, if I'm going to die today, I might as well have a little company for a minute. Cuppa? Coffee? Something else?" I stared at him silently and he laughed.

"I'll just surprise ya." He was gone a few minutes, while I cast my eyes around the living room.

It was modern and uncluttered, in a similar style to the pack house. There were a few photographs on the wall, wedding photos, and my stomach ached for the happiness I could see in their pictures. Daisy was pretty much wrapped around this bigger, stronger man, gazing into his eyes, with pure desire. *Love.*

It brought more tears, because I wanted that so badly, with Asher. Not because he was the Alpha, not even because he was a wolf, *but because he was mine.* I could feel it, just like I knew my tattoo had grown.

I couldn't feel it, nor had I looked, but I just knew. Because our bond grew so much stronger this morning, when he treated me with such care, and then I ran out on him.

A cup of tea waved in front of my face, startling me from my thoughts, so I took it.

"Thanks."

Ned had placed a tray with milk and sugar on the table between us. It was so English and civilised, that it was at odds with this place, and his appearance, which I was starting to learn had led me to misjudge him.

"I don't know what to do," I finally said, as he sat back with a jumbo mug of his own tea.

"I can't promise to know the answers, love, but I'll listen if that helps. Daisy is on her way back as well. I sent her a text." Another work day screwed up, because of me.

"God, I'm sorry, I'm screwing up both your lives now." He laughed.

"I think we can handle a little disruption here and there, Mina. Now tell me what's going on."

I stared at him, a small smile on my face at the thought of talking about this with him.

"I came here to girl talk with Daisy." He snorted, pulling a face.

"Hell, I have no practice at that, but try me. I'm not talking about men's butts or anything, though."

I couldn't hold back my giggles, I'd imagined him to be gruff, and scary, and he was actually kind of funny.

"Our bond isn't working," I said, sipping the tea, while I leapt from the ledge and told him the truth. It was actually pretty nice; the tea, I mean. Ned was frowning.

"In what way is it not working? A bond's a bond, right?"

I shook my head. "Because I'm such a mess, it's taking time. It's kind of... partway through." He brushed his hand over his face, looking shocked.

"I didn't even know that could happen. You guys screwed yet?"

It didn't gross me out, or scare me to hear him ask that, nor did I feel like he'd overstepped by asking something so intimate. Instead, I just shook my head.

"We're close, I think. I want to."

"But you're scared, and that makes sense, love. From the little Daisy told me, you have every reason to distrust men, even though we're mostly all good." He grinned again. He was easier to talk to than anyone

I'd met in a year, even Asher, because there was no expectation from him.

"His tattoo is growing, but mine has only just started," I stated, not knowing how far mine had progressed since we last looked. His eyebrows shot up.

"Ours happened overnight, but then of course we fucked like rabbits for damn near twenty-four hours. Talk about chafing... *Ahem*... I mean, I didn't know it could happen gradually, but that's better than not at all, right?"

I shook my head, because that was the point, wasn't it?

"It's hurting him, weakening him." Ned's eyebrows shot together this time. They were actually pretty expressive, and kind of fascinating.

"*In what way?*" He asked carefully, casually nursing that huge mug of tea. My mouth snapped shut as I realised my mistake.

"I shouldn't be telling you this."

He leaned forward a little. "The way I hear it, we're days away from a pack annihilation by the Somerset pack, so if my Alpha isn't up to the job, I need to know. I might need to get Daisy the hell out of here first. I won't let her get hurt." Oh god, I was making it worse, instead of better.

"No! I mean, it's not that bad," I tried, and failed to make things better, to undo my foolish error.

He sighed, sitting back again.

"Don't panic, love, I'm not looking to act on this." I didn't know what that even meant, but I was full of nerves again.

"Mina, how far has your tattoo actually progressed?" I shrugged, desperate to know the answer myself.

"I haven't looked today since... I mean, *I haven't looked today*." He winked at me.

"Want me to, that is if you feel safe, I could take a pic for you, that's all." I stared at him, my hands shaking. Could I be brave enough to bare my back to this stranger? This man whose house I was in, when nobody knew where I was?

My phone had buzzed a few times, so when I lifted it out of my pocket, I spotted three missed calls, and four text messages. *All from Asher.* My heart felt like it would beat out of my chest, even as it felt like it was breaking into pieces.

"If I've overstepped, you can just say no, Mina. I'm not about making things worse for you." I sighed, steeling myself.

"No, you're right, we should check it, but you'll stay where you are, right?" He nodded, smiling gently at me.

"I'm mated, love. I have no desire to touch another woman, willingly or otherwise."

I sighed, opening the camera app for him. At least, if nothing else, I'd have a picture to remember this experience by when I was gone, and it disappeared.

I stood up, slipping my jacket off, and dropping it on the sofa. Turning around, I awkwardly caught the back of my t-shirt, and slid it up my back, the cool breeze of the moving fabric causing a shiver.

Ned made a hmmmm sound, and I heard the camera click several times.

"Okay, love, you can sit back down." I lowered my top, and tucked it into my trousers, then turned to sit back down, reaching for my phone which was extended back in my direction. Ned made sure our fingers didn't even touch.

Once I had it back, I looked at the picture on the screen, and gasped.

"It's beautiful," I said, wanting to stroke my finger over it, knowing the phone would just read that as a swipe, and move the picture.

Ned cleared his throat.

"It's almost complete, Mina," he pointed out, and I enlarged the image, moving it around on the screen. The wolf had a head, and a torso, but then it faded away. There were swirls, with tendrils, starting to weave across my back, almost like ivy.

"It's different, from Daisy's, I mean." Ned was saying, and I looked up at him.

"Different how? I mean, apart from the obvious."

He shrugged, frowning a little.

"Hers is a wolf, but there's no, uh, foliage. Yours has leaves and stuff too." I frowned, wondering why it was different. Perhaps because I was human, rather than wolf.

The phone rang in my hand and I jumped, fumbling it and catching it, then fumbling it again, before I finally caught it.

"Fuck!" I blurted, and then looked at Ned apologetically, although he was laughing.

"I can see why Daisy likes you," was all he said. Asher rang off again, while I stared miserably at my phone.

"You need to do something, love. Talk to him, or put him out of his misery. He needs to know where he stands."

"What happens if we break the bond?" I asked Ned, and his face dropped.

"Seriously? I have no idea, but it can't be good. You'll lose that connection between you, and it'll never come back. He'll go back to being an unmated wolf, and you'll go back to being just you. Even if the two of you ended up together after that, it'd never be like it could be."

I hated that thought, the idea that we could never get it back.

"Would it stop me pulling his power away?" I asked Ned, hoping it could fix that, if nothing else.

He leaned forward in his chair.

"Doing what now?" His eyes darted around, and his jaw clenched.

"So he's half an Alpha right now?" *Was there something calculating in his eyes now?*

"Until the bond forms, he's not... himself," I finally said. "He's still the Alpha." He was up and pacing.

"I knew I could feel something was different, when we were at the pack house. His pull wasn't as strong. Normally we can feel it, almost always pushing at our shoulders like we need to kneel before him, but it wasn't like that. I thought he was just distracted, but this..."

What had I done? Had I just put Asher directly in danger with his own pack?

I frantically sent a message to Asher, my heart thudding in my chest as I started to panic.

Me: *Break the bond. It's the only way to save you.*
Asher: *Answer the phone, Mina.*
It rang again, and I rejected the call.
Me: *I can't. I'm sorry. Break the bond. Ned knows, I'm sorry.*
Asher: *Knows what? Come on, baby, please come back to me.*
Me: *He knows I'm leaching your power away. I didn't mean to let him know, but now I'm scared he'll want to challenge you. Please. Break the bond.*
Asher: *I'm coming to get you. Don't go anywhere.*

Fuck. I grabbed my bag, and shoved my way past Ned, running from the house like I was being chased. I heard him calling my name a few times, but then he gave up, and I kept running.

Asher

WHAT THE ACTUAL FUCKING fuck? I'd tried calling her so many times, and she was at fucking Ned's house? She didn't even know him, but of course, she went looking for Daisy, didn't she?

"No sign of her anywhere near the house, boss." Derek reappeared, after I'd sent them both looking for her.

"She's at Ned's," I said dully. "She wants to break the bond."

Derek stared at me, comprehension coming faster to him than it did for me.

"Ah man, she heard us." I nodded.

"She thinks she's doing the right thing."

He raised his eyebrows at me, a wary look on his face.

"Is she?"

"No! This isn't how we fix this. She needs to complete the bond with me, not run from it." I just had to find her first, but would charging down to Ned's just scare her even more?

"Boss, if you drag this out for another day, you'll lose the pack. If anyone finds out-"

"Ned knows."

Derek swore, running his hands through his floppy dark hair.

"Fuck, this is bad. This is really fucking bad."

"You might think I've already come to that conclusion, D," I said sourly.

Jase reappeared at that moment, naked because he'd shifted to search the grounds.

"She went down the hill, Alpha." I appreciated him sticking to formality, even though he clearly barely felt my power anymore, none of them did.

"She's at Ned's," I said quietly.

"She told Ned. He knows about him." Derek jerked a thumb in my direction, and I let out a low growl at his rudeness.

"*Sorry*." He looked sheepish.

"What's the plan, Alpha?" Jase asked, slipping into his spare clothes. I took a deep breath, and stared at them both, hoping I looked more confident than I felt.

"We retrieve them both." They were staring at me with near identical expressions.

"Both?"

I shrugged, heading for the door.

"If Ned's planning to challenge me, we might as well get it over with. I'm sure I can take him." They exchanged an incredulous look.

"You're doubting me?"

"Fucking hell, look, at the risk of you being even more of an ass than normal, I don't want Ned as my fucking Alpha. I chose this pack because I chose you, so if he challenges you, I'm with you." Derek glared at me, even as he spoke his words of support.

Jase cursed. "Don't leave me out, I've been itching for a fight." I stared at both of them.

"Against Ned? One of our committee members? Mated husband to Daisy, who I know you both like? You know it'll destroy her if he dies."

Ned suddenly appeared in the doorway, and we all tensed, ready for a fight.

"Alpha." He nodded at us. "I tried to catch up with her, but she ran. She's spiralling."

We all stared at him, caught in a bizarre holding pattern, waiting for the attack that would surely come any moment.

"For fuck's sake, Alpha, we need to get your mate back now before she leaves pack grounds. She's fragile. I'm worried that if she gets out, she might keep running." He looked frustrated as fuck, and I sure as hell could understand that feeling.

I stared at this huge, hulking man, who could probably tear my wolf in half right now.

"Ned."

He lowered his head, under his own power, since he felt none of mine right now.

"I understand, Alpha, and I bear no challenge. I just want to help." *Fuck. Me.*

We drew him in on the plan, and off the four of us went, to hunt down my wayward woman.

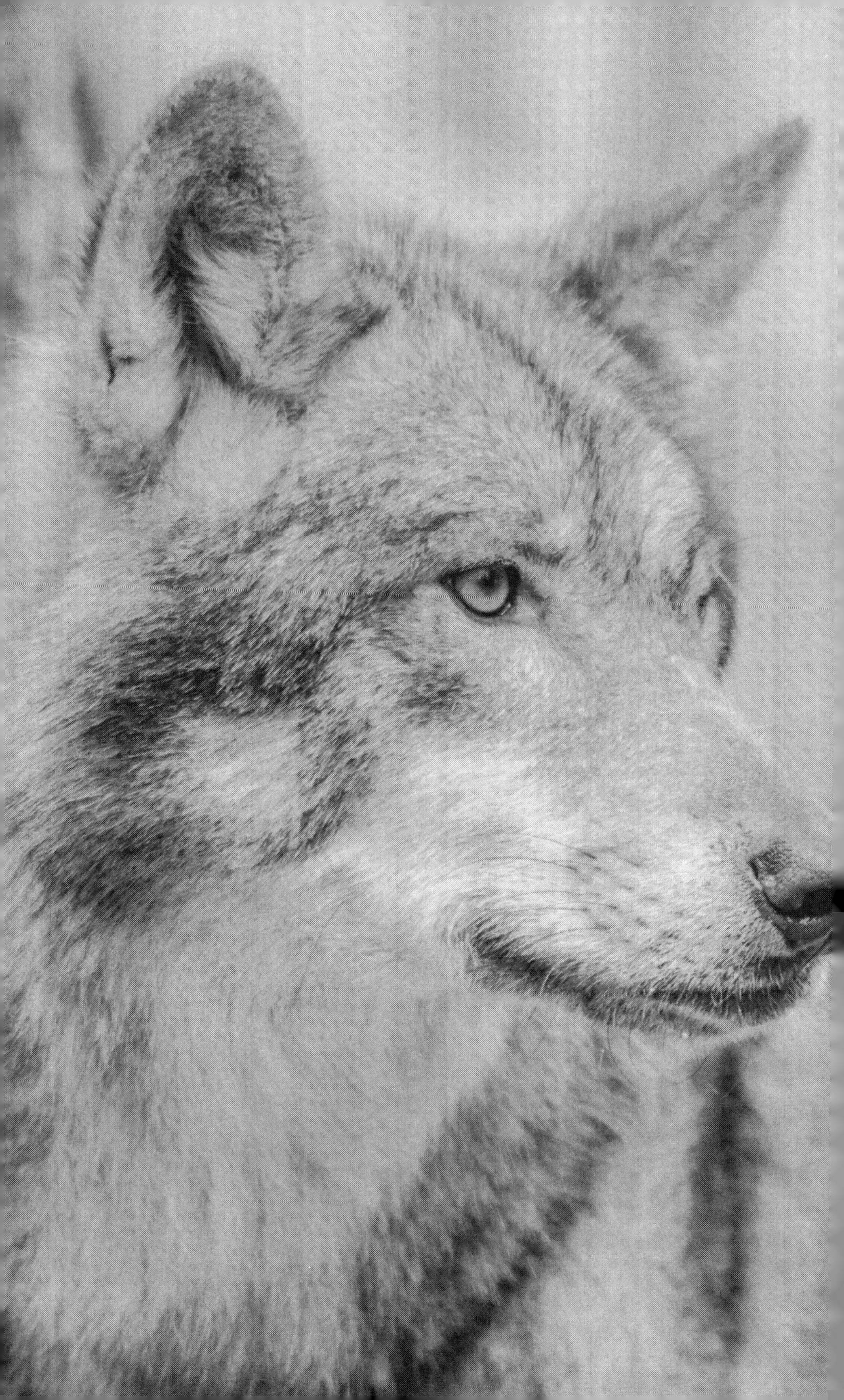

Chapter Forty-Two

Mina

It was the strangest thing. I'd been so sure that when I reached the boundary of the pack land, near Mac's shop, I'd keep running, but I didn't, I couldn't.

We were so close, and surely fixing the bond rather than breaking it, would be the best way to fix all of this. I didn't want to lose him, even just being away from him for this short time was enough to tell me that.

"Nice cup of coffee, love?" Mac was standing outside the coffee shop, smiling at me, and I nodded, not knowing what else to do with myself. I followed him into the quiet store, and hopped up onto the bar stool at the counter.

"Latte?" I nodded again, and he busied himself making a drink for me, remembering my previous drink order. Once he slid it in front of me, my hands went to my bag.

"No, love, I stuck it on the Alpha's tab." He chuckled, then he leaned back against the inner counter, busying himself drying tall latte glasses, as they came out of the steam cleaner.

"Rough day?" He finally asked, doing his best impression of a bartender. I choked out a laugh.

"You could say that. I'm... at a crossroads, I suppose."

He nodded sagely. "Not an easy place to be. All but one route is the wrong one, so which do you take?"

I stared at him as I mulled that one over. It was almost as if he knew what was happening, or the conflict I was going through.

"I want to take the right one," I finally said, staring down at my latte.

He chuckled. "We all do, love. The question is, do you know which one is the right one?" I sighed, because of course I did. I'd always known, hadn't I?

"I'm hoping it's the one I want, more than anything."

He grinned when I looked at him, then nodded over my head. I turned my head to follow his gaze, *and Asher stood in the doorway of the shop.*

He was breathing hard, his fists clenched at his sides, wearing nothing but sweats. My heart thudded in my chest, but it wasn't fear. It was relief, it was excitement, it was seeing everything I needed waiting right there for me.

I watched him nod at Mac, and I knew, I just knew he'd told him that I was here. Thank god. I turned back around to look at Mac, and he gave me a sheepish grin.

"Take the right path, love." I nodded, sliding off the stool. Asher tensely watched me approach him, his chest still heaving with his breaths.

I stopped a few feet away, staring up at him, my lip between my teeth.

"I don't want to break the bond," I whispered, and his body seemed to relax in an instant, a bigger breath rushing out of him.

"Thank god."

"I want to complete it, Asher. *Right now.*"

Asher

FUCK, SHE DIDN'T LEAVE. She stayed right fucking here, where I'd be able to find her. When I got Mac's text, I rushed here in wolf form because I knew I had to get here fast, before she tipped over that edge, but that was the thing about Mac. He knew how to keep a person grounded.

He kept her talking, maybe even talked some sense into her. He kept a bunch of lockers on the pack side of his shop, with spare clothes for any of us who shifted and ran here. It was the only reason I didn't just flash my fucking junk at any patrons he had in his shop, because he really didn't like that.

She stood before me; her lip still caught between her teeth. She said what?

"I want to complete it, Asher. Right now." *Fucking hell*.

My entire body surged with need and I closed the distance, crushing her to me, as I slammed my lips down on hers, my tongue thrusting into her mouth. She tried to press closer to me, returning my kiss just as desperately. *Fuck yes*.

As soon as we broke the kiss, I swept her up into my arms, and turned, nodding at Mac as I left. I could hear him chuckling, as I ran.

I headed to the clubhouse, and pack community hall, because it was empty for now. It had a lounge, but more importantly it had bedrooms upstairs. It was mostly used as a temporary housing opportunity for new pack members, not that we'd had any in so long.

I carried her up to the master suite there; the one designated only for the Alpha and his mate. I kicked the door closed behind me, striding to the bed with her.

Ignoring the urge to throw her down, and cover her with my body, I turned, and sat down, pulling her with me so she straddled my lap, my hard cock caught beneath her. She was breathing fast, trembling and wide-eyed, but excited.

"*I love you, Asher*," she whispered, before she leaned in to kiss me. Her sweet lips teased mine, and I went right into bastard mode, my hand cupping the back of her head and holding her tight, so I could plunder her mouth with my tongue.

She was actually moving in my lap, rocking against me. Her hands were on my shoulders, her nails digging in as she kissed me back just as hard. God yes, at last.

"Baby, I really need to be inside you, right now." I pulled back just millimetres to whisper that to her, bracing myself for her to change her mind. Panic, *run*, but she just smiled.

"Yes." Fucking hell!

She trailed her fingers over my face, tracing my eyebrows, my cheekbones, taking in every detail, and that scent, her arousal? That was fucking drowning me. It was all around us, filling the room, driving me wild with need.

I lowered my hands to her hips, deliberately sliding her against my cock again and again, groaning at the friction, and the sounds she made, every time it pressed me against her clit. I was watching her for her reaction, and finally she just raised an eyebrow.

"Well? Are you ever going to get inside me?"

A frustrated roar rumbled through my chest as I stood up, turning to drop her lightly on the bed. I carefully lowered myself over her, bracing with my arms, so I didn't trap her.

"This okay?" She nodded, then groaned.

"Yes. God, yes, Asher, I trust you. I want you." I was blown away, because she'd grown so different every day. Was that because my power, and strength, had been flowing out of me, and into her?

Had this confidence come only because I was within her already, and would it disappear when I took it all back? Could I really do that to her? I never wanted to see her weak again.

"Please, Asher, *please*." She was writhing beneath me, so I helped free her from her clothes, one annoyingly fucking clingy garment at a time.

When we reached her underwear, I fisted the fabric and tore it away in one swift motion, while she gasped, and then giggled.

Pushing her to settle back, I started to run my lips and tongue all over her body, working both of those fucking nipples into stiff nubs, making her groan when I rubbed my thumbs back over them. I continued to rub them between my fingers, pinching, and tweaking, while she wriggled and writhed, then I worked lower with my kisses.

Her legs parted on their own, and I sucked her clit into my mouth, wrenching a scream from her. Yeah, that was the sound I wanted to hear; screams of fucking pleasure, because of me.

I brought my hands down, to help me tease her apart, sliding my tongue through her pussy lips, making her tremble, as her hands wrapped around my hair once more. I didn't care, she could pull it all out, and I wouldn't give a fuck.

Lifting my head to watch her, I teased her entrance with a finger. Just one, sliding it deep inside her, while her hips lifted, and she moaned. She was so wet, so excited.

I slid that finger out, and then went back in with two, pumping them slowly as she writhed, and gasped, and choked out my name a few times. She was really ready, trusting me to give this to her at last.

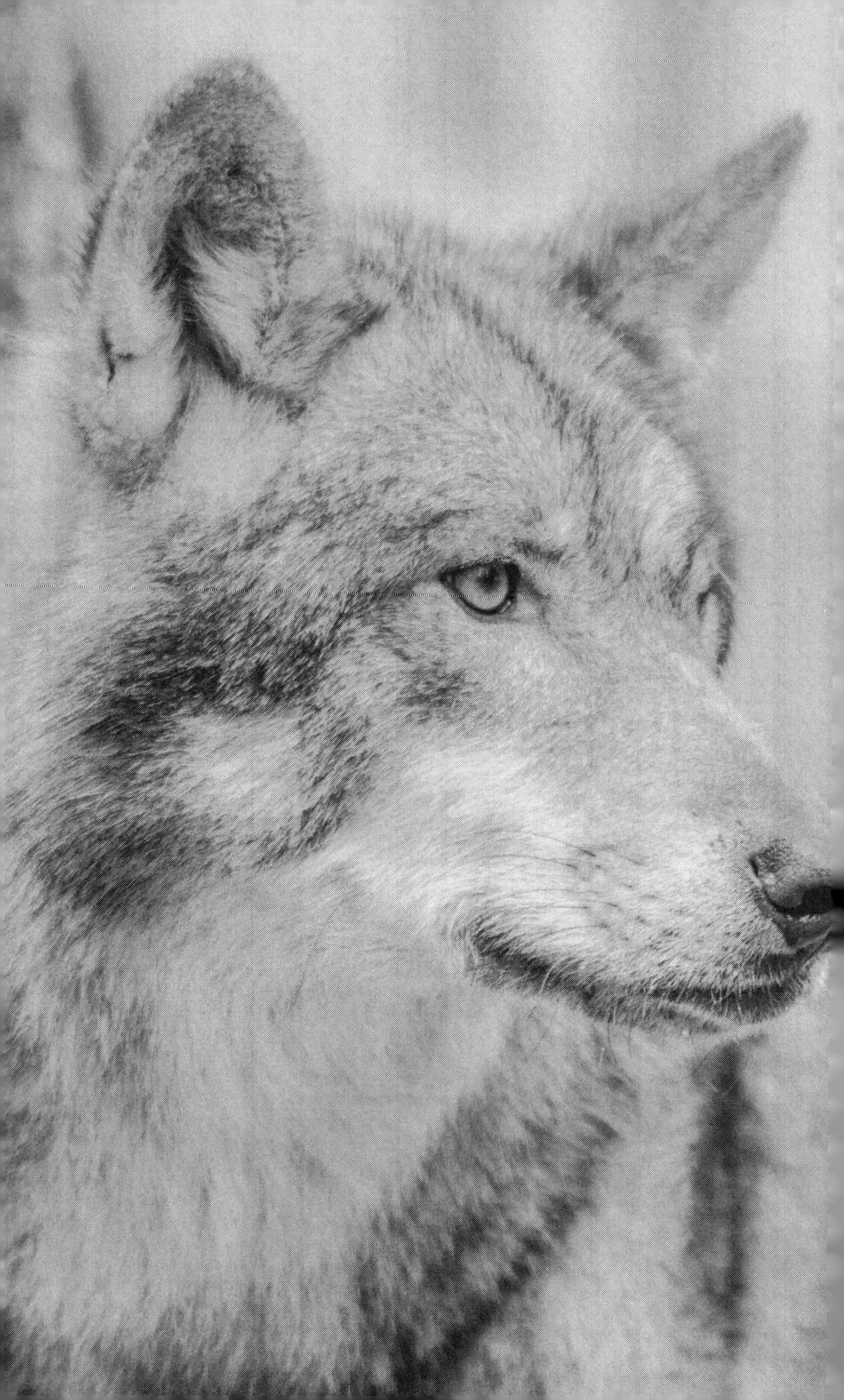

Chapter Forty-Three

MINA

I COULDN'T BELIEVE HOW amazing it felt; his fingers were inside me, and it didn't hurt, and it didn't scare me. They slid back and forth, and the friction made my insides clench and twist.

I knew I was pulling his hair, but neither of us seemed to care. He sucked on my clit again, jamming his fingers in deep, and I felt my body unravel, a scream bursting out of me, as my whole body jerked up off the bed. Ripples of pleasure rolled over me, and chased every thought from my head, except him, except what he was doing.

Asher didn't stop, working his way back up my body to thrust his tongue into my mouth, as one arm braced him, and the other went back to my nipple, twisting it lightly, making me moan. I could taste myself in our kiss, and it made everything more real.

"Please," I gasped, when he paused to take a breath.

His eyes were on mine as he reached down between us, his thumb brushing over my clit, before he took himself in hand. He dragged the head of his cock back and forth across my entrance, and each silky slide made me moan. *Yes, please.*

He pressed inside me, just a little, waiting, watching me. The self-control it must have taken for him to stop and wait was mind-blowing. I nodded, and he quirked a brow.

"Asher, please!" I gasped desperately, and he complied. He jerked his hips, and suddenly he was fully inside me, and I felt every inch of him, filling me, stretching me. My breath hissed out, and he brought both hands up to my face, brushing his thumbs against my cheeks.

"I love you, Mina." His lips came down gently onto mine, and when I opened up, his tongue slipped inside, a languid slide of flesh against flesh.

His hips started to move, matching the rhythm, stroking me inside, and my arms went from his hair to his shoulders, my nails digging into his skin. That brought a shudder from him, and his hips sped up.

He started thrusting hard, pulling almost all the way out just to plunge back in, harder than before. I lifted my legs, bending my knees, and he moved, the angle shifting and each thrust hitting harder, deeper.

Every inch of my body was singing, and I felt another orgasm rapidly building inside me. The friction, the closeness, the repeated pounding against my clit, combined with his body over mine, his lips on mine, his tongue stroking in sync with his cock, was blissful and amazing.

I found myself pulling him closer, I wanted to feel his body sliding against mine as he took what I'd freely given, and he obliged, pressing closer, pulling back to stare in my eyes. He was smiling, and he could see when I started to go over that edge again.

Lowering his head to my throat, he kissed my skin, and ran his tongue over my flesh. Oh... *the marking*... I'd forgotten.

He braced himself, using one hand to lift my hips more, his thrusts growing more frenzied, each one slamming him deeper inside than I could ever have imagined. His teeth brushed my skin, and then I felt him bite. I let out a yell, my back practically inverting as my whole body erupted, and I came harder than ever before.

He made a guttural growling sound, and I felt his body jerking at mine as his own climax hit, his juices spurting inside me, coating me. His tongue swirled over the stinging bite on my neck, and as he pressed kisses to it, I felt it start to go numb.

My body was exhausted; my arms dropped from around his neck, and my legs slid back down. He pulled back to look at me, his face showing that intense satisfaction that I'd seen before, only more so than ever. He ran his tongue over his lips, a flash of red telling me that my blood was on his lips.

"Fuck, I love you, baby."

I smiled, trying to slow my breathing, still tingling all over.

"I love you, Asher." He buried his face in my neck again, as we both waited for our bodies to recover.

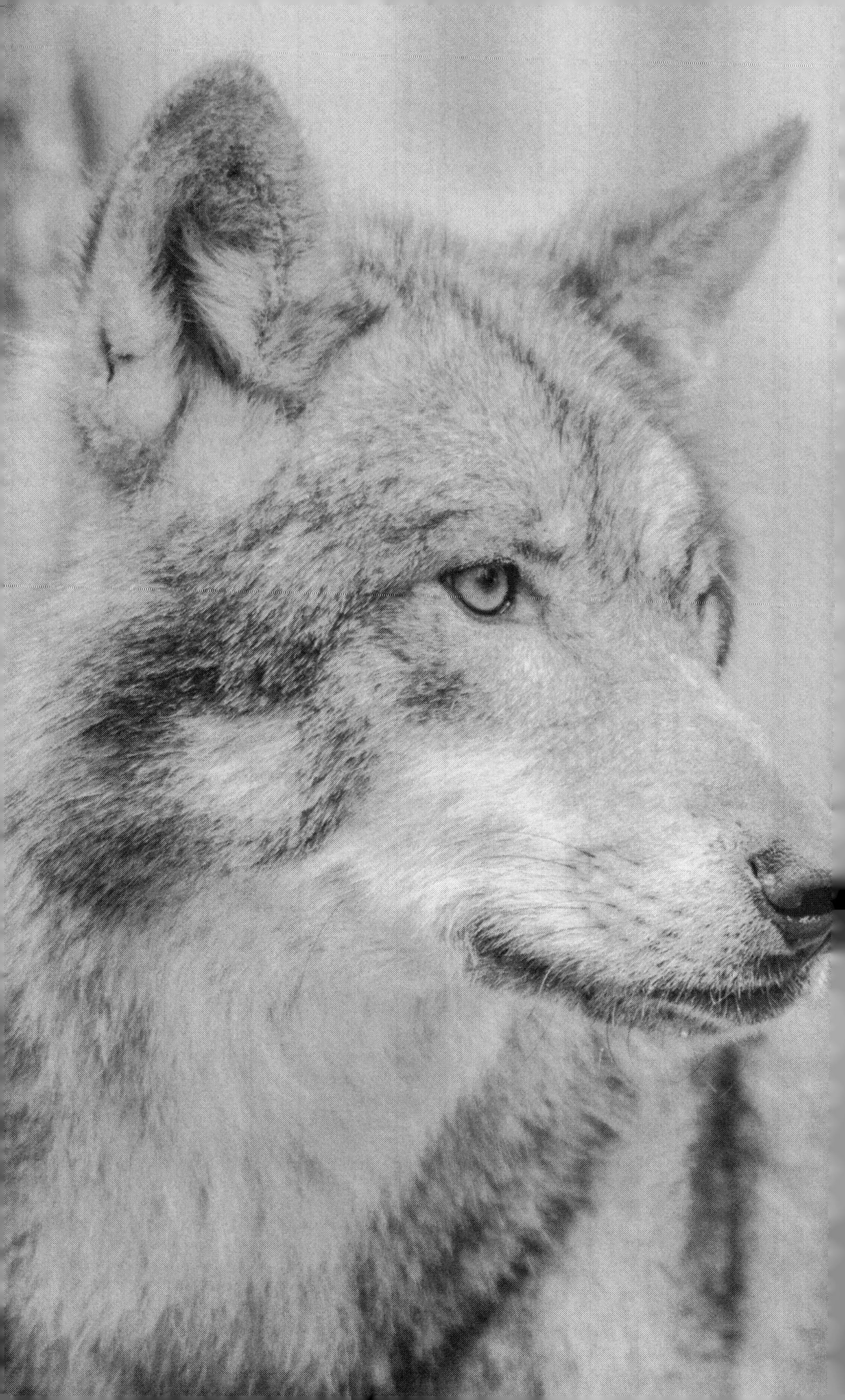

Chapter Forty-Four

ASHER

Fuuuuuuck. If anyone had told me it'd be that good, I'd have laughed it off. How could sex be better than it had ever been before? I guess I'd never experienced its best yet, not before today.

She had fallen asleep very quickly after we mated. *Mated.* Such a strange word in the human world, but it was how wolves apparently bonded; the marking would have helped her sleep, while her body was accepting the mark.

I stared at it, the jagged teethmarks already morphing, shifting, by the time she woke, it would be complete.

She looked so peaceful, her breathing slow and even, one hand over her stomach, the other still half clenched in the bedding. Her legs were relaxed, partially spread still, and I moved to gather the covers, pulling them over her.

As much as I hated to hide her body from me, I didn't want her to get cold. She was mine to protect. *Mine.*

I rolled back onto the bed, and sighed happily, because I could feel the bond completing. We were normally asleep for this part, the boys had said.

Maybe because she was who she was, I was like a livewire, I could feel shocks running through me. It was power, raw power surging through me, almost making me come, all over again.

Mina moaned in her sleep, and I turned to watch her again. I only moved my head, because the rest of me had started to grow heavy, like I was about to pass out.

Mina

WHEN I WOKE UP, he was sleeping quietly beside me. He twitched in his sleep, and wriggled closer to me, his hand coming up to rest on my stomach.

He'd covered me up, but his hand slipped beneath the covers, and I welcomed his touch. How could this even be happening?

Suddenly his touch was like a drug to me, and I wanted it all the time. My neck tingled where he'd bitten, it didn't hurt, but it felt… strange.

I put my fingers up, brushing over it, expecting to feel torn skin, or indentations, but it was smooth. *Huh.* Maybe the mark was symbolic. I stared at his throat, where he didn't have a mark, where I hadn't marked him, because I was just human, right?

There was a need welling inside of me, a desire to see him wearing my mark too. I felt it like a burning urge; *mark him, he's mine.*

Before I knew what I was doing, I'd moved and straddled him, my naked body pressed to his. He groaned, but didn't wake. I'd expected his big hands to come up, to grab me and hold me, but he seemed to be deeply asleep.

I leaned down, taking the opportunity to press my face to his throat, breathing him in. His scent seemed almost like a part of me, and I suddenly needed to taste him too. I ran my tongue up the column of his throat, tasting the slight saltiness of his skin, feeling desire humming through me.

Giving in to instinct, I sank my teeth into the soft part of his neck, biting down hard. He gasped, his whole body jerking against me as he woke.

"Mina! Fuck!" He grabbed my hips, lifting me and lowering me down, and then he was inside me again. He felt so much bigger from this angle, almost too big.

He started thrusting up into me, frenzied, urgent, not just thrusting up, but lifting me and pulling me down as he thrust, so he hit so hard and deep inside me that it dragged a grunt from me each time.

I released his flesh, running my tongue over his skin again, tasting the coppery tang of his blood. It didn't gross me out, in fact, it seemed to complete me. I ran my tongue up his throat again, and then he was pulling my face to his, and kissing me hard.

When I pulled back because I really needed to breathe, he shot me a wicked grin, taking his thrusts into overdrive, his hands holding my thighs, and his thumb suddenly pressing down on my clit.

We came at the same time, both yelling out, and then I collapsed down on him, my energy spent. He chuckled, rolling me over, and then he lay back, reaching to pull the covers around me once more.

"As ways to wake up go, that's about the best fucking possible way," he finally said, when he could breathe.

"I'm sorry, I don't know what happened. I just needed to bite you like that, to mark you too." He nodded, laughing a little breathlessly.

"It's a mate bond thing, but who knew you'd need to mark me, even though you aren't a wolf." I shrugged.

"If I'm wearing your mark, you're sure as hell wearing mine."

He chuckled. "Thank god." I gave him a sidelong glance, before dragging my drained body into a foetal position, facing him.

"Is it done?"

He shrugged, turning on his side to face me.

"It actually *is* my first time, the bonding, so I have no idea. Do you feel different?" I chewed my lip.

"I feel shagged to bits."

He laughed, looking happier and more carefree than ever.

"That's gonna be your new normal, baby. Be prepared to be riding my cock a lot." I shrugged a shoulder.

"I think I can live with that."

He traced my lips with his finger.

"I think I'm going to doze again, baby. Do you need anything before I do?" I shook my head, slipping a hand out from under the covers to take his, pulling it back under to hold it in mine.

"Sleep, Asher, I'll watch over you."

His smile had barely left his face, and he was out, sleeping like the dead. I could see his mark from my position. I'd drawn blood, I knew that because I'd tasted it, and it had felt normal. Like a part of a natural process, that I had somehow instinctively understood.

I could feel everything in my body tingling, not the aftershocks of my orgasm, but something else, something primal. It energised me, burning through me, making me so warm I had to throw off the covers.

Asher was snoring softly, and I glanced at his mark again, and the blood was gone. I leaned up on my elbow, looking closer.

It seemed to be shifting, a pattern moving over his skin, flowing, dissipating, and his skin was smooth again. *Fascinating*. I fell asleep watching the pattern flow hypnotically.

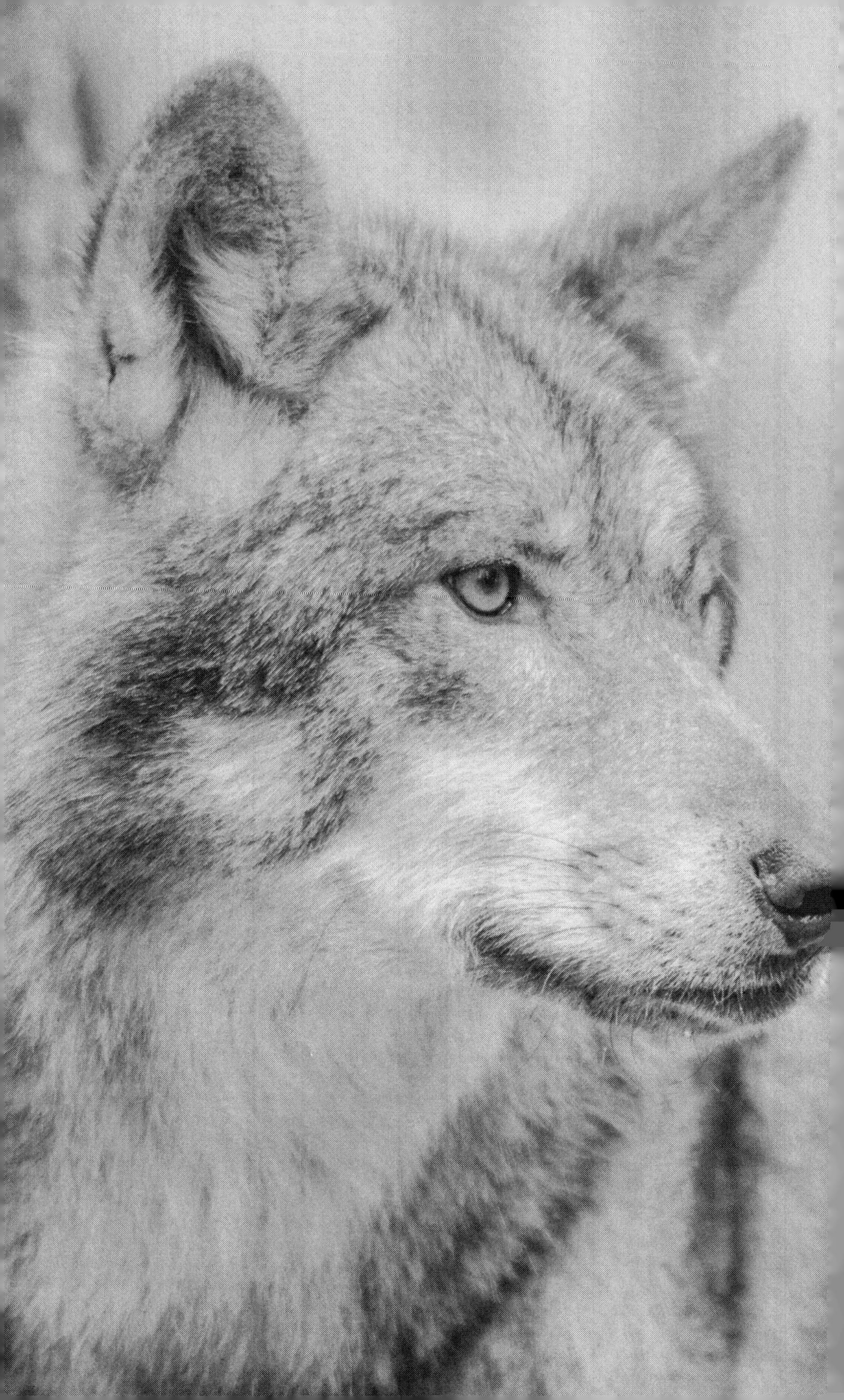

Chapter Forty-Five
ASHER

When I woke again, I felt different; stronger, stronger than I ever had. It flowed through me almost in waves, before it settled into my soul. *I felt like I could do anything.*

I was still pretty much in shock, because Mina, wow, she'd gone from untouchable to incorrigible, from unsure to certain, and from being afraid of sex and being marked, to relishing both and instigating it the second time. She'd actually marked me. *Fuck.*

The feeling of waking with her teeth in my flesh was so intense and erotic, that I'd had to be inside her immediately. Had to fuck our way through the process.

I glanced over at her, and she was sleeping again. I'd worn her out, and wasn't that just how it should be?

~ Boss, you there?

I groaned. Fucking Derek.

~ What?

I practically barked at him.

~ We have news.

Fucking great, because god forbid I get to hide out with my new mate, for more than two fucking seconds. I growled as I slid out of the bed, and started dressing.

I hated to wake Mina, but I sure as fuck wasn't leaving her here. I was dressed before she started to awaken naturally.

"Baby? We need to get back." She stretched, a fluid motion that had my cock waking up.

"Fuck, if you keep doing that, I'm just going to fuck you again. We need to get back, the guys have news." She blinked, sitting up in a smooth move.

"Then we should go. Why are you taking so long?" She was out of bed, and slipping back into her trousers, while I shook my head, bemused. When she turned to grab her t-shirt, I stopped her. *Wow...*

"What is it?" She asked, when my hands settled on her shoulders, stopping her from dressing.

"Your tattoo, it's complete, and it's stunning." I trailed my fingers over the intricate design, which was of a stunning white wolf, almost shimmering at my touch, and yet there was still more to it. Ivy, and other leaves and flowers, twisting and sprawling across the whole of her back, over her shoulders, and around her sides.

I turned her around, and I could see how they wove across her stomach, around her breasts, and hid each and every one of her scars.

"Didn't you see?" I asked her, pointing down, and watching her mouth drop open, as she looked back at me.

"It's everywhere!" She said with delight.

"It's so intricate, and wow, it's perfect for you, Mina."

She grabbed at my t-shirt.

"What about yours?" I shrugged, trying to shake her off for the moment.

"We can look when we get back. Okay okay, or we can check now!" I laughed, as she pulled it up, starting with my back.

"Ohhh, it's magnificent!"

"Well, thanks baby, I like to think it's pretty big." She snorted, slapping my shoulder.

"I'm serious, Asher. It's all over your back, and it's this massive wolf, and his eyes, wow, they're like your eyes, the blue green, the intensity."

I felt frustrated as fuck, because we needed time to explore each other, to learn about the changes we'd just gone through. I really didn't want to rush a moment of this.

She'd moved around to check my front.

"Yours is just on your back," she said at last. Interesting. I wondered why they were so vastly different.

Maybe Daisy and Ned could compare with us, verbally, of course. *If he so much as looked at Mina, he'd be dead.*

Mina

WE HAD A CAR waiting when we stepped outside, with Derek in the driving seat. He welcomed us, sounding more formal than he normally did. It was like he knew we'd completed the bond, without even being told.

We sat in the back together, my hand in Asher's, as he drove us back to the pack house. As we walked inside, something interesting happened.

Jase stepped out of the kitchen.

"Oh great, you're... *fuck*..."

He seemed to be pressed down by some kind of invisible force, eventually dropping to his knees, his head lowered.

"Alpha, congratulations." He gasped those words out while Asher just stared at him. He looked from him to Derek, who flinched, and lowered his head, but didn't bend completely like Jase.

It was strange, and we stayed that way for a long minute, a bizarre tableau of still life, and then Asher groaned.

"Fuck's sake, are we done yet?" The two men snorted, finally able to raise their heads again, Jase struggling up from his knees.

"Yep, I'm guessing the bond worked," Jase said lightly, trying not to look directly at Asher, as if he'd crumple again beneath his power.

Asher grinned, marching past them both and heading for coffee, pouring us both one. The coffee machine was just always on in this house. Someone clearly made it their job to keep it filled, and ready. As a result, there was always coffee.

We sat around the table, the four of us.

"So, what's this news?"

Asher

DEREK AND JASE WERE both smiling back at me.

"For once it's good news. Seems Neil had an update from his bird from Somerset." Mina gasped, reaching for my hand and leaning close, waiting for something scary, even though he'd said it was good news. I chuckled, tucking her under my arm, while the other two shared a wide-eyed look.

"Uh, well, the challenge against us has been postponed indefinitely." What? I couldn't believe it, we'd been days away from attack or annihilation, maybe both. It didn't make any sense.

"What led to this sudden change?" I asked, looking from one of them to the other. They were smirking now.

I decided to let them have their fun, so I waited.

"Well, Alpha, it seems that earlier today every wolf in your pack was driven to their knees, bowing their fucking heads, in a move unseen in most packs ever. She was uh, he was boffing her at the time. Literally fell from the bed, mid-fuck, to kneel for his Alpha."

Mina and I stared at each other. *They felt our bond?*

"Yeah, it seems that seeing every wolf forced into a bow by their Alpha, was enough for her to warn her pack, and suddenly they've got pressing business, and also his wife's up the spout, and he's calling it family business, or some shit." He was grinning widely, and I laughed.

"You all felt it?"

Derek looked cranky.

"Yes, even I was driven to my fucking knees, boss, I didn't like it much, but I'd say your hold over your pack is restored. Stronger, in fact, than ever, and I wouldn't be surprised if more lone wolves don't start turning up, and wanting in. They'll feel your power from quite some way away."

Wow. All of this because I'd mated. No longer did I appear to be the Alpha nobody could rely on, or didn't want. It was one thing to demonstrate my Alpha power over wolves in my presence, but I'd never heard of it happening spontaneously like that, with them being affected no matter where they were.

Mina looked elated, like we'd dodged certain death, and I suppose, from her perspective, without knowing pack laws yet, she could have expected far worse than would have happened.

"So he's safe?" She asked them, squeezing my hand. They laughed.

"I think right now, everyone's praying that he doesn't decide to go on the offensive. Fifty of us might not seem like many, but the Alpha's strength boost made all of us stronger too. We're a far bigger threat than we were six hours ago." Jase looked proud as punch.

I stood up, pulling Mina with me.

"Okay, good. Anything else to report?"

They both sighed, resigned to the fact that I wasn't sticking around for the moment.

"No, boss, all in hand. You go take care of your lady. I'll get the crew in to cook today, so you can uh, focus."

I laughed. "Thanks guys, for having my back through all of this. Now, if you'll excuse us, I need to shower with my lady. *My mate.*"

They were whispering among themselves as we left the table and I led Mina upstairs.

She followed me into our room, and dumped her bag on the sofa. Nobody was sleeping on that fucking thing ever again. I kicked the door shut and fixed my eyes on my beautiful mate.

"With the greatest of respect, my Mina, get the fuck out of those clothes before I shred them for you." She smirked at me.

"You'll have to catch me first!" She turned, running for the bathroom, and I caught her just inside the door.

I lifted her t-shirt off, pushing her against the wall, my mouth on hers, my tongue demanding entry immediately. She didn't hesitate, wrapping her arms around me, and kissing me back, pushing against me. I pulled back to look at her.

"At some point, I plan to lay you out, and spend so long teasing and pleasuring you, that you're begging me to fuck you. But for right now, I don't have anywhere near that kind of patience."

I shoved her trousers down, and kicked them aside, slipping mine off and stepping out of them. I turned the shower on, and then I lifted her, pulling her legs around my waist.

I pressed her up against the tile wall, laughing when she gasped at the chill against her.

"I'm gonna warm you up, baby, don't worry."

And I held her against that wall, and fucked her until we were both exhausted, and the water no longer soothed, but felt like pesky hot needles.

I wrapped my mate in a towel, and took her to the bedroom to care for her some more.

Mina

I MADE ASHER ROLL onto his stomach, so I could inspect his tattoo. It was intricately detailed, and elegant, and there was a strength about the way it flowed, like it had been drawn by a masculine hand.

I traced my fingers over the lines, watching the colours swirl and shift beneath my touch, and Asher groaned.

"My god, keep doing that, please." I was happy to comply. I was sitting naked in our bed. We'd just had rampant sex yet again, this time in the shower, and he'd gently dried me with a towel, before suggesting we rest a while.

I couldn't rest though. I felt happy, alive, rejuvenated. I felt healed, like the damage from before had been washed over, by a healing power; a warmth. I felt strong now. I looked down at my own tattoo, across my stomach and chest.

It was as if the mate bond had known what I wanted to hide. For every scar on my body, there was now an ornate flower covering it, the raised, puckered flesh looking like the textured centre of the flower. I ran my fingers over it.

I noticed mine didn't react to my touch, but maybe that was because I wasn't a wolf. I shrugged, and went back to stroking my fingers over Asher's, before he started complaining.

Later, after we'd had a perfectly nice meal, cooked by the unseen staff, and left by the door for us like room service, we sat together on the bed.

"I feel like a new person." I finally said it out loud, putting it into words. Asher grinned, nudging me with his shoulder.

"It was worth the effort then." I gazed at him, my man.

"What if it hadn't been?"

He looped his arm around me, pulling me against him.

"Then we'd have tried again."

"What happens next?" I asked him, and he shrugged.

"We go back to our lives, but with you living here with me. We get married. Maybe there will be babies."

I stared at him, a sidelong look.

"What about Teddy and Trav?"

He smirked, a deadly, evil smirk.

"They won't get to have babies."

I giggled. "I mean, they get out tomorrow or the next day, I'm lost on what day it is at this point."

"I know exactly when they're getting out. They'll be tracked, snatched, dragged here, and we'll gut them like the pigs they are." I gasped, wriggling away to look at him.

"Really?" Asher frowned.

"I don't know what the problem is. They hurt my mate, and I couldn't stop them, so I'll kill them instead."

"You'll go to prison! I don't want you away from me." Asher was laughing.

"Nobody will see us take them."

I chewed my lip. "If you kidnap them and bring them here, it's premeditated murder, Asher. The worst, but, if we lured them here, if it looked like they came here of their own free will... wouldn't that be self-defence? Protecting your land against trespassers? Involuntary manslaughter?"

He was staring at me open-mouthed.

"Who took law classes, and never told me?"

"I wanted to be a lawyer before all of this. I studied until... I couldn't, and then I realised how much I love plants, and nature. How they seem to grow for me. It replaced that interest, but I still know things, still remember the easy stuff."

He pulled me into his lap, crushing me against him.

"And how do we get them here, sweet girl? Bear in mind, your answer may get you punished..." I gasped, peeking up at him.

"I... punished?" He grinned.

"So?"

"I was going to suggest that we let them know I'm here. They swore revenge on me when they got out, that they'd finish what they'd started. I was afraid before, but now I'm not. They're nothing, and they can't hurt me now."

Asher was growling softly.

"I think I'm going to have to punish you, for this need to put yourself in harm's way, even if you are right." I stared up at him nervously.

"Like... how?"

His grin widened, and a tingle worked its way up my spine.

"You'll see."

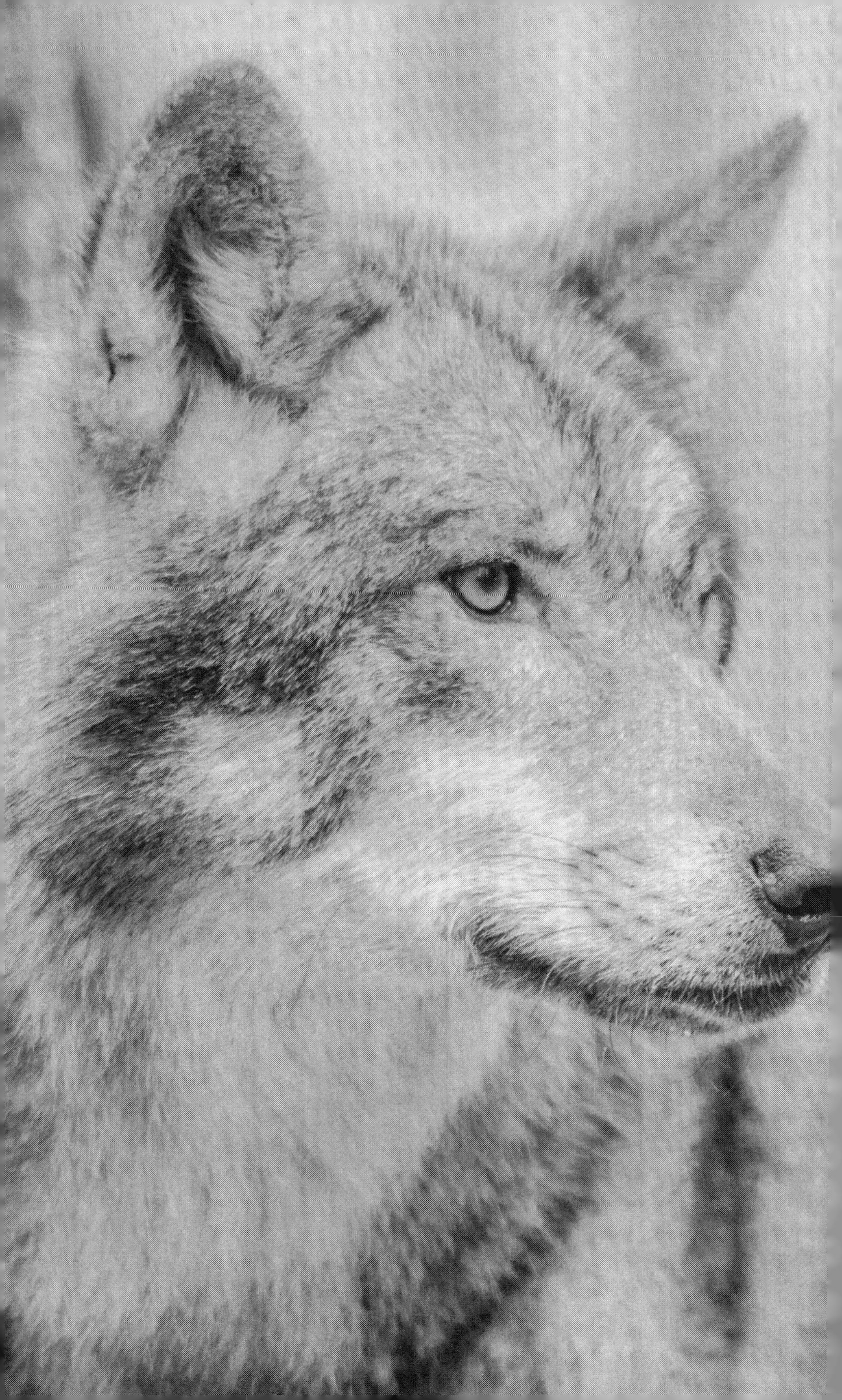

Chapter Forty-Six

Asher

She was right, I mean of fucking course she was. I used mindspeak to tell the boys. They'd make it happen, and they'd make sure we knew the second they crossed into our territory. From there, they were going to meet an angry pack of wolves. When we were done with them, there wouldn't be any pieces of them big enough for worms to eat.

In the meantime, I needed to discourage this reckless behaviour in my mate. I didn't ever want her risking herself for anything, or anyone. *Trouble is, I think she'll enjoy this a little too much.*

I stripped the robe from her shoulders, and dragged her down the bed, still finding it remarkable that she didn't resist, just giggled.

She no longer feared anything with me, no touches, no holds, no part of my body or hers. I spread her before me, and licked her to her first orgasm.

From there, I used my fingers to finger-fuck her, while I sucked on her clit.

After that one, I went on to torture her fucking nipples, bringing her to the brink, before I went down on her once more, and wrenched orgasm number three from her.

She was a quivering mess, gasping my name over and over. Begging. Pleading. I don't think even she knew what for, at this point.

When I drove her to the next one, I slipped a thumb into her tight asshole as I pushed her over the edge. Her eyes were glazed, as I moved back up the bed.

"More? Or has baby learned her lesson?" She turned to look at me, her movements slow and languid, her eyes as wide as I've ever seen them.

"Huh?" I chuckled.

"Yeah, I think that was enough, for now." I fell back to catch my own breath.

Finally she turned to look at me.

"If that was a punishment, I must misbehave more often." *I knew it!* I laughed.

"And maybe next time I'll deliberately not do that, or I'll just take you close, and stop." Her eyes narrowed dangerously.

"You wouldn't."

"Try me."

Mina

WE'D HAD WORD AT last; they were out. It was almost two days since the bonding, and I'd never felt so strong, and in control. Complete. Powerful, even.

I thought I'd been sapping this power from Asher, but maybe it had always been mine, the whole time.

"You ready, baby?" He asked me, shooting me a grin, as he and his fellow shifters stood before me. It seemed he'd had many offers to help, but he kept them all at the sidelines.

Two wolves were tracking each of them, although they'd apparently stayed together, and were already on their way here. They had no idea what would be waiting for them.

Me, and five huge wolves, ready to tear them to pieces. Derek, Jase, Daisy, and Ned; the four backing up my mate, Asher.

He wanted a piece of each of them, of course, and I wanted to be there. Wanted to see them beg for their lives, and then lose. I also needed them to see me strong, and brave, and see the proof that I had survived them.

I was dressed in black jeans, and a t-shirt, with a thin black jacket. My tattoos were hidden, and I half wished they could see them, but that would have given them too much power.

They couldn't even see my mark. It had settled into a shimmer, just below the skin, that any wolf could see, but humans couldn't. Mine was in the shape of an ornate letter 'A', while Asher's was, unsurprisingly, an 'M'.

Now that I'd mated with a wolf, I could see any wolf's mark, so I'd seen Daisy's 'N' shaped one, when we sat together, and giggled, and compared stories. It seemed that her mate had a kinkier side, and enjoyed tying her up. I wasn't entirely sure I wouldn't enjoy that myself.

Since Asher had freed me from all of my fears and inhibitions, I felt like the attack had never happened. The slate had been washed clean, and I was whole again. *Clean.*

Asher had a mindspeak channel open with his pack, so he could communicate with all of them. It was pretty amazing, and I wished so hard that I could hear them, join them. They mostly stood in silence, waiting for the right information.

Asher saw my agitation and took my hand, holding it in his. I leaned against him, resting my head against his chest.

~ *They're approaching, Alpha. Five minutes out.*

I lifted my head, and looked around. That was weird.

~ *They're armed. With knives. Stupid fuckers.*

I gasped, and Asher looked at me, bemused.

"You can hear them, can't you?" I nodded, my eyes wide.

"How are you sharing it with me?"

He shrugged, pulling a face.

"Not a fucking clue, but it's a good thing. You need to be involved." I nodded, resting my head against his chest again, in case proximity was key to the power giving me access.

~ *First fucker just jumped the fence, Alpha, and now the other. Game on.*

~ *They're gonna wish they were never born.*

~ *Save a piece for us, please, Alpha. I'm feeling like teaching those two wankers how to treat a lady.*

Yes, that was a female. I turned to look at Daisy, wide-eyed, and she laughed.

"You can hear us?" I nodded, and she shrugged.

"I've been wanting to get my claws into them, ever since you told me."

Asher squeezed my hand.

"Let's go."

My heart picked up speed, because it was happening. We started running, heading for the trail where I'd hiked before, because that was where they'd been led. It was the most hidden area for the attack.

It was on pack land, but if a helicopter happened to be flying over, and caught footage of huge wolves ripping men to shreds, that wouldn't matter a damn bit.

They weren't going to shift, until it was time to attack. The two bastards wouldn't know shifters were even a thing, until they were about to die.

It looked odd; me, dressed normally, with a whole bunch of bare-chested men, with no shoes, and one woman, who wore a vest too.

~ *They're on the trail, repeat, they've hit the trail.*

~ *Fast movers, for pointless fucking asses.*

~ *They'll move fast once the Alpha's gunning for them. They're so dead.*

There were so many voices, chatting in my head, and it was a strange sensation. It was like a group chat on a phone, but we could just all hear each other. I wondered if I could interact with them too.

~ *Are we close yet?*

I directed that at Asher, and he turned to look at me, a big grin on his face.

~ *Nearly there, baby.*

"Amazing," I heard Jase mutter, and Ned laughed.

"You didn't expect her to be ordinary, did you?"

We reached the start of the trail, at a different point from where they were joining it.

They'd come in from the road, which only came near the trail at a single location, which meant they were probably halfway up the trail.

~ *You're almost on them, Alpha. They're just over the hill there.*

My heart thudded in my chest, and I looked at Asher.

~ *Let me go alone.*

I said, and he shot me a glare.

~ *Not happening. They're armed.*

I laughed.

~ *So what? I've got all of you with me. I couldn't be safer! Let me head them off, I need to do this, please.*

~ *Alpha, we're all within shifting distance. We'll all cover your mate.*

One of the other wolves said, and others piped up to agree.

He lowered his head, growling with frustration, then he nodded.

"Be careful, and keep on the channel. If you need us, we're just two fucking seconds away." I nodded, and glanced at the others, taking in how fierce they all looked on my behalf. I walked on ahead. *Alone.*

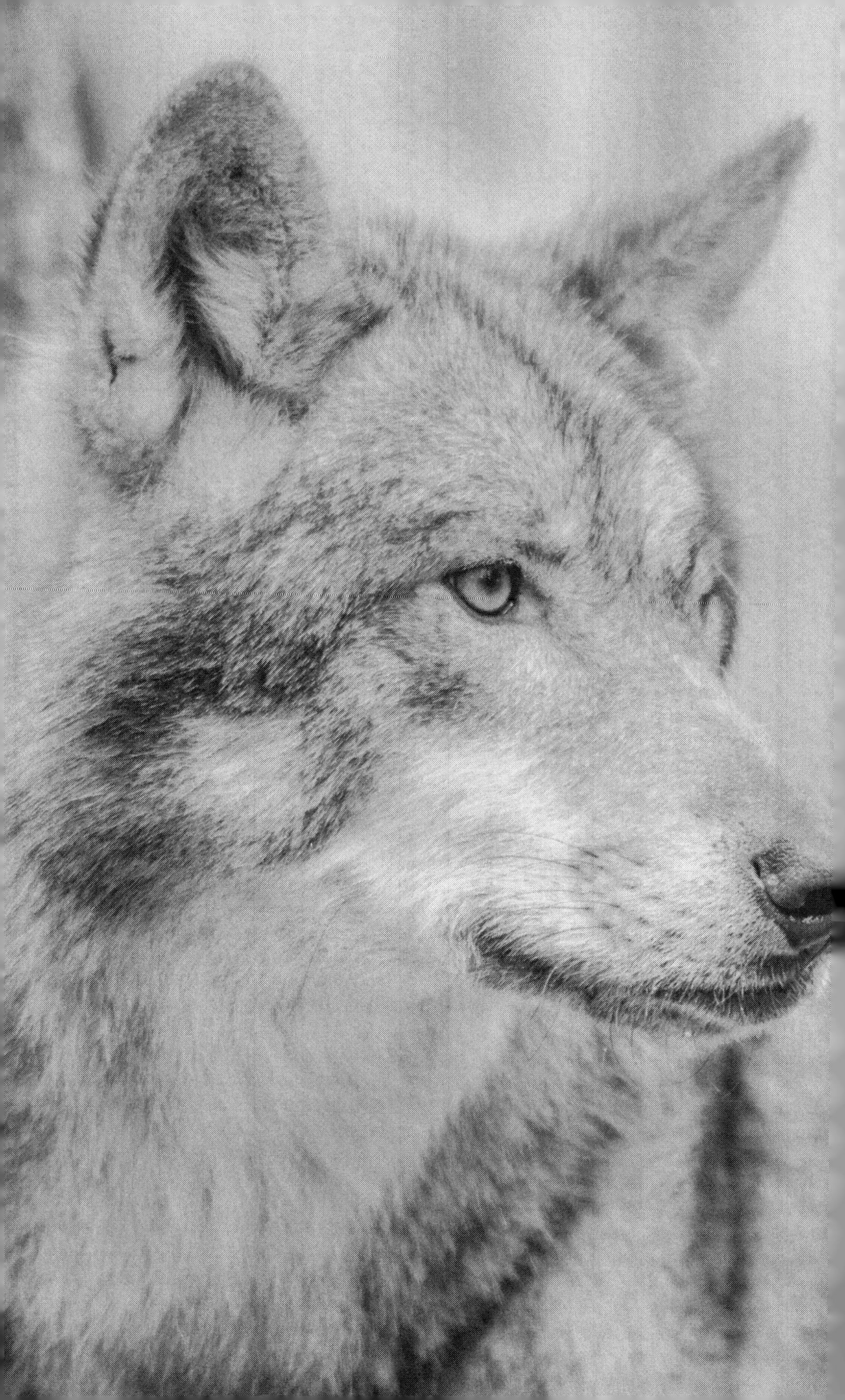

Chapter Forty-Seven

MINA

Even though I'd stepped away from my safety net, I could still sense it all around me. I could feel the attention, and approval, of around fifty damn wolves, in my head, and I'd never felt stronger.

As I crested the hill, I saw them; two clumsy figures, stumbling up the hill. They were only a metre away when they realised I was standing there.

"Well, look who's here," Teddy said, pulling a knife from his pocket and brandishing it in a way that I'm sure made him feel like a man.

"Yeah, mate. The little slut who got us banged up. Looks like she's just dished herself up on a fucking plate for us."

Teddy laughed, punching Trav's shoulder and walking ahead, until he was just in front of me.

"You know what? I'm going to enjoy fucking you up. This time, whore, when I'm done fucking you, I'm going to tear you open with this fucking knife. Oh look, I upgraded." He waved his hunting knife in the air, looking so proud of his ingenuity.

I stared at him, staying silent as Trav came closer, pulling his own knife out; the same damn knife. Did they go to a hardware store together? Losers.

"I'm going first this time," he said, raking his eyes all over my body. It would have scared me, before.

~ *Mina, you have five minutes.*

Asher's voice commanded in my head, and I blinked.

~ *I only need two.*

I felt his amusement through the connection, and not just his. It gave me the strength I needed.

"See how terrified she is of us? Cat got your tongue, huh? I've got somewhere to stick that fucking mouth of yours. Yeah, Trav you can fuck her first, 'cos I'm going to fuck her mouth."

I sighed, rolling my eyes at them, at their pathetic attempts to scare me.

"Do you two losers ever shut the fuck up?" They exchanged a look, shocked into silence for a moment.

"What? Who the fuck do you think you are?" Teddy grabbed the front of my clothes, and I just stared at him, amazed to realise that I felt no fear.

"I'm alive, but you won't be for much longer." I stepped into him and slammed my knee up, catching him as hard as I could in the nuts, enjoying his agonised scream, and the way he fell away from me, curling up on the floor. I kicked his knife away, and turned to Trav.

"Sorry, he went first, after all. But don't worry, you're next."

"I'll fucking carve you up, bitch. I'm not afraid of you." His attention suddenly shifted, and he looked warily behind me.

"Who the fuck are you?"

Asher walked up behind us, to join me.

"I'm her fucking man, and you? You're about to be chopped fucking liver." He threw a savage punch, knocking Trav down, and then turned to slam his foot into Teddy's back, making him yell out in pain.

I pulled him back. "Asher, wait, you know what?" He looked at me with his eyebrows raised.

"I'm done, let the others have their fun." He practically glared at me.

"Their lives are mine, as your mate. I intend to make them scream for mercy." I shook my head, tugging on his arm again.

"I don't want you all covered in their blood and guts, because then I won't let you have sex with me." He laughed, and let me drag him back.

~ *Sic 'em, guys. All yours.*

A rush of excitement and energy came back at us through the connection, and then the air sizzled with the shifting of multiple wolves in one area. You could actually see a glow from each one as they shifted, and it was magical, beautiful.

"What the *fuck*?"

"Trav... Trav, *run!*"

As the snarling of wolves started, and their screams grew louder, we turned and walked away. By the time we were back at the house, we knew the outcome.

~ *So fucking dead. Did you see the squirrelly one crying?*

~ *Let them try attacking anyone now, with no arms.*

~ *Did you see his leg go flying?*

Asher closed the connection at that point, seeing me flinch with each new message.

"Thank you." He opened the door, letting me in before him.

"You're welcome, baby, I don't want you hearing any more of that. They can still hear each other, but I've pulled us out of the connection."

"You can link them all like that?"

He laughed, as he headed for the kitchen, sitting me at the breakfast bar, kissing me on the tip of my nose.

"Seems so. I don't know if I could before the bond, but now, a lot of things are easier. We've had four wolves come and ask to join us too, since the bond kicked in. The builders among the pack are already working on plans for housing."

Wow, so much had changed. He looked at me, as he passed me a coffee, sweetened to perfection as always.

"What I'm wondering is how you managed to connect with us."

I frowned at him. "Don't be ridiculous, I thought you let me in, or our bond did."

He shook his head. "It wasn't anything I did." I shrugged, maybe we'd never know, but it had helped.

"They're all great, you know."

"The pack?"

I nodded. "I feel like I'm finally home, you know?" He smiled widely.

"You are, baby. We'll get the rest of your things, and then you'll never have to live anywhere without me."

I sighed happily. *Perfect.*

A knock at the door turned our heads in that direction, and Asher shrugged.

"Another pack member, I guess. Only Jase or D would let themselves in right now." He disappeared to answer the door, and returned with a woman. *A beautiful woman*, with long raven black hair, and eyes that almost seemed to glow.

"It's true," she said, staring at me. We both looked at her, confused as hell, and Asher cleared his throat.

"This is Astrid, she's the mate of Sammy. You probably don't remember which one he is, I'm sorry. I'll introduce you all properly, I promise."

I scrutinised her, wondering why she wasn't with the others.

"You're not a wolf either?" She laughed.

"Don't be silly. Do I look like a wolf?" I laughed in response.

"I like her already." She glanced at the coffee pot and gestured.

"May I?" Asher nodded, sitting back down with me.

"What brings you here, Astrid? Waiting for Sammy to return?" Clearly he was out killing rapists with the others then.

She grinned. "No, I'm here to meet the other witch in the pack. It's about damn time too, I was getting lonely." We stared at each other in shock. *Witch?*

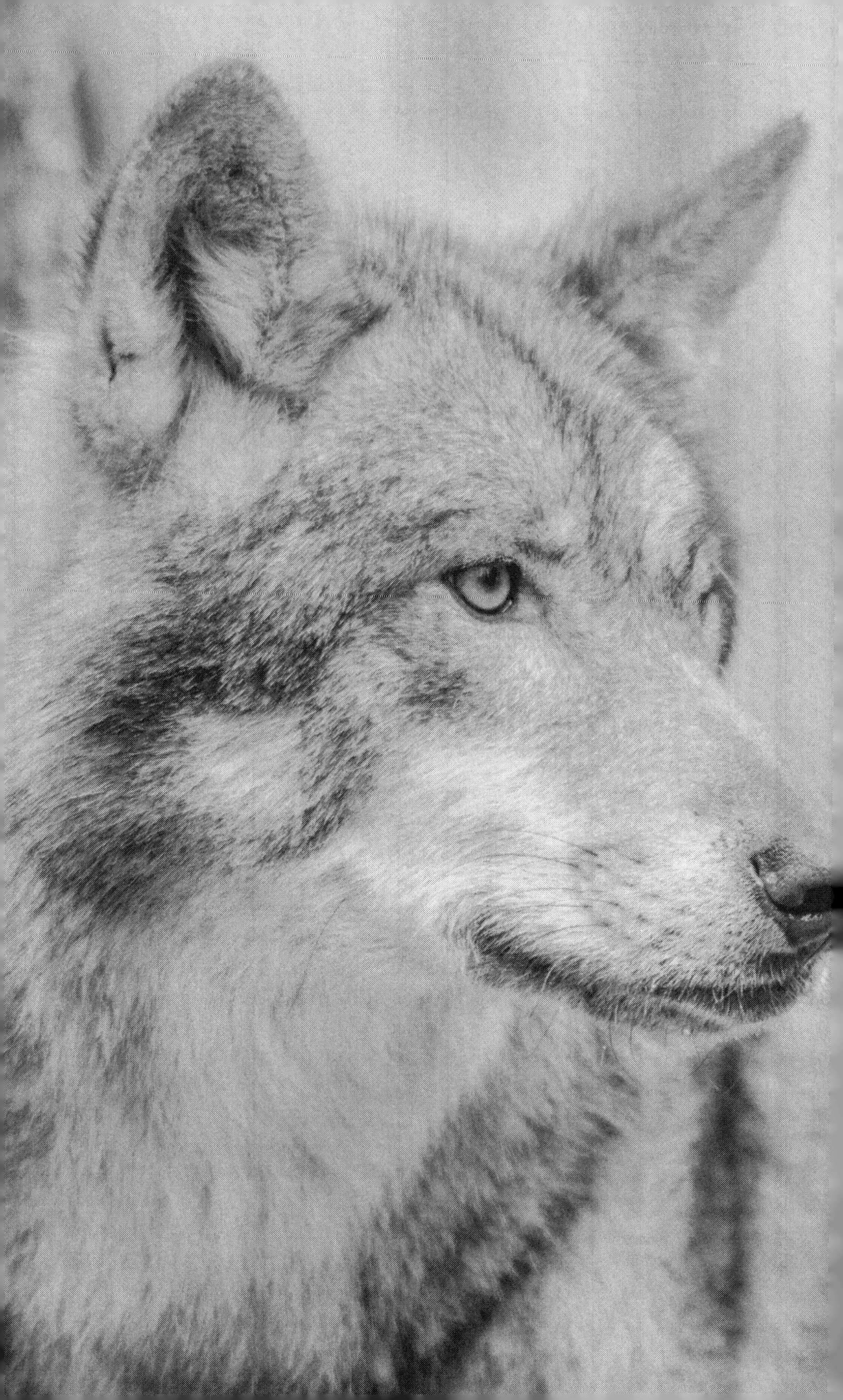

Chapter Forty-Eight
Asher

MEET THE *OTHER* WITCH. She'd said that, and she was looking right at Mina. *My Mina.*

"Witch?" Mina finally asked, frowning at her.

Astrid nodded.

"I wasn't sure at first. I was picking something up, and I wasn't sure what, and then the bond kicked in. While the wolves all crashed to their knees, I felt something too, not the Alpha's power, but yours."

Mina snorted. "I'm human, trust me. I'm actually the weirdo in the pack." She giggled into her hand.

"Mina, I know a witch when I sense one, and I can sense it right now. How else could you have broken through to join the mindspeak channel?" She was grinning widely, apparently understanding all kinds of shit we didn't yet.

I frowned at her. "You can hear it too?" She laughed, waving her hand.

"I've been listening all evening. Once Sammy explained it to me, I just tuned in. It was nice, not having to be left out of it."

Mina's hands were trembling, and I put mine over them.

"Baby, it's okay."

"How can I be a witch? I'm just a normal person, aren't I?" Mina was chewing that damn lip again.

Astrid smiled, lifting her hands.

"Who knows. We're born to our power; it's not hereditary, it's not given, it's born. I was the only witch in my family, and of the coven, they're all the only witch they ever knew, until they found each other. We can help you learn about your powers."

I put my hand on the back of Mina's neck, stroking her skin lightly, trying to give her strength.

"You're basing this entirely on her ability to connect with us via mind-speak?" I asked, both women turning to look at me. Astrid looked almost insulted.

"You think I'm only guessing? I think I know how to sense a witch's power, thank you very much, Alpha."

Mina snorted. "Is there a way to check? I mean, if I had powers, why would I have been unable to defend myself against... if I... I mean, why have I never seen any sign of powers?"

She grinned, unconcerned by our disbelief.

"It normally takes something to awaken it fully in a dormant witch. The bond itself may even have been the catalyst. I know one thing, though, your tattoos will be different. Am I right?" We looked at each other. *The tattoos.*

She started giggling.

"Oh my god, you both just have it written all over your faces. The Alpha's covers his back, his wolf, and yours, Mina, you'll have the ethereal white wolf. That's what we witches have, it's your inner wolf spirit, the part that connects you to the Alpha's wolf. But your tattoo also goes further, right, it covers your front too? It's more elaborate?"

Mina

I WAS IN SHOCK! The tattoo was different because I was a witch, a fucking witch? How could I be twenty-eight-years-old, and not know I'm a fucking witch?

The tattoo had been a shock, because of how different it was, but we'd just assumed it was because I was human, or so damaged when he bonded with me.

"We had no idea," I said, turning to look at Asher, who looked as wide-eyed as me.

"It could be why the Alpha's power over his wolves is so strong now. A witch will fuel him up with her power, so I'd say you're pretty well matched. The only question is which element you're powered by. I'm a fire witch, so my tattoo has flames. I can show you part of it, if you like?" I nodded eagerly.

She stood up and lifted her light floaty shirt, showing us her stomach. It was covered with intricate, delicate flame designs, with little wisps of fire here and there.

"Wow, it's beautiful!" I leaned across the counter to look more closely, and she giggled.

"So, 'fess up. What's yours?" I stared at Asher.

"I have no idea. I'll do what you did." I lifted my shirt, and showed my stomach, which I now no longer hated, because it was interwoven with leaves and flowers, bringing nature to me.

"An earth witch! How perfect! We don't have one in our coven yet. We're mostly fire and water, with one air witch, so you'd complete us. Oh *please*. Please come, and meet the coven." I lowered my t-shirt, feeling energised by her excitement.

"I'd like that. Can you arrange it please?" She nodded eagerly.

"I'll send a group text in a minute! They'll all want to see your tattoo, it's so different. Do you have any questions before I leave you alone? I'm guessing as you're newly mated, I'm probably cramping the Alpha's style here."

Asher snorted, covering his face with his hand.

"*Jesus, this is my penance,*" he muttered, and I elbowed him, making him laugh.

"Would my being an earth witch affect how plants grow for me?" I asked, wondering if I finally had the answer to that question. Astrid smiled.

"But of course, you command the earth, and whatever grows in it. I can make fire do amazing things. The others are all uniquely gifted, but now with all four elements, we will be stronger than ever. *Alpha, how do you feel about having more witches in your pack?"*

Asher groaned dramatically.

"Are you all gonna sit around here all the time, keeping my mate from me?" I elbowed him again.

"Hey! Stop beating me up, woman, I'm just saying."

Astrid laughed. "I was hoping to introduce the coven to some of the wolves. If any others find their mates here, you could massively strengthen your pack, by including us. Witches and wolves seem to make good partnerships, mated or not."

Asher nodded, looking a bit overwhelmed.

"I'll get my Beta to introduce you all to the building team. Feel free to move them onto the land, it's not like we don't have the room. If they don't find mates here, they're still welcome to stay."

I suddenly felt a wave of joy and excitement. *I'm a witch, and there's a coven, and I'm mated to an Alpha wolf.*

I'm not broken anymore, I'm finally complete.

THE END

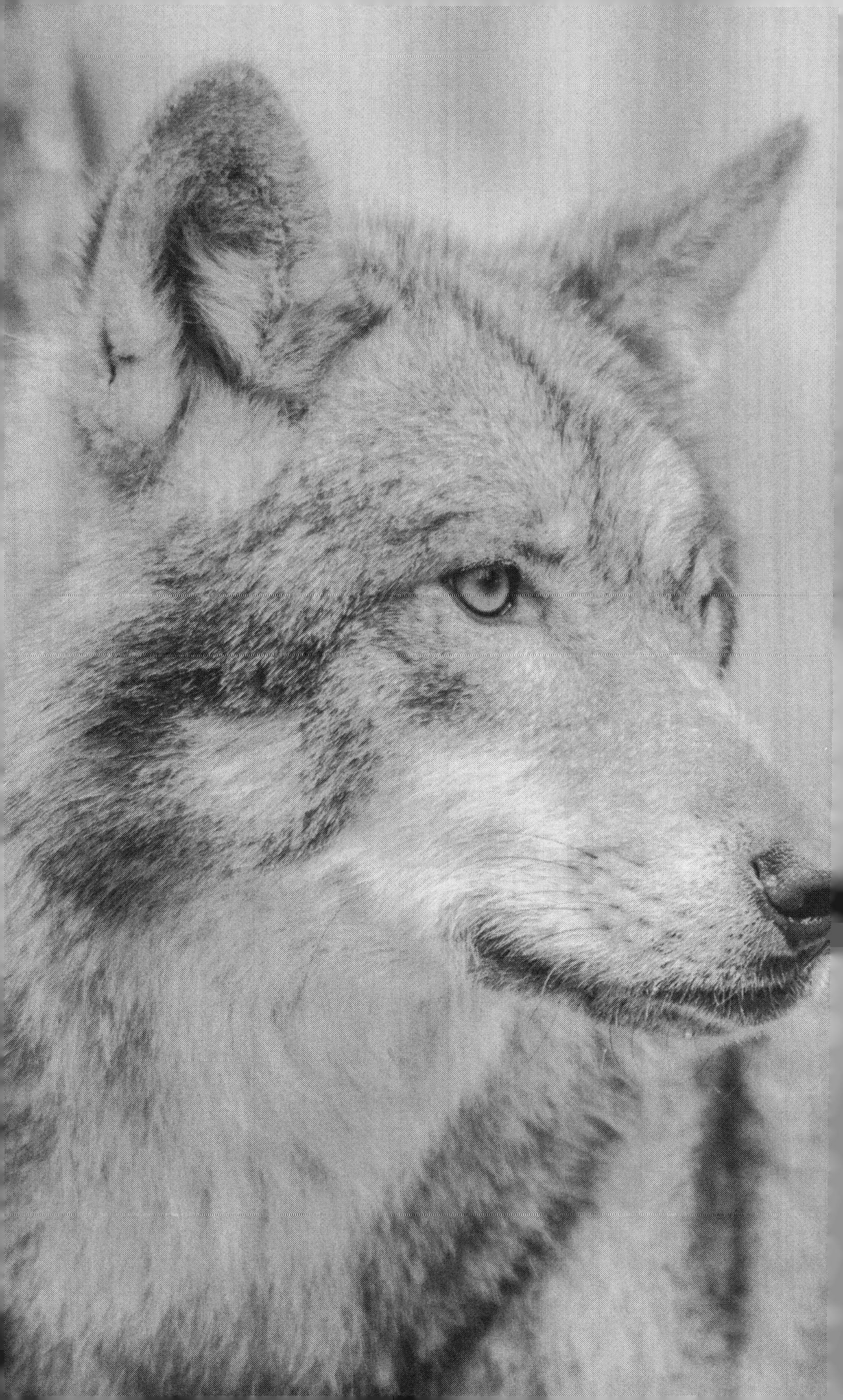

Also by Mia Fury on Amazon/KU

The Bennett Crime World Series
1. At Their Mercy – mybook.to/AtTheirMercy
2. Show No Mercy – mybook.to/ShowNoMercy
3. Cry For Mercy – mybook.to/CryForMercy
4. Worthy Of Mercy – mybook.to/WorthyOfMercy
5. Bleed For Mercy – mybook.to/BleedForMercy
6. Bringer of Mercy – mybook.to/BringerOfMercy

Hughes Stalker Duet
1. Norton's Obsession – mybook.to/NortonsObsession
2. Nico's Mistake – mybook.to/NicosMistake

Wolves of the Wiltshire Pack
1. Asher – mybook.to/Asher_Wolves1
2. Derek – mybook.to/Derek_Wolves2
3. Jase – mybook.to/Jase_Wolves3

New very dark standalone:
Burning Depravity – mybook.to/BurningDepravity

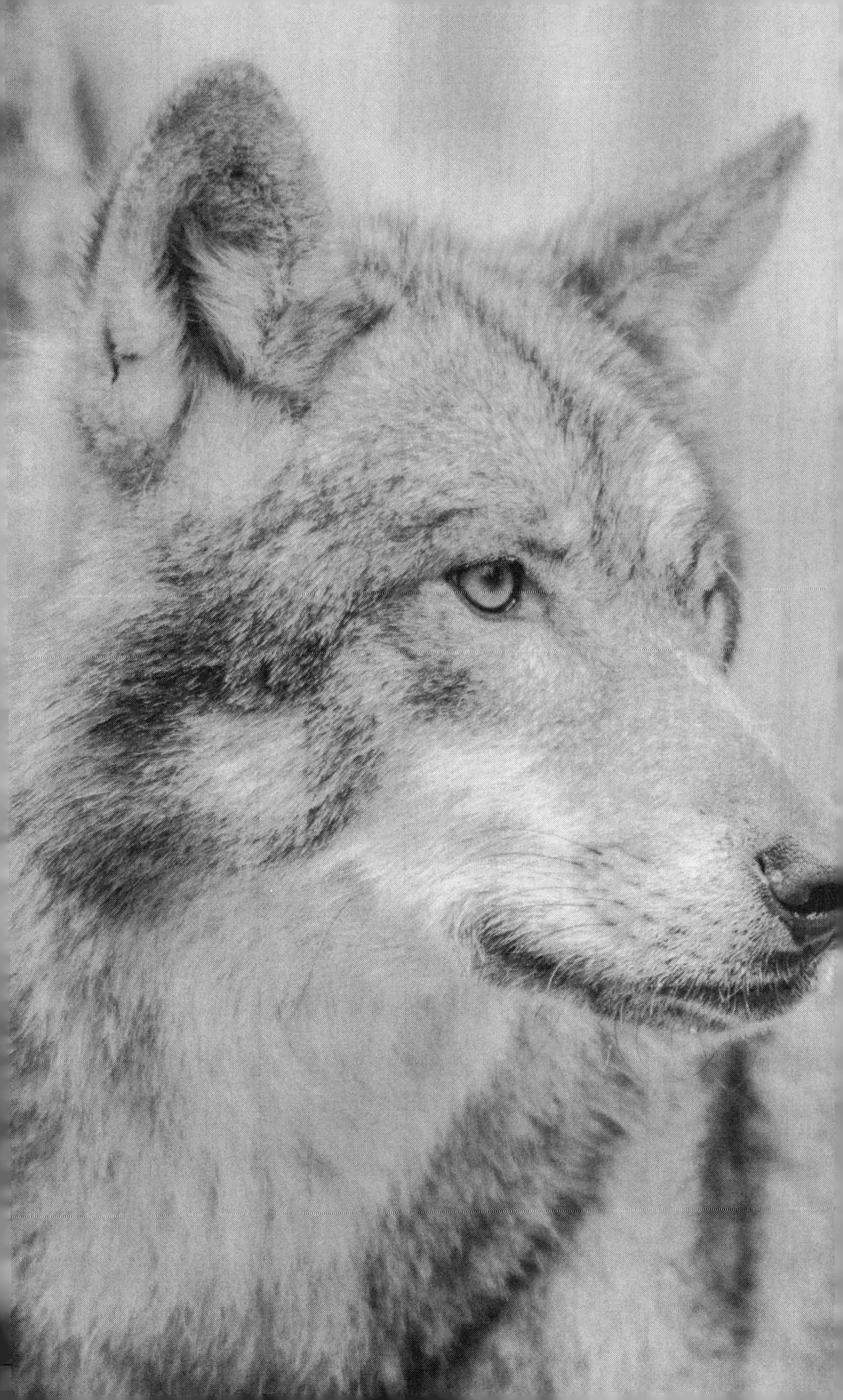

Acknowledgements

LET'S SEE IF I can keep this brief for once! This is the part where I list all of the people who help me get through the days, and make words for you to read and enjoy!

My family, especially my amazing husband, who empowers me to do something as terrifying as sharing my creations with you.

My Street / ARC Team, who lift me up and keep me going when the little confidence I have dissipates and leaves me wondering what the hell I'm doing; Crystal, Gloria, Alexis, Victoria, Juliet, Sarah, Stacie, Tai, Holly, Kelley, and Wren.

My cover artist, Anya, who I couldn't do this without, and would never want to, because first and foremost, she's one of my dearest friends.

You're all amazing, and I see you, and I love you. To all who read this or any of my other books, you make this worth doing. I appreciate every one of you, thank you.

Printed in Great Britain
by Amazon